FRAGMENTS

DAN WELLS

HarperCollins *Children's Books*

YA

First published in hardback in the USA by HarperCollins *Publishers* Inc. in 2013
First published in Great Britain by HarperCollins *Children's Books* in 2013
HarperCollins *Children's Books* is a division of HarperCollins*Publishers* Ltd,
77-85 Fulham Palace Road, Hammersmith, London, W6 8JB.

www.harpercollins.co.uk

1

Copyright © 2013 by HarperCollins *Publishers*

ISBN 978-0-00-746523-1

Dan Wells asserts the moral right to be identified as the author of the work.

Printed and bound in England by Clays Ltd, St Ives plc.

MIX
Paper from
responsible sources
FSC **FSC® C007454**
www.fsc.org

FSC™ is a non-profit international organisation established to promote
the responsible management of the world's forests. Products carrying the
FSC label are independently certified to assure consumers that they come
from forests that are managed to meet the social, economic and
ecological needs of present and future generations,
and other controlled sources.

Find out more about HarperCollins and the environment at
www.harpercollins.co.uk/green

This book is dedicated to everyone who ever admitted they were wrong. It's not a sign of weakness or a lack of dedication, it's one of the greatest strengths a person—human or Partial—can have.

PART 1

CHAPTER ONE

"**R**aise a glass," said Hector, "to the best officer in New America."

The room came alive with the clink of glass and the roar of a hundred voices. "Cornwell! Cornwell!" The men tipped their mugs and bottles and drained them in gurgling unison, slamming them down or even throwing them at the floor when the booze within was gone. Samm watched in silence, adjusting his spotting scope almost imperceptibly. The window was murky, but he could still see the soldiers grin and grimace as they slapped one another on the back, laughed at ribald jokes, and tried not to look at the colonel. The link would be telling them everything about Cornwell anyway.

Hidden in the trees on the far side of the valley, well outside the effective range of the link, Samm had no such luxury.

He twisted the knob on his tripod, swiveling the microphone barely a fraction of a millimeter to the left. At this distance even a small change of angle swept the sound across a vast portion of the room. Voices blurred through his earbuds, snatches of words and conversations in a quick aural smear, and then he was listening to another voice, just as familiar as Hector's—it was Adrian, Samm's old sergeant.

". . . never knew what hit them," Adrian was saying. "The enemy line shattered, exactly as planned, but for the first few minutes that made it all the more dangerous. The enemy became disoriented, firing in all directions at once, and we were pinned down too fiercely to reinforce him. Cornwell held the corner through the whole thing, never flinching, and all the time the Watchdog was howling and howling; it nearly deafened us. No Watchdog was as loyal as his. She worshipped Cornwell. That was the last major battle we saw in Wuhan, and a couple of days later the city was ours."

Samm remembered that battle. Wuhan had been taken almost sixteen years ago to the day, in March 2061, one of the last cities to fall in the Isolation War. But it had been one of Samm's first enemy engagements; even now he could remember the sounds, the smells, the taste of the gunpowder sharp in the air. His head buzzed with the memory, and phantom link data coursed through his brain, just enough to stir his adrenaline. Instincts and training surfaced almost immediately, heightening Samm's awareness as he crouched on the darkened hillside, prepping him for a battle that existed only in his mind. This was followed almost immediately by an opposite reaction—a calming wave of familiarity. He hadn't linked to anyone in days, and the sudden feeling, real or not, was almost painfully comfortable. He closed his eyes and held on to it, concentrating on the memories, willing himself to feel them again, stronger, but after a few fleeting moments they slipped away. He was alone. He opened his eyes and looked back through the scope.

The men had brought out the food now, wide metal trays heaped high with steaming pork. Herds of wild pigs were common enough in Connecticut, but mostly in the deep forest away from Partial settlements. They must have hunted pretty far afield for a feast like this. Samm's stomach rumbled at the sight of it, but he didn't move.

Far away the soldiers stiffened, only slightly but all in unison, warned by the link about something Samm could only guess at. *The colonel*, he thought, and twisted his scope to look at Cornwell: He was as bad as ever, cadaverous and rotten, but his chest still rose and fell, and there didn't seem to be anything immediately wrong. A twinge of pain, perhaps. The men in the room were ignoring it, and Samm chose to do the same. It wasn't time yet, it seemed, and the party continued. He listened in on another conversation, more reminiscing about the old days in the Isolation War, and here and there a story about the revolution, but nothing that fired Samm's memory as profoundly as the sergeant's story. Eventually the sight of the pork ribs and the sound of chewing became too much, and Samm carefully dug a plastic bag of beef jerky from his pack. It was a pale imitation of the juicy ribs his former comrades were enjoying, but it was something. He turned his eyes back to the scope and found Major Wallace right as he stood up to speak.

"Lieutenant Colonel Richard Cornwell is unable to speak to you today, but I'm honored to say a few words on his behalf." Wallace moved slowly, not just his walk but his gestures, his speech—every motion was measured and deliberate. He looked as young as Samm, like an eighteen-year-old human, but in real time he was nearing twenty—the expiration date. In another few months, maybe only a few weeks, he'd start to decay just like Cornwell. Samm felt cold, and pulled his jacket tighter around his shoulders.

The party grew as quiet as Samm, and Wallace's voice carried powerfully through the hall, echoing tinnily in Samm's earbuds. "I've had the honor of serving with the colonel my entire life; he pulled me out of the growth tank himself, and he put me through boot camp. He's a better man than most I've met, and a good leader to all his men. We don't have fathers, but I'd like to think that if we did, mine would be something like Richard Cornwell."

He paused, and Samm shook his head. Cornwell *was* their father, in every sense but the strictly biological. He had taught them, led them, protected them, done everything a father was supposed to do. Everything Samm would never have the chance to do. He tweaked the zoom on the spotting scope, pushing in as close on the major's face as he could. There were no tears, but his eyes were gaunt and tired.

"We were made to die," said the major. "To kill and then to die. Our lives have but two purposes, and we finished the first one fifteen years ago. Sometimes I think the cruelest part wasn't the expiration date, but the fifteen years we had to wait to find out about it. The youngest of you have it worst, because you'll be the last to go. We were born in war, and we earned our glory, and now we sit in a fading room and watch each other die."

The roomful of Partials stiffened again, harder this time, some jumping to their feet. Samm swung his scope wildly, looking for the colonel, but the tight zoom on the major's face made him lose his bearings, and he searched helplessly for a few panicked seconds, listening to shouts of "The colonel!" and "It's time!" Finally Samm pulled back, reset the scope, and zoomed in again from nearly a full mile away. He found the colonel's bed, in a place of honor at the front of the room, and watched as the old man shook and coughed, flecks of black blood dribbling from the corners of his mouth. He looked like a corpse already, his cells degenerating, his body rotting away almost visibly as Samm and the other soldiers watched. He sputtered, grimaced, hacked, and lay still. The room was silent.

Samm watched, stone-faced, as the soldiers prepared the final death rite: Without speaking a word, the windows were thrown open, the curtains cleared, the fans turned on. Humans met death with crying, with speeches, with wailing and gnashing of teeth. The Partials met it as only Partials could: through the link. Their bodies were designed for the battlefield: When they died, they released a burst of data to warn their fellow soldiers of danger, and when they felt it, those soldiers would release more data of their own to spread the word. The fans churned at the air, blowing that data out into that world so that everyone would link it and know that a great man had died.

Samm waited, tense, feeling the breezes blow back and forth across his face. He wanted it, and he didn't; it was both connection and pain, community and sadness. It was depressing how often those two came together these days. He watched the leaves flutter on the trees below him in the valley, watched the branches sway gently as the wind brushed past them. The data never came.

He was too far away.

Samm packed up his scope and the directional microphone, stowing them in his pack with their small solar battery. He searched the site twice, making sure he'd left nothing behind— the plastic bag of food was back in his satchel, the earbuds were stowed in his pack, his rifle was slung over his shoulder. Even the marks of the tripod in the dirt he kicked smooth with his boot. There was no evidence he had ever been here.

He looked one last time at his colonel's funeral, pulled on his gas mask, and slipped back into exile. There was no room in that warehouse for deserters.

CHAPTER TWO

The sun beat down through the gaps in the skyline, mapping out a pattern of ragged yellow triangles on the broken streets below. Kira Walker watched the road carefully, crouched beside a rusted taxi at the bottom of a deep urban canyon. Grass and scrub and saplings stood motionless in the cracked asphalt, untouched by wind. The city was perfectly still.

Yet something had moved.

Kira brought her rifle to her shoulder, hoping for a better view with the telescopic sight, then remembered—for the umpteenth time—that her scope had been broken in the cave-in last week. She cursed and lowered the gun again. *As soon as I'm done here, I'm going to find another gun store and replace the stupid thing.* She peered down the road, trying to separate shape and shadow, and raised her gun again before cursing under her breath. *Old habits die hard.* She ducked her head and scuttled to the back end of the taxi; there was a delivery truck a hundred feet down sticking halfway into the street, which should be able to hide her movements from whatever—or whoever—was down there. She peered out, stared for nearly a minute at the unmoving street, then gritted her teeth and ran. No bullets or clatters or roars. The truck did its job. She trotted up behind it, dropped to one knee, and peeked out past the bumper.

An eland moved through the underbrush, long horns curling into the sky, its long tongue picking at shoots and greens growing up through the rubble. Kira stayed still, watching intently, too paranoid to assume that the eland was the same thing she'd seen moving before. A cardinal screeched overhead, joined moments later by another, bright red streaks spinning and diving and chasing each other through the power lines and traffic lights. The eland nibbled at the small green leaves of a maple sapling, peaceful and oblivious. Kira watched until she was certain there was nothing else to see, then watched some more just in case. You could never be too careful in Manhattan—the last time she'd come here she'd been attacked by Partials, and so far on this trip she'd been chased by both a bear and a panther. The memory made her pause, turn, and check behind her. Nothing. She closed her eyes and concentrated, trying to "feel" a nearby Partial, but it didn't work. It never had, not in any way she could recognize, even when she had spent a week in close contact with Samm. Kira was a Partial, too, but she was different—she appeared to lack the link and some of their other traits, plus she aged and grew like a normal human. She didn't really know what she was, and she had no one she could turn to for answers. She didn't even have anyone to talk to about it—only Samm and the mad Partial scientist Dr. Morgan knew what she was. Kira hadn't even told her boyfriend—her best friend—Marcus.

She shivered uneasily, grimacing at the uncomfortable confusion that always followed her questions about herself. *That's what I'm here to find,* she thought. *Answers to the questions.*

She turned and sat on the broken asphalt, leaning against the truck's flat tire and pulling out her notebook again, though at this point she had the address memorized: Fifty-fourth and Lexington. It had taken her weeks to find the address, and several more days to make it here through the ruins. Maybe she was being too cautious. . . .

She shook her head. There was no such thing as "too cautious." The unsettled areas were too dangerous to take any chances, and Manhattan was more dangerous than most. She'd played it safe and she was still alive; she wasn't going to second-guess a strategy that had proven itself so successful.

She looked at the address again, then up at the weather-beaten street signs. This was definitely the right place. She tucked the notebook back into her pocket and hefted her rifle. Time to go inside.

Time to visit ParaGen.

The office building had once had glass doors and floor-to-ceiling windows, but glass didn't last long since the Break, and the entire ground floor now stood naked to the elements. It wasn't the ParaGen headquarters—that was out west somewhere, on the other side of the country—but it was something. A financial branch, located in Manhattan solely to interface with other corporations' financial branches. It had taken her weeks of searching even to find that the office existed. Kira picked her way through the pellets of shattered safety glass, and the mounds of siding and facade sloughed off from the building's upper floors. Eleven years of neglect had filled the floor inside with dirt, thick enough that small weeds and grasses were already beginning to sprout through. Low benches, once upholstered in sleek vinyl, had been weakened by sun and rain and torn apart by what looked like cats' claws. A wide desk that had probably held a receptionist was now weathered and sagging, the epicenter of a loose scattering of yellowed plastic ID tags. A plaque on the wall named dozens of businesses in the building, and Kira browsed the weather-beaten listings until she found ParaGen: the twenty-first floor. Three elevator doors stood in the wall behind the reception desk, though one was hanging crooked in its frame. Kira ignored them and went to the stairway door in the back corner. There was a black panel in the wall next to it, a sensor pad for a magnetic lock, but with no electricity it was meaningless—the hinges would be the biggest problem. Kira leaned against it, pushing gently at first to test it, then harder as the ancient hinges resisted the force. Finally it gave way, and she walked in to look up the towering stairwell.

"Twenty-first floor," she sighed. "Of course."

Many of the older buildings in the world were too treacherous to climb around in, devastated in the first winter after the Break: The windows broke, the pipes burst, and by spring the rooms and walls and floors were full of moisture. Ten freeze-thaw cycles later, the walls were warped, the ceilings were drooping, and the floors were crumbling to pieces. Mold got into the wood and carpets, insects dug into the cracks, and a once-solid structure became a precarious tower of crumbs and fragments; rubble that hadn't fallen down yet, waiting for a kick or a step or a loud voice to bring it crashing to the ground. Bigger buildings, though, and especially ones this new, were far more durable—their bones were steel girders, and their flesh sealed concrete and carbon fiber. The skin, so to speak, was still weak—glass and plaster and Sheetrock and carpet—but the building itself was sturdy. Kira's stairwell was particularly well preserved, dusty without being filthy, and the extra staleness to the air made her wonder if it had stayed more or less sealed since the Break. It gave the stairwell an eerie feeling, like a tomb, though there was nobody buried in it that she could see. She began to wonder if there was, higher up—if someone had been walking the stairs when RM finally claimed them, and they had been sealed in here ever since—but by the time she reached the twenty-first floor, she still hadn't seen any bodies. She thought about going on to look for some, to satisfy twenty-one floors of pent-up curiosity, but no. There were bodies enough in a city this size; half the cars on the street held skeletons, and the homes and offices held millions more. One body more or less in an old forgotten stairwell wouldn't change anything. She pried open the door with a squeal of hinges and walked into the ParaGen office.

It wasn't the main office, of course; she had seen that in a photograph a few weeks ago: herself as a child, her father, and her adopted guardian, Nandita, standing before a great glass building framed by snowy mountains. She didn't know where it was, she didn't remember the photo being taken, and she certainly didn't recall knowing Nandita before the Break, but there it was. She had been only five when the world ended, maybe only four in the photo. What did it mean? Who was Nandita, really, and what connection did she have to ParaGen? Had she worked there? Had her father? She knew he'd worked in an office, but she'd been too young to remember more. If Kira was really a Partial, was she a lab experiment? An accident? A prototype? Why hadn't Nandita ever told her?

That was the biggest question of all, in some ways. Kira had lived with Nandita for nearly twelve years. If she'd known what Kira really was—if she'd known the whole time and never said a word—Kira didn't like that at all.

The thoughts made her queasy, just as they had on the street outside. *I'm fake,* she thought. *I'm an artificial construct that thinks she's a person. I'm as fake as the faux-stone finish on this desk.* She walked into the front office and touched the peeling reception desk: painted vinyl over pressed plastic board. Barely even natural, let alone real. She looked up, forcing herself to forget about the discomfort and focus on the task at hand. The reception area was spacious for Manhattan, a wide room filled with splitting leather couches and a rugged rock structure, probably a former waterfall or fountain. The wall behind the reception desk showed a massive metal ParaGen logo, the same one on the building in the photo. She opened her bag, pulled out the carefully folded picture, and compared the two images. *Identical.* She put the photo away and walked around to the back of the reception desk, picking carefully through the papers strewn across the top of it. Like the stairwell, this room had no external opening and had thus stayed closed off from the elements; the papers were old and yellowed, but they were intact and neatly ordered. Most of it was unimportant clutter: phone directories and company brochures and a paperback book the receptionist had been reading, *I Love You to Death,* with the image of a bloody dagger on the cover. Maybe not the most politically correct thing to be reading while the world ended, but then again the receptionist hadn't even been here during the Break. She would have been evacuated when RM got really bad, or when it was first released, or maybe even as early as the start of the Partial War. Kira tapped the book with her finger, noting the bookmark about three quarters through. *She never found out who was loving whom to death.*

Kira glanced again at the directory, noting that some of the four-number phone extensions started with 1, and some with 2. The office took up two floors of the building, maybe? She flipped through the pages and found in the back a section of longer numbers, ten digits each: several starting with 1303 and others with 1312. She knew from talking to adults, people who remembered the old world, that these were area codes for different parts of the country, but she had no idea which parts, and the directory didn't say.

The brochures were stacked neatly in a corner of the desk, their front covers adorned with a stylized double helix and a picture of the building from Kira's photo, though from a different angle. Kira picked it up to look more closely and saw similar buildings in the background, most notably a tall, blocky tower that seemed to be made of great glass cubes. In flowing script at the bottom of the page was the phrase: "Becoming better than what we are." Inside were page after page of smiling photos and sales pitches for gene mods—cosmetic mods to change your eye or hair color, health mods to remove congenital illness or shore up your resistance to other diseases, even recreational mods to make your stomach flatter or your breasts larger, to improve your strength or speed, your senses or reaction time. Gene mods had been so common before the Break that almost all the survivors on Long Island had them. Even the plague babies, the children so young during the Break that they couldn't remember what life was like before it, had been given a handful of gene scrubs when they were born. They'd become standard procedure in hospitals around the world, and ParaGen had developed a lot of them. Kira had always thought she'd had the basic infant mods, and had occasionally wondered if she had something more: Was she a good runner because of DNA from her parents, or because an early gene mod had made her so? Now she knew it was because she was a Partial. Built in a lab as a human ideal.

The last half of the brochure talked about the Partials directly, though it referred to them as BioSynths, and there were far more "models" than she had expected to find. The military Partials were presented first, more as a success story than an available product: one million successful field tests for their flagship biotechnology. You couldn't "buy" a soldier model, of course, but the brochure had other, less humanoid versions of the same technology: hyperintelligent Watchdogs, bushy-maned lions rendered docile enough to keep as pets, even something called the MyDragon™, which looked like a spindly, winged lizard the size of a house cat. The last page at the end promoted new kinds of Partials—a security guard based on the soldier template, and others to be looked up online. *Is that what I am? A security guard or a love slave or whatever kind of sick garbage these people were selling?* She read through the brochure again, looking for any clue she could find about herself, but there was nothing else; she threw it down and picked up the next, but it turned out to be the same interior with an alternate cover. She threw that one down as well and cursed.

I'm not just a product in a catalog, she told herself. *Somebody made me for a reason—Nandita was staying with me, watching me, for a reason. Am I a sleeper agent? A listening device? An assassin? The Partial scientist who captured me, Dr. Morgan—when she found out what I was, she nearly exploded, she was so nervous. She's the most frightening person I've ever met, and just thinking about what I might be made her terrified.*

I was made for a reason, but is that reason good or evil?

Whatever the answer, she wouldn't find it in a company brochure. She picked one back up and stowed it in her pack, just in case it ever came in handy, then hefted her rifle and walked to the nearest door. There wasn't likely to be anything dangerous this high up, but . . . that dragon in the picture had made her nervous. She'd never seen one alive, not the dragon or the lion or anything else, but it didn't hurt to be careful. This was the enemy's own lair. *They're artificial species,* she told herself, *engineered as dependent, docile pets. I've never seen one because they're all dead, hunted to extinction by real animals who know how to survive in the wild.* Somehow, the thought depressed her and didn't do much to calm her fears. She was still likely to find the rooms full of corpses—so many people had died here that the city was practically a tomb. She put a hand on the door, summoned her courage, and pushed.

The air on the other side rushed in to meet her, fresher and more rich than the dead air in the lobby and the stairs. The door opened into a short hallway lined with offices, and Kira could see at the end long banks of windows broken out and open to the air. She peeked through the door of the first office, propped open by a wheeled black chair, and caught her breath in surprise as a trio of yellow-brown swallows took sudden flight from their nest in a bookcase. A warm breeze from the glassless window touched her face, stirring the wisps of hair that weren't tied back in her ponytail. The room once had floor-to-ceiling windows, and so was now like a recessed cave in the side of a cliff, and she looked out warily on the overgrown ruins of the city below.

The name on the door said DAVID HARMON, and he had kept his workspace sparse: a clear plastic desk, a shelf of books crusted over with bird droppings, and a faded whiteboard on the wall. Kira shouldered her rifle and stepped in, looking for some kind of records she could search through, but there was nothing—not even a computer, though she wouldn't be able to search it anyway without electricity to power it. She stepped close to the bookshelf, trying to read the titles without touching the excrement, and found row upon row of financial reference guides. David Harmon must have been an accountant. Kira glanced around a final time, hoping for a last-minute revelation, but the room was empty. She stepped back into the hallway and tried the next office.

Ten offices later she had still found nothing that shed any more light on her mysteries: a handful of ledgers, and the occasional filing cabinet, but even those were either empty or filled with profit statements. ParaGen had been obscenely wealthy: She knew that with certainty now, but almost nothing else.

The real information would be on the computers, but the office didn't seem to have any. Kira frowned, disturbed, because everything she'd heard about the old world said that they relied on computers for everything. Why didn't the office have any of the flat screen monitors or metallic towers that she was used to seeing nearly everywhere? She sighed and shook her head in frustration, knowing that even if she found the computers, she wouldn't know what to do with them. She'd used some at the hospital, medicomps and scanners and so on when a treatment or a diagnosis called for one, but those were mostly isolated machines with a singular purpose. Computers in the old world had been part of a vast network capable of communicating instantly, all over the world. Everything had been on computers, from books to music to, apparently, ParaGen's vast scheming plans. But these offices didn't have any computers. . . .

But this one has a printer. She stopped, staring at a side table in the last office on the floor—a bigger office than the rest, with the name GUINEVERE CREECH on the door: probably the local vice president or whatever their ranks were called. There was blank paper scattered around the floor, wrinkly and discolored from past rainstorms blowing through the broken window, and a small plastic box on a side table by the desk. She recognized it as a printer—there were dozens in the hospital back home, useless now because they had no ink, and she'd been tasked once with moving them from one storage closet to another. In the old world they'd used them to write out documents directly from a computer, so if there was a printer in this room, there must have been a computer as well, at least at one time. She picked the thing up to examine it more closely: no cord, or even a place to put one, which meant it was wireless. She set it back down and knelt on the floor, looking under the side table; nothing there. Why had someone gone through and removed all the computers—was it to hide their data when the world fell apart? Surely Kira couldn't be the first person to think of coming here;

ParaGen had built the Partials, for goodness' sake, and they were the world experts in biotech. Even if they didn't get blamed for the Partial War, the government would have contacted them about curing RM. *Assuming, of course, that the government didn't know that the Partials carried the cure.* She pushed the thought away. She wasn't here to entertain conspiracy theories, she was here to uncover facts. Maybe their computers had been seized?

She looked up, scanning the room from her hands and knees, and from this vantage point saw something she hadn't before: a shiny black circle in the black metal frame of the desk. She moved her head and it winked at her, losing and catching the light. She frowned, stood, then shook her head at the stupid simplicity of it all.

The desks *were* the computers.

Now that she saw it, it was obvious. The clear plastic desks were almost exact replicas, in large scale, of the medicomp screen she used at the hospital. The brain—the CPU and the hard drive and the actual computer—were all embedded in the metal edge, and when turned on, the entire desk would light up with touch screens and keyboards and everything else. She got down on her knees again, checking the base of the frame's metal legs, and shouted in triumph when she found a short black cord plugged into a power socket in the floor. Another flock of sparrows lifted up and flew away at the sound. Kira smiled, but it wasn't truly a victory—finding the computers meant nothing if she couldn't turn them on. She would need a charging unit, and she hadn't packed one when she hastily left East Meadow; she felt stupid for the oversight, but there was no changing it now. She would have to try to scavenge one in Manhattan, maybe from a hardware store or electronics shop. The island had been considered too dangerous to travel on since the Break, so most of it hadn't been looted yet. Still, she didn't relish the thought of hauling a fifty-pound generator up those twenty-one flights of stairs.

Kira blew out a long, slow breath, gathering her thoughts. *I need to find out what I am,* she thought. *I need to find out how my father is connected to this, and Nandita. I need to find the Trust.* She pulled out the photo again, she and her father and Nandita all standing in front of the ParaGen complex. Someone had written a message on it: *Find the Trust.* She didn't even know exactly what the Trust was, let alone how to find it; she didn't even know who'd left her the photo or written the note on it, for that matter, though she assumed from the handwriting that it was Nandita. The things she didn't know seemed to settle on her like a great, heavy weight, and she closed her eyes, trying to breathe deeply. She had pinned all her hopes on this office, the only part of ParaGen she could reach, and to find nothing of use in it, not even another lead, was almost too much to bear.

She rose to her feet, walking quickly to the window for air. Manhattan stretched out below her, half city and half forest, a great green mass of eager trees and crumbling, vine-wrapped buildings. It was all so *big,* overwhelmingly big, and that was just the city—beyond it there were other cities, other states and nations, entire other continents she had never even seen. She felt lost, worn down by the sheer impossibility of finding even one small secret in a world so huge. She watched a flock of birds fly by, oblivious to her and her problems; the world had ended, and they hadn't even noticed. If the last of the sentient species disappeared, the sun would still rise and the birds would still fly.

What did her success or failure really mean?

And then she raised her head, set her jaw, and spoke.

"I'm not giving up," she said. "It doesn't matter how big the world is. All that gives me is more places to look."

Kira turned back to the office, going to the filing cabinet and pulling open the first drawer. If the Trust had something to do with ParaGen, maybe a special project that was connected to the Partial leadership, like Samm had implied, this financial office would have had to process some money for it sooner or later, and there might be a record she could find. She wiped the dirt from the table screen and started pulling files from the cabinet, searching through them line by line, item by item, payment by payment. When she finished with a folder, she swept it onto the floor in the corner and started on a new one, hour after hour, stopping only when it had grown too dark to read. The night air was cold, and she thought about starting a small fire—on top of one of the desks, where she could contain it—but decided against it. Her campfires down in the streets were easy to hide from anyone who might be watching, but a light up here would be visible for miles. She retreated instead to the foyer at the top of the stairs, closing all the doors and setting up her bedroll in the shelter of the reception desk. She opened a can of tuna and ate it quietly in the dark, picking it up with her fingers and pretending it was sushi. She slept lightly, and when she woke in the morning, she went straight back to work, combing through the files. In midmorning she finally found something.

"Nandita Merchant," she read, a jolt through her system after searching for so long. "Fifty-one thousand one hundred and twelve dollars paid on December 5, 2064. Direct deposit.

Arvada, Colorado." It was a payroll statement, a massive one that seemed to include employees from the entire multinational company. She frowned, reading the line again. It didn't say what Nandita's job was, only what they'd paid her, and she had no idea what that represented—was it a monthly wage, or a yearly? Or a one-time fee for a specific job? She went back to the ledgers and found one for the previous month, flipping through it quickly to find Nandita's name. "Fifty-one thousand one hundred and twelve dollars on November 21," she read, and saw the same on November 7. *So it's a biweekly salary, making her yearly . . . about one point two million dollars. That sounds like a lot.* She had no frame of reference for old-world salaries, but as she glanced over the list she saw that $51,112 was one of the highest figures. "So she was one of the bigwigs in the company," Kira muttered, thinking out loud. "She earned more than most, but what did she do?"

She wanted to look up her father, but she didn't even know his last name. Her own last name, Walker, was a nickname she'd earned from the soldiers who'd found her after the Break, walking mile after mile through an empty city, searching for food. "Kira the Walker." She'd been so young that she couldn't remember her own last name, or where her father worked, or even what city they'd lived in—

"Denver!" she shouted, the name suddenly coming to her. "We lived in Denver. That was in Colorado, right?" She looked at Nandita's listing again: Arvada, Colorado. Was that near Denver? She folded the page carefully and stowed it in her pack, vowing to search later for an old bookstore with an atlas. She looked back at the payroll report, searching for her father's first name, Armin, but the payments were organized by surname, and finding a single Armin among the tens of thousands of people would be more trouble than it was worth. At best, finding his name would confirm what the photo already suggested: that Nandita and her father had worked in the same location at the same company. It still wouldn't tell her what they did or why.

Another day of research turned up nothing she could use, and in a fit of petulance she snarled and threw the last folder out the broken window; as soon as she threw it she berated herself for doing something to attract the attention of anyone else who might be prowling the city. The odds were against it, of course, but that didn't make it smart to tempt fate. She stayed back from the window, hoping that whoever saw it would chalk the errant paper up to wind or animal activity, and moved on to her next project: the second floor.

It was really the twenty-second floor, she reminded herself, as she trudged up the stairway to the next door. This one, oddly, was only barely closed, and when she pushed it open she stepped into a sea of cubicles. There was no reception area here, and only a handful of offices; everything else was low partitions and shared workspace. Many of the cubicles had computers, she noticed, or obvious docks where a portable computer could be plugged in—there were no fancy desk-screens on this floor—but what really caught her attention were the cubicles that had empty cables. Places where a computer should be, but wasn't.

Kira froze, surveying the room carefully. It was windier in here than on the floor below, thanks to a long wall of broken windows and the lack of office walls to break up the airflow. The occasional piece of paper or swirl of dust blew past the cubicle partitions, but Kira ignored them, looking instead at the six desks nearest to her. Four were normal—monitors, keyboards, organizers, family photos—but in two of them the computers were gone. Not just gone, but ransacked; the organizer and photos had been pushed aside or even knocked on the floor, as if whoever took the computers was in too great of a hurry to bother preserving anything else. Kira crouched down to examine the nearest one, where a picture frame had fallen facedown. A layer of dirt had collected over and around it, and with time and moisture mushrooms had taken root in the dirt. It was hardly surprising—after eleven years of open-air access, half the buildings in Manhattan had a layer of soil inside of them—but what stood out to her was a small yellow stem, like a blade of grass, curling out from beneath the photo. She looked up at the windows, gauging the angle, and guessed that yes, for a few hours of the day this spot would get plenty of sunlight, more than enough to nurture a green plant. There were other blades of grass around it as well, but again, that wasn't the issue. It was the way the grass grew out from underneath the photo. She picked up the photo and tipped it away, exposing a small mass of beetles and mushrooms and short, dead grass. She sat back, mouth open, stunned at the implications.

The photo had been knocked off the table *after* the grass had already started to grow.

The act hadn't been recent. The picture frame had enough dirt and muck on top of it, and around the edges, to show that it had lain there for several years. But it hadn't been lying there the full eleven. The Break had come and gone, the building had been abandoned, the dirt and weeds had collected, and *then* the cubicle had been raided. Who could have done it? Human, or Partial? Kira examined the space under the desk, finding a handful of other cables but no clear evidence of who had taken the CPU they were connected to. She crawled into the next cube over, the other one that had been looted, and found similar remains. Someone had climbed up to the twenty-second floor, stolen two computers, and lugged them all the way back down again.

Why would someone do it? Kira sat back, puzzling through the possibilities. If somebody wanted information, she supposed it was easier to haul the computers down the stairs rather than haul a generator up. But why these two and none of the others? What was different about them? She looked around again and noted with surprise that these two cubicles were the closest to the elevator. That made even less sense than anything else: After the Break, there would have been no power to make the elevators run. That couldn't be the connection. There weren't even names on the cubicle walls; if someone had targeted these two computers specifically, they had to have inside knowledge.

Kira stood up and walked through the entire floor, going slowly, watching for anything else that looked out of place or looted. She found a printer missing, but she couldn't tell if it had been taken before or after the Break. When she finished the central room, she searched the handful of offices along the back wall, and gasped in surprise when she found that one of them had been completely gutted: the computer gone, the shelves emptied, everything. There was enough corporate detritus to make it look like a once-functioning office—a phone and a wastebasket and various little stacks of papers and so on—but nothing else. This office had far more shelving than the others as well, all empty, and Kira wondered just how much, exactly, had been stolen from it.

She paused, staring at the empty desk. Something else was different about this one, something she couldn't quite put her finger on. There was a small desk organizer knocked onto the floor, just as there had been in the cubicles, which implied that the office had been raided with the same sense of anxious haste. Whoever had stolen these items had been in an awfully big hurry. The now-empty cables all hung in the same way, though the office had far more of them than the cubicles. She racked her brain, trying to figure out what was bothering her, and finally hit on it: the small office had no photos. Most of the desks she'd been scouring for the last two days had held at least one family photo, and many of them had more: smiling couples, groups of kids in coordinated outfits, the preserved images of families now long dead. This room, however, had no photos at all. That meant one of two things: first, that the man or woman who worked here had no family, or didn't care enough about them to display photos. Second, and more tantalizing, whoever had taken the equipment had also taken the photos. And the most likely reason for that was that the person who'd taken the photos was the same person who'd once worked in the room.

Kira looked at the door, which read AFA DEMOUX, and below it in thick block letters, IT. Was "IT" a nickname? It didn't seem like a very nice one, but her understanding of old-world culture was sketchy at best. She checked the other doors and found that each followed the same pattern, a name and a word, though most of the words were longer: OPERATIONS, SALES, MARKETING.

Were they titles? Departments? "IT" was the only one written all in capital letters, so it was probably an acronym, but Kira didn't know what it stood for. *Invention . . . Testing.* She shook her head. This wasn't a lab, so Afa Demoux wasn't a scientist. What had he done here? Had he come back for his own equipment? Was his work so vital, or so dangerous, that someone else had come back after to take it? This wasn't a random looting—no one hiked up twenty-two stories for a couple of computers when there were plenty to be had at ground level. Whoever had taken these had taken them for a reason—for something important that was stored in them. But who had it been? Afa Demoux? Someone from East Meadow? One of the Partials?

Who else was there?

CHAPTER THREE

"**T**his hearing is now in session."

Marcus stood in the back of the hall, craning to see over the crowd of people filling the room. He could see the senators well enough—Hobb and Kessler and Tovar and a new one he didn't know, all seated on the stage behind a long table—but the two accused were out of his sight. The city hall they used to use for these sessions had been trashed in a Voice attack two months ago, before Kira had found the cure for RM and the Voice had reintegrated with the rest of society. Without the hall, they'd taken to using the auditorium of the old East Meadow High School instead; the school had been closed a few months before, so why not? *Of course,* Marcus thought, *the building is the least of the things that have changed since then.* The old leader of the Voice was one of the senators now, and two of the former senators were the ones on trial. Marcus stood on his tiptoes, but the auditorium was packed, standing room only. It seemed like everyone in East Meadow had come to see

Weist and Delarosa's final sentence.

"I'm going to be sick," said Isolde, clutching Marcus's arm. He dropped down from his toes to stand flat on the ground, grinning at Isolde's morning sickness, then grimacing in pain as her grip tightened and her fingernails dug into his flesh. "Stop laughing at me," she growled.

"I wasn't laughing out loud."

"I'm pregnant," said Isolde, "my senses are like superpowers. I can smell your thoughts."

"Smell?"

"It's a very limited superpower," she said. "Now seriously, get me some fresh air or I'm going to make this room a lot grosser than it already is."

"You want to go back out?"

Isolde shook her head, closing her eyes and breathing slowly. She wasn't showing yet, but her morning sickness had been terrible—she'd actually lost weight instead of gained it, because she couldn't keep any food down, and Nurse Hardy had threatened her with inpatient care at the hospital if she didn't improve soon. She'd been taking the week off work to relax, and it had helped a bit, but she was too much of a political junkie to stay away from a hearing like this. Marcus looked around the back of the auditorium, saw a seat near an open door, and pulled her toward it.

"Excuse me, sir," he said softly, "can my friend have this chair?"

The man wasn't even using it, just standing in front of it, but he glowered at Marcus in annoyance. "It's first come, first served," he said lowly. "Now stay quiet so I can hear this."

"She's pregnant," said Marcus, and nodded smugly as the

man's entire demeanor changed in seconds.

"Why didn't you say so?" He stepped aside immediately, offering Isolde the seat, and walked off in search of somewhere else to stand. *Works every time,* thought Marcus. Even after the repeal of the Hope Act, which had made pregnancy mandatory, pregnant women were still treated as sacred. Now that Kira had discovered a cure for RM, and there was a real hope that infants would actually survive more than a few days, the attitude was even more prevalent. Isolde sat down, fanning her face, and Marcus positioned himself behind her seat, where he could discourage people from blocking her airflow. He looked back up at the front of the room.

". . . which is just the kind of thing we're trying to stop in the first place," Senator Tovar was saying.

"You can't be serious," said the new senator, and Marcus focused his concentration to hear him better. "You were the leader of the Voice," he told Tovar. "You threatened to start, and by some interpretations actually started, a civil war."

"Violence being occasionally necessary isn't the same thing as violence being good," said Tovar. "We were fighting to prevent atrocity, not to punish it after the fact—"

"Capital punishment is, at its heart, a preventative measure," said the senator. Marcus blinked—he'd had no idea that execution was even being considered for Weist and Delarosa. When you have only 36,000 humans left, you don't jump right to executing them, criminal or not. The new senator gestured toward the prisoners. "When these two die for their crimes, in a community so small *everyone* will be intimately aware of it, those crimes are unlikely to be repeated."

"Their crimes were conducted through the direct application of senatorial power," said Tovar. "Who exactly are you trying to send a message to?"

"To anyone who treats a human life like a chip in a poker game," said the man, and Marcus felt the room grow tense. The new senator was staring at Tovar coldly, and even in the back of the room Marcus could read the threatening subtext: If he could do it, this man would execute Tovar right along with Delarosa and Weist.

"They did what they thought was best," said Senator Kessler, one of the former senators who'd managed to weather the scandal and maintain her position. From everything Marcus had seen, and the inside details he'd learned from Kira, Kessler and the others had been just as guilty as Delarosa and Weist—they had seized power and declared martial law, turning Long Island's tiny democracy into a totalitarian state. They had done it to protect the people, or so they claimed, and in the beginning Marcus had agreed with them: Humanity was facing extinction, after all, and with those kinds of stakes it's hard to argue that freedom is more important than survival. But Tovar and the rest of the Voice had rebelled, and the Senate had reacted, and the Voice had reacted to that, and on and on until suddenly they were lying to their own people, blowing up their own hospital, and secretly killing their own soldier in a bid to ignite fear of a fictional Partial invasion and unite the island again. The official ruling had been that Delarosa and Weist were the masterminds, and everyone else had simply been following orders—you couldn't punish Kessler for following her leader any more than you could punish a Grid soldier for following Kessler. Marcus still wasn't sure how he felt about the ruling, but it seemed pretty obvious that this new guy didn't like it at all.

Marcus crouched down and put a hand on Isolde's shoulder. "Remind me who the new guy is."

"Asher Woolf," Isolde whispered. "He replaced Weist as the representative from the Defense Grid."

"That explains that," said Marcus, standing back up. *You don't kill a soldier without making every other soldier in the army an enemy for life.*

"'What they thought was best,'" Woolf repeated. He looked at the crowd, then back at Kessler. "What they thought was best, in this case, was the murder of a soldier who had already sacrificed his own health and safety trying to protect their secrets. If we make them pay the same price that boy did, maybe the next pack of senators won't think that kind of decision is 'best.'"

Marcus looked at Senator Hobb, wondering why he hadn't spoken yet. He was the best debater on the Senate, but Marcus had learned to think of him as the most shallow, manipulative, and opportunistic. He was also the one who'd gotten Isolde pregnant, and Marcus didn't think he could ever respect the man again. He certainly hadn't shown any interest in his unborn child. Now he was showing the same hands-off approach with the sentence. Why hadn't he picked a side yet?

"I think the point's been made," said Kessler. "Weist and Delarosa have been tried and convicted; they're in handcuffs, they're on their way to a prison camp, they're paying for—"

"They're being sent to an idyllic country estate to eat steaks and stud for a bunch of lonely farm girls," said Woolf.

"You watch your tongue!" said Kessler, and Marcus winced

at the fury in her voice. He was friends with Kessler's adopted daughter, Xochi; he'd heard that fury more times than he cared to count, and he didn't envy Woolf's position. "Whatever your misogynist opinion of our farming communities," said Kessler, "the accused are not going to a resort. They are prisoners, and they will be sent to a prison camp, and they will work harder than you have ever worked in your life."

"And you're not going to feed them?" asked Woolf.

Kessler seethed. "Of course we're going to feed them."

Woolf creased his brow in mock confusion. "Then you're not going to allow them any fresh air or sunshine?"

"Where else are they going to work at a prison farm but outside in a field?"

"Then I'm confused," said Woolf. "So far this doesn't sound like much of a punishment. Senator Weist ordered the cold-hearted killing of one of his own soldiers, a teenage boy under his own command, and his punishment is a soft bed, three square meals, fresher food than we get here in East Meadow, and all the girls he could ever ask for—"

"You keep saying 'girls,'" said Tovar. "What exactly are you envisioning here?"

Woolf paused, staring at Tovar, then picked up a piece of paper and scanned it with his eyes as he talked. "Perhaps I misunderstood the nature of our ban on capital punishment. We can't kill anyone because, in your words, 'there are only thirty-five thousand people left on the planet, and we can't afford to lose any more.'" He looked up. "Is that correct?"

"We have a cure for RM now," said Kessler. "That means we have a future. We can't afford to lose a single person."

"Because we need to carry on the species," said Woolf with a nod. "Multiply and replenish the Earth. Of course. Would you like me to tell you where babies come from, or should we get a chalkboard so I can draw you a diagram?"

"This is not about sex," said Tovar.

"You're damn right it's not."

Kessler threw up her hands. "What if we just don't let them procreate?" she asked. "Will that make you happy?"

"If they can't procreate, we have no reason to keep them alive," Woolf shot back. "By your own logic, we should kill them and be done with it."

"They can work," said Kessler, "they can plow fields, they can grind wheat for the whole island, they can—"

"We're not keeping them alive for reproduction," said Tovar softly, "and we're not keeping them alive as slaves. We're keeping them alive because killing them would be wrong."

Woolf shook his head. "Punishing criminals is—"

"Senator Tovar is correct," said Hobb, rising to his feet. "This is not about sex or reproduction or manual labor or any of these other issues we've been arguing. It's not even about survival. The human race has a future, like we've said, and food and children and so on are all important to that future, but they are not the most important. They are the means of our existence, but they cannot become the reason for it. We can never be reduced—and we can never reduce ourselves—to a level of pure physical subsistence." He walked toward Senator Woolf. "Our children will inherit more than our genes; more than our infrastructure. They will inherit our morals. The future we've gained by curing RM is a precious gift that we must earn, day by day and hour by hour, by being the kind of people who deserve to have a future. Do we want our children to kill one another? Of course not. Then we teach them, through our own example, that every life is precious. Killing a killer might send a mixed message."

"Caring for a killer is just as confusing," said Woolf.

"We're not going to care for a killer," said Hobb, "we're going to care for everybody: old and young, bond and free, male and female. And if one of them happens to be a killer—if two or three or a hundred happen to be killers—we still care for them." He smiled mirthlessly. "We don't let them kill anybody else, obviously; we're not stupid. But we don't kill them, either, because we're trying to be better. We're trying to find a higher ground. We have a future now, so let's not start it by killing."

There was a scattering of applause in the room, though Marcus thought some of it felt obligatory. A handful of people shouted back in disagreement, but the tenor of the room had changed, and Marcus knew the argument was done; Woolf didn't look happy about it, but after Hobb's words he didn't look eager to keep calling for execution, either. Marcus tried to get a look at the prisoners' reactions but still couldn't see them. Isolde was muttering, and he stooped back down to hear her.

"What did you say?"

"I said he's a stupid glad-handing bastard," Isolde snapped, and Marcus backed away with a grimace. That was not a situation he wanted any part of. She insisted that her encounter with Hobb had been willing—she'd been his assistant for months, and he was very handsome and charming—but her attitude had soured significantly in the months since.

"It doesn't look like we're going to be deliberating any

further," said Tovar. "I call for a vote: Marisol Delarosa and Cameron Weist will be sentenced to a life of hard labor on the Stillwell Farm. All in favor."

Tovar, Hobb, and Kessler all raised their hands; a moment later Woolf did the same. A unanimous vote. Tovar leaned down to sign the paper in front of him, and four Grid soldiers walked in from the wings to escort the prisoners out. The room grew noisy as a hundred little conversations started up, people arguing back and forth about the verdict and the sentence and whole drama that had unfolded. Isolde stood up, and Marcus helped her into the hall.

"All the way outside," said Isolde. "I need to breathe." They were ahead of most of the crowd and reached the outer doors before the main press of people. Marcus found them a bench, and Isolde sat with a grimace. "I want french fries," she said. "Greasy and salty and just huge fistfuls of them—I want to eat every french fry in the entire world."

"You look like you're going to throw up, how can you even think about food?"

"Don't say 'food,'" she said quickly, closing her eyes. "I don't want food, I want french fries."

"Pregnancy is so weird."

"Shut up."

The crowd thinned as it reached the front lawn, and Marcus watched as groups of men and women either wandered off or stood in small groups, arguing softly about the senators and their decision. "Lawn," perhaps, was misleading: There used to be a lawn in front of the high school, but no one had tended it in years, and it had become a meadow dotted with trees and crisscrossed with buckling sidewalks. Marcus paused to wonder if he'd been the last person to mow it, two years ago when he'd been punished for playing pranks in class. Had anyone mowed it since? Had anyone mowed anything since? That was a dubious claim to fame: the last human being to ever mow the lawn. *I wonder how many other things I'll be the last to do.*

He frowned and looked across the street to the hospital complex and its full parking lot. Much of the city had been empty when the world ended—not a lot of people eating out and seeing movies while the world collapsed in plague—but the hospital had been bustling. The parking lot spilled over with old cars, rusted and sagging, cracked windows and scratched paint, hundreds upon hundreds of people and couples and families hoping vainly that the doctors could save them from RM. They came to the hospital and they died in the hospital, and all the doctors with them. The survivors had cleaned out the hospital as soon as they settled in East Meadow—it was an excellent hospital, one of the reasons the survivors had chosen East Meadow as a place for their settlement in the first place—but the parking lot had never been a priority. The last hope for humanity was surrounded on three sides with a maze of rusted scrap metal, half junkyard and half cemetery.

Marcus heard a surge of voices and turned around, watching Weist and Delarosa emerge from the building with an escort of Grid soldiers and a crowd of people, many of them protesting the verdict. Marcus couldn't tell if they wanted something harsher or more lenient, but he supposed there were probably different factions calling for each. Asher Woolf led the way, slowly pushing through the people and clearing a path. A wagon was waiting to take them away—an armored car rigged with free axles and drawn by a team of four powerful horses. They stomped as they waited, whiffling and blustering as the noise of the crowd grew closer.

"They look like they're going to start a riot," said Isolde, and Marcus nodded. Some of the protestors were blocking the doors of the wagon, and others were trying to pull them away while the Grid struggled helplessly to maintain order.

No, thought Marcus, frowning and leaning forward. *They're not trying to maintain order, they're trying to . . . what? They're not stopping the fight, they're moving it. I've seen them quell riots before, and they were a lot more efficient than this. More focused. What are they—?*

Senator Weist fell to the ground, his chest a blossom of dark red, followed almost immediately by a deafening crack. The world seemed to stand still for a moment, the crowd and the Grid and the meadow all frozen in time. What had happened? What was the red? What was the noise? Why did he fall? The pieces came together one by one in Marcus's mind, slowly and out of order and jumbled in confusion: The sound was a gunshot, and the red on Weist's chest was blood. He'd been shot.

The horses screamed, rearing up in terror and straining against the heavy wagon. Their scream seemed to shatter the moment, and the crowd erupted in noise and chaos as everyone began running—some were looking for cover, some were looking for the shooter, and everyone seemed to be trying to get as far away from the body as they could. Marcus pulled Isolde behind the bench, pressing her to the ground.

"Don't move!" he said, then sprinted toward the fallen prisoner at a dead run.

"Find the shooter!" screamed Senator Woolf. Marcus saw

the senator pull a pistol from his coat, a gleaming black semi-automatic. The civilians were fleeing for cover, and some of the Grid as well, but Woolf and some of the soldiers had stayed by the prisoners. A spray of shrapnel leaped up from the brick wall behind them, and another loud crack rolled across the yard. Marcus kept his eyes on the fallen Weist and dove to the ground beside him, checking his pulse almost before he stopped moving. He couldn't feel much of anything, but a wave of blood bubbling up from the wound in the man's chest told Marcus the heart was still beating. He clamped down with his hands, applying as much pressure as he could, and cried out suddenly as someone yanked him backward.

"I'm trying to save him!"

"He's gone," said a soldier behind him. "You need to get to cover!"

Marcus shrugged him off and scrambled back to the body. Woolf was shouting again, pointing through the meadow to the hospital complex, but Marcus ignored them and pressed down again. He hands were red and slick, his arms coated with warm arterial spray, and he shouted for assistance. "Somebody give me shirt or a jacket! He's bleeding front and back and I can't stop it all with just my hands!"

"Don't be stupid," said the soldier behind him. "You've got to get to cover." But when Marcus turned to look at him, he saw Senator Delarosa, still in handcuffs. She was crouched between them.

"Save her first!" said Marcus.

"He's over there!" cried Woolf, pointing again to the buildings behind the hospital. "The shooter's in there, somebody circle around!"

Blood pumped thickly through Marcus's fingers, staining his hands and covering the prisoner's chest; blood from the exit wound flowed steadily from the man's back, spreading out in a puddle and soaking Marcus's knees and pants. There was too much blood—too much for Weist to ever survive—but Marcus kept the pressure on. The prisoner wasn't breathing, and Marcus called again for help. "I'm losing him!"

"Let him go!" shouted the soldier, loud and more angry. The world seemed drenched in blood and adrenaline, and Marcus struggled to stay in control. When hands finally jutted forward to help with the bleeding, he was surprised to see that they were not the soldier's, but Delarosa's.

"Somebody get over there!" Woolf was shouting. "There's an assassin somewhere in those ruins!"

"It's too dangerous," said another soldier, crouching low in the brush. "We can't just charge in there while a sniper has us pinned down."

"He's not pinning you down, he's aiming for the prisoners."

"It's too dangerous," the soldier insisted.

"Then call for backup," said Woolf. "Surround him. Do something besides stand there!"

Marcus couldn't even feel a heartbeat anymore. The blood in the victim's chest was stagnant, and the body was inert. He kept the pressure on, knowing that it was useless but too stunned to think of anything else.

"Why do you even care?" asked the soldier. Marcus looked up and saw the man talking to Senator Woolf. "Five minutes ago you were calling for an execution, and now that he's dead you're trying to capture his killer?"

Woolf whirled around, shoving his face mere inches from the

soldier's. "What's your name, Private?"

The soldier quailed. "Cantona, sir. Lucas."

"Private Cantona, what did you swear to protect?"

"But he's—"

"What did you swear to protect!"

"The people, sir." Cantona swallowed. "And the law."

"In that case, Private, you'd better think good and hard the next time you tell me to abandon them both."

Delarosa looked at Marcus, her hands and arms covered in her fellow prisoner's blood. "This is how it ends, you know."

They were the first words Marcus had heard her speak in months, and they shocked him back to consciousness. He realized he was still flexing his arms against Weist's lifeless chest. He pulled back, staring and panting. "How what ends?"

"Everything."

CHAPTER FOUR

"**I** think it was the Grid," said Xochi.

Haru snorted. "You think the DG killed the man who used to represent them in the Senate."

"It's the only explanation," said Xochi. They were sitting in the living room, nibbling on the last remnants of dinner: grilled cod and fresh-steamed broccoli from Nandita's garden. Marcus paused on that thought, noting that he still thought of it as Nandita's garden even though she'd been missing for months—she hadn't even been the one to plant this crop, Xochi had done it. Xochi and Isolde were the only ones left in the house, and yet in his mind it was still "Nandita's garden."

Of course, in his mind this was still "Kira's house," and she'd been gone for two months. If anything, Marcus spent more time here now than before she'd left, always hoping she'd turn up at the door one day. She never did.

"Think about it," Xochi went on. "The Grid's found nothing, right? Two days of searching and they haven't found a single piece of evidence to lead them to the sniper: not a bullet casing, not a footprint, not even a scuff mark on the floor. I'm no fan of the Grid, but they're not inept. They'd find something if they were looking, therefore they're not looking. They're covering it up."

"Or the sniper's just extremely competent," said Haru. "Is that a possibility, or do we have to jump straight to the conspiracy theory?"

"Well, of course he's competent," said Xochi. "He's Grid-trained."

"This sounds like a circular argument," said Isolde.

"Weist was part of the Grid," said Haru. "He was their own representative on the council. If you think a soldier would kill another soldier, you don't know much about soldiers. They're ferociously vindictive when one of their own gets attacked. They wouldn't be covering this up, they'd be lynching the guy."

"That's exactly what I mean," said Xochi. "Whatever else Weist did, he killed a soldier in cold blood—maybe not personally, but he gave the order. He arranged the murder of a soldier under his own command. The Grid would never just let that slide, you said it yourself: They'd hunt him down and lynch him. The new Grid senator, Woolf or whatever, Isolde said he was practically screaming for the death penalty, but then they didn't get it, so they went to plan B."

"Or more likely," said Haru, "this is exactly what the Grid says it is: an attempt on Woolf or Tovar or someone like that. One of the senators still in power. There's no reason to kill a convicted prisoner."

"So the sniper just missed?" asked Xochi. "This amazingly

competent super-sniper, who can evade a full Grid investigation, was aiming for one of the senators, but he's just a really crappy shot? Come on: He's either a pro or he's not, Haru."

Marcus tried to stay out of these arguments—"these" meaning "any argument with Haru"—and this was exactly why. He'd seen firsthand the way the soldiers had reacted to the attack, and he still had no idea if it was a conspiracy or not. The soldier had tried to pull Marcus off Weist, but did he do it because he was trying to save Marcus, or because he was trying to keep Marcus from saving Weist? Senator Woolf seemed practically offended by the attack, as if killing the prisoner had been a personal insult against him, but was that genuine or was he just playing up the ruse? Haru and Xochi were passionate, but they were too quick to jump to extremes, and Marcus knew from experience that they'd argue back and forth for hours, maybe for days. He left them to it, and turned instead to Madison and Isolde, both cooing quietly over Madison's baby, Arwen.

Arwen was the miracle baby—the first human child in almost twelve years to survive the ravages of RM, thanks to Kira's cure self-replicating in her bloodstream. She was asleep now in Madison's arms, wrapped tightly in a fleece blanket, while Madison talked softly with Isolde about pregnancy and labor. Sandy, Arwen's personal nurse, watched quietly in the corner—the Miracle Child was too precious to risk without full-time medical attention, so Sandy followed mother and daughter everywhere, but she had never really fit into their group socially. There were more in their retinue as well: To help protect the child, the Senate had assigned them a pair of bodyguards. When a crazed woman—the mother of ten dead children—had tried to kidnap Arwen the day Madison first brought her to the outdoor market, they had doubled the guards and reinstated Haru to the Defense Grid. There were two guards here tonight, one in the front yard and one in the back. The radio on Haru's belt chirped softly every time one of them checked in.

"Any luck with that?" asked Madison, and Marcus snapped back to attention.

"What?"

"The cure," said Madison. "Have you had any luck with it?"

He grimaced, glancing at Isolde, and shook his head. "Nothing. We thought we had a breakthrough a couple of days ago, but it turned out to be something the D team had already tried. Dead end." He grimaced again at his own word choice, though this time he managed to avoid glancing at Isolde; better to let that reference disappear in shame than call any more attention to it.

Isolde looked down, rubbing her belly the way Madison always used to. Marcus worked as hard as he could—everyone on the cure teams did—but they were still no closer to synthesizing the cure for RM. Kira had figured out what the cure was and was able to obtain a sample from the Partials on the mainland, but Marcus and the other doctors were still a far cry from being able to manufacture it on their own.

"Another died this weekend," said Isolde softly. She looked up at Sandy for confirmation, and the nurse nodded sadly. Isolde paused, her hand on her belly, then turned to Marcus. "There's more, you know—the Hope Act is gone, none of our pregnancies are mandatory anymore, and yet there are more now than ever before. Everyone wants to have a child, trusting that you'll have figured out how to manufacture the cure reliably by the time they come to term." She looked back down. "It's funny—we always called them 'infants' in the Senate, back before the cure, like we were trying to hide from the word 'child.' When all it was was death reports, we never wanted to think of them as babies, as children, as anything but subjects in a failed experiment. Now that I'm . . . here, though, now that I'm . . . making one of my own, growing another human being right inside of me, it's different. I can't think of it as anything besides my baby."

Sandy nodded. "We did the same thing in the hospital. We still do. The deaths are still too close, so we try to keep death distant."

"I don't know how you can do it," said Isolde softly. Marcus thought he heard her voice crack, but he couldn't see her face to tell if she was crying.

"You have to have some kind of progress, though," Madison told Marcus. "You have four teams—"

"Five," said Marcus.

"Five teams now," said Madison, "all trying to synthesize the Partial pheromone. You have all the equipment, the samples to work from, you have everything. It . . ." She paused. "It can't be a dead end."

"We're doing everything we can," said Marcus, "but you have to understand how complex this thing is. It doesn't just interact with RM, it's part of the RM life cycle somehow—we're still trying to understand how it works. I mean . . . we still don't even understand why it works. Why would the Partials have the cure for RM? Why would it be part of their breath, in their blood? As near as we could gather from Kira before she left, the

Partials don't even know they have it, it's just part of their genetic makeup."

"It doesn't make sense," said Sandy.

"Not unless there's some larger plan," said Marcus.

"It doesn't matter if there's some huge hypothetical plan," said Madison. "It doesn't matter where the pheromone came from, or how it got there, or why the sky is blue—all you have to do is copy it."

"We have to know how it works first—" said Marcus, but Isolde cut him off.

"We're going to go take it," said Isolde. There was an edge in her voice Marcus hadn't heard before. He raised his eyebrows in surprise.

"You mean from the Partials?"

"The Senate talks about it every day," said Isolde. "There's a cure, but we can't make it on our own, and babies are dying every week, and the people are getting restless. Meanwhile right across the sound there are a million Partials who make our cure every day, without even trying. It's not 'will we attack the Partials,' it's 'how much longer will we wait.'"

"I've been across the sound," said Marcus. "I've seen what Partials are capable of in a fight—we wouldn't stand a chance against them."

"It doesn't have to be an all-out war," said Isolde, "just a raid—in and out, grab one guy, done. Just like Kira and Haru did with Samm."

That got Haru's attention, and he looked up from his argument with Xochi. "What about me and Samm?"

"They're talking about whether the Grid's going to kidnap

another Partial," said Madison.

"Of course they're going to," said Haru. "It's inevitable. They've been stupid to wait this long."

Great, thought Marcus. *Now I'm stuck in a conversation with Haru whether I like it or not.*

"We don't have to kidnap one," said Xochi. "We could just talk to them."

"You were attacked last time," said Haru. "I've read the reports—you barely made it out alive, and that was with a Partial you trusted. I'd hate to see what happens with a Partial faction you don't know anything about."

"We can't trust all of them," said Xochi, "but the other thing you must have seen in the reports is that Samm disobeyed his commander to help us. Maybe there are more Partials who share his perspective."

"If we could really trust them," said Haru, "we wouldn't have to rely on the one disobedient outlier to help us. I'll believe in peace with the Partials as soon as I see them raise a finger to help us."

"He talks big," said Madison, "but he wouldn't trust a Partial even then."

"If you remembered the Partial War," said Haru, "you wouldn't either."

"So we're back to the beginning," said Isolde. "Nobody in charge wants to make peace with them, and nobody in the hospital can make the cure without them, so our only option is war."

"A small attack," said Haru. "Just slip in and grab one and they won't even notice."

"Which will mean war," said Marcus, sighing as they dragged

him into the argument. "They're already in a war with each other, and that's probably the only reason they haven't attacked us yet. The group we ran into across the sound was studying Kira to try to solve their own plague, their built-in expiration date, and there is clearly a faction of them that believes humans are the key and will stop at nothing to turn us all into experiments. The instant they win their civil war, they'll come down here with guns blazing and kill or enslave us all."

"So then war is inevitable," said Haru.

"Almost as inevitable as you using the word 'inevitable,'" said Marcus.

Haru ignored the jab. "Then there's no reason for us to not raid them. In fact, it's better to do it now, while they're distracted; we'll grab a few, extract enough of the cure to last us as long as we'll need, kill them, and get out of Long Island before they ever have a chance to come after us."

Sandy frowned. "You mean leave Long Island completely?"

"If the Partials start invading again, we'd be stupid not to run," said Haru. "If we didn't need them for the cure, we'd have done it already."

"Just give us time," said Marcus. "We're close, I know we are."

Marcus expected Haru to argue, but it was Isolde who responded first. "We've given you a chance," she said coldly. "I don't care if we synthesize it, steal it, form a treaty, or whatever you want, but I'm not going to lose my baby. People are not going to go back to how it used to be, not now that they know there's a cure. And it doesn't sound like the Partials are going to wait forever. We're lucky we're not looking down the business end of a Partial invasion already."

"You're in a race," said Haru. "Make more of the cure, or war is inevitable."

"Yeah," said Marcus, standing up. "You said that. I need some air—the entire future of the human race resting on my shoulders is a little much all of a sudden." He walked outside, glad that nobody stood up to follow him. He wasn't mad, at least not at them; the truth was, the future of the human race *was* resting on his shoulders, on all their shoulders. With barely 35, 000 people left, it wasn't like there was anybody else to rest it on.

He pushed open the back door and walked into the cool evening air. Twelve years ago, before the Break, there would have been electric lights all over the city, so bright they blotted out the stars, but tonight the sky was filled with twinkling constellations. Marcus looked up at them, breathing deeply, pointing out the few he remembered from school: Orion was the easiest, with his belt and his sword, and there was the Big Dipper. He closed one eye and traced the handle with his finger, looking for the North Star.

"You're going the wrong way," said a girl's voice, and Marcus jerked in surprise.

"I didn't realize anyone was out here," said Marcus, hoping he hadn't looked too stupid when he jumped. He turned to see who it was, wondering suddenly who would be hiding in Xochi's backyard, and yelped in terror when a woman stepped out of the shadows with an assault rifle. He stumbled backward, trying to find his voice—trying just to process the unexpected appearance—and the woman held her finger to her lips. Marcus backed into the side of the house, steadying himself against the wall. The gesture, and the gleaming gun barrel, caused him to close his mouth.

The girl stepped forward, smiling like a cat. Marcus could see now that she was younger than he'd surmised at first—she was tall and slender, her movements full of power and confidence, but she was probably no more than nineteen or twenty years old. Her features were Asian, and her jet-black hair was pulled back in a tight braid. Marcus smiled back at her nervously, eyeing not only the rifle but the pair of knives he now saw clipped to her belt. Not one knife—a pair of knives. *Who needs two knives? How many things does she have to cut at once?* He was in no hurry to find out.

"You can talk," said the girl, "just don't scream or call for help or anything. I'd prefer to get through the evening without running—or, you know, killing anybody."

"That's great news," said Marcus, swallowing nervously. "If there's anything I can do to keep you from killing anybody, you just let me know."

"I'm looking for someone, Marcus."

"How do you know my name?"

She ignored the question and held out a photo. "Look familiar?"

Marcus peered at the photo—three people standing in front of a building—then held out his hand to take it, looking at the girl for permission. She nodded and held it closer, and he took it from her hand, holding it up to the starlight. "It's kind of—"

She flicked on a small flashlight, training it on the image. Marcus nodded.

"—dark, thank you." He looked closer at the photo, uncomfortably aware of the girl's gun so close beside him. The picture showed three people, a man and a woman with a little girl between them, no more than three or four years old. Behind them was a great glass building, and Marcus realized with a start that the sign on the side of it said PARAGEN. He opened his mouth to comment on this, but realized with another shock that the woman in the picture was someone he'd known for years.

"That's Nandita."

"Nandita Merchant," said the girl. She flicked off the light. "I don't suppose you know where she is?"

Marcus turned back to face her, still trying to figure out what was going on. "Nobody's seen Nandita in months," he said. "This is her house, but . . . she used to go out on salvage runs and stuff all the time, looking for herbs for her garden, and the last time she went out, she never came back." He looked at the picture again, then back at the girl. "Are you with Mkele? Or forget who you're with, who are you? How do you know who I am?"

"We've met," she said, "but you don't remember. I'm very hard to see if I don't want to be."

"I'm getting that impression," said Marcus. "I'm also getting the impression that you're not exactly the East Meadow police. Why are you looking for her?"

The girl smiled, sly and mischievous. "Because she's missing."

"I suppose I walked into that one," said Marcus, suddenly aware of how attractive this girl was. "Let me rephrase: Why do you need to find her?"

The girl flicked on the flashlight again, first blinding Marcus and then angling it away toward the photo in his hand. He looked at it again.

"Look closely," said the girl. "Do you recognize her?"

"It's Nandita Merchant," said Marcus. "I already—"

"Not her," said the girl. "The child standing next to her."

Marcus looked again, holding the image close, peering intently at the little girl in the center. Her skin was light brown, her pigtails dark as coal, her eyes bright and curious. She wore a brightly colored dress, the kind a little girl would wear to a park on a summer day. The kind he hadn't seen in twelve years. She looked happy, and innocent, and her face was slightly scrunched as she squinted one eye against the sun.

There was something familiar about that squint. . . .

Marcus's mouth fell open, and he nearly dropped the photo in shock. "That's Kira." He looked up at the mystery girl, more confused now than ever. "That's a picture of Kira from before the Break." He looked at it again, studying her face; she was young, her round face soft with baby fat, but the features were still there. That was Kira's nose, Kira's eyes, and the same way Kira squinted in the sun. He shook his head. "Why is she with Nandita? They didn't even meet until after the Break."

"Exactly," said the girl. "Nandita knew about this, and never told anyone."

That was a weird way to phrase it, thought Marcus. *Not "Nandita knew Kira," but "Nandita knew about this."* "Knew about what?"

The girl flicked off her flashlight, slipped it into a pocket, and plucked the photo from Marcus's hand. "Do you know where she is?"

"Kira or Nandita?" asked Marcus. He shrugged helplessly. "The answer's no to both, so it doesn't matter. Kira went looking for . . ." Kira was looking for the Partials, and he'd been careful never to tell anybody, but he supposed it didn't matter in this case. "You're a Partial, aren't you?"

"If you talk to Kira, tell her that Heron says hello."

Marcus nodded. "You're the one who caught her; the one who took her to Dr. Morgan."

Heron didn't respond, tucking the photo away and glancing into the shadows behind her. "Things are going to get very interesting on this island, very soon," she said. "You're familiar with the expiration date Samm talked about?"

"You know Samm, too?"

"Kira Walker and Nandita Merchant are vital to the solution of the expiration date, and Dr. Morgan is determined to find them."

Marcus frowned, confused. "What do they have to do with it?"

"Don't get distracted by details," said Heron. "It doesn't matter *why* Dr. Morgan wants to find them, just that she does, and she is going to, and Partials have only two ways of doing things: my way, and everybody else's way."

"I'm not a big fan of your way," said Marcus, eyeing the rifle. "Do I even want to know everybody else's way?"

"You've seen it before," said Heron. "It was called the Partial War."

"In that case, I like your way better," said Marcus.

"Then help me," said Heron. "Find Nandita Merchant. She's somewhere on this island. I'd do it myself, but I have business elsewhere."

"Off the island," said Marcus, and ventured a guess. "You're looking for Kira."

Heron smiled again.

"What do I do if I find her?" Marcus asked. "Assuming . . . that I look for her at all, because you're not the boss of me."

"Just find her," said Heron. She took a step backward. "Trust me, you don't want to do this their way." She turned and walked into the shadows.

Marcus tried to follow her, but she was gone.

CHAPTER FIVE

Kira crouched low in the brush, staring through her new rifle scope at the door of the electronics store. This was the fourth one she'd visited, and every one had been previously scavenged. Normally this wouldn't have been strange, but the ParaGen offices had made her wary, and her closer investigations had all proven the same thing: The scavenger, whoever he was, had come recently. This was more than just eleven-year-old looting from the end of the world—someone in the wilds of Manhattan had been collecting computers and generators within the last few months or so.

She'd been watching this place for nearly an hour and a half, focusing her energy, trying to be as cautious in tracking the looter as he was being in hiding his tracks. She watched a few minutes more, scanning the storefront, the neighboring storefronts, the four stories of windows above them—nothing. She checked the street again, empty in both directions. No one was here; it was safe to move in. She checked her pack, clutched her assault rifle tightly, and raced across the broken road. The door had been glass, and she leapt through the shattered opening without pausing; she checked her corners, gun up and ready for action, then carefully sighted down each aisle. It was a small store, mostly speakers and stereo systems, and most of that was long gone, thanks to the original looting. The only person here was the skeletal remains of the cashier, holed up behind the counter. Satisfied that it was safe, she slung her rifle over her shoulder and got down to business, examining the floor as carefully as she could. It didn't take her long to find them: footprints in the dust, clear imprints that could only have been made long after the storefront was destroyed and the building had filled with dirt and debris. The prints here were even clearer than they'd been before, and she measured one with her hand—the same huge shoe size she'd seen before, maybe size fourteen or even fifteen. The prints were also shockingly well preserved: Wind and water would naturally erode the prints over time, especially those in the centers of the aisles, but here there had been almost no erosion at all. Kira dropped to her knees, examining the prints as gently as she could. The others had been made within the last year; these might have been made within the last week.

Whoever was stealing generators was still out there doing it.

Kira turned her attention to the shelves, trying to deduce from their condition, and from the placement of the footprints, exactly what the scavenger had taken. The main concentration of prints was, predictably, in the corner where the generators had been displayed, but the more she looked, the more she saw a deviation in the pattern: He had taken at least two trips to the opposite side of the store, one slow as if he were looking for something, and one firm, the prints deeper, as if he'd been carrying something heavy. She glanced over the shelves, her eyes sliding past dusty plastic phones still tethered to the metal frames, past slim notebook computers and tiny music players like Xochi used to collect. She followed the trail carefully through the rubble on the floor, ending at a low, empty shelf near the back. He'd definitely taken something. Kira bent down to brush away the dirt from the shelf tag, and struggled to decipher the weathered writing: HAM. Ham? No electronics store would sell ham. She peered closer, picking out the faded, filthy word that followed: RADIO. HAM radio, the "ham" all in capital letters. Another acronym, like IT, that she'd never come across before.

Computers, generators, and now radios. Her mysterious scavenger was putting together quite the collection of old-world technology—and he was obviously an expert, as he'd known precisely what the thing on this shelf had been without having to clean up the tag first like she had. More than that, though, he'd taken some very specific equipment from the ParaGen offices, which couldn't possibly be a coincidence; he wasn't just grabbing certain kinds of technology, he was grabbing specific pieces of it. He was gathering old computers from ParaGen, and the generators to be able to access them. And now he was gathering radio systems, but who was he trying to call?

Manhattan was a no-man's-land, empty, an unofficial demilitarized zone between the Partials and the human survivors. No one was supposed to be here, not because it was forbidden but because it was dangerous. If something happened to you out here, either side could get you, and neither side could protect you. It wasn't even great territory for a spy, since there was nothing interesting to observe and report on—except, she supposed, the ParaGen files. She was looking for them, and this scavenger was doing the same—and he'd gotten there first. Now, thanks to him, there weren't any generators left for her to take back to the ParaGen offices, and no guarantee that the computers left there would have the information she needed. She'd hoped to find a generator to get the top executive's desk computer running again, to see if it contained what she was looking for, but this mysterious scavenger was obviously searching for the same things, and he had ignored the executive's computer completely. Most likely, the scavenger had everything she was looking for. If she wanted to read those records, she'd have to find the scavenger himself.

She had to find out what ParaGen was doing with the Partials, with RM, with her, but there was another reason she was here. Nandita's last note had told her to find the Trust—the Partial leaders, the high command who gave all the others their orders—and while she wasn't going to find them here, she might, again, find some clues as to where to start her search. But . . . could she trust Nandita? Kira shook her head, frowning at the ravaged store. She used to trust Nandita more than anyone in the world, but learning that Nandita had known her father before the Break, had known Kira herself, and never once told her . . . Nandita had deceived her, and Kira had no way of knowing what her intentions were in telling Kira what to do next. But it was the only clue she had. She had to keep looking for information about ParaGen, scary mysterious scavenger or not—that was where the answers would be, and this new stranger was where she had to look for them. Whether he was a Partial or a human or double agent or whatever, it didn't matter, she had to find him and learn what he knew.

Another thought came to her then, the mental image of a column of smoke. She'd seen it last time she was here, with Jayden and Haru and the others: a thin trail of smoke rising up from a chimney or a campfire. They'd gone to investigate it and run into Samm's group of Partials, and in the rush to get back out, she'd forgotten that they'd never actually learned where the smoke was coming from. She'd assumed it was part of the Partial camp, but her experiences with them later made that seem almost laughably wrong—the Partials were far too clever to leave such an obvious sign of their presence, and far too hardy to need a campfire in the first place. It seemed more likely that the smoke came from a third party, and the Partials had shown up to investigate it the same time the humans did; their two groups had annihilated each other before either could find out what was going on. *Maybe.* It was a long shot, but it was better than anything else she had to go on. Certainly better than staking out hardware stores in a vain hope the scavenger would hit one while she was watching it.

She'd start with the same neighborhood they'd been investigating back then, and if he'd moved on—which seemed likely, after the massive firefight they'd held just a few blocks away—she'd look for more clues about where he might have headed next. There was somebody in this city, and she was determined to find him.

Finding the source of the smoke plume was harder than Kira had planned. It wasn't there anymore, for one thing, so she had to go by memory, and the city was so big and confusing that she couldn't remember clearly enough without jogging her memory visually. She had to go back, all the way south to the bridge they'd crossed on, and find the same building, and look out the same window. There, at long last, the landscape looked familiar—she could see the long strip of trees, the three apartment buildings, all the signs that had led her to the Partial attack those many months ago. That was where she'd first met Samm—well, not "met him" so much as "knocked him unconscious and captured him." It was strange how much things had changed since then. If she had Samm here, now . . . Well, things would be a lot easier, for one thing.

But even as she thought it, she knew it was more than that. Staring out the window over the leafy city, she wondered again, for the hundredth time, if the connection she had felt between them had been the Partial link or something deeper. Was there any way to know? Did it even matter? A connection was a connection, and she had precious few of those these days.

But this wasn't the time to think about Samm. Kira studied the cityscape, trying to fix in her mind exactly where the smoke had been coming from, and how to retrace her steps to find it. She went so far as to pull out her notebook and sketch out a map, but without a clear sense of how many streets there were, and what they were called, she didn't know how useful the map would be. The buildings here were so tall, and the streets so narrow, the city was almost like a labyrinth, a maze of brick-and-metal canyons. Last time they'd had scouts to lead the way, but on her own Kira worried that she'd get lost and never find anything.

She finished her map as best she could, noting key landmarks that might help her navigate, then descended the long stairway and set out through the city. The streets were rough, filled with jumbled cars and spindly trees, their leaves fluttering in the soft wind. She passed an ancient car accident, a dozen or more vehicles piled together in a desperate bid to flee the plague-ridden city; she didn't remember passing the pileup before, which made her nervous that she was following the wrong path, but soon she turned a corner and spotted one of her landmarks, and continued up the road more confidently. The center of each street was the easiest to travel in, less filled with debris than edges and sidewalks, but they were also the most visible, and Kira was too paranoid to leave the thicker cover. She hugged the walls and fences, stepping carefully through heaps of shifting rubble fallen down from the towering buildings. It was slow going, but it was safer, or at least that was what Kira told herself.

Here and there Kira spotted a bullet hole in a car or a mailbox, and she knew she was on the right track. They had run through here with a sniper behind them; Jayden had even been shot through the arm. The thought of Jayden sobered her, and she paused to listen: birds. Wind. Two cats yowling in a fight. It was foolish to think that there would be a sniper here now, but she couldn't help herself. She ducked down behind a crumbling stairway, breathing heavily, telling herself that it was just nerves, but all she could think about was Jayden, shot through the arm—shot through the chest in the East Meadow hospital, bleeding out on the floor where he'd sacrificed himself to save her. He'd been the one to force her through her fear, to tell her to get up when she was too afraid to move. She gritted her teeth and stood up again, moving forward. She could be afraid all she wanted, but she wouldn't let it stop her.

She reached the apartment complex when the sun was high in the sky: five buildings that had looked like three from her vantage point back in the skyscraper. It was the same place. There was a wide lawn around and between them, now filled with saplings, and she pushed through it carefully as she passed the buildings. *This was the one we passed first, and this was the one we went into. . . .* She came around the side and looked up, seeing the massive hole they'd blown in the wall three stories up. A vine wound around a dangling floor joist, and a bird perched on a crooked shard of rebar. The violence was gone, and nature was reclaiming it.

They had come here looking for the source of the smoke, and they'd chosen that apartment building because it looked out on what they assumed was the back of the occupied house. Kira kept her rifle up as she walked, rounding the first corner, then the next. This would be the street, and if she'd guessed correctly on her map, the house she was looking for would be six doors down. One, two three, four . . . no. Kira's jaw dropped, and she stared in shock at the sixth townhouse in the row.

It was an empty crater, blown to pieces.

CHAPTER SIX

"**T**his Senate meeting will now come to order," said Senator Tovar. "We extend an official welcome to all our guests today, and we look forward to hearing your reports. Before we begin, I've been asked to announce that there's a green Ford Sovereign in the parking lot with its lights on, so if that's yours, please . . ." He looked up, straight-faced, and the adults in the room all laughed. Marcus frowned, confused, and Tovar chuckled. "My apologies to all the plague babies in the room. That was an old-world joke, and not even a very good one." He sat down. "Let's start with the synthesis team. Dr. Skousen?"

Skousen stood, and Marcus placed his binder on his lap, ready in case the doctor asked him for anything. Skousen stepped forward, stopped to clear his throat, then paused, thought, and stepped forward again.

"I take it from your hesitance that you don't have any good news," said Tovar. "I guess let's move on to whoever's ready to not give us the next bad report."

"Just let him speak," said Senator Kessler. "We don't need a joke in every single pause in conversation."

Tovar raised his eyebrow. "I could make a joke when someone's talking, but that seems rude."

Kessler ignored him and turned to Skousen. "Doctor?"

"I'm afraid he's correct," said Skousen. "We have no good news. We have no bad news either, aside from the continued lack of progress—" He paused, stammering uncertainly. "We . . . have had no major setbacks, is what I'm saying."

"So you're no closer to synthesizing the cure than you were last time," said Senator Woolf.

"We have eliminated certain possibilities as dead ends," said Skousen. His face was worn and full of lines, and Marcus heard his voice drop. "It's not much, as victories go, but it's all we have."

"We can't continue like this," said Woolf, turning to the other senators. "We saved one child, and almost two months later we're no closer to saving any more. We've lost four more children in the last week alone. Their deaths are tragedies on their own, and I don't want to gloss over them, but that's not even our most pressing concern. The people know we have a cure—they know we *can* save infants, and they know that we're *not*. They know the reasons for it, too, but that's not exactly mollifying anyone. Having the cure so close, but still unattainable, is only making the tensions on this island worse."

"Then what do you propose we do?" asked Tovar. "Attack the Partials and steal more pheromone? We can't risk it."

You might not have a choice soon, Marcus thought. *If what Heron said is true . . .* He squirmed in his seat, trying not to imagine the devastation of a Partial invasion. He didn't know where Nandita was, or Kira, and he certainly didn't want to hand them over to the Partials even if he could, on the other hand . . . a Partial invasion could mean the end of the human race—not a slow fade, dying off because they couldn't reproduce, but a bloody, brutal genocide. The Partials had proven twelve years ago that they weren't afraid of war, but genocide? Samm had insisted so fiercely that they weren't responsible for RM. That they felt guilty for causing, even inadvertently, the horrors of the Break. Had things changed that much? Were they ready to sacrifice an entire species just to save themselves?

They're asking me to do the same thing, he thought. *To sacrifice Kira, or Nandita, to save humanity. If it comes right down to it, would I do it? Should I?*

"We could send an ambassador," said Senator Hobb. "We've talked about it, we've chosen the team—let's do it."

"Send them to who?" asked Kessler. "We've had contact with exactly one group of Partials, and they tried to kill the kids who contacted them. *We* tried to kill the Partial who contacted *us.* If there's a peaceful resolution in our future, I sure as hell don't know how to reach it."

They were the same arguments, Marcus realized, that he and his friends had bandied around in Xochi's living room. The same circular proposals, the same obvious responses, the same endless bickering. *Are the adults just as lost as the rest of us? Or is there really no solution to this problem?*

"From a medical standpoint," said Dr. Skousen, "I'm afraid I must advocate—against my wishes—the . . ." He paused again. "The retrieval of a fresh sample. Of a new Partial, or at the very least a quantity of their pheromone. We have some remnants of the dose that was used on Arwen Sato, and we have the scans and records of the pheromone's structure and function, but nothing can replace a fresh sample. We solved this problem last time by going to the source—to the Partials—and I believe that if we intend to solve it again, we will have to solve it the same way. Whether we get it by force or diplomacy doesn't matter as much as the simple need to obtain it."

A rush of whispers filled the room, soft mutterings like the rustle of leaves. *It wasn't "we" who solved this problem,* Marcus thought, *it was Kira, and Dr. Skousen was one of her biggest opponents.* Now he was advocating the same action without even crediting her?

"You want us to risk another Partial War," said Kessler.

"That risk has already been taken," said Tovar. "The bear, as they say, has already been poked, and it hasn't eaten us yet."

"Being lucky is not the same thing as being safe," said Kessler. "If there's any way to synthesize this cure without resorting to military action, we have to explore it. If we provoke the Partials any further—"

"We've provoked them too much as it is!" said Woolf. "You've read the reports—there are boats off the North Shore, Partial boats patrolling our borders—"

Senator Hobb cut him off, while the audience whispered all the more wildly. "This is not the right venue to discuss those reports," said Hobb.

Marcus felt like he'd been shot in the gut: The Partials were patrolling the sound. The Partials had kept to themselves for eleven years—a quick recon mission here and there, like Heron had done, but always undercover, so much so that the humans hadn't even known about it. Now they were openly patrolling the border. He realized his mouth was hanging open, and he closed it tightly.

"The people need to know," said Woolf. "They're going to find out anyway—if the boats get too much closer, every farmer on the North Shore's going to see them. For all we know small groups of them have landed already; our watch along that shore is anything but impenetrable."

"So our cold war's heated up," said Skousen. He looked gray and frail, like a corpse from the side of the road. He paused a moment, swallowed, and sat down with a barely controlled *thunk*.

"If you'll excuse me," said Marcus, and realized that he was standing. He looked at the binder in his hands, unsure of what to do with it, then simply closed it and held it in front of him, wishing it was armor. He looked at the Senate, wondering if Heron was right—if one of them, or one of their aides, was a Partial agent. Did he dare to talk? Could he afford not to? "Excuse me," he said again, starting over, "my name is Marcus Valencio—"

"We know who you are," said Tovar.

Marcus nodded nervously. "I think I have more experience in Partial territory than anyone in this room—"

"That's why we know who you are," said Tovar, making a rolling motion with his hand. "Stop introducing yourself and get to your point."

Marcus swallowed, suddenly not sure why he'd stood up—he felt like somebody needed to say something, but he didn't feel at all qualified to say it. He wasn't even sure what it was. He looked around the room, watching the faces of various gathered experts and politicians, wondering which of them—if any—was a traitor. He thought about Heron, and her search for Nandita, and realized that whatever he was trying to say, he was the only one who knew enough to say it. The only one who'd heard Heron's warning. *I just need to figure out how to phrase it without looking like a traitor myself.* "I'm just saying," he said at last, "that the Partials we encountered were conducting experiments. They have an expiration date—they're all going to die—and they're just as invested in curing that as we are in curing RM. More so, maybe, because it's going to kill them sooner."

"We know about the expiration date," said Kessler. "It's the best news we've had in twelve years."

"Not counting the cure for RM, of course," said Hobb quickly.

"It's not good news at all," said Marcus. "Their expiration date is like pushing us out of the frying pan and into the . . . molten core of the Earth. If they die, we die; we need their pheromone to cure ourselves."

"That's why we're trying to synthesize it," said Woolf.

"But we can't synthesize it," said Marcus, holding up his binder. "We could spend a couple of hours telling you everything we've tried, and all the reasons it hasn't worked, and you wouldn't understand half the science anyway—no offense—but that's beside the point, because it hasn't worked. 'Why' it hasn't worked doesn't matter." He dropped the binder on the table behind him and turned back to face the senators. Seeing them again, staring at him silently, made Marcus feel suddenly queasy, and he smiled to cover it up. "Don't everybody cheer at once, I have some bad news, too."

Tovar pursed his lips. "I don't know how you're going to top the first bit, but I'm excited to hear it."

Marcus felt the attention of the entire room bearing down on him and bit back the urge to make another wisecrack; he cracked jokes reflexively when he got too nervous, and he was more nervous now than he'd ever been. *I shouldn't be doing this,* he thought. *I'm a medic, not a public speaker. I'm not a debater, I'm not a leader, I'm not . . .*

. . . I'm not Kira. That's who should be here.

"Mr. Valencio?" asked Senator Woolf.

Marcus nodded, steeling his determination. "Well, you asked for it, so here it is. The leader of the Partial faction we ran into, the one who kidnapped Kira, was some kind of a doctor or a scientist; they called her Dr. Morgan. That was the reason they sent that Partial platoon into Manhattan all those months ago, and they kidnapped Kira because Dr. Morgan thinks the secret to curing Partials is somehow related to RM, which means it's related to humans. Apparently they'd experimented on humans before, back during the Partial War, and if they think it will save their lives, they'll kidnap as many more of us as they need, which might just be Kira again, but for all we know it's all of us. They're probably having the same meeting right now, on the other side of the sound, trying to decide how they can grab a few of us to experiment on—or if those reports you mentioned are true, they already had their meeting and might very well be putting their plan into motion."

"That's classified information," said Senator Hobb. "We need—"

"If you'll permit me to recap," Marcus interrupted, holding

up his hand, "there is a group of super-soldiers"—he put down his first finger—"trained specifically in military conquest"—he put down his second finger—"who outnumber us, like, thirty to one"—third finger—"who are desperate enough to try anything"—fourth finger—"and who believe that 'anything' in this case means 'capturing human beings for invasive experimentation.'" He folded down his last finger and held his fist silently in the air. "Senators, the information might be classified, but it's a pretty good bet the Partials will be unclassifying it a lot sooner than you think."

The room was quiet, every eye focused on Marcus. Several long, heavy moments later, Tovar finally spoke.

"So you think we need to defend ourselves."

"I think I'm scared to death, and I need to learn how to stop talking when everyone is staring at me."

"Defending ourselves is not a viable option," said Woolf, and the other senators stiffened in surprise. "The Defense Grid is well trained and as well equipped as a human army can possibly be. We have watches on every coast, we have bombs on every remaining bridge, we have ambush sites already mapped and ready to go at every likely invasion point. And yet no matter how well prepared we are, it will barely be a speed bump if a sizeable faction of Partials initiate an invasion. That's an inescapable fact that cannot possibly be news to anyone in this room. We patrol this island because it's all we can do, but if the Partials ever actually decide to invade, we will be conquered within days, if not hours."

"The only remotely good news," said Marcus, "is that their society is, if you'll pardon the comparison, even more fractured than ours. The mainland was practically a war zone when we were over there, which could be the only reason they haven't attacked us already."

"So they kill each other and our problem solves itself," said Kessler.

"Except for the RM," said Hobb.

"Taking everything Mr. Valencio has said into account," said Woolf, "we only have one real plan that has any hope of success. Step one, we sneak into that mainland war zone, hope nobody notices us, and grab a couple of Partials for Dr. Skousen to experiment on. Step two, we evacuate the entire island and get as far away as possible."

The room was quiet. Marcus sat down. Leaving the island was crazy—it was their home, it was their only safe haven, that was why they'd come here in the first place—but that wasn't really true anymore, was it? In the wake of the Partial War, this island had been like a sanctuary; they'd escaped from the Partials, they'd found a new life, and they'd started to rebuild. But that safety didn't really have anything to do with the island, now that Marcus thought about it. They'd been safe because the Partials had ignored them, and now that the Partials were back—now that there were boats in the sound, and Heron hiding in the shadows, and the vicious Dr. Morgan trying to turn them all into experiments—that illusion of safety had melted away. Nobody had to say it out loud, nobody had to make an official decision, but Marcus knew it was done. He could see it in the faces of everyone in the room. The instant evacuation was broached as a possibility, it became a certainty.

The side door opened, and Marcus caught a glimpse of the

Grid soldiers guarding the other side. They stepped aside and a large man stepped in: Duna Mkele, the "intelligence officer." It occurred to Marcus that he didn't know who, exactly, Mkele worked for; he seemed to have free access to the Senate, and some measure of authority over the Grid, but as far as Marcus could tell, he didn't really answer to either group. Regardless of how those relationships worked, Marcus didn't like the man. His presence was almost always a sign of bad news.

Mkele walked to Senator Woolf and whispered in his ear; Marcus tried to read their lips, or at least judge the reaction on their faces, but they turned their backs on the crowd. A moment later they walked to Tovar and whispered to him. Tovar listened solemnly, then looked at the crowd of people watching him. He turned back to Woolf and spoke in a loud stage voice obviously intended to carry throughout the room.

"They already know the first half; you might as well tell them the rest."

Marcus saw clearly the stern look that passed over Mkele's face. Woolf looked back unapologetically, then turned to face the crowd.

"It appears our timetable has been accelerated," said Woolf. "The Partials have made ground on Long Island, near Mount Sinai Harbor, approximately five minutes ago."

The meeting hall erupted in noisy conversations, and Marcus felt his stomach lurch with a sudden, terrifying fear. What did it mean—was this the end? Was this an invasion force, or a brazen raid to steal human test subjects? Was this Dr. Morgan's group, Dr. Morgan's enemies, or some other faction altogether?

Was Samm with them?

Did this mean Heron's plan had failed? They couldn't find Kira and Nandita through stealth and investigation, so it was time for a full invasion? He felt a moment of horrifying guilt, as if the entire invasion was his fault, personally, for failing to heed Heron's warning. But he hadn't seen Kira in months and Nandita in over a year; what could he have done? As the crowd roared in fear and confusion, as the reality of the situation sank into him, Marcus realized that it didn't matter. He wasn't ready to sacrifice anyone; he'd rather go down fighting than sell his soul for peace.

For the second time that day Marcus felt himself standing, heard his voice calling out. "I volunteer for the force that goes out to meet them," he said. "You need a medic—I volunteer."

Senator Tovar looked at him, nodded, then turned back to Mkele and Woolf. The room continued to buzz with fear and speculation. Marcus collapsed back into his chair.

I really need to learn to keep my mouth shut.

CHAPTER SEVEN

Kira picked through the ruins of the town house, overwhelmed by the chaos: Walls had fallen in, floors and ceilings had collapsed, shards of furniture had separated and scattered and clustered again in random piles. Wood and books and paper and dishes and twisted chunks of metal filled the crater and spilled far into the street, thrown by the force of the blast.

The home had definitely been inhabited, and recently. Kira had seen a lot of old-world debris in her life; she had grown up surrounded by it, and it had become familiar: framed photos of long-dead families, little black boxes of media players and game systems, broken vases full of brittle stems. The details varied from house to house, but the feel was the same—forgotten lives of forgotten people. The debris from this home was different, and distinctly modern: stockpiles of canned food, now burst and rotting in the rubble; boarded windows and reinforced doors; guns and ammunition and handmade camouflage. Someone had lived here, long after the world was destroyed, and when someone else—the Partials?—had invaded their privacy, they blew up their own home. The pattern of the destruction was too complete, and too contained, to be an outside attack; an enemy would have used a smaller explosive to breach the wall, or a larger one that would have caught the neighboring houses as well. Whoever had destroyed this home had done their work pragmatically and with devastating thoroughness.

The crater reminded her, the more she thought about it, of a similar explosion she'd seen last year—before the cure, before Samm, before everything. She'd gone on a salvage run with Marcus and Jayden, somewhere on the North Shore of Long Island, and a building had been rigged to explode. It had been a booby trap, much like this one seemed to be—not designed to kill but to destroy evidence. *What was the name of that little town? Asharoken; I remember how Jayden made fun of the name. And why were they looking in that building, anyway? It had been flagged by a preliminary salvage crew, and the soldiers had gone back to investigate; they'd had specialists with them, like a computer guy or something. Something electronic?* Her breath caught in her throat as the memory returned: It was a radio station. Someone had set up a radio station on the North Shore, and then blown it up to keep it secret. And now someone had done the same thing here. Was it the same someone?

Kira stepped back reflexively, as if the demolished building could somehow contain another bomb. She stared at the wreckage, summoned her courage, and walked in, placing her feet carefully in the unstable ruins. It didn't take long to find the first body. A soldier dressed in a gray uniform—a Partial—was lodged under a fallen wall, a fractured corpse in the crumpled remains of composite body armor. His rifle lay beside him, and she pulled it from the rubble with surprising ease; the action moved stiffly, but it moved nonetheless, and the chamber still held a bullet. She popped out the clip and found it full—the soldier hadn't fired a single round before he died, and his fellow soldiers had neither recovered his gear nor buried his body. *That means the bomb took them by surprise,* Kira thought, *and it killed them all. There was no one left to recover the fallen.*

Kira searched further, sifting cautiously through the fallen beams and bricks, and found at last the old familiar sight—the blackened fragments of a radio transceiver, just like in Asharoken. The two situations were too similar to dismiss: A group of scouts investigate something suspicious, find a fortified safe house full of communications equipment, and die in a defensive trap. Kira and the others had assumed the site in Asharoken belonged to the Voice, but Owen Tovar denied it then and now. The next most likely candidates were the Partials, yet here was a group of Partials caught in the same trap. *Another Partial faction, then,* thought Kira. *But which belongs to Dr. Morgan—the spies with the radio, or the scouts that attacked it? Or neither? And how does this connect to ParaGen?* Whoever had taken the computers from the offices had also taken the radios from the store, and now here were fragments of both in one place. There had to be a connection. It seemed likely that the faction collecting radios was the same faction that was establishing these radio stations throughout the ruins. But what were they doing? And why would they kill so freely to hide it?

"What I need is a clue," said Kira, frowning at the devastation. She was talking to herself more and more these days, and she felt foolish to hear her voice ringing out through the empty city. On the other hand, hers was the only voice she'd heard in weeks, and it was oddly soothing every time she spoke. She shook her head. "Gotta talk to somebody, right? Even if it does make me look pathetic." She bent down, examining the bits of paper sprinkled throughout the rubble. Whoever had made the safe houses and planted the bombs was still out there, and finding them would be all but impossible now that they'd blown up all the evidence. Kira laughed dryly. "But I suppose that's kind of the point."

She pulled one of the papers from the debris at her feet; it was a fragment of old-world newspaper, wrinkled and yellow, and the headline was just barely legible. DETROIT PROTEST TURNS VIOLENT, she read. The smaller words in the body of the article were only barely legible, but Kira deciphered the words "police" and "factory," and several references to Partials. "So the faction collecting radios is also collecting articles about the Partial rebellion?" She frowned at the paper, then rolled her eyes and dropped it back to the ground. "Either that, or *every* newspaper from right before the Break talked about Partials, and this means nothing." She shook her head. "I need something concrete. You know, aside from all the actual chunks of concrete." She kicked a piece of rubble, and it skittered away across the crater, bouncing off the fallen radio antenna with a clang.

She walked over to the examine the antenna; it was large, probably several yards tall when it was still straight, but as thin as cable. It must have been pretty sturdy to have stood up straight, but the explosion and the fall had twisted it into tight creases and curls. Kira pulled on it, trying to drag it out from the fallen

77

bricks and Sheetrock that held it half-buried. It moved about three feet before catching on something; she strained against it, but it refused to budge any further. She dropped the antenna, panting with exertion, and looked for more . . . anything. She found more news clippings, three more decaying Partial bodies, and a nest of garter snakes curled under the shelf of a fallen solar panel, but nothing that told her where the bombers had gone, or if they might have another radio station elsewhere in the city. She sat down beside another solar panel to rest, pulling out a canteen of water, when suddenly it occurred to her:

Why were there two banks of solar panels?

This type of solar panel was called a Zoble, and Kira knew them well; Xochi had installed one on their roof at home to run her music players, and there were several more at the hospital. They could draw a lot of power and transfer it very efficiently, and they were incredibly rare. Xochi had only been able to afford hers through her "mother" and her connections to the farms and the fresh food market. To find one in Manhattan wasn't necessarily bizarre—demand was less, after all, with no other scavengers to compete with—but to find two, rigged to the same building, spoke of abnormally high power needs. She scoured the crater again, on her hands and knees this time, searching for the capacitor that stored all this energy, and found instead the broken shards of a third Zoble panel.

"Three Zobles," whispered Kira. "Why do you need all that juice? For the radio? Can they possibly need that much?" She'd used walkie-talkies back home that fit snugly in the palm of her hand, running off tiny rechargeables. What kind of radio needed three Zoble panels and a five-meter antenna? It didn't make sense.

Unless they were powering more than just a radio. Unless they were powering, say, a collection of stolen ParaGen computers.

Kira looked around, not at the crater but at the street behind her and the cold, lifeless buildings beyond. She felt exposed, as if a spotlight had just been pointed at her, and she stepped into the shadow of a fallen wall. *If there were really something valuable under here,* she thought, *whoever was protecting this place would have come to dig it up by now. The extra juice was here to power the radio and the computers, and whoever I found collecting radios and computers was doing it in the last few months—long after this building exploded. They're still out there, and they're up to something weird.*

She looked up at the roofline, and the darkening sky beyond it. *And all I have to do to find them is to find what they need: a giant antenna and enough solar panels to run their radio. If there are other such sites in the city, I won't be able to see them from down here.*

"Time to go up."

Kira's plan was simple: climb the tallest building she could find, get a good view of the city, and watch. If she was lucky she'd see another smoke trail, though she had to assume her targets had learned their lesson after the last time; more likely, she'd just have to study the skyline as closely as she could, in all directions and in all angles of sunlight, hoping to catch a glimpse of a giant antenna and a bank—or banks—of solar panels.

"Then I just have to keep notes, find them on my map, and check them out in person," said Kira, talking to herself as she climbed another flight of stairs. "And hope I don't get blown up, like everyone else has so far."

The building she'd chosen was relatively close to the ParaGen building, maybe a mile southwest—a massive granite skyscraper proudly proclaiming itself the Empire State Building. The outer walls were overgrown with vines and moss, like most of the city, but the inner structure seemed stable enough, and she'd only had to shoot one lock to get into the main stairway. She was on the 32nd floor now, slowly rounding the railing to the 33rd; according to the signs in the lobby, she had fifty-three to go. "I've got three liters of water," she told herself, reciting her supplies as she climbed, "six cans of tuna, two cans of beans, and one last MRE from that army supply store on Seventh Avenue. I need to find another one of those." She reached the landing of the 34th floor, stuck out her tongue, and kept climbing. "That food had better last me a while, because I don't want to make this climb any more often than I have to."

What felt like hours later she collapsed on the 86th floor with a gasp, pausing to drink more water before checking out the alleged "observatory." It had a great view, but the walls were mostly windows, and almost all had been shattered, leaving the entire floor drafty and frigid. She trudged back to the stairway and ended up on the 102nd floor, at the base of a giant spire that continued up another two or three hundred feet. A plaque at the door congratulated her for climbing 1,860 individual stairs, and she nodded as she caught her breath. "Just my luck," she gasped. "I'm going to have the best glutes left on the planet, and there's nobody here to see them."

While the 86th floor had been wide and square, with a slim balcony around the perimeter of the building, the 102nd floor was small and round, almost like a lighthouse. The only protection between observers and the street below was a circle of windows, mostly intact, but Kira couldn't help but lean out one of the broken ones, feeling the rush of the wind and the insane thrill of the mind-numbing height. It was the kind of view she'd always imagined the old-world people had seen from their airplanes, so high up the world itself seemed distant and small. More importantly, it gave her an amazing view of the city—there were other buildings that were taller, but only a few, and their view wouldn't be any better than this one. Kira dropped her bags and pulled out her binoculars, starting with the southern view and scanning the skyline for radio antennas. There were far more than she expected. She blew out a long, slow breath, shaking her head and wondering how she'd ever be able to find the one building she needed out of the thousands that filled the island. She closed her eyes.

"The only way to do it," she said softly, "is to do it." She plucked her notebook from the back of her bag, found the closest antenna to the south, and starting taking notes.

CHAPTER EIGHT

The farthest antenna Kira found was so far north she suspected it might be beyond the borders of Manhattan island, in the region called the Bronx; she hoped she didn't have to go that far, as the proximity to the Partials still made her nervous, but if she had to do it, she swore that she would. The answers she stood to gain made any risk worth it.

The closest antenna was the giant spire on top of her own building, but there was no one in the building with her. Well— she didn't think there was anyone else in the building with her who could be using it, but it was an awfully big building. "Maybe I'm being paranoid," she told herself, climbing up to check the antenna. She stopped and corrected herself. "Maybe I'm being *too* paranoid. A little bit is probably pretty healthy." The antenna turned out to be completely unpowered, and she was surprised at how relieved she felt. She studied the city, taking notes on each new antenna she found, and watched as the setting sun revealed new solar panels one by one, winking slyly as the fading light hit just the right angle, then sliding again into darkness. At night she slipped down a few floors to find an enclosed room, and bundled herself warmly in her sleeping bag. This high in the sky the buildings were remarkably clean—no windswept dirt, no budding shoots, no paw prints in the dust. It reminded her of home, of the buildings she and others had worked so hard to keep clean: her house, the hospital, the school. She wondered, not for the first time, if she would ever see any of them again.

On the fourth day her water ran dry, and she made the long climb down to street level looking for more. A park at the end of a long city block drew her attention, and she found what she was looking for—not a pool or puddle but a subway entrance, dark water lapping at the steps. In the old world the subway had been for transportation, but somehow it had flooded; the tunnels were now an underground river, slow but still flowing. Kira brought out her purifier and pumped three more liters, refilling her plastic bottles, always keeping a wary eye on the city around her. She found a grocery store and stocked up on several cans of vegetables, but stopped and grimaced when she found one that had swollen and burst—these cans were now more than eleven years old, and that was getting close to the shelf life of most canned foods. If some of these were already spoiling, she was better off not risking any of them. She sighed and put them back, wondering if she had the time to hunt live game.

"At least some snares," she decided, and set a few simple rope traps near the top of the subway entrance. There were prints around the mouth of it, and she figured some of the local elands and rabbits were using it as a watering hole. She climbed back up to her observatory, set a few more snares for birds, and got back to work. Two nights later she had goose for dinner, roasted over a smokeless survival stove and turned on a spit made of old wire hangers. It was the best she'd eaten in weeks.

Five days and three water trips later she found her first big break—a gleam of light in a window, a tiny speck dancing redly for just a second, and then it was gone. Was it a signal? Had she only imagined it? She sat up straighter, watching the spot intently through her binoculars. A minute went by. Five minutes. Just as she was about to give up, she saw it again: a movement, a fire, and a closing door. Someone was letting out smoke; maybe their cook fire had gotten out of hand. She scrambled to identify the building before night fell too completely, and saw the dancing flame three more times in the next half hour. When the moon rose she looked for smoke, but there was nothing; they had dispersed it, or the wind had, too effectively to be seen.

Kira stood up, still staring toward the building now invisible in the darkness. It was one of the many she'd identified as a likely target—its roof was covered with solar panels, ringing a central antenna so large she thought it must have been an actual radio station. If someone had gotten that old equipment running again, they'd have a more powerful radio than either of the two she'd seen blown up.

"Do I go now, or wait for morning?" Staring into the darkness, she realized she still wasn't sure what her plan was—knowing where the bad guys were hiding wouldn't do her any good if she triggered a bomb as soon as she stepped inside. She could try to catch one of them, maybe in a larger version of her rabbit snares, and ask questions, or she could try to slip in when the bomb wasn't armed—which, she supposed, was only when the mysterious bombers themselves were inside. That didn't sound safe at all.

"The best thing to do," she whispered, crouching lower in the window, "is exactly what I'm doing now—watch and wait and hope I can learn something useful." She sighed. "It's gotten me this far."

But the question remained: Should she go tonight or wait for morning? A journey through the city would be more dangerous in the dark, but her targets had proven to be incredibly cautious—if they knew a flash of light and a trail of smoke had given away their position, they might move to a new location, leaving another booby trap in their wake, and Kira would lose them. Had the fire been an accident? Would it make them nervous enough to run? Kira had no way of knowing, and the uncertainty made her nervous in turn. This was one situation where the slow, cautious approach was too risky—she'd already lost five days; better to go now, she decided, than to take the chance of losing her only good lead. She packed her things, checked her rifle, and began the long descent through the pitch-dark bowels of the stairwell.

Feral cats prowled the lower levels, searching for food with bright, nocturnal eyes. Kira heard them moving in the shadows, waiting and watching and pouncing; the hiss of predators and the struggling of prey.

Kira scanned the street carefully before leaving the building, then moved softly from car to car, keeping to cover as much as possible. The building with the campfire was about three miles north, uncomfortably close to the giant forest of Central Park.

Wild animals lived throughout the city, but the park was home to most of the big ones. Kira traveled as quickly as she dared, keeping her flashlight off and using the moon to see. The pale light made shadows deeper and more ominous; it also made the ground look smoother than it really was, and Kira stumbled on the rough terrain anytime she tried to move too fast. She skirted the west side of the park, watching for animals, but there were none out in the open. This was bad news: If there were deer out, it would at least give the predators something better to hunt than her. Feral house cats were hardly the most dangerous predators in the city.

A shadow shifted in her peripheral vision, and Kira whirled around to look. Nothing. She paused to listen . . . yes . . . there it was. A deep thrum, almost too low to hear. Something very big was breathing nearby, not just breathing but purring, almost growling. Something very good at hiding.

Kira was being hunted.

Before her was a large plaza, the concrete cracked and buckled and dotted with tufts of tall, dark weeds; the center statue stood solemn and unmoving. Cars circled the edge, their tires long ago turned flat and deflated. Kira backed slowly against a wall, cutting off the predator's lines of attack, holding her breath to listen. The deep breathing was there, a bass rumble of giant lungs filling and exhaling. She couldn't tell where it was coming from.

There are panthers in the city, she thought. *I've seen them during the day—panthers and lions and once, I swear, I saw a tiger. Refugees from a zoo or a circus, well fed by the herds of wild deer and horses that roam Central Park. There are even elephants—I heard them last year. Do they feed on those, too?*

Focus, she told herself. *They're going to feed on you if you don't find a way out of this. Lions or panthers or worse.*

Panthers. A terrifying thought occurred to her: *Panthers are supposed to hunt at night, but I've only ever seen them in the day. Do they hunt in both now, or is this thing in the darkness something worse—something so dangerous the panthers had to change their habits to avoid it? Am I being hunted by a nocturnal panther, or are the panthers hiding, scared in their dens, to escape the creature that's hunting me?* Memories of the ParaGen brochure leapt unbidden to her mind—dragons and intelligent dogs, engineered lions and who only knew what else they'd done. They'd designed the Partials as the ultimate soldiers—had they designed an ultimate predator as well?

Kira stole a glance back down the street where she'd come, shaking her head at the long string of derelict cars and delivery vans; this creature could be hiding behind any one of them, waiting for her to pass by. It was the same with the plaza in front of her. Her best bet lay across the street, in the lobby of what might once have been a shopping mall: fallen mannequins, faded posters of bodies and faces, rack upon rack of ragged clothes. The beast could be in there, too—for all she knew the cluttered hallways could be its den—but there were doors as well, human-size and closed, and if she could get inside one and close it again behind her, she would be safe. Safe until it went away, safe until morning if it took that long. She heard the same rumbling growl, closer now than ever, and set her jaw fiercely.

"It's now or never." She leapt to her feet, charging across the broken street to the mall beyond, dodging around the corner of a car as a rush of air tore past behind her. She imagined giant claws swiping inches from her back, and struggled to regain her footing as she raced in through the shattered glass facade of the building. Debris clattered in her wake, far more than she could ever dislodge by herself, but she didn't dare look back; she raised her gun over her shoulder, firing wildly behind her, turning again as she reached a cracking pillar. The interior of the mall was bigger than she'd expected, glistening metal stairways climbing up and down in pairs, a vast courtyard yawning wide in the center of the floor below her. It was too dark to see the bottom or the top; too dark to see much of anything. The door she'd been aiming for was on the other side; she turned to the right, skirting the pit, and brought her gun back in front of her, switching on the light. The thing seemed to be scrabbling on the slick floor; Kira found the first door she could and sprinted straight toward it.

The light beam jerked wildly as she ran, up and down, back and forth, shining back from the tiled floor and the metal stairs and the mirrored plates across the walls. In a flash of reflected light the wall before her showed her own image, a massive black shape bearing down from behind, and then the beam jerked again and the scene was gone, a strobing nightmare of light and darkness and fear. She fixed her eyes on the doorway, running like she'd never run before, and moments before she got there she lowered her rifle, sighted on the doorknob, and fired a semi-automatic burst. The lock blew clear, the door fell open, and Kira dove through without a pause, slamming her hand against the left wall to help propel her toward the right and another open door. She grabbed at this one as she passed, slamming it closed behind her, and leaned against it just as something hit it from the other side, cracking it loudly; still, though, it held, and Kira braced herself tightly against it as the thing came back for another hit.

She looked around wildly, aiming the rifle awkwardly with one hand to shine its light on the room, and saw a large wood desk. Claws scraped across the other side of the door—it was pawing at the barrier now, not smashing it, and she took the risk, jumping over the desk and heaving against it, pushing it back to block the door. The scratching turned to thumping; the door shook, and suddenly Kira was deafened by a massive roar. She lost her footing, dropped her rifle, and threw herself against the desk again, slamming it up against the door just as the thing on the other side slammed it again, shaking the room. The desk held. Kira fell back, reaching for the rifle's light, and brought it up to illuminate the top half of the door, riven with cracks and splintered away from the frame. Something moved beyond it, nearly as tall as the ceiling; the light reflected against a huge amber eye, narrowing to a slit as the light blinded it. Kira reeled at the sheer size of it, scooting away almost involuntarily. A massive paw clawed at the gap in the door, giant claws gleaming silver in the halogen beam, and Kira fired a burst from her rifle, clipping it in the toe. The creature roared again, but this time Kira roared back, cornered and furious. She climbed on the desk, sighted straight through the broken doorway, and fired at the wall of fur and muscle before her. It howled in rage and pain, thrashing wildly at the door, and Kira ejected the spent clip, slapped in another one, and fired again. The creature turned and fled, disappearing into the darkness.

Kira stood frozen in the doorway, her knuckles white as bone as they clutched the rifle. A second became a minute; a minute became two. The monster didn't return. The adrenaline rush wore off and Kira began to shake, subtly at first and then harder, faster, shaking uncontrollably. She climbed down from the desk, nearly falling to the floor, and collapsed in the corner, sobbing.

The dawn light didn't reach through the maze of walls and doorways, but Kira could hear the sounds of morning: birds singing to greet the sun, bees buzzing through the flowers in the asphalt, and yes, even the distant trumpet of an elephant. Kira stood up slowly, peering through the cracked doorway. Her light was still on, though the batteries were failing; the room beyond was covered in sprays and smears of blood, but the creature itself was gone. She pulled back the desk, carefully opening the door; it was lighter out here, and she saw a beam of sunlight on the cluttered floor of the mall. Red-brown footprints led out to the street and into the plaza, but Kira didn't bother following them. She took a drink from her canteen, sloshing the cold water on her face. It had been stupid to go out at night, she knew, and she promised herself she would never do it again.

She shook her head, working out the kinks in her back and arms and fingers. The men she was chasing were probably too far away to have heard the gunfire last night, but if she was unlucky with the echoes, who was to say what could have happened? It didn't change her plan—she had already been in a rush to find their building, and it was only more urgent now. She pulled her map from her backpack, locating herself and her quarry and planning out the best route to take. With a sigh and another sip of water, she set off through the city.

Kira traveled cautiously, wary now not only of Partial patrols but of giant hairy claw monsters; she saw movement in every shadow, and had to force herself to stay calm and levelheaded. When she arrived at the right neighborhood, it took her a few hours to positively identify the building with the antenna, though most of that was her fear of being seen. She ended up climbing another building's staircase to get a bird's-eye view, and from there spotted the antenna easily. The buildings here were shorter, only three or four stories for most of them. Knowing what she was looking for, it was easy to spot some of the more subtle clues that the building was inhabited—many of the windows were boarded over, especially on the third floor, and faint tracks in the built-up dirt showed that someone had recently used the front steps.

This was the tricky part. She didn't dare to move in until she knew who lived there, where they were, and whether the bombs were set to explode. The most likely scenario, at least to her, was that this was some kind of outpost for a faction of Partials—and not a faction friendly to Dr. Morgan, since their last meeting at the other outpost had gone so destructively. That didn't automatically mean that these Partials were friendly to humans, though, and Kira didn't want to walk into a trap. She would watch, and wait, and see what happened.

Nothing happened.

Kira watched the building all day and night, holed up in the apartment across the street. She ate cold cans of beans and huddled under a moth-eaten blanket to avoid starting a fire. Nobody went in and nobody went out, and when night fell there were no fires in the windows, no smoke rising up through a crack in the boards. Nothing happened the second day either, and Kira was beginning to get nervous—they must have left before she got there, or slipped out a back way. She crept down to the street and did a quick perimeter check, searching for other entrances and exits, but nothing looked used, either generally or recently. If they'd left at all, they'd done it through the front door. She settled back in to watch it.

That night, someone came out.

Kira leaned forward, careful to stay out of the moonlight in the window. The man was large, easily seven feet tall, with the heft and girth to match. He probably outweighed Kira by two hundred pounds. His skin was dark, but probably no darker than her own; it was hard to tell in the faint light of a cloudy moon. He opened the front door cautiously, lifted a small cart through the door and down the stairs, and carefully locked the door behind him. The cart was full of jugs, and Kira guessed he was off to retrieve water. He wore a heavy pack full of something she couldn't identify, and she couldn't see his weapon. *Safer to assume the worst, then,* she thought, as there could easily be a high-caliber handgun or submachine gun hidden in the folds of his loose-fitting trench coat.

Kira grabbed her things quietly, packing in the dark, and stole down the stairs to follow him. He was already at the corner when she reached the street, and she waited until he rounded it before slipping out after him, stepping as lightly as she could through the rubble in the street. She peered around the corner and saw him walking slowly, pulling the cart behind him. He moved strangely, almost like a waddle, and Kira wondered if it was just his bulk or some other factor. He reached the end of the block and stepped into the street without pausing, as if completely unconcerned that he would be seen or, worse, eaten. How had he survived this long without running into that nocturnal monster? He disappeared around a low wall, and Kira crept after him.

He stood at the mouth of a subway tunnel, filling his plastic jugs with a long-tubed pump similar to her own. He huffed as he worked, as if the exertion was too much for him, but the rest of his mannerisms spoke of long familiarity and expertise. He'd done this often enough to be very good at it.

Was he a Partial? Kira stayed motionless in the shadows observing him, trying to . . . not to listen, not to smell, but to *feel* him, in the way that she'd been able to feel Samm. The link. It was more emotional than informational; if she linked with this man at all, it would be through feeling the things he felt. She examined her emotions closely: She was curious; she was tired; she was sure of her purpose. Did any of that come from him? What would he be feeling? He was muttering to himself, not angrily but simply talking, the way she had started talking to herself. She couldn't hear the words.

The more she watched him, methodically filling the jugs, the more she realized that his size suggested he was human. The Partials had been engineered not just as soldiers but as specific soldiers: the infantry were all young men, the generals were all older men, and Samm had said that their doctors were women and their pilots were petite girls designed to fit easily into small vehicles and tight cockpits. The military contractors had saved billions of dollars building undersized jets. Obviously there were exceptions—Kira had no idea what role Heron was intended to fill, the tall, leggy supermodel who'd captured her for Dr. Morgan—but did one of the templates include this man? He was huge, especially now that she saw him from ground level. Some kind of super-soldier among super-soldiers? A heavy-weapons specialist, maybe, or a close-combat expert? Samm hadn't mentioned anyone like that, but there had been a lot of things he'd never mentioned. Kira concentrated as hard as she could, willing herself to detect this giant through whatever version of the link she possessed, but she felt nothing.

Aside from his size was the simple fact that he was winded. He'd walked only a couple of blocks, and yet he was huffing like he'd just run a marathon. That didn't make sense for a physically perfect super-soldier, but it was perfect for an overweight human.

He was illuminated fairly well, thanks to a large moon and a cloudless sky, and Kira quietly pulled out her binoculars to look at him more closely. She was barely thirty yards away, crouched behind a rusting car, but she wanted to confirm his weaponry at the very least. There was nothing on his legs or hips, no holsters or knives, and there seemed to be nothing in the cart but plastic jugs. He finished filling a jug and lifted it, turning toward her as he placed it in the cart, and for just a moment his coat fell open and she saw his chest and sides: He had no weapons in there either, no shoulder holsters or bandoliers or anything. Kira frowned. No one would travel in the wilderness unarmed, so his weapon must be concealed, but why conceal it if you thought you were alone—

In a flash Kira realized that she had walked into a trap: This man, big and slow and unarmed, had been sent outside as bait, while the others circled around to cut off her escape. She dropped to the ground, lowering her profile in case anyone tried to shoot her right there, and looked around wildly for the attackers. The city was too dark; there could be snipers in a hundred different windows and doorways and shadows around her, but she couldn't see deep enough into any of them. Her only hope was to run, just like with the monster in the plaza. The building behind had some kind of storefront, maybe an old pizza place; there would be a back room at the very least, probably a basement, and if she was lucky a stairwell that accessed the rest of the building. She could slip in, find another exit, and slip out before they had a chance to close their trap.

The man by the subway stairs was stretching, his backpack lying gently on the ground beside him. Was he prepping for a strike? She had to go now. Kira scrambled to her feet and bolted toward the storefront, bracing herself for the impact of bullets in her back. Behind her she heard a yelp, like a cry of fear, but she didn't turn around. At the back of the old pizza place was a thin wooden door, and beyond it an office; Kira dove through and slammed it closed behind her, switching on her light to look for another exit. There was none.

She was trapped.

CHAPTER NINE

Kira swept her arm across the metal desk in the center of the room, clearing away decades-old dust and thick stacks of papers. Last was a thin computer monitor, which she knocked aside on her backswing before flipping the desk on its side, diving behind it for an extra layer of shielding. She crouched low behind the barrier, her rifle tucked into the side of her face, the barrel trained squarely on the door; if the knob so much as twitched, she could put a whole clip into whoever stood beyond it. She waited, barely daring to breathe.

She waited.

A minute went by. Five minutes. Ten minutes. She imagined another gunman on the far side of the door, lying in wait as carefully as she was. Which one of them would break first? There were more of them, and they had the advantage; they had more room to maneuver, and more people to do it with. But she wasn't going to give up that easily. If they wanted her, they had to come in and get her.

Ten more minutes went by, and Kira shifted her weight painfully from one leg to the other. She blinked sweat from her eyes, feeling them red and raw, but still she refused to move. Another ten minutes. Her throat was parched and painful, her fingers cramped around the handgrip of her gun. Nothing moved. No sound disturbed the night.

Kira's flashlight flickered, sick and yellow as the batteries started to fail. They'd been weak for a few days, and she hadn't found any replacements yet. Ten minutes later the light winked out for good, and Kira closed her eyes uselessly against the utter blackness, listening with every ounce of her focus: for the doorknob, for the creak of floorboards or the squeak of shoes, for the click of a gun as it readied to fire. Ten more minutes. Twenty. An hour. Were they really this patient?

Or was there nobody there?

Kira rubbed her eyes, thinking back on the attack. She had assumed there was a trap—it was the most logical explanation—but she hadn't actually seen anyone. Was it really possible that the man outside, unarmed and alone in a dead city full of monsters, was really the only one? It was extremely unlikely, but yes, it was possible. Was she ready to bet her life on that possibility?

She lowered her gun, whimpering silently at the ache in her stiff shoulders. She moved as quietly as she could to the side of the room, out of the line of fire that would come through the door, and listened again. All was quiet. She reached out with one hand, hugging the wall tightly, and touched the doorknob. Nobody shot her. She took a breath, gripped the knob tightly, and threw it open as fast as she could, yanking her hand back and rolling away from the opening. No gunfire, no shouts, no noise at all but the creak of the door. She stared at the dark black doorway, trying to work up the courage to go through it, and decided to try one more thing; she picked up the monitor she'd knocked off the desk, found a good stance, and heaved it out the door, hoping to draw the fire of anyone lurking on the other side. The monitor clattered to the ground, the screen cracked, and the silence returned.

"Nobody shoot me," she said, just in case, and slowly came around the corner of the door frame. The pizza place beyond was as empty as ever, and out in the street the sagging metal cars reflected shafts of moonlight. She crept outside, rifle up and ready, checking her corners and watching for an ambush, but she was alone. On the far side of the street stood the subway entrance, and beside it the large man's cart, motionless and abandoned. A jug lay on the ground nearby, dropped on its side, the water now long spilled out. A few feet away, where he had laid it against the wall of the subway entrance, was the man's bulging backpack.

Kira walked a full circuit of the intersection, running from car to car for cover, before approaching the backpack. It was enormous, practically as big as she was, and she couldn't help but think of the shattered craters of the previous two houses she'd seen. Did she really want to open a bomber's backpack? He could have left it here as a trap specifically to kill her . . . but honestly, he'd had so many easier opportunities to just shoot her if he really wanted her dead. Or were explosives the only weapon he knew? Maybe he really didn't have a gun at all.

She circled the bag warily, rubbing her face with her palm, trying to make a decision. Was it worth it? The nocturnal monster still haunted her—the one time she'd taken a major risk, she'd nearly died. But her caution was costing her time, and time wasn't a resource she could afford to spend this freely. The answers she was looking for—what is the Trust? How are the Partials connected to RM? Who am I, and what plan am I a part of? Those were the answers that could save the human race or destroy it. As dangerous as her choices were, she still had to make them. She slung her rifle behind her shoulder and reached for the bag—

—and heard a voice.

Kira scrambled back, ducking behind the wall of the subway entrance. The voice was soft, but it carried well in the midnight silence—a faint muttering from a side street, maybe half a block down and closing. She gripped her rifle, looking for somewhere to run, but she was trapped in the open. Instead she crept slowly to the side, keeping the subway entrance between her and the speaker. As he drew nearer, the muttering got louder and louder until at last she understood the words.

"Never leave the backpack, never leave the backpack." It was the same phrase, over and over: "Never leave the backpack." She peeked out and saw the large man from before, trudging up the street with his same waddling gait. "Never leave the backpack." His hands twitched, and his eyes darted back and forth across the street. "Never leave the backpack."

Kira wasn't sure what it was; something about the way he walked, or spoke, or rubbed his hands together—probably a combination of all that and more—that made her decide. She'd wasted enough time. She had to act. She slung her rifle back over her shoulder, spread her hands wide to show that they were empty, and stepped out from her hiding place, between him and the backpack.

"Hello."

The man jerked to a stop, his eyes wide with horror, and he turned and bolted back the way he had come. Kira stepped forward to follow, not certain if she should, when suddenly he stopped, bending low at the waist as if wounded, and shook his head violently. "Never leave the backpack," he said, turning toward her, "never leave the backpack." He saw her again and ran a few more steps away, as if it were an involuntary reaction, but then he stopped again, turning and eyeing the backpack with a pained, terrified expression. "Never leave the backpack."

"It's all right," said Kira, wondering what was happening. This wasn't at all what she'd expected. "I'm not going to hurt you." She tried to look as harmless as possible.

"I need the backpack," he said, his voice practically dripping with desperation. "I'm not supposed to ever leave the backpack, I always take it with me, it's everything I have."

"Are these your supplies?" she asked, stepping to the side. The move gave the man a better view of the backpack, and he surged forward five more steps, his hand reaching out as if to snatch it away from her from fifty feet away. "I'm not here to steal from you," she said slowly. "I just want to talk. How many others are there?"

"That's the only one," he pleaded. "I need it, I can't lose it, it's everything I have—"

"Not the backpack," she said, "other people: How many other people are with you in the safe house?"

"Please give me the backpack," he said again, creeping

forward. He stepped into the light, and she could see tears in his eyes. His voice was hoarse and desperate. "I need it, I need it, I need the backpack. Please give it back to me."

"Is it medicine? Do you need help?"

"Please give it back," he muttered, over and over. "Never leave the backpack." Kira considered for a moment, then stepped to the side, moving twenty feet away to the other side of the water cart—far enough that he could come up and grab the backpack while still staying well outside her reach. He rushed forward and collapsed on it, clutching it and crying, and Kira looked again for an ambush—for snipers in the windows, or men coming up behind him in the street. He seemed to be completely alone. *What's going on here? Could this be the bomber who'd been so hard to track, who'd set traps so cunning that even Partials didn't find them until it was too late?*

He didn't seem eager to talk about anything but the backpack, though, so she focused on that.

"What's in it?"

He answered without looking up. "Everything."

"Your food? Your weapons?"

"No weapons," he said firmly, shaking his head, "no weapons. I'm a noncombatant, you can't shoot me, I don't have any weapons."

Kira took a small step forward. "Food, then?"

"Are you hungry?" He seemed to perk up at this, his head rising.

Kira thought carefully, then nodded. "A little." She paused, then gestured toward her own pack. "I have some beans if you want some, and a can of pineapple I found in a drugstore."

"I have lots of pineapple," he said, climbing slowly to his feet. He brushed off his hands and hefted the backpack up onto his shoulders. "I like fruit cocktail best: It has pineapples and peaches and pears and cherries. Come back to my house and I'll show you."

"Your house," she said, thinking back to the craters. She was more sure now than ever that this man was no Partial; if anything, he seemed like a giant child. "Who else is back there?"

"Nobody," he said, "nobody at all. I'm a noncombatant, you can't shoot me. We'll eat fruit cocktail in my house."

Kira thought about it a moment longer, then nodded. If this was a trap, it was the weirdest one she'd ever encountered. She put out her hand to shake. "My name is Kira Walker."

"My name is Afa Demoux." He placed the fallen water jug on the cart, gathered his pump, and began towing it all back to the safe house. "You're a Partial, and I'm the last human being on Earth."

Afa's safe house turned out to be an old TV station, old enough to contain some equipment from before the days of computerized entertainment. Kira had done salvage runs on a handful of local news stations back on Long Island, and their systems had been arcane but small: cameras, cables, and little bits of computer equipment feeding everything into the cloud. This building had that as well—every TV station probably did, she thought, given the old world's obsession with the internet—but it had older devices as well: broad banks of manual mixing equipment, a room of mysterious broadcasting machines designed to send everything into the sky, to be picked up by remote antennas instead of beamed directly through satellite links. This was why the building still had its enormous antenna, and that was why Afa lived here. She knew this because he told her, over and over, for nearly an hour.

"The cloud went down," he said again, "but radios don't need the cloud—it's a point-to-point communication system. All you need is a radio, an antenna, and enough electricity to run it. I can broadcast to anyone, and they can broadcast to me, and we don't need a network or a cloud or anything. With an antenna this big I can broadcast all over the world."

"That's great," said Kira, "but who do you talk to? Who's out there?" There had to be more survivors than just Long Island— she'd always hoped but never dared to believe.

Afa shook his head—broad and brown-skinned, with a bushy black beard salted liberally with gray. Kira guessed that he was Polynesian, but she didn't know the individual islands well enough to guess which one. "There's nobody out there," he said. "I'm the last human on Earth."

He did live alone; that much, at least, was true. He had converted the TV station into a twisting warren of stored equipment: generators, portable radios, stockpiles of food and explosives, and pile after pile of papers. He had stacks of files and folders, bundles of news clippings held together by twine, boxes of yellowed printouts next to more boxes of scraps and receipts and notarized documents. Thick binders overflowed with photos, some of them glossy, some of them printed on weathered office paper; other photos bulged from boxes or spilled out of rooms, entire offices filled floor to ceiling with records and filing cabinets and always, everywhere, more photos than she'd ever imagined. Those few walls not covered with cabinets and bookshelves and tall stacks of boxes were papered over with maps: maps of New York State and others, maps of the United States, maps of the NADI alliance, maps of China and Brazil and the entire world. Covering the maps was a dense nest of pushpins and strings and crooked metal flags. They made Kira dizzy just looking at them, and all the time, on every surface, even crunching and rustling underfoot, were the papers and papers and papers that defined and bounded Afa's life.

Kira pressed him again, setting down her can of fruit cocktail. "What are you doing here?"

"I'm the last human on Earth."

"There are humans on Long Island," she said. "What about them?"

"Partials," he said quickly, waving his hand to dismiss the idea. "All Partials. It's all here, all in the files." He gestured around grandly, as if the mounds of unordered papers were plain evidence of universal truth. Kira nodded, irrationally grateful for this fleck of insanity—when he had first called her a Partial it had scared her, truly disturbed her. He'd been the first human ever to say the words out loud to her, and the accusation—the knowledge that someone might actually know, might actually say it—had shaken her to the core. Knowing that Afa was merely delusional, thinking everyone in the world was a Partial, made it easier to bear.

Kira pressed again, hoping that more specific questions might draw out a more specific answer. "You used to work for ParaGen."

He stopped, his eyes locked on hers, his body tense, then returned to his eating with forced nonchalance. He didn't answer.

"Your name was on a door at the ParaGen office," she said. "That's where you got some of this equipment." She gestured around at the rows of computers and monitors. "What are they for?"

Afa didn't answer, and Kira paused again to watch him. There was something wrong with his mind, she was certain— something about the way he moved, the way he talked, even the way he sat. He didn't think as quickly, or at least not in the same ways, as anyone Kira had met before. How had he survived on his own like this? He was cautious, certainly, but only about certain things; his home was miraculously well defended, filled with ingenious traps and security measures to keep himself hidden and his equipment safe, but on the other hand, he'd gone outside unarmed. *The best explanation,* Kira told herself, *is that there's somebody else with him. Based on what I've seen, there's no way he's capable of defending himself this well, and certainly no way he could set up all this equipment. He's like a child. Maybe whoever's really running this safe house uses him as an assistant?* But as much as Kira had tried, she hadn't been able to see or hear anyone else in the building. Whoever it was was hiding too well.

Talking about ParaGen just makes him clam up, she told herself, *so I need to try a different tactic.* She saw him eyeing her half-eaten can of fruit and held it out to him. "Do you want the rest?"

He grabbed it quickly. "It has cherries in it."

"Yes, it does. Do you like cherries?"

"Of course I like cherries. I'm human."

Kira almost laughed, but managed to stop herself. She knew plenty of humans who hated cherries. Sharing the fruit seemed to undo the nervousness she'd caused by mentioning ParaGen, so she probed him about a new topic. "It's very brave of you to go out at night," she said. "A few nights ago I got attacked by something huge; I barely got away with my life."

"It used to be a bear," said Afa, his mouth full of fruit cocktail. "You need to wait till it catches something."

"What happens when it catches something?"

"It eats it."

Kira shook her head. "Well, yeah, but I mean why do you need to wait for that to happen? What does that mean?"

"If it's eating something, it's not hungry," he said, staring blankly at the floor. "Wait until it eats, and then go outside to get water while it's busy. That way it won't eat you. But always remember to take the backpack," he said, pointing in front of him with his spoon. "You can't ever leave the backpack."

Kira marveled at the simplicity of his plan, but even so, his answer sparked a dozen new questions: How did he know when the monster had eaten? What did he mean that it "used to be" a bear? What was so important about the backpack, and who had told him all these strategies in the first place? She decided to pursue the latter question, as it seemed like the best opportunity to broach the topic again.

"Who told you not to leave the backpack?"

"Nobody told me," he said. "I'm a human. Nobody's in charge of me, 'cause I'm the only one left."

"Obviously nobody's in charge of you," said Kira, frustrated by the circular conversation, "but what about your friend? The one who warned you not to lose the backpack?"

"No friends," said Afa, shaking his head in a strange, loose sort of way that shook his entire torso as well. "No friends. I'm the last one."

"Were there others before? Other people with you, here in the safe house?"

"Just you." His voice changed when he said it, and Kira was struck by the thought that he might very well have been completely alone—that she might be the first person he'd spoken to in years. Whoever had saved him and taught him to survive, whoever had set up this and the other radio stations—whoever had rigged them with explosives—was probably long dead, lost to Partials or wild animals or illness or accident, leaving this fifty-year-old child all alone in the ruins. *That's why he says he's the last one,* she thought. *He watched the last ones die.*

Kira spoke softly, her voice tender. "Do you miss them?"

"The other humans?" He shrugged, his head bouncing on his shoulders. "It's quieter now. I like the quiet."

Kira sat back, frowning. Everything he said confused her more, and she felt as if she was even further now than before from understanding his situation. Most confusing of all was the name on the door at ParaGen—Afa Demoux had had an office, an office with his name on it, and ParaGen didn't strike her as the kind of place that let a mentally handicapped man have an office just to keep him entertained. He had to have worked there; he had to have done something, or been something, important.

What had it said on his door? She struggled to remember, then nodded as the word came back: IT. *Was it just a cruel joke? Call the weirdo "it"? That could explain why he didn't want to talk about ParaGen.* But no; it didn't make sense. Nothing she knew about the old world suggested that kind of behavior, at least not so officially in a major corporation. The letters on the door had to mean something else. She watched his face as he finished the can of fruit, trying to guess his emotional state. Could she bring up ParaGen again, or would he just go silent like before? Maybe if she didn't mention ParaGen, and just asked about the letters.

"You seem to know a lot about . . . I-T." She winced, hoping that wasn't a stupid question—or worse, an insulting one. Afa's eyes lit up, and Kira felt a thrill of success.

"I was an IT director," he said. "I used to do everything—they couldn't do anything without me." He smiled broadly, gesturing at the computers arrayed around the room. "See? I know every-thing about computers. I know everything."

"That's amazing," said Kira, barely containing her grin. Finally she was getting somewhere. She scooted forward. "Tell me about it—about I-T."

"You have to know how everything works," he said. "You have to know where everything is; some's in the cloud, and some's in the drives, but if it's the wrong kind of drive, then it won't work without power. That's why I have the Zobles on the roof."

"The solar panels," said Kira, and Afa nodded.

"Zobles and Hufongs, though those are a lot harder to find, and they break a lot. I turned the generators in room C into capacitors to hold extra electricity from the Hufongs, and they can hold on to it for a while, but you have to keep them cycling or they run down. Now," he said, leaning forward and gesturing with his hands, "with the right kind of electricity you can access any drive you need. Most of what I have here is solid state, but the big ones, the ones in that corner, are disc-based servers—they use a lot more electricity, but you can store a lot more data, and that's where most of the sequences are."

He kept going, more rapidly and with more animation than anything he'd done or said before. Kira reeled at the sudden burst of information, understanding most of the words but only about half the concepts; he was obviously talking about the digital records, and the different ways they were stored and powered and accessed, but he spoke so quickly, and Kira had such a poor background in the subject, that most of his meaning flew right over her head.

What stood out to her more than anything was the sudden, almost shocking proficiency he had with the topic. She'd assumed he was slow, too childlike to do more than fetch water on somebody else's instructions, but she saw now that her first impression had been wildly wrong. Afa had his quirks, certainly, and she didn't doubt that there was something off about him, but on at least one subject the man was brilliant.

"Stop," she said, holding up her hands, "wait, you're going too fast. Start at the beginning: What does I-T mean?"

"Information technology," said Afa. "I was an IT director. I kept everyone's computers running, and I set up the servers, and I maintained cloud security, and I saw everything on the network." He leaned forward, staring at her intently, stabbing the floor with his finger. "I saw *everything*. I watched it all happen." He leaned back and spread his arms, as if to encompass the entire room, maybe the entire building, in his gesture. "I have it all here, almost all of it, and I'm going to show everyone, and they're going to know the whole story. They're going to know exactly how it happened."

"How what happened?"

"The end of the world," said Afa. He swallowed, his face turning red as he raced to speak without pausing for breath. "The Partials, the war, the rebellion, the virus. Everything."

Kira nodded, so excited her fingers started to tingle. "And who are you going to tell?"

Afa's face fell, and his arms dropped to his sides. "No one," he said. "I'm the last human being left alive."

"No, you're not," said Kira firmly. "There's an entire community on Long Island—there are nearly thirty-six thousand humans left there, and goodness knows how many more on other continents. There *have* to be more. What about me?"

"You're a Partial."

The accusation, again, made her uncomfortable, especially since she couldn't counter it with a flat refusal. She tried a misdirection instead. "How do you know I'm a Partial?"

"Humans don't come to Manhattan."

"You're here."

"I was here before; that's different."

Kira ground her teeth, caught again in Afa's circular, self-referential arguments. "Then why did you let me into you house?" she asked. "If the Partials are so bad, why trust me?"

"Partials aren't bad."

"But—" Kira frowned, exasperated by his simple, matter-of-fact answers, which seemed to make no sense. "You're out here alone," she said. "You hide, you protect yourself like crazy, you blow up your radio stations anytime anyone gets too close to them. You've got a huge community to the east, and a huge community on the north, and you don't join either of them. If the Partials aren't bad, why keep yourself separate?" It occurred to her, as she said it, that the question applied equally well to her. She'd been out here alone for months, avoiding Partials and humans alike.

Not avoiding them, she told herself, *saving them. Saving both of them.* But the thought still bothered her.

Afa scraped the last bits of fruit from his can. "I stay here because I like the quiet."

"You like the quiet." Kira laughed, more helpless than amused, and stood up from the floor, stretching and rubbing her eyes. "I don't understand you, Afa. You collect information that you do and don't want to show anyone; you live in a giant radio tower and yet you don't like talking to people. Why do you have the radios, by the way? Is it just part of the information gathering? Are you just trying to know everything?"

"Yes."

"And you didn't think that maybe somebody else could benefit from all this information you're putting together?"

Afa stood up. "I have to go to sleep now."

"Wait," said Kira, abashed by his discomfort. She'd been arguing with the brilliant IT director, almost yelling at him in her frustration, but here she was confronted with the child again, awkward and slow, a tiny mind in a giant body. She sighed, and realized how tired she was, as well. "I'm sorry, Afa. I'm sorry I got upset." She reached toward his hand, hesitating as she watched his eyes. They had never touched, Afa always keeping his shy distance, and she realized with a rush of emotion that she hadn't touched anyone—not a single human contact—in weeks. Afa, if she understood his situation correctly, hadn't touched anyone in years. Her hand hovered over his, and she saw in his eyes the same mixture of fear and longing that she felt in herself. She lowered her palm, resting it on his knuckles, and he flinched but didn't move away. She felt the pressure of his bones, the softness of his flesh, the leathery texture of his skin, the warm beat of his pulse.

She felt a tear in the corner of her eye and blinked it away. Afa began to cry, more like a lost child than anyone she'd met in ten years, and Kira drew him into an embrace. He hugged her back tightly, sobbing like a baby, nearly crushing her with his massive arms, and Kira let her own tears run freely. She patted him softly on the back, soothing him gently, luxuriating in the sheer presence of another person, real and warm and alive.

CHAPTER TEN

Marcus ran as fast as he could through the forest, trying to keep his feet under him and his head from cracking into low-hanging branches and vine-crusted poles. The soldier beside him fell abruptly, red blood blossoming on his back as a bullet brought him down. Marcus faltered, instinctively turning to help the fallen soldier, but Haru grabbed him and dragged him forward, crashing headlong through the trees.

"He's gone," Haru shouted. "Keep running!"

More shots flew past them, whistling through the leaves and exploding against trunks and old boards. This part of Long Island had been heavily wooded even before the Break, and in the twelve years since then, nature had reclaimed the neighborhood, tearing down rotten fences and collapsing old roofs and walls, filling the lawns and gardens with new growth. Even the sidewalks and streets were cracked and split by a dozen years of freezes and thaws, and trees had sprung up in every gap and rift and crevice. Marcus leapt over a crumbling brick retaining wall and followed Haru through a living room so filled with vines and brush it was almost indistinguishable from the world outside. He dodged a sapling sprouting up through the floorboards, and cringed as another Partial bullet whooshed past his ear and shattered the glass in a picture frame not ten feet in front of him. Haru turned down a sagging hallway, dropping a live grenade just around the corner, and Marcus's eyes went wide in terror as he leapt over it, putting on an extra burst of speed he didn't know he had. He tumbled out the far side of the house just as it exploded. Haru hauled him to his feet again with an urgent grunt.

"If they're as close behind as I think they are, that got at least one of them," said Haru, puffing as he ran. "Either way it's going to slow down anyone who followed us into the house, and it's going to make them think twice about following us into the next one."

"Sato, you all right?" A woman's voice cut sharply through the trees, and Marcus recognized it as Grant, the sergeant of this squad of Grid soldiers. Haru ran a little faster to catch up, and Marcus snarled with exhaustion as he struggled to keep up.

"Just dropped a frag in that last house," said Haru. "Medic and I are fine."

"Grenades are fun, but you're gonna miss 'em when they're gone," said Grant.

"It didn't go to waste," Haru insisted. Another soldier beside them twisted and fell in midstride, claimed by another bullet, and Marcus ducked involuntarily before sprinting forward again. They'd been running like this for nearly an hour, and the forest had become a nightmare of death unmoored from the familiar rules of cause and effect. Bullets came from nowhere, people lived one second and died the next, and all they could do was run.

"We need to make a stand," said Haru. He was in better shape than Marcus, but fatigue was more than evident in his voice.

Grant shook her head almost imperceptibly, conserving her energy as they ran. "We tried that, remember? We lost half the squad."

"We didn't have a good ambush point," said Haru. "If we can find a good spot, or if we can regroup with more soldiers, we might have a chance. The one thing we did accomplish was to get a good look at their forces, and they're not very big. We outnumber them, and we know the terrain better—there's got to be a way to make this work."

Another bullet flew past, and Marcus stifled a scream. "You have an absolutely heartwarming level of optimism."

"There's a work farm near here," said Grant, "on the grounds of an old golf course. We can make a stand there."

They redoubled their efforts, discarding grenades here and there as they ran, hoping the erratic explosions would deter their pursuers enough to buy a few precious extra seconds. Marcus saw a sign for a golf course and marveled at Grant's presence of mind—he was too scared and frantic even to notice their environment, let alone recognize it. A voice from the trees called out for them to halt, but they barreled forward as Grant shouted back, "Partials behind us! Hold your positions and fire!" Marcus followed the soldiers past the line of cars that marked the edge of the parking lot, and dove to the ground behind the largest truck he could find.

A man in rough farming clothes crouched next to them, clutching a shotgun. "We heard the reports on the radio. Is it true?" His eyes were wild with fear. "Are they invading?"

Grant readied her assault rifle as she answered, checking the clip for ammo and then slapping it back into place. "Full-scale. The Grid base in Queens is gone, and the watch posts on the North Shore are reporting Partial landing craft from there all the way out to Wildwood."

"Mother of mercy," the farmer muttered.

"Incoming!" shouted another soldier, and Grant and Haru and the rest reared up, bracing themselves behind the line of cars and firing furiously into the trees. Ten or so farmers, already gathered by the radio reports, joined them with grim looks. Marcus threw his hands over his head and ducked lower, knowing he should help but too terrified to move. The Partials returned fire, and the cars shook with the staccato rhythm of bullet impacts. Grant shouted more directions, but she stopped mid-word with a sickening gurgle, falling to the ground in a red mist of blood. Marcus moved to help her, but she was dead before she even landed.

"Fall back," Haru hissed.

"She's dead," said Marcus.

"I know she's dead, fall back!" Haru emptied his ammo clip into the forest, then dropped behind cover to reload. He glared at Marcus fiercely. "The farm's back there somewhere, and anyone left in it is not a fighter—if they were, they'd be out here. Find them and get them out of here."

"And go where?" asked Marcus. "Grant said the Partials are everywhere."

"Go south," said Haru. "We'll try to catch up, but get the civilians moving now. You'll need all the time you can get."

"Going 'south' won't be enough," said Marcus. "This isn't a raid, it's an invasion. Even if we make it to East Meadow, they'll be right on our heels."

"You want to stay here then?" asked Haru. "I don't know if they're here to capture us or kill us, but neither one sounds pleasant."

"I know," said Marcus, "I know." He glanced toward the farmhouse, trying to work up his courage to run. Haru rose, turned, and fired again into the trees.

"This is what I get for volunteering," said Marcus, and ran for the farm.

CHAPTER ELEVEN

Afa slept on a king-size bed on the seventh floor of the building, in what looked like it used to be a dressing room. Kira tucked him in like a child before searching for a room of her own, eventually finding a vast, dark studio with stadium seats on one side and half of a stylized living room on the other. A talk show set, she guessed, though the logo on the back wall didn't spark any memories. She knew that talk shows existed, because someone had watched one in her house—her nanny, maybe—but she doubted she could recognize even that one's logo. Afa had filled the chairs with boxes, each carefully labeled, but the talk show couch was empty, and she checked it for spiders before laying down her bedroll and going to sleep. She dreamed of Marcus, and then of Samm, and wondered if she'd ever see either of them again.

There was no natural light in the building, thanks to Afa's logical insistence on blackout curtains, and even less light in the studio, but Kira had been fending for herself for too long, and jerked awake at the same time as always. She found her way to a window and peeked out, seeing the same familiar sight that greet her every morning: ruined buildings laced with green, and tinged with blue light as the dark sky turned pale in the sunrise.

It didn't sound like Afa was awake yet, and Kira took the opportunity to skim through some of his files, starting with the boxes in the studio. They were numbered 138 through 427, one box per chair with more ringing the walls, back-to-back around the entire perimeter of the room. She started with the nearest box, number 221, and pulled out the page on top, a folded print-out with a faded military letterhead.

"'To whom it may concern,'" she read. "'My name is Master Sergeant Corey Church, and I was part of the Seventeenth Armored Cavalry in the Second Nihon Invasion.'" The First Nihon Invasion was one of the early major defeats for the NADI forces in the Isolation War, the world's failed attempt to take back Japan from a suddenly hostile China. She remembered learning about it in school in East Meadow, but didn't remember much of the details. The Second Nihon Invasion was the one that worked—the one where they went back with two hundred thousand Partial soldiers and drove the Isolationists back to the mainland, kicking off the long campaign that finally ended the war. It was the reason the rest of the Partials had been built. Kira read more of the letter, some kind of battlefield report, recounting the man's experience fighting alongside the Partials; he referred to them as "new weapons" and said that they were "well trained and precise." Kira had grown up knowing Partials only as bogeymen, the monsters that had destroyed the world, and even having met Samm—even knowing that she herself was some kind of a Partial—it was strange to see them referred to so positively. And yet so clinically, as if they were a new kind of Jeep from the quartermaster. The master sergeant mentioned that they seemed "insular," that they kept to themselves and ignored the human soldiers, but that was hardly a negative—a bit ominous, in light of their eventual rebellion, but not immediately threatening or scary.

"This is how it started," she said out loud, setting it down and picking up another paper from the same box. It was another combat report, this time from a Sergeant Major Seamus Ogden. He talked about the Partials the same way, not as monsters but as tools. She read another document, then another, and the attitude was the same in each one—it wasn't that they thought the Partials were harmless, it was that they barely thought of them at all. They were weapons, like bullets in a clip, to be spent and used and forgotten.

Kira moved to another box, 302, pulling out a newspaper clipping from something called the *Los Angeles Times*: PARTIAL RIGHTS GROUPS PROTEST ON CAPITOL STEPS. Beneath it in the box was a similar clipping from the *Seattle Times*, and beneath that another from the *Chicago Sun*. The dates in this box were all from late in 2064, just a few months before the Partial War. Kira would have just turned five. Obviously the Partials would have been all over the news at the time, but she didn't remember her father ever talking about them; now that she knew he'd been working for ParaGen, that made more sense. If he'd worked with them, or even helped create them, he would have had a different attitude from the rest of the world—probably a pretty unpopular attitude. *At least I hope he had a different attitude,* she thought.

Why else would he raise one as his daughter? She vaguely remembered her nanny as well, and a housekeeper, but they never talked about Partials either. Had her father asked them not to?

Had they even known what Kira really was?

Kira turned to the earliest numbered boxes in the room, finding number 138 and pulling out the top piece of paper. It was another newspaper clipping, this time from the financial section of something called the *Wall Street Journal*, describing in vague terms the awarding of a massive military contract: In March of 2051 the US government contracted ParaGen, a budding biotechnology company, to produce an army of "biosynthetic soldiers." The focus of the article was entirely on the cost of the project, the ramifications for stockholders, and the impact this would have on the rest of the biotech industry. There was no mention of civil rights, of diseases, of any of the massive issues that had come to define the world right before the Break. Only money. She searched through the rest of the box and found more of the same: a transcript from a news interview with ParaGen's chief financial officer; an internal ParaGen memo about the company's new windfall contract; a magazine called *Forbes* with the ParaGen logo on the cover and the crisp silhouette of an armed Partial soldier in the background. Kira flipped through the pages of the magazine, finding article after article about money, about technologies being used to make more money, about all the ways the Isolation War, despite being "a terrible tragedy," would help heal the American economy. Money, money, money.

Money had a place in East Meadow society, but that place was a small one. Almost everything they needed was free: If you wanted a can of food, a pair of pants, a book, a house, whatever it was, all it cost you was the effort to go out and find one. Money was used almost exclusively for fresh food, things like wheat from the farms and fish from the coastal villages—things you had to work for—and even then, most of those commodities were traded in kind, through a barter system in the marketplace. Nandita and Xochi had built a lucrative business trading herbs for fresh food, and Kira had always eaten well because of it. Money, such as it was, was usually just work credits: government vouchers for her time spent in the hospital, her reward for performing a vital service that didn't actually produce a tradable commodity. It was enough to keep her in fresh fish and vegetables for lunch, but not much else. It was a minor, almost insignificant aspect of her life. The documents in box 138 described a world in which money was everything— not just the means of sustaining life but the purpose of living it. She tried to imagine being happy about the war with the Partials or the Voice, rejoicing because it would somehow bring her extra work credits, but the idea was so foreign she laughed out loud. If that was how the old world worked—if that was all they really cared about—maybe it was better that it had fallen apart. Maybe it was inevitable.

"You're real," said Afa.

Kira spun around, startled, hiding the magazine behind her guiltily. Would he be mad at her for looking at his records?

"Did you say I'm . . ." She paused. "Real?"

"I thought you were a dream," said Afa, shuffling into the room. He stopped at one of the boxes and sifted through it idly, almost as if he were petting an animal. "I haven't talked to anyone in so long—and then last night there was a person in my house, and I thought that I'd dreamed it, but you're still here." He nodded. "You're real."

"I'm real," she assured him, placing the magazine back into box 138. "I've been admiring your collection."

"It has everything—almost everything. It even has video, but not in this room. I have the whole story."

Kira stepped toward him, wondering how long he'd stay talkative this time. "The story of the Partial War," she said, "and the Break."

"That's just part of it," said Afa, picking up two stapled sheaves of paper, examining his own pen marks in the upper corners, and then reordering them in the box. "This is the story of the end of the world, the rise and fall of human civilization, the creation of the Partials and the death of everything else."

"And you've read all of it?"

Afa nodded again, his shoulders slack as he moved from box to box. "All of it. I'm the only human being on the planet."

"I guess that makes sense, then," said Kira. She stopped by a box—number 341—and pulled out some kind of government report; a court order, by the look of it, with a round seal stamped in the corner. She wanted answers, but she didn't want to pressure him again, to freak him out by saying or mentioning anything he didn't want to remember. *I'll keep it generic for now.* "How did you find it all?"

"I used to work in the clouds," he said, then immediately corrected himself: "In the cloud. I lived my whole life up there, I could go anywhere and find anything." He nodded at a box of dusty clippings. "I was like a bird."

I saw your name at ParaGen, she wanted to say again. *I know you have information about the Trust: about RM, the expiration date, what I am.* She'd been looking for these answers for so long, and now they were right here, split into boxes and trapped in a failing brain. *Is it just from the loneliness? Maybe his brain works fine, he just hasn't spoken to someone in so long he's forgotten how to interact with people.* She wanted to sit him down and ask him a million questions, but she'd waited this long; she could wait a little longer. *Win him over, don't freak him out, get him on your side.*

She read a bit of the court order in her hand, something about the words "Partial Nation" being declared a sign of terrorist sympathy. Students couldn't write or say them on school campuses, and anyone caught using them in graffiti was subject to prosecution as a threat to national security. She waved it lightly, grabbing his attention. "You've got a lot about the last days before the war," she said. "You've really worked hard to put this together. Do you have anything . . ." She paused, almost too cautious to ask. She wanted to know about the Trust, which Samm had implied was part of the Partial leadership, but she worried that if she just blurted it out, like she had with ParaGen, he might shut down again. "Do you have anything about the Partials themselves? The way they're organized?"

"They're an army," said Afa. "They're organized like an army." He was on the floor now, looking at two of his boxes and the papers in them; every third or fourth one he frowned at and moved to the other box.

"Yes," said Kira, "but I mean, the leaders of the army—the generals. Do you know anything about where they are now?"

"This one died," said Afa, holding up a paper without looking away from his boxes. Kira walked to him and took it carefully; it was an article from the *New York Times*, like some of the others she'd seen, but printed out from a website instead of clipped from a real paper. The headline read NORTH ATLANTIC FLEET SUNK IN LOWER BAY.

Kira looked up, surprised. "They sank a Partial fleet?"

"The Partials didn't have a navy," said Afa, still sorting his papers. "That was a human fleet, sunk by the Partial Air Force, just off the shore of Brooklyn. It was the biggest military strike in the war, in retaliation for the death of General Craig. I have one about him, too." He held up another page, and Kira snatched it away, poring over the information: "'General Scott Craig, leader of the Partial uprising and former mouthpiece of the Partial rights movement, was assassinated last night in a daring strike by human commandos—' We killed him?"

"It was a war."

"And then they destroyed an entire fleet." She counted up the ships in the article, a massive group sailing north to attack the concentration of Partial forces in New York State. The ships had been undermanned, their crews already ravaged by the plague. "Twenty ships, and they just . . . killed everyone on them."

"It was a war," said Afa again, taking the papers from her hands and dropping them back in the box.

"But it didn't have to be," said Kira, following him across the room. "The Partials didn't want to kill everyone—you said yourself that they weren't evil. They wanted equality, they wanted to live normal lives, and they could have done that without killing all those thousands of people on those ships."

"They killed billions of people," said Afa.

"Do you know that for sure?" Kira demanded. "You have all these documents and articles and everything else—do you have something about RM? About where it came from?"

"I'm the last human being on the planet," he said loudly, walking more quickly to stay ahead of her, and Kira realized that she was practically shouting at him. She backed off, forcing herself to calm down; he had to have something about the virus, but she'd never find it without his help. She need to keep him, and herself, calm.

"I'm sorry," she said. "I'm sorry I got loud. I'm very . . ." She took a deep breath, collecting herself. "I've been looking for some very important answers, and you've found them, and I just got overexcited."

"You're still real," he said, backing into a corner. "You're still here."

"I'm here and I'm your friend," she said softly. "You've done an amazing thing here—you've found all the information I need. But I don't know your system; I don't know how it's organized. Will you please help me find what I'm looking for?"

Afa's voice was soft. "I have everything," he said, his head nodding up and down. "I have almost everything."

"Can you tell me who created RM?" She clenched her fists, forcing herself not to get loud or aggressive.

"That's easy," said Afa. "It was the Trust."

"Yes," said Kira, nodding eagerly, "the Trust, keep going. The Trust are the Partial leaders, the generals and the admirals and the people who made the decisions, right? You say they made RM?" That was completely the opposite of what Samm had told her; he'd insisted that the Partials had nothing to do with it, but she'd already suspected that might be a lie—not Samm's lie, but one that had been told to him by his superiors. If the cure for RM was in their breath, manufactured in their own bodies, then the connection between the Partials and the virus was undeniable. To learn that they had created it and released it was an easy jump to make.

And yet Afa was shaking his head.

"No," he said, "the Trust aren't the Partial generals—they aren't even Partials. They're the scientists who made the Partials."

Kira's mouth dropped open in shock. "The scientists? ParaGen? Humans?" She struggled for words.

Afa nodded. "The Partial generals still follow the Trust; I don't know why. That's where they get all their orders."

"The Trust," said Kira, forcing the word out. "The Trust created RM."

Afa nodded again, never stopped nodding, rocking his whole body slowly back and forth.

"So the people who destroyed the human race were . . . humans." She groped for a chair, realized they were all full of documents, and sat heavily on the floor. "But . . . why?"

"I know everything," said Afa, still rocking back and forth. "I know *almost* everything."

CHAPTER TWELVE

Kira stared at Afa. "What do you mean, you know almost everything?"

"Nobody knows everything."

"I know," said Kira, struggling to keep her temper from flaring up. "I know you don't know *everything*, but you have so much." She picked up a handful of printouts from the nearest box, shaking them tightly in her fist. "You have hundreds of boxes in this room alone, and more all over the building. You have files in every room, you have cabinets in the hallways, you have at least twenty salvaged computers in the room we ate dinner in last night. How can you have so much—the entire history of the Partials—and not have a scrap about the people who made them?"

"I have scraps," said Afa, holding up his hand. He shuffled out of the corner, jogging awkwardly to the nearest door. "I have scraps in my backpack—I'm never supposed to leave my backpack." He ran down the hall, shouting over his shoulder, and Kira followed close behind. "I'm never supposed to leave my backpack. It has everything." Kira caught up with him in the cafeteria, the makeshift computer lab where they'd eaten fruit cocktail the night before. He crouched down in front of his massive backpack and zipped it open, revealing thick sheaves of paper.

"That's what's in the backpack?" she asked. "More papers?"

"The most important papers," said Afa, nodding. "All the keys to the story, the biggest steps, the biggest players." He thumbed through the papers with lightning speed, his fingers guided by an obvious familiarity. "And the biggest players of all were the Trust." He pulled out a slim brown folder, holding it in the air with a flourish. "The Trust."

Kira took it gingerly, as she might have touched a baby in the old maternity ward. It was thin, maybe twenty or thirty sheets of paper at the most—pathetically slim next to the massive bulk of papers bursting out of the overstuffed bag. She opened it and saw that the top sheet was an email printout, framed by layers of meaningless symbols. At the top of the page was the name she hadn't dared to hope for:

Armin Dhurvasula.

Armin.

Her father.

The email was date-stamped November 28, 2051, and the list of recipients was illegible—another string of random symbols. She read it breathlessly: "'So it's official. The government has placed an order for 250,000 BioSynth 3s. We're building the army that will end the world.'" She looked at Afa. "He knew?"

"Keep reading." He was more lucid now than before, as if the familiar topic had rejuvenated his mind.

"'A quarter million soldiers,'" she continued. "'Do you have any idea how ridiculous that is? That's a small city of completely new beings, not technically human but still intelligent, still self-aware, still capable of human feeling. It was one thing when we were making a few thousand Watchdogs, but this is a new humanoid species.'" These were his words—her own father's words. She had to fight not to cry as she read them. "'The government—even our own board of directors—talks about them like property, but that's not how most people will see them, and that's not how they'll see themselves. At best, we're reverting to the worst excesses of "partial people" and human slavery. At worst, we're making humans completely obsolete.'"

Kira shook her head, her eyes locked on the page. "How could he know all this? How could he know it and not do anything to stop it?"

"Keep reading," said Afa again, and Kira swallowed her tears.

"'I don't know where this is going to end, but I know that there's nothing we can do at this point to keep it from starting. The wheels are already moving, the technologies are already proven—Michaels and the rest of the board could do this with or without us. We can't stop it, but we need to do something to tweak it. I don't want to say anything else, even on an encrypted server. We're having a live meeting tonight at nine in Building C. My office.'

"'The first thing we'll do is figure out exactly who we can trust.'"

Kira fell silent, reading and rereading the email until the words seemed to blur and lose meaning. She shook her head. "I don't understand."

"That's the first instance of the word," said Afa, standing and pointing at the final sentence. "He said they had to figure out who they could trust. From what I've been able to piece together, they formed the group that night, in that secret meeting, and they started using the word Trust as a code word."

"He said they were trying to tweak something," said Kira. "What does that mean? Were they trying to tweak the plans for the Partials? Or tweak the Partials themselves?"

"I don't know," said Afa, taking the folder from her hand. He sat down and began laying out the papers on the floor. "Everything they did was encrypted—that's what all this gobbledygook is up here, and down here. I got through as much of it as I could, but they were being very careful." He arranged another printout carefully on the floor in front of him. "This is the next one, though it doesn't say much. I assume it's in code, but not machine code, or I could have cracked it. They gave themselves pass codes and phrases so they could talk without their bosses understanding them."

Kira sat down across from him and turned the document around. It was another email, from her father like the last one, but this time he was talking about company parking spaces. Afa had circled several words: Trust. Parallel. Failsafe.

"What do these mean?"

"I'm pretty sure 'Parallel' was the name of their plan," said Afa. "Whatever they started coming up with that night. Or maybe a second plan, designed to go along with the first. The 'Failsafe' I'm not sure about, because they talk about it in different ways: Sometimes they're trying to create something called a 'Failsafe,' sometimes it seems like they're trying to work against it, and I can't figure it out."

"So what is this email saying?"

Afa took it from her hands, touching some of the marked words. "If I've deciphered their code the way I think I have, they're saying that the plan is underway, and they've started work on the Failsafe, and they need to lie low and wait before holding another meeting." He shrugged. "I can't read any more than that. I'm the last human being left alive."

Kira nodded, recognizing from his phrase that the moment of lucidity was passing; in a few more minutes Afa would be back to his old, mumbling self again. She pressed him, trying to learn as much as she could before he slipped away. "Where did you get this?"

"I pulled it out of the cloud. It was encrypted, but I knew most of the keys."

"Because you worked at ParaGen." She held her breath, praying that he wouldn't shut down at the mention of it. He paused, staring, motionless, Kira clenching her fist in desperation.

"I was the IT director in the Manhattan office," he said, and Kira breathed a sigh of relief. "I'd been watching this grow for years, from one piece to the next. I didn't know where it would go. I didn't know how far."

"You got this from the office computers," said Kira, looking up at the rows of computer drives lining the cafeteria. "Is there any way to get the rest?"

"It's not in these computers," he said, shaking his head," it's in the clouds." He corrected himself, and Kira saw another gap in his comprehension begin to widen: "In the cloud. The network. Do you know how the cloud works?"

"Tell me."

"It's not just up in the sky," he said. "Every piece of data is stored in a computer somewhere—a little one like these, or a big one called a server. It's like a . . . an ant farm. Did you ever have an ant farm as a kid?"

"No," said Kira, motioning with her hand for him to keep going. "Tell me about them."

"It's like, a bunch of rooms, and a bunch of roads all running between them. You could make something on one device, and people could see it on the others because it traveled along through the little roads. Every device had a road. But the cloud is down." He looked at the floor and saw the papers, as if noticing them for the first time, and began cleaning them up. He was silent for too long, and Kira spoke again, trying to pull him back.

"If all these things are in the cloud, how do we bring it back up?"

"You can't," he said, and his voice was still strong—still "present." "It's gone forever with the power grid. The cloud only works if every piece works—every computer from here to the one you want to talk to, like links in a chain. When the power went down, the cloud went with it. All the roads in the ant farm got filled in, and none of the rooms can talk to each other."

"But the rooms are still there," said Kira. "The data is still there, on a computer somewhere, just waiting for us to power it up. If we can find the right computer and hook it up to a generator, you can read it, right? You know the file system, and the encryption system, and everything?"

"I know everything," he said. "Almost everything."

"So where is the ParaGen server?" she demanded. "Is it here

somewhere? Is it back in the office tower? Let's go get it—I can go get it right now. Just tell me how to find it."

Afa shook his head. "The Manhattan office was financial only. The server we want is too far away."

"Out in the wilderness?" she asked. "Listen, Afa, I can go to the wilderness if that's what it takes. We have to find the rest of these records."

"I can't do it," he said, hugging the folder and staring at the floor. "I'm the last human being left alive. I need to keep the records safe."

"We need to find them first," said Kira. "Tell me where they are."

"I'm the last human—"

"I'm right here, Afa," she said, trying to coax him back into coherence. "We can do this together. You're not alone. Just tell me where the server is."

"It's in Denver," said Afa. "It's on the other side of the continent." He looked back at the floor. "It may as well be on the other side of the world."

". . . moving through the LZ . . ."

The voice rose from the static like a breaching whale, surfacing in a moment of clarity before sinking back down in the deep. White noise filled the room again, a dozen different signals washing over and through one another in Kira's ears. Afa had shut down completely, too spooked by their conversation—or by the thoughts their conversation had brought to mind—to think about anything important. She'd taken him to the food stores and given him fruit cocktail, hoping it would soothe him, and then left him alone to recover. She'd searched through his records for a while, desperate to find what she wanted, but without Afa's guidance the filing system was impenetrable. As she explored, the sounds of static had brought her to the radio room, and she listened helplessly to the whisper of disembodied voices. Lights glowed like dim green stars on the console, hundreds of buttons and dials and switches arrayed before her. She didn't touch them.

She listened.

". . . in B Company. Don't . . . until they get . . ."

". . . orders from Trimble. That's not for . . ."

". . . everywhere! Tell him I don't care . . ."

That last one had been human. Kira had learned to recognize the difference between human and Partial radio traffic, though it wasn't exactly hard: The Partials were more professional, stiffer and colder in the way they talked. It wasn't that they didn't have emotions, it was that they weren't accustomed to expressing them verbally. The link carried all their emotional cues chemically, and their radio communication was too disciplined to need any emotion at all. It was pragmatic, even in the midst of combat. And there was a lot of combat.

The Partials had invaded Long Island.

The human radio transmissions had a desperate, frightened quality that had confused her at first, chopped up as they were into tiny fragments devoid of sense or context. The people on Long Island were tense and terrified, but she couldn't tell why. Soon she began to hear gunfire in the background, all-too-familiar pops and cracks as bullets flew back and forth behind the speakers. Was it the Voice again? Another civil war?

The more she listened, the more obvious it became: It was the Partials. They had begun to mention landmarks she knew, cities she'd visited on Long Island, and the order in which they mentioned them suggested a relentless progress from the North Shore toward East Meadow.

And all Kira could do was listen.

She thought about Afa again, and what she might do to bring him back to normal. In hindsight, his occasional retreats from reality made a lot of sense: He'd been alone for twelve straight years since the break, and pretending to still be alone again might be the only way he could calm down. She laughed now at the irony of it: a man who knew exactly what she needed to know, but so lost, so crazy, he couldn't even talk about it. The voices ebbed and flowed around her.

". . . more room, get back to the . . ."

". . . the farm last night, we haven't counted . . ."

". . . backup. Get me Sato's . . ."

Kira's eyes snapped open, the name shocking her out of her reverie. *Sato? Are they talking about Haru?* When she'd left East Meadow, he was still on work release, dishonorably discharged from the Grid for his role in kidnapping Samm. Had he been reinstated? Were they talking about a different Sato? *Please,* she thought, *don't let it be Madison. Don't let it be Arwen. If they're in trouble . . .* She didn't even want to think about it.

She looked at the control console, not really a single piece but a hodgepodge of salvaged transceivers, all cobbled together with wire and cable and duct tape. There was an old radio station here, underneath it all, but Afa had apparently rebuilt it almost from scratch. It was too dark to see everything clearly, and Kira tried her pocket flashlight before getting frustrated and going to the windows. Afa had walled them all off with cardboard and plywood, and Kira ripped one of the panels away, flooding the room with daylight. She ran back to the radio console and studied it carefully, trying to figure out which of the many speakers the message had come through. *Who said "Sato"?*

There was no way to tell for sure, but she narrowed it down to two. The controls seemed to be more or less grouped around the speaker they pertained to, and she searched the knobs for anything that looked familiar. She'd used radios before, of course, small walkie-talkies while out on salvage runs, but those were very simple: a volume and a tuner. Whatever else this had, it had to have those, too, right? She found what she thought was a tuner, on the speaker she thought had mentioned Sato, and turned it gingerly. The white noise poured through unchanged, broken here and there by the snippets from the other radios; she leaned in closer to the speaker, concentrating on its sound and ignoring everything else.

". . . not crossed yet, repeat, the third . . ."

Partials. She let go of the tuning knob and moved to the next speaker, searching for the signal. A radio signal was a delicate thing, a soundless, invisible voice in the sky. To hear it clearly she had to tune her radio to the exact frequency, with enough power, under perfect atmospheric conditions, and she had to hope that the radio sending the signal had enough power as well. Even the size and shape of the antenna could play a part. Finding that lone, weak signal in the midst of all this chatter was—

". . . Sergeant, get to the top of that hill immediately, we need covering fire on the right flank. Over."

"Yes sir, moving out. Over." It was Haru's voice.

"Yes!" Kira shouted, pumping her fist in the air. The signal was still weak—they were probably using handhelds, like the little ones she'd learned on, and they didn't have the wattage to send a clear signal this far from the island. *They must be close*, she thought, *somewhere on the west side of Long Island. The Grid base in Brooklyn? Had the Partials attacked it first?* She tried to remember what she'd learned about Partial tactics from her history classes, wondering what an assault like that would signify. If they were raiding the North Shore that was one thing, but if they were taking out the Grid headquarters, it was in preparation for a full-scale assault. Cut down the defenses, and then secure the island unimpeded. She listened closely to everything Haru's team was saying, then continued to scan the airwaves, listening to pieces of Partial broadcasts, until one caught her attention.

". . . to the top of the hill. Snipers at the ready."

Kira swore. That was a Partial communication, coming in on a different speaker. All the Partial messages had been on different speakers, even the ones from the same voice in the same battle. They were changing their frequencies on the fly to make sure no one could eavesdrop, but they hadn't been counting on Afa's paranoid, overproduced workshop; Kira could hear everything. They knew where Haru's unit was headed and that the Partials were ready with an ambush. And she was the only one who knew about it.

Kira reached for a microphone, but there was nothing—no handhelds, no ceiling mics, nothing. She looked under the console, then raced around to look behind it. *Nothing again.* It was as if Afa had removed them all on purpose, which, she reflected furiously, he probably had. He wasn't trying to communicate with anyone, just to listen. To collect information.

". . . nearing the top, coast is clear here . . ." Haru's voice again. Kira cursed loudly, half a scream and half a grunt of frustration, and dove to her knees by a stack of boxes in the corner, tearing them open in search of a microphone. The first was empty, and she threw it aside. The second was filled with cables, and she tore them out, a giant nest of thick rubber cords, and as soon as she determined it had no mic she threw it behind her, still caught in the web of cables. *I have to warn him.* The third box was speakers and plugs and manuals; the fourth and fifth were old transceivers, half-empty and cannibalized for parts. The speakers behind her erupted in gunfire and screaming and bursts of deafening static, and Kira cried as she dug through the last box and found nothing but more cables.

". . . taking fire!" Haru screamed. "We are taking fire on the hilltop! I've lost Murtry and—" The signal died with a pop and a howl of static, and Kira collapsed on the floor.

"Sato! Sergeant Sato! Do you read me?" The human commander's voice rang through the radio room, buzzy from the fading signal.

Kira shook her head, imagining Madison and Arwen, now husbandless and fatherless. It was nothing new, really—everyone in East Meadow was fatherless, and had been for over a decade—but that was exactly the problem. The Satos had been unique, the first of a new generation: a real family again, after eleven long years. They had been hope. To have lost that—to have heard it happen—broke Kira's heart. She sobbed on the floor, clutching the coils of discarded cabling as if they could comfort her, or protect her, or something. She sniffed and wiped her nose.

I don't have time for this.

Kira was still trying to figure out what to do with the information she had found so far. One thing was clear: She was going to have to gather more information from Afa's records before she could formulate her next move. But now there was a new threat to everything she was trying to save. If the Partials and humans wiped each other out before she could find her answers . . .

She dragged herself to her feet, shrugging off the rubber cables. The radio console was chaotic, but not indecipherable. She could tell which knobs went where, and which controls connected to which speaker. Somewhere on the roof was a bank of antennas, charged and ready, the dozens of transceivers below each tuned to a different frequency. With this equipment she could hear any radio in a thousand-mile radius—more, if Afa had as much power as he said he did. And once she found a microphone—not if, but when—she could communicate back. There would be something in the building, left over from the old days, and if Afa had somehow destroyed them all, then there would be something in the city, in the electronics shops and the stereo stores. Somewhere there would be a mic.

Kira would find it. And she would use it.

"I need a microphone."

Afa wasn't ready for another confrontation, but Kira didn't have time—there were people dying, and she needed to help them. The big man shuffled through his food supplies, peering myopically at shelves of cans. "I don't talk to people," he said, "I just listen."

"I know you don't," said Kira, "but I do. The Partials have invaded Long Island, and I have friends there. I need to help them."

"I don't help the Partials—"

"I'm trying to help the humans," she insisted. She ran her hand through her hair, already tired and worn. She felt torn, even on this seemingly simple issue—she didn't want the humans to die, but she didn't want the Partials to die, either. She wanted to save both, but now that they were engaged in open war, what could she do? "With a mic and your radio station I can feed them information, keep them running circles around each other. At least until I can think of something better."

Afa found a can of refried beans and waddled to the door. "You can't help humans. I'm the only one left—"

"No, you're not," she said loudly, blocking his path. He was head and shoulders taller than she was, and more than three times her weight, but he shrank back from her like a deflating balloon, eyes down, chin tucked in, shoulders hunched and ready for a blow. She softened her voice but kept her stance firm. "There are thirty-five thousand people on Long Island, Afa, thirty-five thousand humans. They need our help—they need your knowledge. Everything you've collected here, they can use that. They're trying to cure RM, and they know nothing about it, but you know so much. For all I know, you have the key to manufacturing the cure somewhere in here, to solving the mystery of the Partials' expiration dates, to averting another war. There's a whole human society left, Afa, and they need your knowledge." She stared at him firmly. "They need you."

Afa shuffled his feet, then turned abruptly and waddled back into the storage room, rounding a stack of cans and coming back along the next aisle. Kira sighed and stepped over, blocking that one as well. "Where are the microphones?"

Afa stopped again, looking nervously at the floor, then turned and retreated again. Kira stayed by the door, knowing he'd have to come past her eventually. "You can't hide forever," she said, "and I'm not just talking about this room, I mean the whole world. You have to move on, or go back, or do *something*. You've collected all this information so you could show it to somebody: Let's go show it to somebody."

"There's nobody to show it to," he said, turning uncertainly in the maze of stacked cans and boxes. "I'm the only human being left alive."

"You know what I think," said Kira, softening her voice even further. "I think the reason you insist you're the last one left is because you're afraid to go meet anyone. If all the humans are dead, then there's no one to talk to, and no one to help, and no one to risk disappointing."

He was in the back of the room now, shrouded in shadow. "I'm the last one left."

"You're the last IT director," said Kira. "At least the last that I know of. With everything you know about computers and networks and radios and solar panels—I mean, seriously, Afa, you're like a genius. You *are* a genius. You've been alone for so long, but you don't have to be. You're helping me, right? You're talking to me, and I'm not scary."

"Yes, you are."

"I'm sorry," she said. "I'm not trying to be. But you have to face this. What are you hiding from, Afa? What are you afraid of?"

Afa stared in silence before whispering his answer, and his

voice was scarred by years of pain and fear. "The end of the world."

"The world already ended," said Kira. "That monster's come and gone." She stepped forward slowly, inching toward him. "In East Meadow we celebrate it—not the end, but the beginning. The rebuilding. The old world is dead and gone, and I know that's so much harder for you than for me. I barely even knew that world." She stepped closer. "But this world is right here. It has so much to give us, and it needs so much of our help. Let the old world go, and help us build a new one."

His face was lost in shadow. "That's what they said in their emails."

"Who?"

"The Trust." His voice was different now, not the halting mush of confusion or the clear window of intelligence, but a distant, almost haunted whisper, as if the old world itself was speaking through him. "Dhurvasula and Ryssdal and Trimble and everyone: They knew they were building a new world, and they knew they were destroying the old one to do it. They did it on purpose."

"But why?" Kira pressed. "Why kill everyone? Why put the only cure in the Partials? Why link humans to the Partials at all? Why leave us with so many questions?"

"I don't know," he said softly. "I tried to know, but I don't."

"Then let's figure it out," she said, "together. But first we have to help them." She paused, remembering the words of Mr. Mkele, words that seemed so unconscionable when he said them. She repeated them now to Afa, bewildered to find how her situation had turned. "Humanity needs a future, and we need to fight for it, but we can't do that unless we save it in the present." She put a hand on his arm. "Help me find a microphone, so we can make sure there's somebody left to give all these answers to."

Afa watched her anxiously, seeming small and childlike in the dark.

"Are you a human?" he asked.

Kira felt her voice catch in her throat, her heart jumping in her chest. What did he need to hear? Would he help her if she said she was human? Would anything else terrify him back into his shell?

She shook her head. What he needed to hear was the truth. She paused, breathing deep, clenching her fist to build up the courage. She'd never said it out loud before, not even to herself. She forced herself to speak.

"I'm a Partial." The words felt right and wrong and true and forbidden and terrible and wonderful at once. To speak a truth, to get it off her chest, brought a thrill of liberation, but the nature of the truth made her shiver uncomfortably. She felt wrong to say it, and immediately she felt guilty for feeling wrong about her own true nature. She didn't. "But I have given my entire life, I have given everything, to save the human race." Her lips parted in a thin smile, and she almost laughed. "You and I are the best hope they have right now."

Afa set down his can of beans, picked it up, then set it down again. He took a step, stopped, and nodded. "Okay. Follow me."

CHAPTER THIRTEEN

Marcus crouched in the lee of a crumbling cinder-block wall—an old garage, he guessed. There was a car inside, visible through a hole in the wall, with the driver's skeleton still sitting at the wheel. Marcus tried to imagine why the man had died here, in the car, still sitting in a closed garage, but it hardly mattered now. If the Partials found his patrol, Marcus would be as dead as he was.

"We can't afford to protect the farms," said Private Cantona. His voice was an urgent whisper, and he never took his eyes off the forest. Marcus had come to hate him, but he couldn't deny he was an effective soldier. "Or the farmers."

"We're not going to abandon them," hissed Haru. He'd been leading the patrol ever since Grant died. He glanced at the four farmers hiding beside the soldiers—two men and two women, eyes wide and terrified. "As near as I can tell, the Partials are capturing every human they can get their hands on. We're supposed to be protecting people, so we're going to protect these people all the way back to East Meadow."

"We're supposed to protect civilians," said Cantona. "That was a work farm—for all we know, these four could be convicts."

"If the Partials want them," said Haru, "then I will die before I give them up."

Marcus looked at the farmers, minimally armed with three guns between the four of them. It seemed unlikely that prisoners would have access to weapons at all, but with a Partial army bearing down on you, who knew? *I'd give them all guns,* he thought, *and hope for the best. When the enemy are Partials, every human is an ally.*

"They're going to get us killed," said Cantona. Their unit, once twenty soldiers strong, had been reduced to seven plus the farmers; half had been wiped out in the ambush, and the rest as they'd retreated, running almost headlong through the forest to stay ahead of the invaders. "They can keep up with us fine," said Cantona. "That's not the problem, it's that they're noisy. They don't know how to stay hidden."

The farmers' faces were sunburned and weathered, but Marcus could see their skin grow pale as they listened to the soldiers argue their fate. He shook his head and butted into the conversation. "They're no worse at it than I am."

"I'm not throwing away our medic."

"But he's right," said Haru. "With Marcus in the group, we'll make enough noise to be found no matter how many civilians we have."

"Well, I'm not that bad," said Marcus.

"It doesn't matter either way," said Haru. "If they haven't heard us talking, then we're out of danger for now—it's getting dark, and they have no reason to hunt down a group of armed soldiers who might be lying in ambush. More than likely the Partials retreated, regrouped, and you can bet they're on their way to another farm."

"Then we don't need to protect them anymore," said Cantona, gesturing again at the farmers. "Either way we cut them loose, tell them to make for East Meadow, and then we try to rejoin our unit."

"I can't raise them on the radio," said Haru. "We have no unit to rejoin with."

One of the other soldiers, a big man named Hartley, held up his hand, and the group fell instantly silent. It was a sign they'd become all too familiar with, and Marcus listened intently, gripping his rifle. The Partials had stronger senses—better hearing, better vision—so they could detect Marcus's group from much farther away, but in a forest this dense, they still had to get close to engage them, and at that distance the humans could sometimes hear them coming. They were no match for a Partial unit, though, with or without warning; the only enemy they'd managed to kill had been distracted by larger forces. Marcus and his group had been running, pure and simple, and they'd still been whittled to a fraction of their former numbers.

They sat in silence, ears perked, rifles ready. The forest around them stared back, as still as a tomb.

Marcus heard one of the watchmen curse suddenly, shouting the first few syllables of a warning, and a little black disk clinked against the wall by his feet. He looked down just in time to see it explode in a blinding flash of light, and suddenly the entire patrol was shouting. Marcus clutched his eyes, grunting at the throbbing pain, seeing nothing but brilliant white afterimages. Guns fired; Haru shouted; people screamed and cried. Marcus felt a splash of hot liquid on his hands and ducked down, cowering against the wall. A body fell against him and he crawled backward, his breathing ragged and terrified. By the time his vision cleared, the fight was over.

Senator Delarosa stood over him, a rifle in one hand and a thick, hooded cloak over her head.

Marcus tried to think. "What?"

"You're lucky it was only two," said Delarosa. "And that we had the drop on them." Her face was grim. "And that we had such good bait."

"Two what?"

"Two Partials," said Haru. He was shaking his head, pounding his ear with the palm of his hand as if it were ringing. "And don't call us bait."

"I don't know what else to call you," said Delarosa, turning and rolling a body over with her foot. Marcus saw that there were several: soldiers, a cloaked figure like Delarosa, and two inert Partials in their unmistakable gray armor. The one by Delarosa's feet groaned, and she shot him again. "You were making enough noise to attract every Partial patrol for miles."

"You used us as bait!" Haru said again, struggling to his feet. Whatever had incapacitated him had left him unsteady. "You knew they were there? How long were you watching?"

"Long enough to be ready when they got here," said Delarosa. "We knew you'd attract a group eventually, so we laid low and let you." She knelt over the body, quickly stripping it of useful equipment: body armor, ammo clips, and several pouches clipped to the chest and shoulders. She turned back as she worked, nodding at the black disk on the ground by Marcus's feet. "That's their flashbang. They thought you were incapacitated, so their guard was down."

Marcus tried to stand up but found himself just as woozy as Haru. He gripped the cinder-block wall for support. A soldier slid to the ground beside him as he shifted, and Marcus realized there was a bullet hole in the soldier's face. "You should have warned us."

Delarosa left the first Partial's equipment in a neat pile and started taking off the body armor. "They would have found you either way; this way they didn't find us until it was too late."

"We could have laid an ambush," said Haru. He glanced around, taking stock, and Marcus did the same: three human soldiers dead, plus one of Delarosa's people. There were at least two more in the trees beyond, keeping watch on the perimeter. "We could have been ready for them and not lost so many people."

"We *were* ready," said Delarosa, moving to the second body. "This *was* an ambush. We had the perfect situation, with a perfect distraction, and we still lost four people and got two of the civilians wounded." She pointed at the farmers. "We had ideal conditions and they still killed twice as many as we did. Would you really want to try that again without the distraction?"

"Your distraction was my men!"

"Are you really going to argue with me about this?" said Delarosa, standing to face him. "I saved your life."

"You let three of us get killed."

"If I hadn't done what I did, you would have all been killed," she snapped back, "or worse still, captured. We are facing a superior foe with better equipment, better training, and better reflexes. If you want to risk a fair fight, you're as blind as the Senate."

"The Senate put you in jail," said Marcus, finally gaining his feet. "You were in a work farm." He frowned. "You were in this work farm?"

Delarosa turned back to the second Partial, pulling the rest of his equipment into a pile beside the first. "Back when it was a work farm, yes. Now it's just a . . . crime scene. Anyone left alive has scattered."

"Did you escape in the attack or shoot your way out first?" asked Haru.

"I'm not here to kill humans," said Delarosa, and stood again, facing him directly. "I was sentenced to a work farm: You're right. Do you remember what for?"

"For killing a human," said Marcus. "That kind of undermines your credibility."

"For doing whatever it takes," she said. She gestured to one of her companions, similarly cloaked and hooded, and he came to collect the piles of equipment. "We're facing the extinction of our species," she said sternly. "That comes before everything else—before kindness, before morality, before law. Things you would never have done twelve years ago aren't just acceptable now, they're required. They're a moral imperative. I will kill a hundred Shaylon Browns before I let the Partials win. I'll kill a thousand."

"That's exactly what I'm talking about," said Cantona. "That's the only way we're going to survive this."

"If you kill a thousand of your own people, the Partials don't even have to fight," said Marcus. "You're doing their job for them."

A bird chirped loudly in the forest, and Delarosa looked up. "That's our cue to leave. Looks like these two had backup." She ran to the edge of the clearing, but Haru shook his head.

"We're not going with you."

"I am," said Cantona. He grabbed a second rifle from a fallen human soldier. "Come on, Haru, you know she's right."

"I'm not abandoning these civilians!"

"Actually," said one of the farmers, "I think I'm going with her, too." He was an older man, made lean and leathery from hard labor. He held up his hunting rifle and took a sidearm from a fallen soldier.

Cantona looked at Delarosa, who nodded and looked back at Haru. "We won't use you as bait again." She turned and melted into the forest. Her people went with her, then the farmer, and last of all Cantona. He paused, waved, and followed her into the trees.

Marcus looked at Haru, then at Hartley, then at the three remaining farmers. They'd armed themselves with rifles and ammo from the fallen soldiers. "Two of you are wounded?"

"We can walk," said one of the women, a fierce look on her face.

"That's great," said Haru, "but can you run?"

They stopped in a schoolyard, panting with exertion. The pursuing Partials had claimed two more of them, leaving only Marcus, Haru, and two farmers. One of them was wounded, a brown-haired woman named Izzy; she leaned heavily against the wall, eyes closed, her breathing ragged. Haru was out of ammo, and Marcus handed him his last clip.

"You can use this better than I can." He paused for breath, then nodded toward Izzy. "She can't go much farther."

"Get her down from the wall," gasped Haru, hiding in the brush. "They'll see us."

"She won't be able to get up again," said Marcus.

"Then I'll carry her."

Marcus and the last farmer, a man named Bryan, pulled the woman gently to the ground, propping her against the wall with her head between her knees. Marcus looked at her bandages—she'd been shot through the shoulder, miraculously missing the vital bones and arteries, but the wound was still bad, and she'd lost a lot of blood. He'd already patched the bandage twice, in quick stops like this, and given her all the painkillers he could without knocking her unconscious. The bandage was soaked with blood, and his eyes blurred from exhaustion as he started changing it again.

"I'm starting to wish we had a band of guerrillas using us as bait," said Haru.

Marcus frowned. "That's not funny."

"It wasn't meant to be."

"You could do it right," said Bryan. "The ambush, I mean. Enough guns in the woods, with a good clear shot, and you wouldn't have to risk the bait at all."

"You certainly could," said Haru, still panting for air, "you certainly could." He pulled out his radio and tried again, his voice hoarse with desperation. "This is Haru Sato, I have a medic and two civilians pinned down at the"—he looked up—"Huntsman

Elementary School. I don't know which city. If there is anyone out there, anyone at all, please respond. We don't know how widespread this attack has been, we don't know where to retreat to. We don't even know where we are."

Izzy coughed: harsh, racking coughs that shook her body until she retched on the ground. Marcus leaned out of the way, then finished bandaging her arm.

"I think something's wrong with your radio," said Bryan. "When's the last time you got a call? In or out?"

"Not since the snipers," said Haru, staring listlessly at the radio. It didn't have any bullet holes, but it was pretty dinged up. Marcus wouldn't be surprised if it was broken.

"Let me see it," said Bryan, and stood up to take it. His head rose above the level of the surrounding brush and he jerked suddenly, a puff of red mist flying out from the side of his ear.

Marcus and Haru instantly dropped to the ground, flat on their stomachs. Unsupported by Marcus's arm, Izzy slumped to the side, unconscious.

"Looks like this is it," said Marcus. "Either your murderer swoops in to our rescue, or we get to say hi to Dr. Morgan."

"You'll forgive me for hoping it's the murderer."

"You'll love Dr. Morgan," said Marcus. "She hates humans almost as much as you hate Partials."

Haru looked at the playground. "We've got about three feet of brush coming up through the asphalt, rising to six or seven if we can make it to what I assume used to be a soccer field." He looked at Izzy. "I don't think we can carry her."

"I'll grab her and run," said Marcus. "You cover me. Those taller saplings are only—"

"No," said Haru, "but that's exactly what we're going to

pretend we're doing." He pointed behind them, a few feet past them along the base of the school wall. Marcus saw the black rectangle of a broken basement window. "You drag her in there," said Haru, gathering a pile of broken asphalt chunks. "I'll do my best to make it look like we're crawling across the field."

Marcus nodded. "How much time will that buy us?"

"Enough," said Haru. "If it works. We'll find another door and slip out of the building on the far side."

Marcus sighed, looking at the ominous black hole of the basement window. "If I get eaten by badgers or whatever the hell's down there, I'm going to pretend like this wasn't our only viable option."

"Go."

Marcus rolled Izzy onto her back, brought her arms over her head, and grasped both wrists with his left hand; with his right elbow, on his stomach, he started crawling across the broken asphalt toward the window. The rough edges ripped into his clothes, and a bullet winged off the wall above his head. He kept low, trying not to shake the bushes. Haru threw rocks into the field, keeping the arc low so the Partials couldn't see them; when they landed, they shook the brush. Marcus thought it must have worked, because the next sniper shot slammed harmlessly into the bushes about twenty feet out from the wall.

He reached the window and peered in; the air inside was dank, like a cave, and Marcus smelled wet dog. Unless recently abandoned, the basement had become an animal lair, though the dogs probably didn't use this entrance; the ground around it was loose, not packed like a high-traffic passage would be. He couldn't see much, and decided it was safer to crawl in himself before pulling the sick woman after him.

He was only halfway in when Haru scrabbled to a stop next to the window, breathing heavily. "Pretty sure the game is up," he said. A bullet slammed into the brick wall above him. "Yep. Get out of the way."

Marcus slithered the rest of the way through, dropping to the floor and immediately slipping in several inches of slick mud. He stood up and pulled Izzy through, listening as more bullets exploded against the wall. As soon as the window was clear, Haru launched himself through, landing with a strangled groan in the mud.

"It smells like dead dogs in here."

Marcus searched his pockets for a light, holding Izzy with one arm. "And I'm pretty sure that's not all mud."

"No lights," said Haru. "Follow me." He stepped forward with a squelch, a dim silhouette in the basement darkness, and Marcus followed as carefully as he could. In addition to five or so inches of liquid mud, the basement was filled with metal desks, stacks of worm-eaten books, and row after row of old laptop computers, tethered with rusty metal cables to rolling metal cabinets. Haru led them cautiously through the maze, and as Marcus's eyes adjusted to the dark he saw a door appear in the wall before them. Haru tried it, the knob clicking open, when suddenly the room got even darker. The light source behind them had been abruptly obscured, and Marcus dropped to the ground.

Bullets ripped through the air, muzzle flashes lighting up the room in deafening staccato bursts. The flimsy wooden door shredded under the onslaught, and Marcus was just able to see

Haru dive for cover behind the nearest laptop cabinet.

"They're really determined," said Haru. "I've wanted to kill you before but never this bad."

Haru returned fire on the open window, and the shooter ducked out of the way. Marcus took the opportunity to surge forward, dragging Izzy through the door. When he got to safety Haru stopped, trying to conserve their final bullets, and the shooter came back to the window, laying down a thick stream of suppressive fire. Haru fired his last few bullets, driving the Partial back into cover, and dove through the mud at the bottom of the door.

"I don't actually agree with what I'm about to say," said Marcus, "but we're safe. At least for now."

Haru nodded, wiping mud from his face "As long as we still have bullets—and as long as they know we still have bullets—they're not following us through there. But you can bet they're coming around through another entrance." He looked up, and Marcus could feel his eyes burning through him, even in the dark. "Time to decide, Valencio. You want to die hiding or pulling a trigger?"

"Where's the option for 'soaked in my own urine'?"

Haru laughed. "I'm pretty sure that comes free with either package." He sniffed. "Besides, we're already soaked in something's urine. No one's going to know the difference."

"Try the radio," said Marcus. "You never know."

Haru pulled it from his belt, holding it up in the darkness. "You have a better chance of reaching God on this thing than anyone still living on Earth."

"Then I'll pray." Marcus took the radio and thumbed the

button. "This is Marcus Valencio, assuming anyone out there can hear me. I'm . . . hiding in a muddy tunnel full of dog urine and Haru Sato, though I'm not sure which is worse. I have a wounded civilian and what appears to be an entire brigade of vengeful Partials. They've been chasing us for miles, whittling us down from twenty soldiers to two. I don't know if they're trying to conquer the island, raid it, or just kill us for fun. I don't even know who's around to hear this—for all I know we're the last humans left." He let go of the button, and the radio crackled instantly to life.

"If I had a nickel for every time I've heard that lately," said the radio. The voice was scratchy and clipped, and so sudden Marcus almost dropped the handset. Haru stood up, his eyes wide.

"Who is this?" asked Marcus, staring at Haru in wonder. He shook his head, clicked the button, and asked again. "Who is this? Repeat, who is this? We require immediate assistance, and backup, and . . . saving of our lives." He let go of the button and shrugged helplessly. "They'd better not say no just because I screwed up the radio protocol."

The radio crackled to life again. "Partial radio traffic says that they're looking for you, specifically, Marcus. Dr. Morgan wants you for something."

Marcus froze, suddenly realizing why the voice sounded so familiar. "Kira?"

"Hey, babe," said Kira. "Miss me?"

"What?" Marcus stumbled for words. "Where are you? What's going on? Why is Dr. Morgan looking for me?"

"Probably because she wants me," said Kira. "The good news is, she has no idea where I am."

"Well that's a relief," said Haru derisively. "I'm so glad Kira's safe."

Marcus thumbed the radio button. "Haru says hi."

"Don't worry," said Kira, "I've got good news for him, too: there's a Grid army advancing on your position."

"There is?"

"Head out of the building and south," said Kira. "You'll meet a Grid battalion coming the other way, just two minutes out at the most."

"Hot damn," said Haru. "Let's get out of this muck." He lifted Izzy into a fireman's carry and started making his way down the hall.

"Wait," said Marcus, running to catch up with him. "Where are you? What's going on?" The radio was completely silent, and Marcus ran back to where he'd been standing before. It must have been a sweet spot for reception, because the radio crackled to life again.

". . . now. Repeat, you have to go now. The battalion has a small arsenal of rocket-propelled grenades, and they intend to bring down the entire building."

"Wait!" screamed Marcus. "We're not out yet!"

"Then go!"

He turned and ran, catching up to Haru at the base of the stairs. They ran up, testing the door cautiously before opening it into a wide school hallway. There didn't seem to be any Partials, and Haru pointed at a pair of loosely hanging doors. "There."

They ran out of the south side of the building, sprinting across the open street to the cover of a residential street beyond. No shouts rose behind them, no bullets flew past their heads.

Marcus swerved around a corner, Haru close behind with Izzy on his shoulders; he lifted the radio to his mouth and screamed into it as he ran.

"Kira? Kira, can you hear me? What's going on?"

"How old was I when you met me?" said Kira's voice. "Go that many channels up."

Five, Marcus thought, *we met in school the first year here.* He set it for five, then paused. *They didn't organize a school the first year here. I met her when we were six.* He flipped the channel dial one more slot up. "What's going on?"

"This is a trick that will only work once," said Kira. "They're listening to your frequencies, but I'm listening to theirs; I told you there was a Grid battalion close by, and I had a friend here give them a false report with the same information. The two Partials hunting you have fallen back, but they won't stay gone long, and the battalion to your south is at least six miles away. You have to get there fast, because they are hunting you specifically and they will come after you when the realize they've been tricked."

"So—" He slowed, trying to catch his breath. "What do I do now?"

"I'll help you as much as I can," said Kira, "but we don't have a lot of options. We've been listening to Morgan's communication, and here's the bad news: They're not just invading the island, they're conquering it. Inside of two days, every human on Long Island will be a Partial prisoner."

PART 2

CHAPTER FOURTEEN

The first alarm sounded at four in the morning. Afa had rigged the first-floor doors and windows with small electric alarms, wired to his bedroom and a few of the main research rooms, and the small jingle woke Kira almost instantly. She was still on the couch in the film studio, where she'd been for just over a week—the most permanent sleeping arrangements she'd had in ages. The alarms were persistent but quiet, designed to alert the occupants without letting the intruders know that anything was amiss. Kira was on her feet in seconds, pulling on her shoes and then grabbing her gun. If she had to flee, those were the essentials.

Of course, with Afa poised to blow up the entire building, even fleeing barefoot and unarmed wasn't the worst-case scenario.

Kira met Afa in the hall, both silent; he shut off the alarm and listened. If it was a false alarm, maybe wind or a stray cat pawing at the glass, the building would stay silent. Kira listened with her eyes closed, praying that nothing would—

Beep. Beep.

Afa shut it off again, permanently this time, jogging heavily down the hall to another bank of switches. The solar panels on the roof stored massive amounts of electricity, more than enough to power their jury-rigged security systems at night. Afa woke up a sleeping monitor, the picture jerking to life like a slide show, just in time to see a black-clad figure in body armor slip through the window. The helmet was round and faceless, the too-familiar calling card of the Partial army, though this armor was battle-scarred and damaged to the point that Kira wondered if it was salvaged. The brief outline of the intruder's body against the moonlit street beyond showed that it was female, though the second form climbing in behind her was probably male. Kira glanced at Afa, his face of rictus of anxiety and indecision: His other safe houses he'd simply blown up when they were threatened, but this was his headquarters, his main library of documents, his life's work. He didn't want to blow it up.

But then again, he wasn't exactly a clear thinker in stressful situations.

Kira and Afa were on the seventh floor, and there were two full levels of security measures before any ground-level intruders reached the important stuff. The first story was the explosives, enough to bring the entire building down, and Kira carefully placed herself between Afa and the manual trigger for the bombs. They watched on scratchy, closed-circuit cameras as the intruders—only two—picked their way carefully through the rooms and hallways, from one camera to another, the different angles and monitors giving their path a crazed, disjointed trajectory. Left to right on the third monitor; right to left on the first. Top to bottom on the second and fourth simultaneously, one in front and one behind. They moved slowly, rifles at the ready, colorless shapes in the darkness. Their helmets seemed to provide augmented night vision, and the two figures were seamlessly coordinated in their movements. A surefire sign of the link at work. They were most definitely Partials.

Kira checked her ammunition carefully, never taking her eyes off the monitors; she might be able to drop one of the Partials if she surprised him, but the odds of beating two in concert were minuscule. If she didn't run now, she'd probably wake up back in Dr. Morgan's lab, stretched out naked on an operating table while the mad doctor cut her open to find her secrets.

She took a step to run but forced herself to stop. *Breathe,* she told herself. *Breathe deep. Stay calm. Nobody in the world is more paranoid than Afa—he knows how to protect his home. Give him time. There's still another floor between us.*

The final camera showed them at the stairs, testing the door and then slowly coming up. The first floor was devoid of traps because Afa didn't want the bombs to trigger accidentally by a stray animal, but Kira hoped the Partials would misread it as a lack of security entirely. Would they be less cautious on the second floor? She held her breath, and the Partials' feet disappeared into the darkness at the top of the stairs. There were no cameras on the second floor, just sensors and automated booby traps.

A red light flashed on the wall panel, and Kira heard a violent clatter shake the building. "Antipersonnel mine," said Afa. "It's called a Bouncing Betty—when someone walks by, the mine jumps up about four feet in the air, like a ball from a Little

League pitching machine, and then explodes out, like this, in a ring." He demonstrated with his hands, showing an expanding halo of destruction in a single plane. "Nails and shrapnel and buckshot, right at gut level. They're wearing armor, but it can still do a lot of damage without bringing down the building frame." Kira nodded, her stomach queasy, watching the next light in the row. If the Bouncing Betty had stopped them, no more lights would come on. The threat would be over, and all they had to do was clean it up. Kira prayed—

The second light came on.

"They're moving through the east hallway," said Afa, his hands curled in front of him like an infant's, weak and fetal. His face was streaked with sweat.

"How do we get out?" asked Kira. There was a fire escape, she knew, but it was laden with traps as well, and she hoped there might be a faster way down. Afa swallowed, staring at the lights, and Kira asked again, "How do we get out?"

"They're in the east hallway," he said, "coming up on the shotguns. They're motion-sensored, not wired like the mines— they won't know what's coming until it's too late." The third red light came on, and Kira heard a distant crack. She waited, gritting her teeth in desperation, and the world paused.

The fourth light blinked to life.

"No," Kira muttered, shaking her head. Afa was looking up and down the hall, his hands opening and closing on some imaginary tool. He had no guns, and barely tolerated Kira's; he did everything by trap, distant and impersonal. If they made it up here, he was helpless.

"Afa," said Kira, grabbing his elbow. "Look at me." He kept

searching for something, moving his head, and Kira placed herself firmly in his field of vision. "Look at me: They're going to come up here, and they're going to kill us."

"No."

"They're going to kill you, Afa, do you understand me? They're going to kidnap me and kill you, and burn this entire building to the ground—"

"No!"

"—with all your records in it. Do you understand? You will lose everything. We have to get out of here."

"I have my backpack," he said, pulling away from her and snatching up the massive backpack from the floor, never more than a few feet away from him. "I never lose the backpack."

"We need to take it and go," said Kira, pulling him toward the studio. She had a few seconds to grab her things and then they had to run, as far and as fast as they could. She thought about the radio station upstairs, about Marcus and the way she'd helped him. Dr. Morgan had taken control of East Meadow, and every other population center on the island, and it was all Kira could do to use the radios and keep Marcus one step ahead of his pursuers. She was about to lose it all. Afa resisted, pulling away to go back to the sensor panel, and Kira ran to the studio without him, quickly gathering her things to flee.

"They've passed the conference room," he said. "They're moving slowly. They're past the second Bouncing Betty in the east hallway, moving on to the—there's more now."

Kira stood up, her bag half-packed with the last of her survival gear. "What?"

"One in the east hallway and one in the west. There's another group." He spluttered, his voice growing wilder and higher. "I didn't see anyone else come in! I've been watching the monitors—I would have seen them come in!"

Kira snapped her pack closed, leaving the bedroll and sprinting back down the hall. "It's not more," she said. "They've split up." She pointed at the seventh light. "There's a central hallway here, right? It's the same on every floor. This is a two-man kill team just like a dozen others I've been following on the radio—they don't need a second team, they just split up the first—" She paused, midsentence. "They're split," she said again, as if it meant something entirely different this time. "They're alone. Afa, where do the separate hallways join the third floor?"

"The stairs," he mumbled.

"Yes," said Kira, placing herself in his eye line again. "I know it's the stairs, but I need specifics. You built this entire system, Afa, you know where they're going next. This one." She pointed at a red dot. "Where will that dot reach the third floor?"

"The back stairs," he said, practically stuttering in fear. He reached for the manual bomb trigger and she stopped him, pulling his hand away. "The service stairs. They come up from the delivery room in the back."

"Perfect," said Kira. She wrapped his hand around his backpack and pushed him gently away from the control panel. "You need to save this backpack, do you hear me? Do not blow up the building—if you blow it up, you will lose your backpack."

"I can never lose the backpack."

"Exactly. You find whatever escape route you have planned and you take it—you run far away, and you don't come back for a week. If the Partials go away, I'll be here be waiting. Now go!"

Afa turned and ran down the hall, and Kira shouldered her pack and ran the other way, swinging around the last doorway and practically throwing herself down the stairs. Sixth floor. Fifth floor. If she could reach the third floor first—if she could get there while the Partials were still split up, still alone, right where she knew they were coming—she could ambush the first and retreat before the second arrived as backup. She had a chance to kill both of them, but it was only a chance. Fourth floor.

Third.

She slowed, placing each step carefully, listening at the corner before moving around it. The stairwell was clear. She dropped to her knee, raising the rifle to her cheek, peering around the corner into the second floor. Moldy carpet stretched away in the darkness. The metal door had been completely removed, hauled upstairs as armor for one of Afa's mini bunkers—that was where Kira would retreat, she decided. Kill the first, fall back to a bunker, and wait for the second to make a mistake. If the Partials even made mistakes.

The second floor was empty, but the signs of chaos were clear. A pattern of holes in the walls and blackout curtains showed that the latest round of Bouncing Betties had gone off exactly as planned, but there didn't seem to be any bodies. The floor was dimly lit by the holes in the curtains, and a small flame flickered in the wall near the back. Kira waited, trying to remember what the last trap on the floor had been—something incendiary, she thought, and it obviously hadn't gone off. The Partial was still inside.

Kira waited at the top of the stairs, her rifle aimed and ready. As soon as a Partial appeared in the doorway, it was as good as dead.

She waited.

Maybe I was too noisy, she wondered. *It heard me coming and went the other way—or worse, it's waiting for me. I could retreat back up the stairs, but then I lose my advantage. I can't take both Partials at once. If there's any chance I can ambush this one, I have to take it.*

How far has the other one gotten? This is the service stairwell, but the other hall leads to the main stairwell. Has the Partial reached it yet? Did it go upstairs? Did Afa get away? She hoped that Afa had been smart enough to run, that he wasn't sitting in the hallway with his finger on the trigger of the bomb, ready in his paranoia to destroy his entire life's work—and he and Kira with it—just to keep it from the Partials. *I need to get back up there,* she thought, *and I need to stay here, and I need to run away. I don't know what to—*

And then she knew, as firmly and as strongly as if she'd seen it with her own eyes, that there was a Partial creeping toward her on the third floor.

The third-floor doorway, like the second, had been cannibalized for Afa's bunker. The door was open, and the Partial would have a clear shot at her as soon as it came around the corner. *It's the link,* she thought, *it's the only way I could know this so clearly. It's broadcasting everything we're doing. I don't have the full complement of sensors that Samm described, but apparently I have enough to sense where they are—and maybe enough to give myself away.* She patted her jacket, wishing she had something she could throw—a grenade or even a rock to distract them with—but all she had was the rifle, and by the time she had a clear shot with that, it would be too late. She had to move. She shifted to the balls of her feet, ready to race down the stairwell to the first floor, when she got a second impression, as clear as the first, that there was another Partial in the stairwell below her. They hadn't paused inside the doorway, waiting, they'd jumped ahead and completely encircled her. There was nowhere to go but into the second floor, still rigged with one last trap. She jumped to her feet and ran.

The Partial agents didn't shout to each other, for the link warned them of danger in much more effective silence, but Kira still felt it in her head like a chemical scream: SHE'S RUNNING. Feet clattered on the stairs behind her, and Kira fired a burst from her rifle into the stairwell below, keeping the second Partial from sniping her as she raced past into the second-floor death trap. Kira tumbled through the open door and scrambled back to her feet, looking around wildly for the final trap, but Afa had hidden it too well. A Partial pounded through the door behind her and Kira spun, tracking shots across the wall in a deadly line headed straight for the attacker's chest. The Partial—obviously a woman, but with her face obscured behind a visored helmet—paused when she saw Kira, then converted her charge into an acrobatic roll; she pulled her rifle in close to her chest, tucked herself into a ball, and somersaulted under Kira's spray of bullets before Kira had time to correct its course. The Partial came up just feet away from her, firing almost immediately, and Kira had to dive to the side to stay clear. The Partial followed with uncanny speed, pressing the attack, lashing out with a devastating kick that knocked Kira's rifle from her hands. Kira stumbled into a conference room, recovered her feet, and sprinted past the rotting wooden table to the second door at the far end of the room, just three steps ahead of the Partial. She came back into the hall and ran back to the door, only to collapse with a crash as the Partial tackled her from behind, knocking the air from her lungs. Kira fought for breath, wrestling madly with the Partial, managing to connect a solid elbow slam to the side of the attacker's helmet. She reeled back and Kira rolled away, crawling another few feet before the Partial, already on her feet, kicked her thigh out from under her. Kira grunted in pain, falling to the side, and when she looked up the Partial was a few feet away, her boot raised over a tiny trip wire, her hand pointed to a spot above Kira's head. Kira looked up and saw the nozzle of Afa's incendiary trap, a flamethrower aimed directly at her head. All the Partial had to do was stomp down, and a jet of flame would roast Kira alive. She cringed, staring at the Partial's featureless visor, and heard a male voice cry out.

"Kira!"

Kira froze. She'd know that voice anywhere. Her jaw dropped as he stepped out of the stairwell, his helmet in his hands.

"Samm?"

CHAPTER FIFTEEN

"I wasn't going to kill her," said the female Partial. She stepped away from the trip wire and took off her helmet, and Kira recognized her as well: jet-black hair, gorgeous Chinese features, and dark eyes that glittered with a terrifying genius. This was Heron, the Partial who'd captured her before and taken her to Morgan. The girl smirked dismissively, looking at Kira the way someone would stare at a lost kitten—someone who didn't really like kittens. "I was only trying to scare her."

Samm bent down to help Kira to her feet, and she rose uncertainly, still trying to process what was happening. "Samm?"

"It's good to see you."

"What . . . why are you here?"

"Because we finally found you," said Heron, and pointed at the ceiling. "Everybody knows you're on the radio, but we're the only ones who've figured out you were in Manhattan." She bowed with mock respect. "We chose to keep that information to ourselves."

Samm retrieved Kira's rifle from the floor. "We've known somebody was in this building for a few days, but we also recognized the signs of the same bomber who'd almost blown us up twice already, and so we took our time coming in. We didn't know for sure that you were in here until"—he paused, tilting his head as if calculating—"thirty seconds ago. When I saw your face." He handed Kira the rifle.

Kira took it, puzzled. "You didn't—" She stopped herself, realizing that she'd almost blurted out, right in front of Heron, that she was a Partial. She was going to ask why they hadn't felt her on the link, since she'd been able to feel them so clearly, but she didn't know if Samm had told her or not. She would ask him later, in private.

Kira pushed those thoughts aside and looked back at Samm. "You could have just knocked. . . ." She sighed and shook her head. They couldn't just knock, because if they were wrong, and this had been anyone other than Kira, they'd be exposing themselves to far greater danger: a rival faction of Partials, or Afa's megaton booby trap. *I wonder how far Afa got, if he got away at all.*

"A better answer to your question," said Samm, "is that we're here because we needed to find you. You're in danger."

"Dr. Morgan is trying to find you," said Heron, and paused just long enough to make Kira uncomfortable before adding, "We're here to make sure she doesn't."

Kira looked back pointedly. "You're not with her anymore?"

"I'm with myself," said Heron. "Always."

"But why?"

Heron glanced at Samm, almost imperceptibly, but didn't answer.

"She's helping me," said Samm. "Dr. Morgan has put all her efforts into looking for you."

Kira nodded, phrasing her next question carefully. "How much does she know?"

"I know you're a Partial," said Heron, "if that's what you're asking. Some kind of crazy Partial none of the doctors could identify." She smiled slightly, raising her eyebrow. "I take it you're still keeping this a secret? You never told your human friends before you left them?"

"It's not that easy," said Kira.

"It's the easiest thing in the world," said Heron, "unless . . . You're still trying to play both sides, aren't you? Partial and human at the same time? Trying to save both? Not gonna work."

Kira felt herself growing angry. "You're suddenly the expert on my life?"

Heron raised her hands in mock defensiveness. "Whoa, tiger, where'd all the hostility come from?"

Kira nearly snarled. "The last time I saw you, you were strapping me down to an operating table. You worked for Dr. Morgan then, and I don't see why I should trust you now."

"Because I haven't killed you yet."

"I don't think you understand trust very well," said Kira.

"You can trust her because I trust her," said Samm. He paused. "That is, assuming you still trust me."

Kira studied him, remembering how he'd betrayed her—and how he'd saved her. Did she trust him? A little, yes, but how much? She blew out a long breath of air and gestured helplessly. "Give me a reason."

"I defected from Dr. Morgan's faction when I freed you from the lab," said Samm. "Heron followed us, waited for you to leave, and after we had discussed everything we'd seen, she proposed a plan: finding our own cure for the expiration date. That's why we had joined Morgan's faction in the first place, but her methods had become . . . distasteful."

Kira raised an eyebrow. "That's an understatement."

"The expiration date is going to kill us in less than two years," said Heron, and Kira heard a flash of cold anger in her voice. "Every single Partial in the world, dead. Faced with genocide, Morgan's methods don't seem quite so extreme."

Kira glanced at Heron, then back at Samm. "And yet you still left her."

"We left because of you," said Samm. Kira felt a flush of warmth creep through her body, but listened quietly as Samm continued. "Discovering that you were a Partial changed everything, Kira—you are literally, right now, exactly what we've hoped to be for almost twenty years."

"Lost?"

"Human." Samm tapped the photo of her as a little girl. "You age. You grow. You aren't enslaved to a chemical caste system. Dr. Morgan's preliminary scans of your body suggest that you're not even sterile."

Kira furrowed her brow. "How do you know this?"

"We've been spying on her ever since you left," said Samm, "trying to stay one step ahead. She's looking for you everywhere—the entire Long Island invasion is a last-ditch effort to find you and finish her experiments."

"But how can she not know what I am?" asked Kira.

"Dr. Morgan is convinced that the secret behind our expiration date has something to do with you," said Samm. "She's still experimenting on humans, but her main focus is on two things: She wants to find you, and she wants to find the Trust."

"You mean the rest of the Trust," said Kira. Samm frowned, confused, and Kira explained. "Dr. Morgan is part of the Trust," she said. "McKenna Morgan, specialist in bionanotechnology and human augmentation. She worked at ParaGen for years— I've got her whole résumé upstairs."

Samm frowned. "How could she work at ParaGen if she's part of the Trust? They're not human scientists, they're Partial generals and doctors who stepped up to lead us after the Break."

Kira pursed her lips. "We'd better go upstairs."

Afa was gone, leaving nothing but a smoking hole in the wall of the eighth floor: He'd used a small shaped charge to blow a hole between this building and the adjacent one, and slipped out while Kira was fighting Heron and Samm. He'd taken his backpack, but he hadn't blown them up, and Kira knew he'd come back soon—he couldn't stand to leave his library for long. In the meantime she led Samm and Heron to one of the records rooms, a former sound booth with a wide table and a ring of co-opted filing cabinets. This was where Afa stored his most extensive, most valuable records about the inner workings of ParaGen, and Kira had been going through them steadily during her breaks from the radio. As the Partials grew more canny, and the human army retreated away from effective radio range, those breaks were getting longer and more plentiful.

"This one first," said Kira, hanging her oil lantern on a hook in the wall, and setting out a printed sheet from an old company email. "It's a meeting request from the financial manager to the top staff of the ParaGen labs. This part at the top is a list of email addresses—it's like code names, kind of, that the computer system used to deliver messages to people."

"We're familiar with email," said Heron.

"Hey," said Kira, "this technology is all new to me—I was five when you blew everything up, remember?"

"Go on," said Samm.

Kira looked at the two Partials, noting for the first time how different they were: Samm, like before, was straightforward; he didn't say half of what he felt, but what he did say was simple and utilitarian. He'd explained his taciturn nature as a side effect of the link: It carried most of their emotional information, so their speech didn't need to. Partials used their voices to convey ideas, and their pheromones to convey the social context of those ideas: how they felt about it, how nervous or relaxed or excited they were. For a human observer not connected to the link, it made the Partials seem cold and robotic. Heron, in contrast, was a remarkably human communicator—she used facial tics, voice modulation, slang, even body language in a way Kira hadn't seen from any other Partials. *Well*, thought Kira, *any other Partials but me. I can barely detect the link, though, and I grew up without any access to it at all. I talk like a human because I've been communicating with them my whole life.*

What's Heron's explanation?

Samm was looking at her expectantly, and Kira turned back to the printout. "I've cross-referenced this email list with some of the other records Afa's got in here, and I think these six people are the Trust—maybe not the whole Trust, but I'm pretty sure most of the Trust ringleaders were in this group." She pointed to each address as she named them off. "Graeme Chamberlain, Kioni Trimble, Jerry Ryssdal, McKenna Morgan, Nandita Merchant, and . . ." She paused. "Armin Dhurvasula. Some of those names probably look familiar."

"General Trimble runs B Company," said Samm. "We've known for a while she was part of the Trust—but like I said, the Trust are all Partials, not humans. And this Dr. Morgan—there's probably more than one Dr. Morgan in the world, there's no guarantee this is the same one."

"Take a look at her info page," said Kira, handing him a stack of papers, "printed from the company website. There's a photo."

Heron took the stack, Samm reading over her shoulder as she flipped through it. They paused on the photo, studying it carefully; it wasn't the best quality, but the image was unmistakable. Kira had only been with the doctor for a few minutes, but her face was scarred into her memory. It was the same woman.

Heron set down the papers. "Dr. Morgan is a Partial. She's on the link—we've all felt it. She's been with us since before the Break. She's immune to RM. Hell, she survived a gunfight with Samm in close quarters back when you escaped—that's a sure sign of heightened Partial reflexes. There's no way she's a human."

Kira nodded and dug into another filing cabinet. "One of these records is a report from a corporate investigator; apparently some of the members of the Trust had been giving themselves Partial gene mods. The company leaders flipped out when they found out about it."

"Partial gene mods?" asked Samm. "What does that even mean?"

"Before they got into the business of biosynthetic organisms," said Kira, "ParaGen got its start in biotech, making genetic modifications for humans—they'd fix congenital defects, improve people's strength and reflexes, even do cosmetic mods like breast augmentation. By the Break, nearly every person born in a hospital in America had some sort of genetic modification customs built by ParaGen or another biotech firm. This report doesn't go into detail, but it specifically says 'Partial gene mods.' I think some of the members of the Trust were using the same technology they made for you—us—on themselves."

"They gave themselves the link and then used it to control us," said Heron. Her voice dripped with venom.

"So they made themselves into . . . half-Partials," said Samm. He didn't show it as obviously, but Kira could tell he was just as disturbed as Heron was, though maybe not so angry. He paused, then looked at Kira. "Do you think maybe that's what you are?"

"I thought the same thing," she answered, "but there's no way to know for sure without a closer look at the bioscan Morgan took of me. Every doctor in the room seemed pretty certain I was a Partial, though, not just a hybrid. They spoke of Partial-specific codes written on my DNA. But I'm not ruling anything out."

Heron looked back at the list. "So Morgan's part of the Trust. So is your friend Nandita." She looked up, staring at Kira, and Kira got the sudden sense that she was being analyzed—not by a scientist, but by a predator. She half expected Heron to pounce forward and take a bite from her neck.

Kira looked down, too uncomfortable to hold the girl's gaze. "Nandita left me a message," she said. She fished the photo from her backpack pocket and handed it to Samm. "I found this in my house three months ago; it's the reason I left. That's Nandita, that's my father, Armin Dhurvasula, and that's me in the middle. Kira . . . Dhurvasula." It still felt strange to say it. For all she knew, it might not even be her name. She'd never been officially adopted, as far as she could guess, because all the papers she'd read from the time period implied that Partials weren't legally defined as people. She wouldn't bear her father's surname any more than a dog would, or a television.

Samm stared at the photo intently, his dark eyes flicking back and forth across the image. Heron seemed more interested in the various Trust-related documents scattered across the table. "So your father created you at ParaGen," said Samm. "He knew you were a Partial. And so did your guardian on Long Island."

"But she never told me about it," said Kira. "She raised me like a human—I think my dad did, too. At least I don't remember any reason to think that he didn't. But why?"

"He wanted a daughter," said Samm.

"You were part of their plan," said Heron, shaking her head. "All of us are. We just don't know what it is, and what each member's part was in creating it." She held up another email, one Kira had been looking at the night before. "This says Dr. Morgan was assigned to 'performance and specifications.'"

"I think that means she programmed your super-soldier attributes," said Kira. "Each member of the Trust had a part in the creation of the Partials, and her part was all the extra gizmos that make you what you are—enhanced reflexes, enhanced vision, accelerated healing, stronger muscles, and so on and so on. The rest of the team tried to make you as human as possible; it was

Dr. Morgan who made you . . . more."

"And she's still doing it," said Samm. He set the photo down and looked at Kira somberly. "I've overheard some reports about Morgan messing with the Partial genome, and Heron says she's seen it in person."

Heron raised an eyebrow, still sifting through the pages on the table. "Apparently she can't stop tinkering."

"Is she trying to just work around the expiration date?" asked Kira. "Maybe she can't find the genes that kill you after twenty years, so she's adding in new mods to try to dampen them."

"Maybe," said Samm, "if something like that is even possible. But she's mostly doing more . . . well, like you said: augmentation. Making certain Partials stronger or faster. They say she has a whole squad that can breathe underwater. She's drifting further way from the human template."

"Sounds like she's turned her back on humanity across the board," said Kira. "Or maybe just given up on it."

"She had help at ParaGen," said Heron, picking up another sheet of paper. "Look. Jerry Ryssdal was assigned to the same project, or another part of it."

Kira nodded, marveling at Heron's ability to sort through the information scattered across the table. It had taken Kira days to find these connections, but Heron was putting it all together in a matter of minutes. "I don't know exactly what Ryssdal's contribution was," Kira said, "but I think you're right. Some of them worked in pairs."

"But not all?" Samm prompted.

Kira shrugged. "I honestly have no idea. We're talking about the biggest secrets of an incredibly secretive company, and the even more secretive inner circle that was apparently working both for and against them. Even the basic information is buried in layers of security and coded emails, and I can't even be sure if the clues I've found are real or just disinformation designed to throw people off the trail. Afa's spent years on this, even before the Break, but it's just . . . incomplete. We don't have the answers.

"He's . . ." Kira paused, not certain how to articulate the big man's condition. "He's been alone for a very long time, let's put it that way. I think it kind of broke his brain, but even broken he's a genius. He was collecting information on the end of the world before it even ended. He's got stuff about the Isolation War, and the biotech industry, and the Partials, and . . . everything. He worked for ParaGen, running part of their computer system, which is where most of this stuff comes from." She gestured around the room, and Samm nodded appreciatively.

Heron received the information more passively, seeming to soak it up while studying a full array of documents at once. Her eyes flicked back and forth as she read the papers before her, and a dark frown crept across her face. "This isn't good," she said.

Samm looked up. "What?"

"Morgan is a part of the Trust—we have two conflicting ideas of what the Trust is, but they both say she was a part of it. And the Trust seems to be the group that created the Partials."

"We know all that already," said Kira. "None of it's awesome news, but it's not exactly terrible, either."

"That's because you're not paying attention," said Heron. "Start putting the pieces together: Morgan built the Partials, but she didn't know about the expiration date until the first generation started dying three years ago. Why didn't she know? The cure for RM is built into the Partial pheromone system, but she didn't know about that, either. You're some kind of new-model Partial, and she had no idea you even existed."

The implications hit Kira like a punch to the gut, and she sank into a chair. "That's not good."

"I'm not seeing it," said Samm. "The three things you just mentioned have nothing to do with the physical augmentation package she worked on, so it makes sense that she didn't know about them. Why is this a big deal?"

"Because it means they're not who we thought they were," said Kira. "They're not *what* we thought they were. I've been out here for two months trying to find the Trust because I thought they had it all together—a group of geniuses or whatever with a plan for exactly how everything was supposed to work. Cures for RM, details on expiration, answers to how I fit in, everything. But now that we're finally learning about them, they're just . . ." She sighed, understanding, finally. "If everything Heron is saying about Morgan is true, then they're just as fragmented as everybody else. They kept secrets from each other; they messed with each other's work. I was relying on them for answers, but I'm starting to think they might not have them, either."

"And if they don't have them," said Heron, "nobody does."

Samm paused, lost in thought. Kira thought about the problem from different angles, going through everything she knew about the Trust. Each member of the Trust would still have certain answers to her questions, right? She could still find them, like Nandita had told her to, and she could still learn something. If there wasn't a plan in place, she could make one. The pieces were all here. And perhaps there was a member of the Trust out there who did know it all, who oversaw the project, who could tell her how these pieces fit together. How she fit together.

She had to believe.

Samm broke the silence. "What about the scientists who worked with you directly?" he asked. "Your father, and Nandita: What were their contributions?"

"My father did the pheromone system," said Kira, "which I suppose makes sense—I don't have the full link, but I have a version of it. He may have built it custom."

"Which parts of it do you have?" asked Heron.

"I have no idea," said Kira. "I knew you were waiting for me on the stairs, and you knew I was waiting for you, but right now I can't sense either of you at all."

Heron raised an eyebrow, a motion half-mocking, half-curious. "We knew you were on the stairs because you're about as stealthy as a moose. There was no link data coming from you at all—and there isn't any now."

"But I felt you," said Kira. "I knew exactly where both of you were."

"Interesting," said Heron.

Kira turned to Samm. "What about you?" She thought about the connection she'd felt with him in the lab, and suddenly grew anxious. "Do you feel anything?" She felt stupid for asking, like a schoolgirl, and couldn't bring herself to ask the second part of the question: *Did* you feel anything?

Samm shook his head. "Nothing . . . right now."

"And before?" Heron asked.

"I . . . can't be sure."

What's that look in his eyes? thought Kira. *Why are these stupid Partials so hard to read?*

"Maybe all she can do is receive," said Heron, "with no ability to transmit."

"Or the transmitter's been turned off somehow," said Samm. "I don't know why, though."

"To hide me from other Partials," said Kira, "or to protect me from them. I've never gotten any of the 'command' data you've talked about, either. When Dr. Morgan tried to force you to obey her, I didn't feel a thing."

Samm's expression was dark. "Count yourself lucky."

"I wonder if she's a spy model," Heron mused. "Strength and reflexes slightly boosted, physically attractive, heightened intelligence, human communication skills, and apparently engineered for independence. It fits."

"You have spy models?" asked Kira.

Heron laughed, and Samm cocked his head in the most human expression of confusion she'd seen from him yet. "What do you think Heron is?"

"But if I'm a spy, then what's my mission?" asked Kira. "Am I going to wake up someday with a data download telling me to assassinate a senator? How could they have even planned something like that five years before the Break?"

"I have no idea," said Heron. "I'm just saying it's a possibility."

"Moving on," said Samm. "Dhurvasula built the pheromone system, but what about Nandita?"

"That's another of our big holes," said Kira. "Nandita and one other guy, Graeme Chamberlain, were working on something called the Failsafe. Of all the things that went into making the Partials, this is clearly the most secret. I have absolutely no records that explain what the Failsafe was, or what it did, or even who ordered it."

"What do you know about this Chamberlain?" asked Samm. "I've never heard of him before."

"That I can tell you," said Kira, "but it's going to creep you the hell out." She opened a manila folder and pulled out a single sheet of paper: a death certificate. "As soon as he finished building the Failsafe, he killed himself."

The three fell silent. Kira had gone through Afa's records as thoroughly as she could, and they simply didn't have the information they needed—they raised some tantalizing questions, like this one about Chamberlain, but they never actually answered them. All the most important secrets were still locked away somewhere: Who was the Trust? Why did they create RM? What was the Failsafe?

What am I? Kira thought. *What purpose do I have in all this?* Without more information, there was no way to know.

It was Samm—always pragmatic, always straightforward— who broke the silence again. "We have to go."

"Where?" asked Kira.

"To ParaGen," said Samm. "To wherever they were when they did all this—when they made all these decisions. If the information's not here, that's the only other place it could be."

"That's not going to be easy," said Heron.

Kira nodded. "The ParaGen headquarters were in Denver. I'm not really up on my old-world geography, but I'm pretty sure that's not close."

"It's not," said Heron, "and the road to get there is, by any estimation, hell."

"How horrible could it be?" asked Kira, gesturing around. "We've made it through this, didn't we? Is Denver any worse?"

"We honestly don't know about Denver," said Samm, glancing at Heron, "but most of the Midwest is virtually uncrossable, thanks to Houston. It was the biggest oil and gas refinery in the world at the time of the Break, and without anyone to keep it operating properly, it started to fall apart. Eventually it lit on fire—a lightning strike, maybe, we don't know for sure—and it's still burning ten years later, creating a cloud of toxic fumes a thousand miles wide. The entire Midwest is a toxic wasteland, everywhere those gases have been blown to by the Gulf wind."

Kira raised her eyebrow. "And this is your plan?"

Samm's face remained stony. "I wasn't intending to enjoy it, but if it's the only way, it's the only way."

"It's not the only way," said Heron. "We could call in Dr. Morgan right now and end this entire thing—the search, the war, everything. We know now that even if she doesn't know everything about RM and expiration, she knows more than she's let on, and the information we have might be enough for her to come up with a plan to cure us. And we wouldn't have to cross this nightmare wasteland to do it."

"She'll kill Afa," said Kira.

"Probably."

"She'll kill everybody," said Kira, feeling an edge of steel in her voice. "She wants to solve the expiration date—"

"That's exactly my point," said Heron.

"—but I'm trying to solve them both," said Kira. "Expiration and RM. They're connected through the Partials, and through ParaGen, and if we can find the ParaGen records, we can find the answers we need. If we give up and side with Morgan, the humans die."

"The humans will live," said Heron, "because Morgan will stop killing them looking for you."

"So they'll die in a few decades," said Kira, "but they'll still die. RM won't be cured, and they won't be able to reproduce, and the human race will go extinct."

"Did it ever occur to you that maybe it's time for them to go extinct?" Heron asked. Kira felt like she'd been punched in the face. "Maybe humans are just done," said Heron, "and it's time for the Partials to inherit the Earth."

Kira's voice was a hiss. "I can't believe you would say that."

"That's because you still think you're one of them," said Heron.

"It's because I care about people and don't want them to die!"

"There are Partials dying every day," said Heron. "Do you care about them?"

"I told you, I'm trying to save everyone—"

"And what if you can't?" asked Heron. "A journey across the continent is incredibly dangerous—what if we don't make it? What if we get there and can't find any answers? What if it takes us so long the Partials all die before we get back? I don't want to risk their lives just because you couldn't pick a side!"

Heron's eyes were practically flaring with anger, but Kira met them fearlessly and stared straight back. "I've picked a side," she said darkly. "And everyone's on it. And that's exactly who I'm going to save."

Heron glared at her, practically snarling. Samm spoke with his typical stone-faced demeanor. "If we're going to go, we need to go now—the sooner we leave, the sooner we get back." He looked at Heron. "And we'll need you, or we'll never make it."

Kira looked at them both, steeling her courage. "If we do this, we have to do it right. Any records we find will be stored on computers, under heavy encryption: Do either of you know how to get past that kind of security?"

Samm shook his head; Heron only glared.

Kira blew out a long, low breath. "Then we need to find Afa."

CHAPTER SIXTEEN

Heron found Afa in a nearby drugstore, holed up in the back in a mini safe house he'd obviously prepared years earlier. He refused to come out, insisting, variously, that he was the last human being on the planet, and that he couldn't ever leave his backpack. Heron came back for Kira—probably because beating him unconscious would require dragging him home, and she didn't want to bother with the effort—and Kira tried to calmly talk him out. The last thing they needed was another explosion.

"We need your help," said Kira. It was a small drugstore set back into a larger building, the shelves picked clean of anything edible. The floor was scattered with dirt and animal tracks. Afa was in the back room, the door closed, and from the looks of it something heavy had been shoved in front of the door on the other side. Kira couldn't see any explosives, but that didn't mean they weren't there. "These are my friends, and they need your help. You have to tell us how to get to Denver."

"Denver's gone," said Afa, and Kira recognized the distant

lilt to his voice, the half-absent slur that meant he'd retreated into his protective stupor, perhaps deeper now than she'd ever seen him before. The assault on his building had shocked him profoundly. "I'm the last human being on the planet."

"The people are gone," said Kira, "but the city's still there. The records are still there. We want to help you finish your work—to fill in all the missing pieces about the Trust, and the Partials, and the Failsafe. Don't you want to learn all that?"

Afa paused. "I have everything in my backpack," he said at last. "I never leave my backpack."

"You have almost everything," said Kira. "You don't have the Trust—not their plans, not their formulas, not their secrets or their reasons or anything. We need that information, Afa, it might be the only way to save any of us, humans and Partials."

"Too dangerous," Afa muttered. "You'll burn up. You'll be poisoned."

Kira glanced at Samm, then turned back to Afa's door. "We'll be as safe as possible," she said. "My friends are the best wilderness scouts I know, and I'm pretty handy myself. We can cover ourselves, we can carry our water, we can defend ourselves from wild animals—we can make it. Trust me, Afa, we can get you the records you've been looking for."

"I think you might be overselling us a little," whispered Heron. "The wasteland is going to be hell no matter how well we prepare."

"He doesn't have to know that," Kira whispered back.

The drugstore was silent, everyone listening quietly while Afa thought. Birds wheeled between the broken buildings outside, watched closely by a feral cat perched high in a windowsill. The morning sun turned the rusted cars into fuzzy shadows on the road.

"You could go to Chicago," said Afa.

Kira snapped back to look at the bunker door. "What?"

"ParaGen was in Denver, but their data center was in Chicago," said Afa. His voice was clearer now, more lucid and confident. "Remember what I told you about the cloud? All the information in the cloud was stored somewhere, on a physical computer, and most of that physical storage was in huge central locations called data centers. ParaGen's was in Chicago."

"Why would their data not be in their own offices?"

"Because the cloud made distance meaningless," said Afa. Kira heard a bolt slide back, then another, then two more. The door cracked open, but Afa stayed hidden behind it. "Storing digital information in Chicago was the same as storing it in Denver, or Manhattan, or wherever, because you could access it no matter where you were. As IT director, I worked with the Chicago center all the time, setting up permissions and security and making sure nobody could get the data but us. Unless it was all hard copies, I guarantee it's in the data center."

"If it's that easy," asked Samm, "why haven't you gone to get it before?"

"It's seven hundred twelve miles," said Afa, "more if you can't fly, which you can't. I can't go that far—I have to stay here with my records."

Kira shot another look at Samm. "But we need you, Afa. We can't do this without you."

"I can't go," said Afa.

"We don't need him," said Heron, speaking loud enough that

Afa could hear her—allowing herself to be overheard on purpose, it seemed to Kira. "Data centers run on electricity, obviously, so we'll have to reactivate the auxiliary generator, which won't run for very long. That will be hard enough. Then we'll have to find which servers have the ParaGen files, which ParaGen server has the Trust files, and which Trust files have the information we need, all while navigating the single most powerful security protocols that old-world money could buy."

"I already know all that," said Afa. "I could find it, easy."

Heron smiled.

"So come help us," said Kira.

"I can't leave my records."

"I can do it just fine on my own," said Heron, grinning maliciously, trying to challenge Afa's expertise. "We don't need him."

"You'll never do it," said Afa.

"Once we find the right files," said Heron, "we'll have to decode the data and download it to a portable screen, all before our generator dies, and we'll probably only get one shot at it. It's going to be a pretty amazing feat—getting a computer file out of a ruined building from a long-lost civilization. It'll be like hacking the Giza pyramids."

The door opened slightly wider, and Heron nodded triumphantly.

"You know the wilderness," said Afa. "You're scouts, Kira said so. You don't know computers."

"I know enough."

The door opened even wider. "Do you know how to crack a Nostromo-7 firewall?" said Afa, and Kira noticed the difference in his voice—he was waking up, mentally, enlivened by the idea. Kira had thought Heron was trying to goad him into coming, challenging him by claiming to be better, but really she was geeking him out. She was presenting him a challenge so interesting, and so firmly in his area of expertise, he couldn't help but get excited about it. Kira had done the same with Marcus, more than once, in their medical research.

Samm shook his head, speaking softly. "I don't like this. It's not safe to take him."

"It's not safe to leave him, either," said Kira. "Dr. Morgan's looking for me, too, right? Can you say for sure she's not going to find this radio station eventually? She's not going to go easy on the mentally damaged man she finds here."

"He's not just mentally damaged," said Samm, "he's a paranoid bomber that we can't control or predict. If we take him out into the wasteland, he's as likely to kill us as anything is to kill him."

"What are our other options?" asked Kira. "We can't just ask Morgan, A because she's evil, and B because she doesn't know anything about me or expiration or the Failsafe. If we could find Nandita that'd be great, but the entire Long Island population's been looking for her for months and she's nowhere."

"We could talk to Trimble," said Samm, "assuming B Company doesn't kill us on sight."

"Assuming there's anything left of B Company at all," said Heron. "Morgan's been recruiting them in droves. But Trimble isn't connected to the pheromones or the Failsafe or the expiration, at least not according to anything in the records you showed us. She won't know anything more than Morgan."

Kira's eyes widened. "You know where Trimble is?"

"She's in charge of B Company," said Samm. "She and Morgan have been the main face of the Trust for years—now we know she's not just a messenger, she's apparently one of them."

"B Company hates D Company," said Heron. "Most of the civil war you've seen here on the mainland is a war between them."

Kira grimaced. "Saving the world would be a lot easier if the people we're trying to save would stop killing each other."

Afa's door opened slightly farther, and he peeked one eye out. "You didn't say anything about Nostromo-7s, so I assume you don't know how to get past one. I do."

Samm looked at him and whispered softly, "We shouldn't be doing this."

"He's a good man," said Kira.

"He's insane."

"I know that," hissed Kira. "I don't like it any more than you do, but what else are we supposed to do?" She looked at Heron. "Can you actually do any of that stuff you were talking about? Do you even know anyone who can? Afa's unpredictable, yes, I admit that, but when his mind is working right, he's positively brilliant."

"When his mind is working right," said Samm.

"So we watch him," said Kira. "We keep him away from weapons, we keep him away from anything that explodes, we do whatever it takes to keep him happy and lucid and friendly." She paused. "It's the only way we're ever going to find the information we need."

The Partials stared at her. Samm turned to face the street. "We'll need horses."

"We can make better time on foot," said Heron.

"You and I can," said Samm, "not Kira and definitely not Afa. Listening to him breathe, he's at least three hundred pounds."

Kira raised an eyebrow. "You can tell his weight from his breathing?"

"It's labored and irregular," said Samm. "He'll die of a heart attack before we make it halfway."

"There's a Partial camp not too far northeast of here," said Heron, "an A Company lookout post in the Bronx. They're not exactly friendly with D, but they're not looking for a fight, either. Samm and I can sneak in, steal their horses, and meet you over there"—she pointed—"on the George Washington Bridge."

"You're going to sneak up on a lookout?"

"There are very few people this far south," she said. "All they're here for is to keep an eye on your military base across the bay. We'll be coming from a different angle, and they won't suspect a thing."

"It still seems like it'll be harder than you're making it out to be," said Kira. "I mean, yes, you're Partials, but so are they."

"But none of them are me," said Heron. She turned and walked into the street, slinging her rifle over her shoulder. "If we're going to do this, let's do it. We'll see you at noon tomorrow on that bridge. Be ready." She started walking away.

Kira looked at Samm. "You . . ." She didn't know what to say. "Be safe." She paused. "Come back."

"Noon tomorrow," said Samm. He hesitated, his hand hanging in the air by her arm, then turned and followed Heron.

Kira turned back to Afa, still hidden behind his half-open door. "You hear that?" she asked. "We have a day and a half to get ready for this. We're really going to do it."

"Do you think I'm mentally damaged?"

Kira felt a hot flush steal over her face. "I'm sorry," she said softly. "I didn't know you could hear us."

"I hear everything."

"I think . . ." She stopped, not certain how to say what she felt. "I want us to be realistic, Afa. You're a brilliant man, and I said that, too."

"I heard."

"But you're also . . . inconsistent. Inconsistently capable, I guess. I know that sounds terrible, but—"

"I know what I am," said Afa. "I do my best. But I know what I am."

"You're my friend," said Kira firmly. "I will do everything in my power to help you."

He stepped out from behind the door, the brilliant lucidity gone, looking for all the world like a giant child. "This is my backpack," he said, lifting it onto his shoulders. "I never leave my backpack."

Kira took him by the arm. "Let's get back to your place and pack one for me."

CHAPTER SEVENTEEN

Marcus ran from tree to tree down Kira's old street, eyes searching constantly for anything out of the ordinary—a rustle of leaves, a face or a body, a broken door or window. The Partial army was barely half an hour away, battling what was left of the Grid's desperate last stand. He needed to leave East Meadow altogether, but there was something he had to do first.

Xochi's house was closed and shuttered, like all the other houses in the city. He knocked on the door, eyeing the trees suspiciously—this was, after all, the house where Heron had accosted him.

Marcus heard a bolt slide, and Xochi opened the door. "Come in," she said quickly, bolting it solidly again behind him. The house smelled like basil and nutmeg and coriander, a cacophony of competing aromas. Xochi set down the shotgun she'd been holding, going back to her frenzied packing, and Marcus stood uncomfortably in the middle of the room.

"What brings you here?" asked Xochi, looking up from her

half-filled backpack. "I thought you'd be halfway to our safe house by now." Xochi and Isolde had picked a central point on the island where their group of friends could flee and rendezvous if—or when, really—the Grid defense failed. Marcus didn't answer right away, still trying to think of how to start—he had so many questions, but was this a topic she'd even want to talk about? Xochi frowned, noticing his indecision, and gestured toward the kitchen. "Do you need anything? Water? I got a bushel of lemons I'm not taking with me, I could whip up some lemonade."

"That's okay."

"It takes like thirty seconds, it's fine if you want some—"

"No, thank you," said Marcus. He worked his chin and lips, as if warming up his mouth for the conversation, but it was just a stalling tactic. He still wasn't sure how to start. He sat down, then stood up nervously and gestured to the couch. "Sit down."

Xochi sat solemnly. "What's going on, Marcus? I've never seen you like this before."

"I talked to Kira," he said. Xochi's eyes went wide, and Marcus nodded. "Three weeks ago was the first time, when Haru and I were on the front lines. Six, maybe eight times since. I don't know where she is, but she's been listening to our radios and the Partial radios and feeding us information—nothing that could win us the war, obviously, but enough to keep Haru and me from getting killed."

"Is she okay?"

"She's fine," said Marcus. "Better than we are, at least, though that'll change pretty quick if they can find her. Dr. Morgan is pouring every resource she has into this."

Xochi nodded. "That's what Isolde told me. Apparently this entire invasion is about finding her. Do you know why?"

"I don't," said Marcus. "Kira won't tell me. She's been acting strange ever since Morgan's lab, like they did something to her that she doesn't want to talk about."

"It was a pretty traumatic experience," said Xochi.

"I know," said Marcus quickly, "I know, but I mean . . . Let me ask you this: What's your earliest memory of Kira?"

Xochi played with the straps of her backpack, rolling them into little cylinders as she spoke. "It was at school, the old one by the hospital. I'd been in the farms with Kessler for a couple of years, but we fought like tigers—even then—and so when I turned eight she sent me into East Meadow for school."

Marcus almost smiled at the memory. "You beat up Benji Haul on your first day."

Xochi shrugged. "He had it coming. I spent the afternoon in detention, and Kira was in there for, I can't remember, starting a fire with all the phosphorus from the lightbulbs or something— one of those crazy brainiac schemes you and Kira were always getting into."

"What about Nandita?" asked Marcus.

Xochi frowned. "What about Nandita?"

"When was the first time you met her?" asked Marcus. "Soon after that?"

"Not for another year at least," said Xochi. "I never came here because I was confined to the school—Kessler's orders—and I never saw Nandita there because I always ran and hid when they did presentations or fairs or whatever. I had enough problems with my own fake mom, I didn't need to hang out with anybody else's. Why are you asking about Nandita?"

Marcus leaned closer. "I haven't told you everything," he said. "Do you remember the Partial that followed Samm after we left Morgan's lab? An assassin or something; Samm said she was watching when we got into the boat to come home."

"I remember that it happened, yeah," said Xochi. "Why?"

"Because she was here," said Marcus. "Four or five weeks ago, in this backyard."

"Here?"

"She was looking for Kira," said Marcus, "but she was also looking for Nandita. She had a photo of Kira and Nandita together, before the Break, standing in front of the ParaGen building."

Xochi froze. "Nandita never knew Kira before the Break."

"That's what I thought, too," said Marcus. "Did either of them ever actually say it?"

"She talked about meeting the girls," Xochi spluttered. "She told these little stories about finding each one of them, one by one—"

"What was the story about Kira?"

Xochi stuck out her lower lip, thinking. "She found her on the mainland," she said, "in a refugee camp. A big group of soldiers, US or NADI or whatever, marched in one day with a whole ton of survivors they'd picked up, and Nandita saw Kira cussing out one of the guards because he didn't have any pudding."

Marcus raised an eyebrow. "Cussing him out?"

Xochi laughed. "Have you met Kira? She's a fireball now, and she was a fireball then. Nandita used to call her the Little Explosion. Besides, she was five years old and she'd just spent who knows how long with no one to talk to but soldiers; she probably had a monster vocabulary. The soldier kept apologizing about the pudding, and this skinny little girl kept calling his mother into serious moral question, and Nandita swooped in to teach her some manners." Xochi smiled distantly. "I think she thought the situation was just too adorable to pass up, but she always insisted she did it to teach her."

"To teach her?"

"That's all she's talked about," said Xochi, "the whole time I've known her: She needed to teach her girls. I don't know what—I'm the one she taught herbology."

"If Nandita knew Kira before," said Marcus, "why would she pretend like she didn't?"

"You said the picture was taken in front of a ParaGen building, right?"

"Yeah."

"Well, if she was involved with ParaGen, it's not all that surprising that she'd keep it a secret," said Xochi. "Some ParaGen employees got lynched in the first days after the Break, before the Senate got organized and started imposing order. If I'd worked for the company that made the Partials, even as a janitor, I wouldn't have told anyone."

"But what does that have to do with Kira?" Marcus asked.

"I'm working on that part," said Xochi, pursing her lips. "How about this: Nobody who landed on this island had ever met any of the others. The population of the US dropped from four hundred fifty million to forty thousand. That's like one out of every twelve hundred people—the chances that any of them knew each other were ridiculous, and in the few cases where two survivors did know each other, like Jayden and Madison, Dr. Skousen and his doctors interviewed the living daylights out of them, trying to find anything that might be a correlating factor of survival. If Nandita waltzed in claiming she and Kira went way back, they would never have rested until they found every possible piece of information. And if one of those pieces said that Nandita worked at ParaGen, she was probably very reasonably afraid of being held prisoner and interrogated, or worse—maybe killed, if the people were angry enough."

"'Every possible piece of information,'" said Marcus, half to himself. "I almost wish they'd done it."

"Killed Nandita?"

"Interrogated her," said Marcus. He put his finger on the low wooden coffee table, tracing patterns in the grain of the wood. "Every possible piece of information about the two people the Partials are tearing our island apart to find." He nodded. "Yeah, I kind of wish they'd done it."

"You need to tell the Senate about Heron," said Xochi.

"I've told Mkele," said Marcus. "I'm not stupid. Mkele's looking for Nandita, but I'm not too anxious to tell the Senate that I was in contact with the enemy." He moved his finger slowly around the whorls of a knot. "I guess we're still afraid of being lynched," he said. "Afraid of being caught. Do you know what the others told me?"

Xochi narrowed her eyes. "What others?"

"Your other sisters," said Marcus, "Madison and Isolde. They got evacuated in the first group, to protect the children, so I talked to them quickly before they left. They said Kira wasn't the first girl Nandita adopted."

Xochi cocked her head. "Really? I mean, I never assumed she was until we started talking about that photo, but now it seems kind of weird that she wasn't."

"By the time she had Kira, she already had the other one," said Marcus. "Ariel."

Xochi nodded, as if this piece of information was especially profound. "Ariel moved out a couple of years ago," she said, "before I moved in. I didn't know her well, but she never got along with any of the other girls, and she hated Nandita like you wouldn't believe."

Marcus counted them off on his fingers. "Ariel in Philadelphia, Kira in a refugee camp, Isolde here on the island, and Madison a full year later when Jayden got chicken pox—he stayed in quarantine, Madison stayed here, and the situation worked so well she never moved out. Madison said Nandita fought like a lion to get her moved here instead of somewhere else."

"Why?"

"Anybody's guess," said Marcus. "But Madison does remember the first thing Nandita said when she brought her to the house: 'Now you can teach me.'"

Xochi frowned. "What does that mean?"

"I don't know," said Marcus, standing up, "but there's only one person left to ask." He walked to the door and drew back the bolt. "You head to the rendezvous point. I'm going to go find Ariel."

CHAPTER EIGHTEEN

Kira and Afa were waiting on the George Washington Bridge with a pile of equipment when Samm and Heron finally appeared with the horses, not right at noon but soon thereafter. Afa, of course, had his backpack, stuffed to the seams with originals and copies of all his most important documents. If the worst happened, and his record stash was raided or destroyed, he had enough in his backpack to . . . Kira wasn't sure. To write a really good history book about the end of the world. What they needed now were the answers that would make it all add up: What was the Failsafe? Why did the Trust end the world? And how could they use that knowledge to save what was left?

"This is too much," said Heron, reining up her horse. It nickered, breathing heavily. "We'll have to leave most of it."

"I've planned for that," said Kira, gesturing at some of the boxes. "Afa insisted we bring some of his larger archives, but I told him we might not have room. Remove all that stuff and it's really not too bad."

"We need another horse," said Afa, though he was shying away from the four in front of him. "We need a packhorse, like a . . . shipping horse. A baggage carrier for all my boxes."

"We'll have to leave the boxes behind," said Samm, swinging down from his saddle. He picked through the other supplies, nodding his head in approval. "Food, water, ammunition—what's this?"

"That's a radio," said Kira. "I want to make sure we have some way of communicating, if it comes to it."

"It's too small," said Heron. "We won't be able to talk to anyone with a thing like that."

"Afa's set up repeaters all over this place," said Kira. "That's what the building was in Asharoken, and the one by where we met Samm."

"*Captured* Samm," said Heron, the barest hint of a smile in the corner of her lips.

"Wait," said Samm. "All those rigged buildings, all the explosions, those were radio repeaters?"

"I set them up," said Afa, reorganizing the piles of equipment. "I didn't want anyone to find them."

Samm was stone-faced. "You killed people over radio repeaters?"

"And record depots," said Kira. "Most of them were also temporary safe houses."

"That doesn't make it any better," said Samm.

"You knew he was a paranoid lunatic yesterday," said Heron. "How does this change anything?"

"Because it's wrong," said Samm.

"And it wasn't wrong yesterday?"

"I'm sorry," said Kira. "I've lost friends to those bombs as well."

"Not *those* bombs, *his* bombs."

"And I'm not happy about it either," Kira insisted. "He was overzealous and he killed some innocent people, but you know what? Which side hasn't in this idiotic war?"

"He's not a side," said Samm, "he's a wild card."

"A wild card that we need," said Heron. "We agreed to this yesterday, we're following through with it today. He's unarmed—just don't let him plant a bomb anywhere and you're perfectly safe."

Samm glowered but didn't object, and he and Kira began loading equipment onto the horses.

"We'll need to set up another repeater in the Appalachians," said Afa, carefully placing the radio in his own saddlebag. "We don't have anything set up that can get a reliable signal over a mountain."

"Are you going to rig that one to explode as well?" asked Samm.

"How did you know I brought explosives?" he asked, his brow furrowed. "Kira said I couldn't bring explosives—"

"You can't," said Samm, and searched the pile fiercely, finally pulling a brick of C4 from a pack full of food. He brandished it at Heron. "See? This is what we're getting ourselves into."

"So check the rest and make sure you have it all," said Heron, taking the brick and throwing it over the side of the bridge. They were still over the city, not the water, and it fell silently through the air before splatting on the pavement below.

Samm searched everything they'd brought, including Afa's

backpack, and when he was finally satisfied, they mounted up and rode west, across the bridge and into the untamed mainland beyond: what used to be New Jersey. Kira looked back at the boxes of extra records, forlorn by the side of the road.

"Boxes of old ParaGen emails," she said. "That's going to be a weird surprise for anyone who finds them."

"If someone finds them," said Heron, "then we've done a very poor job of slipping away unnoticed."

Kira had been riding horses for years, mostly on salvage runs in and out of East Meadow, so the first days of the trip were easy for her; Heron and Samm proved to be accomplished riders as well. Afa, to no one's surprise, was not, which made their progress slow starting out. He also made strange, disjointed conversation as they rode, talking here about cats and there about internet firewall subroutines. Kira listened casually, ignoring most of it, having learned over the last three weeks that all Afa really wanted to do was say things out loud; he'd been alone too long to expect a response, and she'd started to suspect that he would talk to himself just as much if there were no one around to hear him. Samm and Heron scanned the horizon, watching the road ahead and the buildings on the side for signs of an ambush. It was unlikely out here—as far as they knew, nobody lived on this side of the city, or indeed anywhere else on the continent— but it was better to be safe than sorry. The road curved north, then south, then north again, winding lazily through the dense suburbs of New Jersey. When night fell they were still in urban terrain, office buildings and stores and apartments on every side. They slept for the night in an auto parts store, the horses tethered to tall racks of rubber tires. Heron took the first turn at watch, and Kira couldn't help but notice that she was watching her and Afa as much as anything that might be approaching from the outside.

Kira woke again in the middle of the night, momentarily disoriented, but as her eyes adjusted and she remembered where she was, she saw Samm was now on watch, perched on a desk in the corner of the room. Kira sat up, hugging her knees in the cold.

"Hey," she whispered.

"Hey," said Samm.

Kira sat, looking at him, not sure what to say or how to say it. "Thanks for coming back."

"You told me to."

"I mean, thanks for coming to find me. At all. You didn't have to."

"You told me to do that, too," said Samm. "We said we'd learn what we could, then get back together and compare notes."

"We did," said Kira, scooting back to rest against the wall. "So. What do you know?"

"I know we're dying."

Kira nodded. "The expiration date."

"You say that," said Samm, "but do you really appreciate what it means?"

"Partials die after twenty years."

"The first wave of Partials arrived at the Isolation War twenty-one years ago," he said. "They were created the year before that. All our leaders, all our front-line veterans, are already dead. The closest thing we have to ancestors." He paused again. "I was in the last group made, and I turn nineteen in a few months.

Heron's been nineteen for a while. Do you know how many of us are left?"

"All we ever talk about is 'a million Partials,'" said Kira. "'There are a million Partials right on the other side of the sound.' I guess that's not true anymore, is it?"

"We've lost more than half."

Kira brought her knees in closer to her chest, suddenly colder. The room felt small and fragile, like a house of sticks ready to crumble in the wind.

Five hundred thousand dead, she thought. *More than five hundred thousand.* The sheer size of the number, nearly twenty times the entire human population, terrified her. Her next thought came unbidden: *It won't be long before we're even.*

Immediately she felt terrible, even for thinking it. She didn't want anyone to die anymore, human or Partial; she certainly didn't want to "get even" with them. She'd been angry at them before, before she started to understand them, but she'd moved past that. Hadn't she? She was one of them, after all. It occurred to her then that she might have to face an expiration date as well—and moments later she realized that she was so different from the other Partials, she might not have an expiration date at all. The first thought terrified her, but the second stunned her with a deep, empty sadness. *The last of Partial left. The last of my people.*

Which side am I on?

She looked at Samm, his back against the wall, one leg hanging off the desk, his rifle resting calmly next to him. He was a protector, a guardian, watching over them while they were helpless; if anybody did come to attack them, not only would he see them first, but they would see him first. He had placed himself in harm's way to protect a girl he barely knew and a man he didn't like or trust. He was a Partial, yet he was a friend.

That's the whole problem, she thought. *We still think there are sides. There can't be, not anymore.*

She felt the sudden urge to crawl up next to him, to help keep watch, to share a bit of body heat in the bitter nighttime chill. She didn't. She pulled her blanket to her chin and spoke.

"We're going to solve it," she said. "We're going to find the Trust, we're going to find their records, we're going to find out not just why they did this but how—how we can reverse the expiration date, how can we synthesize the cure for RM. Whatever I'm supposed to be, and what part I'm supposed to play in it. They knew all this, variously, and once we know it, we can save everyone."

"That's why I came back," said Samm.

"To save the world?"

"I wouldn't even know where to start," he said. His face was a mask of shadow. "I came to help you save it. You're the only one who can."

Kira pulled her blanket tighter around her neck and shoulders. *Sometimes a vote of confidence can be the most nerve-racking thing in the world.*

They packed and left at the first sign of dawn, making sure the horses were well-fed and watered for the day's trip. By noon the city had all but disappeared, and they passed the afternoon in rural country, thick forests slowly but surely overrunning the small towns that nestled in the hills. Afa's constant babbling petered out as well, as if the stretches of untamed wilderness made him uncomfortable. Kira occasionally heard him mutter to himself, but she couldn't hear what he was saying.

Kira didn't know what her horse's name was, since they'd been stolen, so she passed most of her day trying to think of something appropriate. Samm's horse was willful, and stubborn, so she wanted to name him Haru, but she knew none of her companions would appreciate the joke. She reflected that she could just as easily name a stubborn horse Xochi, or Kira for that matter. She searched for something else and settled on Buddy, a boy she'd known in school who fought with the teachers almost on principle, because they were in charge. Samm's horse seemed to have the same attitude. Heron's horse, on the other hand, seemed almost determined to obey her, or perhaps Heron was simply better at controlling it. Calling on the same well of acquaintances, Kira named this one Dug, after a perennial overachiever from her intern program. Her own horse, a bit of a goofy trickster, she named Bobo, and Afa's poor mount she named Odd, or Oddjob, or any number of other permutations as the mood struck her. If Heron was the best at managing her horse, Afa was the worst, and the poor animal seemed at times just as confused as he was, bobbing its head and shuffling sideways and sending Afa into fits of frustrated grumbling. It was almost funny, but it kept them slow, and Kira tried to give him riding tips when she could. It didn't seem to help.

It was near nightfall when they heard a cry for help.

"Hold up," said Samm, reining his horse Buddy to a stop. The others stopped with him, listening on the wind for another sound. Oddjob stamped and snuffled, and Heron shot Afa a dirty look. Kira tried to focus, and heard the voice again.

"Help!"

"It's coming from over there," Samm said, pointing down a gully by the side of the road. There were lakes all through these hills, and tiny rivers and streams had cut paths between them for centuries. The gully in question was thick with trees and underbrush.

"It doesn't matter," said Heron. "We don't have time to stop."

"Someone's in trouble," said Kira. "We can't just leave them."

"Yes, we can," said Heron.

"It's a Partial," said Afa. "I'm the last human on the planet."

"It's not a Partial," said Samm. "I'm not linking with anyone."

"They might be too far away," said Kira.

"Or downwind," said Heron. "I don't like it either way—any humans we meet would likely love to ambush a group of Partials, and we know our faction's not this far west."

"I thought you didn't have a faction anymore?" asked Kira. Heron only glared.

"Heron's right," said Samm. "We can't afford the time or the risk."

"Help!" The cry was distant and garbled, but it sounded like a young woman. Kira clenched her teeth. She knew they were right, but . . .

"She could be dying," she said. "I don't want to fall asleep tonight haunted by some lost girl's dying call for help."

"Do you want to fall asleep at all?" asked Heron, and it was Kira's turn to glare.

"Let's keep moving," said Samm, nudging Buddy with his knees. The horse started forward, and Kira's Bobo followed without waiting to be asked.

"Help!"

"I'm going," said Kira, grabbing the reins and turning Bobo's head toward the side of the road. "You can come if you want."

"Why does she just say 'help'?" asked Afa.

"Because she needs help," said Kira, sliding out of the saddle at the edge of the road. The slope was steep and covered with bushes, and she didn't think the horse could make it in the fading light. She tied his reins to a mile marker and unslung her rifle.

"I think she'd be saying, 'Help me,'" said Afa, "or 'Is anybody out there?'"

"They've heard our hoofbeats," said Samm, who suddenly shook his head and swore. "Kira, I'm coming with you."

Heron stayed on her horse. "Can I have your stuff when you're dead?"

"You're the spy," said Samm, gesturing at the hills below. "Sneak around behind them and . . . I don't know, help."

"It's getting dark," said Heron, "and they're already aware of us, and we don't know where they are, or how many of them there are, or how they're armed, or what they're doing. You want me to sneak behind them by what, magic?"

"Just stay here and watch the horses then," said Kira. "We'll be back soon." She climbed over the railing at the side of the road with Samm close behind her, and they picked their way carefully down the side of the hill. The brush was thick, clutching at her boots, and the hill was steep enough that she found herself grabbing the bushes for support, descending almost on hands and knees. The bottom was no better, with thick scrub reaching all the way to the water line.

They heard the cry again, back in the reaches of a narrow gully, and Kira decided they wouldn't be hidden much longer anyway and called out. "Hang on, we're coming!"

"I don't know how they even got back there," said Samm, fighting through the brush behind her. Almost immediately Kira stumbled into a narrow path, and Samm bumped into her from behind as he did the same.

"An animal track," he said. "Deer?"

"Wild dogs," said Kira, looking at the worn earth. "I've seen this kind of track before."

"I figure this is an injured hunter or something, but who follows a dog trail?"

They heard the cry again, closer now, and Kira could hear that something was wrong with the voice—it was garbled, somehow. She sped up. The gully turned into a steep ravine, a giant wall of rock sprouting up on their right, and as they rounded the edge of it they found a small clearing, maybe seven feet wide at the most, and in the center of it a large tan dog. Kira stopped in surprise, the dog staring at her calmly.

Samm stepped around the corner after her, saw the dog, and swore.

"What?" Kira whispered.

"Help!" said the dog, and gave a terrifyingly human grin. "Help!"

"Fall back," said Samm, but in that instant the bushes around them seemed to explode with more dogs, heavy, muscled monsters that leapt up against their chests and backs to knock them down. Samm went down under two of them, and Kira only barely managed to brace herself in time, keeping her feet but getting a deep bite in the arm instead. Another dog tore at her legs, yanking one out from under her, and she fired her gun wildly as she fell. The nearest dog retreated with a yelp, red wounds blossoming on its shoulder, but another lunged to take its place and snapped hungrily at Kira's throat.

"Samm, help!" Kira cried. She felt sharp teeth clamp down on her leg, and more on her collarbone, her heavy travel vest only barely stopping the beast's fangs from piercing deep into her flesh. Beside her the dogs on Samm were scrabbling and growling, snapping wildly with their teeth, and Kira wondered why they hadn't pinned him down yet like they had with her. She tried to raise her rifle and saw that the dogs had pinned that as well, a massive animal pressing it hard into the ground with his bulk. She fired it anyway, hoping to scare it off; a flurry of dirt exploded from the ground, and a dog on the far side of the clearing leapt aside with a howl of pain, but the massive beast on the rifle only snarled at her, baring scythelike fangs.

The tan dog whose call they'd responded to leapt onto Kira's chest, knocking the air out of her, and lunged for her throat to finish her. But inches before contact he fell aside, and Kira felt a hot gush of blood pour onto her chest. She looked up to see Samm standing over her, his rifle gone and a gore-drenched hunting knife in his hands. He slashed at the dog on Kira's shoulder, but the massive dog jumped into him, knocking him again to the ground. Kira brought her gun up and another dog leapt in to wrestle it away from her, his jaws clamped around the barrel and his heavy paws pressing it flat across her chest—away from the creatures menacing Samm. They were trapped.

She heard a shot behind her, and saw the dog at her feet drop lifeless to the dirt; another shot took the dog on her rifle right through the back, and he slumped over her like a hairy boulder. His eyes even with hers, the life draining out of him, he wheezed out a single word in a horrible, inhuman voice:

"Please."

The dog died, its eyes still open barely four inches from Kira's own. She stared back at it in terror, her mouth working soundlessly, her hands gripping the trapped rifle like a lifeline. She heard another shot, and suddenly the dogs were barking rather than growling, short, clipped sounds of communication. The pack turned and fled, the biggest pausing only to snarl "bastard" before disappearing into the trees.

Heron stepped into view, her rifle still tight against her shoulder. She nodded at Kira and kicked the dead animal off her chest.

Even when she was free, Kira couldn't move.

"Did that dog just call me a bastard?" asked Samm.

"We need to get out before they regroup," said Heron. "Come on."

Kira finally managed to speak. "What?"

"We need to go now," said Samm, reaching down with a muddy, bloody hand. "If they get the drop on us, we're dead."

Kira took his hand, struggling to her feet. "What on earth is going on?"

"Watchdogs," said Heron, leading them back out around the wall of rock. "We used them in the war."

"Hyperintelligent dogs bred for battlefield assistance," said Samm. He retrieved his rifle and fell into line behind Kira, walking backward to keep his gun aimed at the dog pack's path of retreat. "They're bigger and tougher and capable of basic speech. We used them for everything over there. I should have recognized, the moment I heard it's voice, but it's been too long."

"You had talking monster dogs?"

"ParaGen made them," said Samm. "Apparently they've gone feral."

Kira remembered the brochure she'd seen at the ParaGen office: It had mentioned both a Watchdog and a dragon. She looked to the sky, but nothing swooped down to tear her apart with angry talons.

She'd seen the word elsewhere as well, "Watchdog," in some of the battlefield reports she'd read in Afa's library. She shook her head, still numb, stumbling through the dog path. It wasn't just the word—she remembered now another thing, a scene in her mind, one of her only memories of her father. She had been attacked by a dog, a giant one, and he had stepped in the way to save her. Had that been a Watchdog, or something else?

Worse was the realization that this thing—this inhuman, unnatural beast—had come from the same place she had. She looked more human, but her origins were closer to those Watchdogs than to any human she'd ever known.

"You've been on Long Island for twelve years," said Samm. "It's a closed environment. The rest of the world's changed."

"They're circling around," said Heron. "Go!"

Please, the dying dog had said, its face burned into Kira's memory. She shook her head and climbed.

CHAPTER NINETEEN

Ariel McAdams had run away from Nandita's house years ago, living by herself on the south side of East Meadow, but after her infant died—almost every woman on Long Island had a dead infant or two, thanks to the Hope Act—she'd left East Meadow altogether. Marcus had found a vague address in the hospital records, and hanging around to look for it had very nearly cost him his freedom. He kept a portable radio to listen in on military reports and to talk to Kira if she ever called him again, and the news as he left East Meadow was grim. The Partial army moved in barely an hour after he left. He had nowhere to go but away. He checked again the address on his small piece of paper: "An island in Islip." It wasn't much to go on, but it was better than nothing.

He learned from his radio that the Partials had set up a perimeter around East Meadow, catching much of the population before they were able to leave, and sending out search teams to comb the island for stragglers and bring them all back to that central location. Still, the island was very big, and a hundred thousand Partials couldn't look everywhere at once. Marcus stayed low, never lighting fires or walking through open spaces, and managed to avoid them for the first few days. *It won't last,* he thought, *but if I can find Ariel and just hunker down instead of traveling, I can last a lot longer.*

On the evening of the second day, his radio chirped to life; his heart sped up, but he quickly realized it was not Kira, nor was it another guerrilla report from the Grid. It was Dr. Morgan.

"This is a general message to the residents of Long Island," said Morgan. "We did not want to invade, but circumstances forced our hand. We are looking for a girl named Kira Walker, sixteen years old, five feet ten inches tall, approximately one hundred eighteen pounds. Indian descent, light-skinned, with jet-black hair, though she may have cut or dyed it to help disguise her identity. Bring us this girl and the occupation ends; continue to hide her, and we will execute one of you every day. Please don't force us to do this any longer than is necessary. This message will cycle through all frequencies and repeat until our instructions have been complied with. Thank you."

The message ended, and Marcus listened in shock to the static that hung in the air.

After a moment of stunned silence, Marcus twisted the tuning knob, searching for the next frequency up. The message was playing there, just like she'd said it would, and Marcus listened to it again with disbelieving ears. He followed it up the dial four more times, as if he was certain it was all a dream, that it wasn't actually real, but every time it was the same: They wanted Kira. They would kill innocent people to find her. They would stop at nothing.

That night he paced the floor of his makeshift hideout,

thinking about the message. That was what this whole invasion was about, from the beginning; they wanted Kira, and they'd do anything to get her. Why was she so important? Why did they need her so badly?

Why hadn't Kira contacted him?

He had no solar panels for his radio, as those had all been commandeered by the Senate and the Grid in the earliest days after the Break, but he had a hand crank, and he worked it furiously to keep the radio active. His days began to blur together, walking all day in search of Ariel, and cranking all night in the hope that Kira would contact him. When he reached Islip he found an unassuming home to hide in, and connected the radio to an exercise bike; as he pedaled he listened to the hiss of radio static buzzing softly through the house. In his crazier moments he thought about going to Manhattan himself to find her, imagining all sorts of horrible scenarios: She'd been captured by Partials, or eaten by lions, or simply trapped by a collapsing building. It was stupid to travel alone, and he'd been stupid to let her. But stopping Kira was something he'd never been able to do.

The radio buzzed, the wheels squeaked. When the sun began to set, he took a break for water and an apple, grown in a heavy tree in the backyard, and then went straight back to his pedaling. Nighttime, he knew, was the most likely time for a call, when it became unsafe to travel and Kira settled down for the night. He pedaled until after midnight—until his legs burned and his feet throbbed and his hands felt blistered against the handlebars. He crawled to his bed, the radio still crackling in his ears, and fell asleep.

In the morning he rode some more, and when he couldn't

take the walls closing him in, he went outside for air. He rubbed his throbbing calves and set out for a walk, looking again for Ariel. *An island in Islip,* he thought. Islip was huge, but only some of it touched the waterfront. He walked up and down it all day, his radio in his backpack, looking for any sign of human life. On the second day he found an island, and on the third he found an occupied house: a trimmed lawn, a cultured garden, a stained porch that had once been wrapped in vines, now studiously cleaned. Marcus walked up the warping wooden steps and knocked on the door.

The sound of a racking shotgun slide was hardly a surprise, and Marcus didn't even flinch.

"Who's there?"

"My name is Marcus Valencio," said Marcus. "We've met before, though it's been a few years. I'm a friend of Kira's."

A pause, then: "Go away."

"I need to talk to you," said Marcus.

"I said go away."

"Nandita's disappeared—"

"Good riddance."

"Ariel, look, I don't know what kind of falling-out you had with them; I don't know why you hate them so much. I can assure you they don't hate you. But that's not why I'm here— they didn't send me, I'm not going to report back to them or tell you to visit them or anything like that. I'm definitely not trying to find Kira to turn her in to Morgan. I'm just trying to figure something out."

Ariel didn't answer, and Marcus waited. And waited. After a full minute he realized she was probably just ignoring him, and turned to leave, but as he did he saw that she had a small bench on her porch; not a swing, just a low wooden seat to sit and watch the world go by. He brushed away some dirt, sat down, and started talking.

"The first question I need to ask you, assuming you're even listening, is how you met Nandita. I've talked to the other girls she adopted, and they all tell me that by the time they met her, you were already with her. Isolde said something about Philadelphia, that you were there when Nandita found you. That's actually the same place Xochi's from, but I don't know if that means anything. What I want to know is . . . where did you come from, I guess? How did you meet Nandita? Was it just the standard 'lone little kid wandering the streets' kind of story? We have a lot of those on the island—a heartwarming number of them, in a weird kind of way. Your family's dead, your neighbors are all dead, you get hungry or scared or whatever and go out looking for something. For me it was milk—we had plenty of cold cereal in my house, and it was the one thing I knew how to make when I was five, so I ate it every day, for every meal, and it didn't take long to run out of milk. I tried a few other meals, peanut butter and jelly on tortillas, that kind of thing. I couldn't even work the can opener." He laughed, and rubbed a tear from the corner of his eye. "So anyway, I went out looking for milk. I don't know where I expected to find any, and the whole world was just sitting there, you know? A couple of things were burning, like a car and a drugstore, but this was Albuquerque, and there wasn't a lot of foliage to help the flames spread around. A couple of hoses were running, just running and running, making a little stream in a gutter. But no people anywhere. I walked all the way to the nearest store I knew—my uncle's place, a little Abarrotes shop just a few blocks away—but it was locked, and I couldn't get in, so I just kept going, and going, and the entire city was just empty. Not a single living person. I found a Walmart, eventually—walk far enough in a town like that and you'll inevitably find a Walmart—and I went inside to look for milk and there was this guy, I'd never seen him before in my life, filling a wheelbarrow with bottles of water. He looked at me, and I looked at him, and he lifted me up into the wheelbarrow and gave me a pack of lunch meat. He even found some milk in the back of the store, shelf-stable so it hadn't gone bad yet, and I ate a bowl of cereal while he gathered up everything he needed. His name was Tray, I don't know his last name. Tray carried me all the way to Oklahoma City before we finally met up with the National Guard. I lost track of him, and I honestly don't know if he even made it the rest of the way here—I'm ashamed to say I haven't thought about him much in the last few years. I suppose if he's here, he lives in the wilds somewhere, fishing or farming or whatever. I'd have found him if he lived in town. And I don't know why I told you that whole story, except to say that those are the kinds of people we need—those are the kinds of people we are. Nobody survived unless they worked together, and helped each other, and that's what makes RM and the Break the most over-the-top natural selection process of all time. I don't know how Nandita found you, but she found you, and she saved you, and she brought you here, and now she's missing and I'm just trying to figure out what's going on. What did she know, what did she do, why was she here? Why are the Partials looking for her?"

"Nandita didn't find me in a Walmart," said Ariel through

the window. Marcus had lulled himself with the sound of his own talking, and Ariel's voice startled him out of his reverie. The curtains were closed, her voice muffled, but the words were clear. "She came to my house. My parents had been dead maybe twenty-four hours. She came and she took me away."

Marcus furrowed his brow, trying to piece together the puzzle. "You think she may have known that you were there? That she came for you specifically?"

"I think she never let me say good-bye."

Marcus turned to look at her, but the curtains were still drawn tight across the window. "I'm sorry," he said. And then, because there wasn't anything else to say: "That sucks."

Ariel didn't respond.

"The Partials are looking for her," said Marcus. "They're looking for Kira because of what she did a few months ago, I think, but they're looking for Nandita because they think she knows something. She *does* know something—Ariel, I saw a photo, of Nandita and some dude with Kira in the middle. They were at a ParaGen complex. Whatever she knew, it had something to do with Kira, and the Partials have mounted a full assault on us in an attempt to find out what it is. If you know what any of this means . . . please, you have to tell us."

There was no response, not for a while. Marcus could hear Ariel's shallow breathing behind the curtain, and waited. It wasn't like he had anywhere else to go.

"Nandita was a scientist," said Ariel finally. "She did experiments."

"On Kira?"

"On all of us."

▼ ▼ ▼

The inside of Ariel's house was, Marcus discovered, full of planter boxes. "I didn't know you were a gardener," he said, his eyes slowly adjusting to the darkness. With so many Partial patrols out combing the island, Ariel had covered each window as thickly as possible.

"I grew up with Nandita," she said. "Gardening's one of the only things I know."

"Is that why you hate her?"

Ariel's voice dropped. "I told you why I hate her."

"The experiments," said Marcus. He looked at her. "Are you ready to talk about them?"

"No," she said, looking off into the street. "But that doesn't mean it's not time to do it." She closed the door, plunging the room into blackness.

Marcus let his eyes adjust, and focused on Ariel's silhouette. "What kind of experiments? Why didn't the other girls say anything about this?"

Her voice sharpened. "Do you know how much I've tried to move on? To pretend like I have a normal life? I got a job I didn't need just so I'd have something to do with myself all day; I got pregnant two years before the Hope Act said I had to. I'm even weeding this stupid garden because . . . because that's what people used to do, before the Break. I've done everything I could, I've even avoided my own sisters—"

"What happened?" Marcus demanded. "What was so bad?"

"It started with breakfast," said Ariel, looking down at the floor. "Nandita would get up early and make us tea—chamomile and peppermint and things like that. She was an herbalist, obviously, so she had all kinds of stuff in the house, and in her hothouse out back. Some we could touch, like the chamomile, but some were in these little glass droppers, with numbers on the sides like specimen jars, and those we couldn't touch. I didn't think anything about it at the time—we got in trouble just for playing in the hothouse, so it didn't seem out of place—but one morning I got up early and came down to help with the tea, and she was putting whatever was in the droppers into it. I wouldn't have thought anything about it, but when I asked what she was doing, she looked guilty—as guilty as I've ever looked getting caught doing something I shouldn't. She played it off, just a new flavoring or something, but I couldn't forget that look. I snuck down again the next day to look again, and she was doing the same thing again, with different droppers this time, keeping notes on a clipboard. She did it almost every day, but I stopped drinking the tea."

"Did you ever see the clipboard?"

"Once, when I snuck into the hothouse, but I think she knew I'd done it, because I could never find it again. It wasn't just notes on the tea, it was notes about us—how fast we were growing, how healthy we were, our eyesight and hearing and things like that. She always had us play games, like coordination games and memory games, and after I saw that clipboard I couldn't even play those anymore. She wasn't playing with her daughters, she was testing us."

"Maybe she was just . . . keeping track," said Marcus. "I don't actually know how a concerned parent is supposed to act, maybe that's normal."

"It wasn't normal," Ariel insisted. "Everything was a test, or a study, or an observation. She didn't play catch, she threw balls to test our reflexes; we didn't play tag, we ran time trials against each other up and down the street. When one of us cut her finger or scraped her knee, she wrapped it up in a bandage, but not before looking at it closely to see every gory detail."

"Why didn't the other girls say anything about this?" asked Marcus. "I asked them everything I could about Nandita—everything they could remember, everything they did together. They didn't say anything about this."

"I tried talking to them a few times," said Ariel, "but they never believed me. They never saw the droppers or the clipboard, and they thought the races were just fun games."

"You'd seen behind the curtain," said Marcus, "so you saw everything else in a different light."

"Exactly."

"But . . ." Marcus paused, phrasing his next words as carefully as he could. "Is it possible—I'm not calling you a liar or anything of the kind, but isn't it possible—that the things you saw as a tiny little girl were completely innocent, and they just made you . . . paranoid . . . and after that you started seeing something insidious where nothing of the kind was intended?"

"You think I didn't ask myself that a hundred times a day?" asked Ariel. "A thousand times? I told myself I was crazy, that I was ungrateful, that I was making it all up, but every time I did, I saw something else that set me off again. Everything she did was some crazy, messed-up way to control us, to make us act a certain way or think a certain way or I don't even know."

"How can you be sure that was the purpose?"

"Because it said so right on the clipboard," said Ariel. "It was about Madison, and it was a study of control."

"What did it say?"

"It said 'Madison: Control.' Why is this so hard for you to grasp?"

Marcus shook his head. "I guess it's just . . . so incongruous from what I saw. Did you tell anybody?"

Ariel snorted. "Have you ever seen an eight-year-old tell an adult that her mom is trying to control her?"

"But at least you tried—"

"Of course I tried," said Ariel. "I tried everything I could think of, and if I'd known what sexual abuse was, I would have accused her of that, too—anything to get out of that house. But she wasn't hurting any of us, and my sisters were all happy, and I was just Angry Little Ariel. Nobody believed me, and when even my sisters wouldn't believe me, I figured maybe the control was already working, and they'd been brainwashed or mind-zapped or worse. I did the only thing I could think of: I destroyed the hothouse."

Marcus frowned, thinking of the elaborate hothouse in Xochi's backyard. "She rebuilt that thing herself?"

"You're thinking of the new one," said Ariel. "This was at the old house: I smashed it to bits with a crowbar: every piece of glass, every pot, every planter box, every dropper I could find, though I know it wasn't all of them. Nandita practically exploded when she came home, which I would have loved to see. I ran away to an empty house on the other side of town, and made it almost a month before they found me. I expected Nandita to . . . well, I don't know what I expected her to do, but I didn't think she was going to bring me back in. She'd had time to calm down, I guess.

She was still as mad as hell, but she brought me back."

"Because she loved you," said Marcus, hopefully.

"Because she needed me for whatever insane experiment she was running," said Ariel. "She couldn't just start over with somebody new." She sighed and rapped her knuckles on the wooden steps. "That was winter, and in spring we moved to the new place—she claimed it was water damage, but of course she just needed a new hothouse to grow her herbs. I ran away a few more times, but 'children are our most precious resource,' and all that, so they kept bringing me back. The instant it was legal for me to leave, I left, and I've never gone back."

"Maybe the experiments had something to do with RM," said Marcus. "You lived there until, what, sixteen?"

"Yeah."

"So she tracked everything, every physical change, up through and including puberty."

"I assume so."

"I'm just thinking," said Marcus. "Madison has the only live baby on the island. Obviously, it's thanks to Kira finding the cure, but what if it were more than that? It's at least something of a coincidence. Do you think it might have been something Nandita did? A heightened immune system, or a stronger fetal . . . I don't know, I'm grasping at straws here. But maybe it was about reproduction."

"I don't know," said Ariel. "I've spent years trying not to think about it."

"And now Nandita's gone," said Marcus. "Completely disappeared, right off the face of the planet. And you know what that means."

Ariel looked up at him. "What?"

"It means she's not guarding her house," said Marcus. "And maybe she left some of those notes behind."

Ariel narrowed her eyes. "That's in East Meadow—that's under Partial control."

Marcus nodded, a hint of his old scheming grin creeping onto his face. "That's where they're throwing everyone they catch. Which is going to make it awfully easy for us to get there."

CHAPTER TWENTY

"I can't lose this backpack," said Afa. "I'm the last human being on the planet."

"He's getting worse," said Samm. Buddy the horse was tamer now, snuffling as Samm patted his neck. Kira was convinced that he and Bobo were brothers, but it might have just been their coloring. They'd been traveling for a week now, and were in the midst of the Appalachian Mountains. Afa had gone through map after map, circling and underlining little roads and towns and peaks, finally insisting on a detour to the top of Camelback Mountain, an imposing giant promising a thousand-foot climb. There was a radio repeater there, he claimed, and with one of his mini Zoble solar panels he could get it up and running again to keep them in contact with the Long Island radios. Heron, to her credit, didn't object, and they made the trek up a winding road through what looked like an old ski resort. The top, however, brought nothing but disappointment: It wasn't a mountain at all but the leading edge of a massive plateau stretching west as far as the Partials could see. Heron scrounged the place for usable equipment, while Afa collapsed in a heap of maps and faulty calculations, insisting that this was wrong, that the mountain was here, they were just in the wrong place. It took them nearly two hours to calm him down, and then only when they agreed to stop for the night and rig up the Zoble anyway. Mountain or plateau, there was still a radio repeater, and Kira marveled at the massive latticework of the old metal tower. Afa assured them he'd set everything up correctly, but night had fallen before he finished, and there was no way to know for sure until the morning. The waiting, the inability to do anything productive, made Kira antsy. She decided to brush Bobo's coat, and Samm joined her.

"I know that we need him," Samm said, his voice low. "I just don't know if he's going to be much use to us at this point."

"Is that how you think of him?" asked Kira. "Some kind of tool?"

"You know that's not what I meant," said Samm. "I'm telling you that I'm worried. We've only been out here a week, and there are at least three weeks to go before we make it to Chicago, probably more. By the time we get there, he'll be a basket case."

"Then we need to help keep him calm," said Kira, and as if on cue Afa stood up, waddling to the horses with his backpack clutched in his arms.

"We need to go back," he said, trying to pick up Oddjob's saddle with one hand. "All my records—everything we're looking for. I've already found it, we don't need to go to a data center, we need to go back. It's right there. It's safe—"

"Easy, Afa," said Kira, taking the saddle from him as gently as she could. His agitation was spreading to the horses, and Samm did his best to keep them calm. "Come here," she said, taking the big man's hand and leading him back to the fire. "Tell me about your collection."

"You've seen it," he said, "but you didn't see all of it. You didn't see the sound room."

"I loved the sound room," she said, keeping her voice soothing. "That's where you had all the ParaGen emails." She kept him talking, hoping the topic would cheer him up, and after nearly half an hour he seemed to calm down. She laid out his bedroll, and he slept with his arms around the backpack like a teddy bear.

"He's getting worse," said Samm again.

"Which is impressive," said Heron, "considering how bad he was to begin with."

"I'm taking care of him," said Kira. "He'll make it to Chicago."

"You're talking as if the worst that can happen is he falls apart and turns useless," said Heron. "I'm expecting him to snap and kill us. Yesterday he thought Samm was trying to steal his backpack; the day before that, he thought you were trying to read his mind. He's accused me of being a Partial twice today."

"You are a Partial," said Samm.

"All the more reason I don't want him to get violent over it," said Heron. "There are three different chemicals in this repeater station that could be used to build a bomb, and I guarantee this idiot savant knows how to use all three of them. He's every bit as brilliant as you said he is, but he is completely broken, and that is not a combination I am comfortable traveling with."

Kira studied Heron in the firelight, flecks of orange light and deep brown darkness dancing over her. She looked tired, and that by itself made Kira scared. Heron had thus far been invulnerable, more capable than Kira had dared to hope, but if she never slept for fear of a madman's betrayal . . . Kira whispered softly, "What do you want to do?"

"Me?" asked Heron. "I want to go home and save the Partials. I thought I made that clear."

"He has a screen in his pack," said Samm, "and a Tokamin to power it—which might also explain his mental problems, if the radiation's gotten to him. Anyway, maybe he can show us what we need to do when we get to Chicago, in case he doesn't make it."

"I'll talk to him tomorrow," said Kira. "He trusts me most."

"Just stop trying to read his mind," said Heron. "I hear that bugs him."

Kira watched the two Partials—the two *other* Partials, she reminded herself—and wondered. What would happen when they reached Chicago? Would it be infested with Watchdogs, or dragons, or something even worse? Would Afa betray them, or would Heron? No matter how much they bantered, Heron always stayed aloof, always stayed an observer more than a participant. What was she observing? Who was she observing for?

Kira slept against a tree, her back to the fire, her hands on her rifle. In the morning they tested the solar panels, and the radio repeater fired up instantly. Afa had done it all without a hitch. Samm nodded, and though he didn't say it, Kira got the distinct impression that he was impressed—surprised, almost certainly, but still impressed. Kira patted Afa on the back. "Good job."

"The Zobles are extremely durable," he said, though his voice seemed off. "They use a mad cow matrix around doped silicon crystals to increase efficiency." Kira nodded, unsure how much of his response had been meaningful science, and how much was pure gibberish. His intelligent persona was mingling with his childlike one, which might be good or bad in the long run. Kira was worried that whatever mental scaffolding allowed him to function was starting to break down.

"Let's test the radio," she said. He complied, flipping it on and turning the knob carefully, falling into the easy patterns of a technical task he'd done countless times before. He turned, and listened, and turned, and listened, until finally he hit on a man-made—or Partial-made—signal. Kira leaned in closely while Afa fine-tuned the connection.

". . . retreated. Our sources on the island say it's only . . ."

"Partials," said Heron.

"Can you tell which ones?" asked Kira. Afa shushed them, his head cocked toward the speakers.

". . . killing a new one every day."

"Northerners," said Heron. "Trimble's people, from B Company."

"What are they talking about?" asked Kira.

Heron narrowed her eyes. "Probably the expiration date."

"We need to find Marcus," said Kira, and gently pulled Afa away from the tuning dial. She and Marcus had set up a rotating schedule of frequencies back when they'd been communicating during the invasion, hoping it would make them harder to listen in on. She added the days in her head, calculating which frequency they'd be using today, and hoped he was still listening.

She turned the dial and clicked on the microphone. "Flathead, this is Phillips, are you there? Over." She clicked off the mic and waited for a response.

Heron smirked dismissively. "Flathead and Phillips?"

"That was his nickname in school," said Kira. "What can I say? He had a kind of a flat head. I started using it to call him couple of weeks ago, because I knew he'd know it was for him, and nobody else would." She shrugged. "Just another layer of paranoid security. Phillips just seemed like the natural counterpart."

"Flathead and Phillips are two types of screwdrivers," said Afa. "Also Frearson and hexhead and clutch and—"

"Yes," said Samm, touching him reassuringly on the shoulder, "we know."

"Don't touch me!" Afa yelled, whirling to his feet. Samm backed off, and Afa yelled again, his face red with fury. "I never said you could touch me!"

"It's okay, Afa," said Kira, trying to calm him down. "It's okay, just hush—I'm going to call again, so we need it to be quiet." The appeal to technical necessity seemed to work, and Afa sat down again. Kira clicked on the mic. "Flathead, this is Phillips, are you there? Come in, Flathead. Please respond. Over." She clicked off, and they listened to the static.

"And clutch," said Afa softly, "and square head, and Pozi, and Mortorq—"

"Phillips, this is Flathead." Marcus's voice was garbled and staticky, and Afa's hand shot forward to tweak the dial. The voice phased in and out. ". . . in very weak, where . . . you in over a week. Over." Marcus's voice resolved into a clear signal, and Kira waited for him to finish before smiling and clicking on the mic.

"Sorry about the downtime, Flathead, we've been busy. We had to . . ." She paused, considering carefully the best way to tell him where they were without giving everything away to anyone else listening in. "Move. We had to move our base camp; they were too close to finding us. Our communication will be intermittent from now on. Over."

"That's good to hear," said Marcus. "I was worried." There was a long pause, but he hadn't said "over," and Kira wasn't sure if she should try to speak again or not. Just as she reached for the mic button, Marcus spoke again. "Are you still monitoring radio traffic? Over."

"We've had very intermittent access, like I said," Kira answered. "What's up? Over."

There was another pause, and when Marcus spoke again, his voice was pained. "Dr. Morgan's taken over the island. She's conquered the whole thing—not controlling it, not like Delarosa did when she seized power, more like . . . like a zoo, almost. Like a ranch. They're rounding up everyone they can find, trapping them here in East Meadow, and then killing them. A new one every day." His voice had faded to a shattered whisper. "Over."

Kira gasped.

"That's what we heard that other person talking about," said Afa, and Kira shushed him with a curt wave of her hand. She clicked the button to talk, already knowing the answer to her question, but compelled to ask it anyway.

"Why are they killing people?" She hesitated before signing off. "Over."

"They're looking for Kira Walker," said Marcus. He was still refusing to give away her identity, but she could hear the pain in his voice, and hoped no one else was listening in on the frequency.

"I warned you it would get bad," said Heron. She gestured at the radio. "I warned him, too."

"Shut up," said Kira.

"You need to turn yourself in," said Heron.

"I said shut up!" Kira roared. "Give me a minute to think."

"I haven't told anyone where she is," said Marcus, still keeping up the ruse. "Not that I even know where she is, but I haven't told anyone the parts I do know. If she turns herself in . . . it's up to her. I'm not going to make that decision for her. Over."

Kira stared at the radio, as if it could crack open and reveal some miraculous answer inside it. *She's killing someone every day,* she thought. *Every day.* It seemed terrifying, horrible, unconscionable, but . . . Was it really any worse than what was already happening to the Partials? Sure, they weren't being executed, but they were still dying. She had insisted to Heron that this quest was more important than stopping those deaths; it was more important to find ParaGen, to find the Failsafe. To see what answers it held and solve this problem forever, for both sides, not just a Band-Aid but a real, permanent cure. If she was willing to leave the dying Partials behind, she had to be willing to leave the dying humans, too, or it was all an act. It was all lies.

She shuddered, growing weak and nauseated at the thought of so much death.

"I don't want to be in this position," she said softly. "I don't want to be the one who everybody's hunting, who has to choose who lives and who dies."

"You can whine about it or you can fix it," said Heron. "Go back now, and you could save both sides: we have a shot at curing the Partial expiration, and Morgan stops killing humans."

"It saves them for now," said Kira. "I want to save them forever." She paused, still staring at the radio, then turned to Heron. "Why are you here?"

"Because you're too stubborn to turn around."

"But you didn't have to come with us," said Kira. "You've been against this mission from the beginning, but you came anyway. Why?"

Heron looked at Samm. "The same reason you did." She looked back at Kira. "The same reason you trusted me: because Samm trusted me, and that was good enough for you. Well, Samm trusts you, and that's good enough for me."

Kira nodded, watching her. "And if we keep going?"

"I'll think you're an idiot," said Heron, "but if Samm still trusts you . . ."

"Your signal's starting to break up," said Marcus. His voice was growing garbled as well. "Where are you? Over."

"We can't tell you," said Kira. *I can't even tell you who I'm with.* "We're looking for something, and I wish I could tell you more, but . . ." She paused, not certain what to say, and eventually just said, "Over."

They waited, but there was no response.

"Passing atmospheric conditions," said Afa. "Our reception might have been temporarily boosted or broken by clouds or storms or virga."

"I still trust you," said Samm. "If you think this is the way to go, I'll follow you."

Kira looked at him, long and hard, wondering what he saw

in her that she didn't. Eventually she gave up, shaking her head. "What about the Failsafe?"

"What about it?" asked Samm.

"We don't know what it is, but the word means something that can't go wrong—or something designed to jump in and fix things when they do. What if the Failsafe can solve all our problems, and all we have to do is find it and activate it?" She thought about Graeme Chamberlain, the member of the Trust who'd worked on the Failsafe and then killed himself as soon as he was done. She shivered despite the heat. "What if it's something horrible, and right when we think we've fixed everything, the Failsafe jumps out and screws it all up again? We don't know what it is. It could be anything."

"How do you know it even matters?" asked Heron.

"Because it has to," said Kira. "The Trust had some kind of plan. The cure for the human disease is in the Partial pheromones, plus there's me, a Partial something-or-other living in a human settlement. None of this is by accident, and we have to figure out what it all means." She paused. "We have to. It's the same old argument I used to have with Mkele: the present or the future. Sometimes you have to put the present through hell to get the future you want." She held the radio to her mouth. "We're going on," she said simply. "Over."

CHAPTER TWENTY-ONE

Another pack of Watchdogs trailed them from Camelback Mountain to the Susquehanna River but never moved in to attack. Samm tied their food and equipment high in the trees every night, and Heron and Kira did their best to protect the horses. Afa stopped talking to Samm completely, and only barely to Heron; the few times he did, both girls began to suspect he was confusing her for Kira. He was better in the mornings, when his mind was rested, but as each day wore on he became more suspicious, more furtive; Kira began to see a third personality emerge, a dangerous cross between the confused child and the paranoid genius. It was this version of Afa that stole a knife from Kira's gear, and tried to stab Samm with it the next time he got too close to his backpack. They got the knife away from him, but Kira worried that the struggle was even more damaging in the long run, feeding his distrust and paranoia.

As they traveled, Kira thought about her experience with the link—about the times she could sense something, and the times she couldn't. She couldn't quite puzzle it out, but that didn't mean it didn't make sense, just that she didn't yet have all the tools she needed to make sense of it. She tried to concentrate, willing herself to feel Samm's emotions, or to transmit something to him, but it didn't seem to work—unless they were in a high-stress situation, like combat. After a few days of trying and failing, she approached Samm about it directly.

"I want you to teach me how to use the link."

Samm looked at her passively, though she knew he must be sending some kind of link data to reflect his emotional state. Was he confused? Skeptical? She clenched her teeth and tried to sense it, but she couldn't. Or she couldn't tell the difference between that and what she thought she was picking up intuitively.

"You can't learn how to link," said Samm. "That's like . . . learning how to see. Either your eyes work or they don't."

"Then maybe I'm already doing it and I just can't recognize it," said Kira. "Teach me how it works, so I know when it happens."

Samm rode in silence for a moment, then shook his head—a surprisingly human gesture he must have picked up from her or Heron. "I don't know how to describe it because I can't imagine not having it," he said. "It's like not having eyes. You use your eyes for everything—vision is so important to human and Partial function that it colors every other aspect of our lives. Even that—the word 'colors' as a synonym for 'affects.' It's a visual metaphor being used to describe something nonvisual. When you imagine someone trying to function without sight, that's how I imagine someone trying to function without the link."

"But vision fails all the time," said Kira. "Blind people can still function in society, and I bet all of them understand metaphors like 'colors.'"

"But blindness is still considered a handicap," said Samm, "at least among Partials."

"Humans, too."

"Okay then," said Samm. "And no one would argue that blindness is a stylistic difference, it's literally a lessening of ability."

"Take a look at this," said Kira. She widened her eyes, making an exaggerated "surprised" face, and Samm didn't respond. "Did you see it?"

"See what?"

"I just opened my eyes really wide."

"You do that all the time," said Samm. "Different parts of your face and body move constantly while you talk; Heron does it, too. I used to think she had a facial tremor."

Kira laughed. "It's called body language. Most of the social cues that you communicate with pheromones, we communicate with little facial movements and hand gestures. This means I'm surprised." She widened her eyes again. "This means I'm skeptical." She raised her eyebrow. "This means I don't know something." She shrugged, holding her hands to the sides, palms up.

"How do you . . ." Samm paused, in the space where a human would furrow his brow or wrinkle his lips—something to signify confusion—and Kira assumed that he was sending out "I'm confused" data through the pheromone link. "How do you teach that to each other? A new member of your culture, or a new child—how long does it take them to learn all these weird little hand signals?" He tried to emulate the shrug, looking stiff and mechanical.

"That's like asking a Spanish speaker why they bother with all those weird words when it would be so much easier to just speak English," said Kira. "Do you have to teach the link data to new Partials?"

"We haven't had new Partials in years," said Samm, "but no, of course not, and I think I see where you're going with this. Do you really mean to say that this 'body language' is as inherent to human beings as the link is to Partials?"

"That's exactly it."

"But then how—" He stopped, and Kira could only guess what link data he was expressing now. "I was about to say, 'How can you understand each other over the radio when half your communication is visual?' but I suppose the link doesn't transmit over the radio either, so we're even there. But on the other hand, Partials can still understand each other in the dark."

"I'll grant you that," said Kira, "but we also have a lot of verbal cues you don't. Listen to these two sentences: 'Are you going to *eat* that?' Now: 'Are *you* going to eat that?'"

Samm stared back, and Kira almost laughed at what she assumed was his confusion. "I suppose you're going to tell me that the difference in volume changes the meaning of the sentence? We use the link for most forms of emphasis like that."

"I suppose that gives us a leg up on radio communication," said Kira, and waggled her eyebrows. "This may be the key to winning the war."

Samm laughed, and Kira realized that laughter, at least, seemed to be fairly common among the Partials. They probably didn't need it, since they could express enjoyment or humor through the link, but they still laughed anyway. Maybe it was built into some human segment of their custom genome? A vestigial response? "Enough about body language," said Kira. "I want to practice the link, so hit me."

"Hitting you won't make the link easier to detect."

"It's an expression," said Kira. "Send me some link data—start throwing it out there. I need to practice trying to pick it up."

They spent the next few days practicing, with Samm sending her simple pheromonal messages and Kira trying everything she could to feel them, and to recognize which emotions they represented. A couple of times she thought she could sense it, but most of the time she was completely lost.

They passed through the Appalachians on a wide highway marked with a number 80, run-down and crumbling in places, but mostly unbroken. They made better time across the river, leaving the dog pack and, they hoped, any other potential observers far behind them. With less fear of attack they could travel more openly, but the open stretches of farmland only accentuated what Kira understood was a growing agoraphobia in Afa, and he tried to stop at almost every town they passed through, holing up in a bookstore or library and obsessively sorting the titles. Much of the area was covered with long, low hills, and he did better when they could travel between them, comfortably hemmed in by reassuring masses that, while not buildings, at least limited his sight line. Kira hoped that this kind of terrain would continue all the way to Chicago, but as they moved west, the land got flatter and flatter. When they crossed the Allegheny River and the midwestern plains stretched out before them, Afa's mutterings grew more sporadic and disorganized. By the time they crossed the border from Pennsylvania to Ohio, Kira realized he wasn't just talking but arguing, mumbling furiously at a choir of voices in his head.

Afa's lone saving grace in the Midwest were the cities, which were bigger here and more frequent; Heron, on the other hand, grew more cautious in each, always wary of an attack by some unseen force. They stayed on Interstate 80 as much as possible, passing through Youngstown and following it north to a place called Cleveland. Both were eerie, empty cities, lacking the kudzu that gave such a junglelike quality to Kira's home on the East Coast. New York was still and silent, but the vegetation at least gave it a feeling of life. Here the cities were dead, bare and crumbling, eroded by wind and weather, fading monuments in a vast and featureless plain. It made Kira lonely just to look at them, and she was as happy as Heron to leave them behind. Their road took them along the southern edge of a rolling gray sea, which Samm insisted was just a lake; even seeing it on the map, Kira found it hard to believe that it wasn't another part of the ocean she'd left behind. She'd never liked that ocean before, feeling small and exposed on its shores, but now she ached for it. She ached for her friends—for Marcus. Bobo nickered and shook his mane, and she patted him gratefully on the neck. How the old world ever got by without horses, she couldn't understand. You couldn't pet a car.

In a city called Toledo the lake met a wide river snaking up from the south, and they reined in their horses on the edge of it, a ledge off which there was a fifty-foot drop down to the raging river. There was no longer any road before them; the rubble of the I-80 bridge lay in the river far below.

"What happened here?" asked Kira. The precipice was dizzying, the wind whipping through her hair. "The bridge looks too new to just fall apart like this."

"Look at the beams," said Samm, pointing below to the metal infrastructure twisting out of the concrete on their side of the chasm. "This was blown up."

"That should make you happy," said Heron to Afa. Afa was turning in circles on his horse Oddjob, ignoring them and muttering threats that Kira guessed were only half directed at the horse.

"We'll have to go around," said Samm, pulling Buddy's head to the left to head back. Kira stayed near the edge, peering across to the far side. The fallen bridge had made a sort of barrier in the river, not big or tall enough to block its flow, but intrusive enough to send the placid river roiling and bubbling over the rubble before smoothing again on the other side.

"Who would have blown it up?" she asked.

"There was a war," said Heron. "You probably don't remember it, you were pretty young."

Kira did her best not to glare at her. "I know there was a war," she said. "I just don't understand which side had a good reason to blow up a bridge. You told me the Partials focused on military targets, so they wouldn't have done it, and the humans wouldn't have destroyed their own structures."

"That's the attitude that started the war," said Heron, and Kira was surprised by the angry undercurrent in her voice.

"I don't understand," said Kira.

Heron looked at her, a mixture of calculation and disdain, then turned and looked out over the river. "Your tacit assumption of sovereignty. This bridge belonged as much to the Partials as it did to the humans."

"Partials were given property rights in 2064," said Afa, staring at the road as Oddjob turned him around and around. "These rights were never recognized by state courts, and Partials were still unable to get loans to buy anything anyway. *New York Times*, Sunday edition, September 24."

"There's your answer," said Samm, pointing down at the line of broken water as the river rolled over the fallen bridge. "There, sticking out of the water about twenty yards out." Kira looked, following the line of his finger and shading her eyes against the spots of glare off the water.

Where Samm was pointing, Kira saw a metal prong sticking out of the water, lodged somehow in the pieces of the bridge. She pulled out her binoculars and looked again, focusing them in on the metal, and saw that it was the cannon of a tank. The body bulged up, just under the flow of water, wedged between two pieces of concrete and steel. The markings on the side read 328. "There was a tank on the bridge when it went down."

"Probably dozens of them," said Samm. "328 was a Partial armored platoon. I'm guessing the local militia rigged the bridge and blew it when the Partials were crossing, killing as many as they could."

"They wouldn't have done that," said Kira.

"They did that and worse," snapped Heron.

Samm's voice was more gentle. "By the end of the war they

were desperate enough to do anything," he said. "The Partial victory was already decisive, and the release of RM made everything worse. Humans were dying by the millions. Some of them were ready to blow up anything they could—their bridges, their cities, even themselves—if it meant killing even one of us."

"Really great ethics," said Heron.

"What about the fleet off New York Bay?" Kira snapped back, whirling to face her. "I saw it in Afa's documents—twenty human ships brought down, all hands lost, the most devastating attack of the war."

"Twenty-three," said Afa.

"Self-defense," said Heron.

"Are you kidding me?" asked Kira. "What could the Partials possibly be defending themselves from?"

Heron raised her eyebrow. "Why do you keep saying that?"

"What?"

"Saying 'them' instead of 'us.' You're a Partial—you're different, but you're one of us. And you're most definitely not one of them. You keep forgetting it, but your human buddies aren't going to. And they will find out."

"What does that have to do with anything?" asked Kira.

"You tell me," said Heron. "What's your little boyfriend Marcus likely to do to you when he finds out what you are?"

"Easy," said Samm. "Everybody just calm down. This argument is not going to get us anywhere."

"Neither is this bridge," Kira growled, and turned Bobo's head to lead him back down to the highway. She wanted to yell, to scream at them both, even at Afa—that this was their fault, that they had fought this war and destroyed the world before she was even old enough to defend it. But this one part of it, this massive act of destruction, she couldn't even blame on them. That was the worst part of all. "Let's find another way around."

Chicago was flooded.

It had taken them nearly a month to get there, anticipation rising with each new day. All their solar panels were gone, powering a string of radio repeaters behind them—if the records they found included a way to extend the expiration date or synthesize the cure for RM, they could radio it home in seconds instead of traveling another month back through dangerous country. Afa grew more eager as the city appeared before them, a giant metropolis that seemed even bigger, if possible, than New York City. It sat on the shores of another giant lake, curving around the eastern and southern sides, and spread out into the plains as far as Kira could see—towering skyscrapers, elevated trains and monorails, vast factories and warehouses and endless rows of houses and offices and apartments.

All crumbling. All mired in oily, swampy water.

"Is it supposed to look like that?" asked Kira.

"Not a chance," said Samm. They stood on the top of an office complex on the edge of the city, surveying the scene with his binoculars. "It's not all flooded, just most of it; looks like there are rises and falls in the terrain, though nothing huge. I'd bet most of the water's just a few inches deep, maybe a few feet in the worst places. Looks like the lake overflowed its boundaries."

"Chicago had dozens of canals running through the city," said Heron. "Some of your shallow streets are going to be deep rivers, but they should at least be easy to spot."

"Those canals were the most heavily engineered waterways in the world," said Afa proudly, as if he had engineered them himself. "The old-world engineers actually reversed the flow of one of the rivers—those are the glories we used to have, when mankind kept nature under tight control." His eyes glowed, and Kira could only imagine what the thought did to him; after four weeks in a wilderness run wild, a city so fiercely technological must have felt like an answer to a prayer.

"Nature has fought back," said Heron. "Let's hope it hasn't flooded your data center."

"Here's the address," said Afa eagerly, pulling a folded piece of paper from his backpack; another email printout, with a street address circled in red near the bottom. "I've never been here, so I don't know where it is."

Samm looked at the paper, then at the gargantuan city ahead of them. "Cermak Road. I don't even know where to start looking." He glanced back down at his paper, then down at the streets below. "We're going to need a map."

"That tower is probably an airport," said Kira, pointing to a tall concrete pillar near the shores of the lake. "They'll have an old car rental place, and that's bound to have some kind of local road map." The others agreed, and they climbed back down to their horses. The roads to the airport were mostly dry, but the few patches of flooding still proved problematic. Some of the streets were full of shallow standing water, others were merely muddy, but here and there a street had become a moving stream or a rushing river. Manhole covers bubbled with encroaching lake water, pavement buckled from leaking water mains, and sometimes entire streets had caved in and washed away, thanks to overloaded sewer pipes far below. The smell was overpowering, but it smelled like lake, not sewer. Humanity had been gone so long it didn't even smell bad anymore. It took them all day to reach the airport, and they camped for the night in a ground-floor office. The horses they tethered to a rusting X-ray machine. As Kira had suspected, the rental car center had a number of local maps, and they pored over them by the light of Heron's flashlight, planning their route for the following day.

"The data center is here," said Samm, pointing to a spot near the coast, smack in the middle of the thickest part of downtown. "With the lake right there, and canals on every side, I think we'll be lucky if we don't end up swimming there. And we'll have to hope the water's not poisonous this close to the toxic wasteland."

"The horses will never make it," said Kira.

Heron looked at the scale in the corner of the page, trying to calculate distance. "That's a long walk without them. It looks like we can take Highway 90 almost the whole way there; if it's elevated, like some of these have been, we shouldn't have any problems with the flooding until the last few blocks."

"And then what?" asked Kira. "Leave the horses tied up to the freeway? If Chicago's anything like Manhattan, they'll be eaten by lions in the first few hours. Or those freaky talking dogs."

Samm almost smiled. "You're still hung up on those, aren't you?"

"I don't understand how the rest of you aren't," said Kira.

"If we leave them free enough to escape from predators, they won't be there when we get back," said Heron. "If you want horses at all, we have to take the risk."

"How far is it?" asked Kira, looking closer at the map. "We

could leave them here, or upstairs maybe—if they're penned in, they're not in as much danger, and we know we could find them again."

"I don't want to walk," said Afa from the other side of the room, fiddling with his portable screen. Kira didn't even know he'd been listening.

"You'll do fine," she said, but Samm shook his head.

"I don't know if he will. I think he's weaker now than when we started the trip."

"If he can't handle the walk there, he won't be able to handle the walk back home," said Kira. "We leave the horses somewhere safe, and pick them up on the way back."

Heron examined the map, tracing the route with her finger. "We go out here and get straight on 90; it's a toll road, but I've got a few quarters. That links up here, to 94, and goes right into the heart of downtown. We get off on this big interchange here, and it's a straight shot across to ParaGen, maybe only a mile of surface streets." It was hard to tell on the map what kinds of buildings lay along the route, since it was intended for tourists and business travelers; a few key hotels and convention centers were called out, and a handful of famous local restaurants, but nothing that looked convenient to their path. Finally Heron zeroed in on a building shaped like a lopsided circle, just off the highway. "This says 'Wrigley Field.' That's a baseball stadium. There'll be an off-ramp from the highway, and plenty of places to pen the horses in—they'll have food, and they'll be contained and protected."

Kira studied it, then nodded. "I suppose it's our best bet, and if things don't go as planned, we can adapt on the road. Let's get some sleep, and head out at first light."

The airport had several restaurants, and in the back kitchens they were able to scrounge together several cans of sealed food—mostly bulk-size cans of fruit, but one place had a rack of canned chicken, and a sagging Mexican restaurant had some gallon cans of refried beans and cheese sauce. Most of the fruit had turned, and the beans smelled just suspicious enough that they decided not to risk it, but the chicken and cheese made for a tasty if slightly messy meal. They started a fire in a metal garbage can and warmed it up as best they could, serving it on foam trays—so well-preserved they looked like new—and eating with plastic forks from a bag in the back of an old sandwich shop. Afa ignored them, eyes glued to his screen, eating only when Kira placed the food directly in front of his face. He was mumbling about security codes, and they left him to his work.

Kira took the first watch, talking softly to Bobo as he nibbled on an overgrown planter box. Afa was still working when Heron took over at two in the morning, but when Kira woke up at seven he was asleep in his chair, slumped down over the darkened screen. Kira couldn't help but wonder if he'd fallen asleep naturally, or if Heron had somehow knocked him unconscious.

They packed up and rode out, following the map and discovering that Heron was right, and the highway was elevated. They passed through mile after mile of Chicago as if on a bridge through a swamp, looking down at houses and parks and schoolyards all flooded and soggy, the oily surface of the water glinting brightly in the morning sun. Here and there a river moved through the city, evidence of an extremely high water table, and Kira marveled that the city had ever been dry at all. It must have taken an immense effort for the old world to keep the lake and the rivers and even the groundwater in check. Part of her felt proud, as Afa had been the day before, smiling to think that she was a part of such an amazing legacy—a species so intelligent, so capable and determined, that they could hold back the sea and turn rivers around in their paths. To have taken this marshy coastline and turned it into a megacity was a feat to be proud of.

Another part of her thought only of the towering pride. How easy would it be for a civilization so amazing to reach just a little too far? To do something it shouldn't? To make one sacrifice or one compromise or one rationalization too many? If you can build a city so great, what's to stop you from building a person? If you can control a lake, what's to stop you from controlling a population? If you can subjugate nature itself, why should a sickness ever get out of hand?

Kira thought about the Trust: about all their secret plans and hidden intentions. About the Failsafe. What was it? Were they trying to save the world, or destroy it? The answers were in the data center, and the data center was in their grasp.

They followed Interstate 90 on a straight course northwest, until at last it arced farther west to join 94. To their dismay it began to dip down here, not just losing its elevation but literally running below the level of the rest of the city—not under the ground, but sunken into it. What had once been a highway was now a lazy river, with only the tops of the tallest trucks poking out above the water.

"We'll need to double back," said Samm.

"And what," asked Heron, "travel through the surface streets? You saw the sinkholes we passed trying to get to the airport—with this much water covering everything, we'll never know whether we're stepping into solid ground or an underwater pit."

Kira looked behind them, scanning the cityscape, then back at the river. "It's too long for the horses to swim."

"It's miles," said Heron.

"Let's find a boat," said Afa.

Kira looked at him. "Are you serious?"

"You said this road goes straight up to the data center, right? We know it's deep enough for a boat, so let's leave the horses and take one."

Samm nodded. "I have to admit that's a pretty good idea. Let's find something that can float and carry us."

Kira angled Bobo toward the side of the highway and looked off, scanning the city around them. Here at the point of junction the highway was ridiculously wide, dozens of lanes across, and nearly at ground level. The north side was some kind of a rail station, but the south looked like a residential neighborhood, and probably the best bet for finding a small boat. She slid off Bobo's back, stretched her legs, and grabbed her rifle. "One of you come with me. Let's see what we can find over there."

"I'll go," said Samm. He jumped off Buddy and followed Kira, catching up to her quickly with long, easy strides. They clambered over a cement barrier, then another and another, countless different roads and lanes and directions all running into and past and around one another. "It's a good plan," he said.

Kira hoisted herself over another barrier. "The boat? Afa's not an idiot."

"I think I've been unfair to him."

Kira grinned. "Don't get all mushy over one good idea."

"It's not just that," he said, "it's everything. He's been stronger than I expected. Or more resilient, at least." He followed her over the barrier.

Kira nodded absently, scanning the trees at the edge of the road. "He's been through a lot."

"Eleven years alone," said Samm, "running and hiding without anyone to help or share it with. It's no wonder his mind broke." He shrugged. "He's only human."

Kira froze. "Wait," she said, turning to face him. "You're saying he's . . . that it's okay that he's crazy because he's human?"

"I'm saying that he's done much better for himself than a lot of humans would have," said Samm.

"But you think being human is a liability," said Kira. "That being human somehow excuses his deficiencies because hey, at least he's not crapping in his pants all the time."

"That's not what I said."

"But it's what you meant," said Kira. Is that what you thought about me? 'She's pretty smart, *for a human*'?"

"You're a Partial."

"You didn't know that."

"We are engineered to be perfect," said Samm. "We're stronger and smarter and more capable because we were built that way—I don't see why it's so bad to recognize it out loud."

Kira turned away and vaulted the last barrier, splashing down in the thin mud beyond. "And you wonder why all the humans hate you."

"Wait," said Samm, following closely behind her. "What's this really about? You don't normally get this angry."

"And you don't normally make sweeping racist statements

about how stupid humans are."

"Heron does," said Samm. "You never bite her head off."

She spun to face him. "So you should be allowed to hate us, too? Is that the problem—I'm being unfair to you?"

"That's not—" He stopped in midsentence. "Ah."

"'Ah'? What 'ah'?"

"I see what this is about, and I apologize for bringing it up."

"I told you what this is about. Don't try to shift the blame anywhere but your own perfectly engineered shoulders."

"You keep calling the humans 'us,'" he said softly. "You're still identifying with them."

"Of course I'm identifying with them," she said. "It's called human empathy. That's what humans do, we identify with each other—we care about each other. Obviously Heron has no heart whatsoever, but you, I thought, were different. You . . ." Her voice trailed off. How could she explain the betrayal she felt when he talked like that about people she loved? When he continued to not understand how horrible that kind of attitude was? She turned away and started walking.

"I'm sorry," he said behind her. "But Heron is right. You're going to have to figure out who you are."

Kira threw her hands in the air, yelling back without turning around. "So I can 'choose a side'?" She was crying now, and the tears were hot on her cheeks.

"So you can be happy," said Samm. "You're tearing yourself in half."

CHAPTER TWENTY-TWO

It took them an hour to find a boat, never talking to each other beyond simple monosyllables: Here. There. No. It was a small motorboat, maybe twelve feet from stem to stern, mounted on a trailer and packed into a backyard practically overflowing with trucks and off-road vehicles. Kira walked around it, splashing in the shallow water, determining how it was attached, how to unhook it, where they might be able to push a truck or break a fence to get the thing out of the yard. There didn't seem to be a way. She simmered, still angry at Samm, but finally spoke without looking at him.

"I don't think we can get it out."

"I agree." His voice was plain and unemotional, but he was always like that. Was he as mad at her as she was at him? The thought that he might not be made her even angrier than before.

"Whoever lived here was obviously an outdoorsman," said Samm, glancing around at the dirt bikes and camping trailers lying near the immovable boat. "He might have something smaller in his garage."

"Or *her* garage," said Kira, immediately regretting the tone of petulance in her voice. *You can be mad at him without being an idiot, Kira.* She focused on the problem at hand, looking at the truck's tires again, wondering how far it would get if she tried to start it: The tires were flat, and the gas in the tank was twelve years old, so if it started at all, it wouldn't get far. To the end of the street? The end of the driveway? They were only a block from the south fork of the highway river; if they could just get that far, they could dump it in and row it the rest of the way. She tried the door to the house, supposing that if the owners were home when they died, the keys to the truck might be inside. The door was locked, and she pulled her pistol to shoot off the lock when suddenly Samm emerged from the garage, loudly banging a small metal rowboat against the door frame.

"There are oars inside," he said, nodding back toward the garage.

"It's kind of small."

"It's the best I could find," said Samm, "I'm only a Partial." There was no vitriol in his voice as he said it, because there never was, but Kira felt a small surge of anger that could have come from the link—or it could have come from her own raging mind. Whether she felt it or not, he was clearly still thinking about their argument, and the revelation gave her a joint thrill of anger and triumph. She forced herself to keep a cool expression and went inside to get the oars.

By the time they made it back to the highway junction, first rowing and then carrying the boat up the small incline, Heron and Afa were standing alone. "I tied up the horses in the train yard," said Heron.

"She made me get off my horse," said Afa. "I hate that horse."

"You should be glad to be rid of it, then," said Kira. She looked at Heron pointedly. "They're safe?"

"I gave yours a gun just in case."

"Perfect," said Kira. "Ready to go?"

Heron glanced at Samm, then back at Kira, calculating silently. "What happened between you two?"

"Nothing," said Samm. Heron raised an eyebrow.

They slipped the boat back into the water, helping Afa in and positioning him carefully in the center. The boat sank lower under his weight, but it held, and he clutched his backpack tightly to his chest. "We need a bigger boat. I brought all our nacho sauce."

"Yum," said Kira. She wanted to look at Samm, to see if he was rolling his eyes or making some other outward sign of derision over Afa's childlike behavior, but she didn't dare, and she knew he wouldn't be anyway.

"It will get wet," said Afa.

"We won't let it get wet," said Samm. They shoved the boat farther from the shallow, inclined shore, and Heron and Kira piled in after Afa. They took the oars, and Samm pushed them even farther out before getting in himself. He was wet to the waist, and dripped and sloshed all over the bottom of the boat; Afa reached out dispassionately to knock him back over the side, but Kira held him back. They settled in, kept their weight as balanced as possible, and began to row.

The river grew deeper and deeper as they rowed out into it. The lines of cars, stopped or crashed in their drivers' last moments of life, looked like lines of squat brown animals slowly wading into a watering hole: Here was one with just its front tires wet; here was another with its engine submerged; here was one with its only the roof and antenna poking up from the water. They rowed without speaking, the water lapping at the edges of the boat, and soon even the diesel trailers and giant shipping trucks were submerged, with only the very tops shining up through the water like steep metal sandbars.

The edges of the river highway were lined with trees, tall and no longer limited by human supervision; they had reclaimed backyards, parks, and even some portions of the road. Every mile or so they passed under a bridge, the old roadways between one side of the highway and the other, and often these were hung with moss and vines—not kudzu, but something with smaller, darker leaves that Kira didn't recognize. She plucked one off as they glided beneath it, and she saw that it was waxy to the touch. She rubbed it softly between her fingers, wondering what it was called, and dropped it into the water.

The greater hazard below the bridges were the flocks of water-birds that had taken up residence there, streaking the concrete supports with yellow-white droppings. Under the third bridge a roosting flock was disturbed by their passage and flew away, first diving down before swooping away from the water and soaring high into the air. Afa flailed at them, startled by the sight and sound of a hundred swarming birds, almost toppling the boat, but Kira was able to calm him. She handed her oar to Samm and focused her attention on keeping Afa mellow. The river was long, even longer than they had expected, and Kira started to wonder how accurate their map had been. Right as she was ready to turn them around, certain they'd somehow missed their turn, they passed the ballpark Heron had seen on the map. Kira announced that they were close, and listened and nodded reassuringly as Afa told her about the technical specs of the data center.

The road rose above the water only once, an overpass in the final interchange before leaving the highway and entering the city. They carried the boat over it, scanning the city as they did, and Kira pointed out the building she guessed was the data center—a fat brick building with two square towers. They walked down the other side of the overpass and got back in the boat, though they could only row for a few more blocks before the depth became too inconsistent to bother. They waded the final mile, probing the ground before them with sticks to keep from falling into any sudden sinkholes. There were two, and they had to go a full block out of their way to avoid the second one. When they arrived at the data center, Kira smiled proudly—it was the same building she'd spotted from the hill. The water level reached almost to their knees, and Samm looked up at the multistory building.

"I hope the computer you're looking for isn't on the first floor," he said. "Or in the basement."

"I won't know until we get them turned on," said Afa, splashing toward the corner. "The emergency generator should be outside somewhere. Find some paint thinner."

Kira glanced at Samm, then immediately looked away, aiming her question at Heron instead. "Paint thinner?"

Heron shook her head. "Maybe he's doing some home improvement projects."

Afa's answer was lost as he walked around the corner of the building, and Kira and the Partials hurried to catch up.

". . . breaks apart the resin," he said. "It's not an effective long-term solution, because the fumes it puts out are toxic, but it'll get that motor running better than it has in twelve years." He was back in lucid mode again, perhaps more lucid and eager than she had ever seen him—here, in his element, he was all genius with none of the child to slow him down. It made Kira, in contrast, feel like the slow one.

"What are you talking about?" asked Kira, tapping the ground ahead nervously with her stick as she raced to keep up.

"That," said Afa, rounding the back corner of the building. Behind the data center was a series of power poles, cables, and giant metal blocks, once painted gray but now mottled with rust. He splashed up to the gate and wrestled with the locks. "We need to get these started, at least one of them, and the best way is with paint thinner."

"Let me do it," said Heron, pulling a pair of thin metal prods from somewhere on her belt. She inserted them in the lock on the fence, twisted them slightly, and the lock popped open. Afa raced in, nearly losing his balance in the water. The metal blocks were marked with various icons and labels and warnings. Even looking at them, Kira wasn't sure what they were for.

"This place was one of the biggest data centers in the world," said Afa. "If it lost power, half the planet lost their data. It pulled power from the overall power grid like everybody else, but it had all these as backups—if anything happened to the main grid, or even to one of these generators, there were ten other generators on site to pick up the slack. They're diesel-powered, so we just need to find the . . . I don't understand." He sloshed off in another direction, and Kira read the labels on the nearest metal block.

"These aren't power generators," she said, "they're . . . cold generators?"

"It's a cooling system for the data center," Afa shouted. He splashed back, nearly falling as he came. "I've never seen one this big. But where are the generators?"

"Let's look inside," said Heron, and they followed her in. The building was more ornate than Kira expected, an older style of architecture done with brick and plaster and wood paneling. Even the ceilings were vaulted. The first floor of the building was just as flooded as the outside, thanks to the shattered glass and poor seals in the doorways; it came just past their knees, and a coating of dust and debris floated on the top of it like a crust. There were a few offices, but most of the floor was taken up with a single giant room filled end to end with rows of computer towers—not just screens, like the portable computer Afa carried with him, but giant bricks of memory and processing power, each one taller and wider than Kira herself. The first floor had hundreds, lined up like obelisks, bits of wire and insulation floating in the water around them.

"That's not good," said Samm. "We'll never get these running again."

"Then we hope what we want's on another floor," said Afa, and splashed down a row of servers to a large metal tank. "And we hope they have more of these up there with it."

"It's a gas tank," said Kira, and Afa nodded enthusiastically.

"And the generator's right next to it. This is where we need the paint thinner."

"I still don't get that," said Kira.

"Gas degrades over time," said Samm, nodding as if he

understood everything. "The petroleum inside turns into resin, like a thick gum. That is why none of the cars work anymore."

"Everybody knows that," said Kira.

"That is why he's looking for paint thinner," said Samm. "It breaks down resin and turns it back into gasoline. The exhaust would be toxic, like he said before, but the generator would run."

"At least long enough for us to get our data," said Afa. He clambered up on a metal stair and started straining against the valve on the tank.

"I'll open it," said Samm, pushing him gently aside. "You two find some paint thinner."

"Yes, sir," said Kira primly, and managed to stifle a curtsy as she turned to leave. Heron followed her out and spoke softly as they left the building.

"Glad to see you two getting along so well," said Heron. "Anything you want to tell me before you stab Samm in the face?"

Kira didn't answer, scanning the storefronts for anything that looked like it might sell hardware. She took a breath, trying to calm herself. "Do you think humans are inferior?"

"I think everyone's inferior."

Kira stopped, looking back to glare at Heron, then turned again and kept walking. "Do you think that's the answer I'm looking for?"

"It's a fact," said Heron. "Facts are too busy being true to worry about how you feel about them."

"But you're a person, not a fact—how do *you* feel about it?"

"Partials live in a caste system," said Heron. "The soldiers are the best fighters, the generals are the best leaders and problem solvers, the doctors have the most knowledge and manual dexterity. It's how we were built—there's no shame in knowing that you've been outsmarted by a general, because they are designed, from the genetic level, to outsmart everyone." She bowed slightly, an immodest smile creeping over her face. "But I'm an espionage model, and we're designed to beat everyone at everything. Independent operatives who function outside the normal command structure, facing problems in every category and overcoming them without outside assistance. How could I not feel superior when I demonstrably am?" She paused, and her smile turned more serious. "When I suggested that you might be an espionage model as well, that's pretty much the best compliment I can give."

"You don't get it," said Kira. "You or Samm or any of the other Partials." She stopped walking again, throwing up her hands in frustration. "How do you think this is going to end? You kill us and we kill you until nobody's left?"

"I'm pretty sure we'll win," said Heron.

"And then what?" asked Kira. "In two more years you'll all be past your twenty-year limit, and you'll be dead. And if any of us live through the war, we'll die with you, because we need your pheromone to live. And what if we avoid the war? What if we find something in this data center and we cure RM and expiration and we go on with our lives? We'll both live and we'll both hate each other and sooner or later we'll have another war, and we're never going to escape it unless we change the way we think. So no, Heron, I don't like your facts or your attitude or your self-righteous explanation of why it's okay to be a racist, fascist jerk. Damn it, where is there a hardware store?" They turned another corner, and Kira saw a sign that looked promising, storming toward it in waterlogged boots. She didn't bother looking to see if Heron was behind her.

The store was odd, a kind of combination pet store/home repair store, but they did have paint thinner, and Kira loaded up with two gallon cans per fist. When she turned around, Heron was right behind her, and she grabbed four cans as well. They stomped back through the water to the generators, being careful to follow the same exact route in case there were any collapses or sinkholes they'd missed on the way out.

By the time they got back, Samm and Afa had managed to open the gas valve, and Afa was probing the tank with a long piece of rebar.

"Glued almost solid," he said. "This could take a while."

"There are a few more cans in the store if we need them," said Kira, setting the cans heavily on the metal grating near the tank. "I brought a funnel."

"First we need to make sure this is the right tank," said Afa. "Samm looked around, and there are several more on this floor, and from the looks of this wiring there are more upstairs as well."

"That means we can't put it off any longer," said Samm. "We have to figure out which server ParaGen's data is on."

Afa nodded. "Records of which servers are ParaGen's will be found in an administration office; probably upstairs."

They found the nearest staircase and trudged up; Kira exulted in the feeling as she finally stepped up above the water level. The second story held nothing but servers, as did the third, but the fourth had a number of small offices along one row of broken windows. Afa set down his pack and zipped it open, pulling out a Tokamin—a phone-shaped battery that provided nearly perpetual power, but only in small quantities, and the device's benefits had traditionally been negated by the ambient radiation it emitted. The old world had never produced them beyond the proof of concept, and though the survivors on Long Island had toyed with the idea, they'd deemed it too dangerous for practical use. When you only have a handful of humans left, there's no sense giving them cancer. Afa, it seemed, had made his own; Kira stepped back from it, and noticed that Samm and Heron did the same. Afa pressed the button to power it on, and Kira cringed, half expecting a burst of gaseous green energy, but all it did was light up a small doughnut-shaped icon in the center. He plugged it into the desk computer, one of the black-framed glass ones Kira had seen in the Manhattan ParaGen office, and turned it on.

The desk flickered, a five-foot panel of clear glass—on, off, on, on, off. With a final burst of blue light the desk lit up, showing essentially a larger version of Afa's handheld screen. It was like a window had opened into another world, replacing the sheet of glass with a view of a verdant green jungle, so sharp and clear Kira reached out to touch it. It was the same glass, covered with drifts of dust and dirt, and marred here and there by pixelated glitches in the image. Glowing softly in the center was a small box requesting a password, and Afa tried a few simple words before turning back to his pack and rooting around for something.

"Look for notes," he said, gesturing haphazardly at the rest of the room. "Seventy-eight percent of office workers leave their passwords written down near their computers." Kira and Samm scoured the ruined office for pieces of paper, though twelve years of broken windows and full access to the elements had left the room so disheveled she didn't expect to find anything useful. Heron turned instead to the room's few remaining photos, turning them around to see if any had names on the back. While they searched, Afa retrieved a memory stick from his backpack and inserted it into a port in the frame of the desk. Before anyone could find a password, Afa barked a short laugh. "Got it."

Kira looked up. "The password?"

"No, but these desks had a maintenance mode, and I was able to trigger it. I can't see any of the data, and I can't modify anything at all, but this will let me see the settings and, more importantly, the file tree." The image on the screen wasn't even an image anymore; the jungle and the icons had been replaced with scrolling text, broken into branches and offshoots like a word-based root system. Afa's fingers flew across the image, expanding it here, compressing it there, flipping past row after row of names and files. "This is perfect."

"So you're going to be able to find the ParaGen servers?" asked Samm. Afa nodded, his eyes glued to the screen. Samm waited a moment, then asked, "How long?"

"Unless we get really lucky, most of the night," said Afa. "Can you bring me some more of that nacho sauce?"

CHAPTER TWENTY-THREE

Samm stirred the gas tank, and Kira heard a satisfying slosh as the liquid inside slapped against the metal walls. "Sounds like we're ready."

"This should give us enough juice to power the whole floor for most of the day," said Afa. Samm screwed the valve tight on the gas tank, they all stepped back, and Afa flipped the switch to start it. On the fourth try it spluttered, stiff from disuse, and on the seventh it roared angrily to life. Almost immediately the emergency lighting came on, those few bulbs that hadn't burned out or broken, and moments later the klaxons on the ceiling began to sound, two of them blaring an urgent warning that the power supply to the data center had been compromised, and the third merely hissing air and dislodging a cloud of dust.

Heron looked at them through slitted eyes. "That's going to get annoying."

"Let's go," said Afa. "We don't have long."

"I thought you said we had power for most of the day?" asked Kira.

"Power yes, but cooling no. That entire facility next door is just to keep this one cool, and there's no way to get that running again—even if we could get it started, it uses some rare chemicals we're not going to find in the corner doggie hardware store. Without a cooling system, these servers could melt their circuits and each other pretty quickly."

The ParaGen server was two rows over, and about halfway down; physically close to the generator that served it and about eighty other machines. Even with the generator running, the servers didn't seem to have enough power to get going, so Afa sent Kira and Samm around to every other computer on the same circuit with an order to cut the power. It took Kira a while to figure out which of the many cables was for power, but once she found the first one, the rest were simple. She'd done about twenty, still not speaking to Samm, when Afa shouted triumphantly.

"It's on!"

Samm stood to go back, but Kira kept working. If unplugging half of them helped, unplugging the rest would help even more; besides, she was still mad at both Samm and Heron, and didn't want to be around them. How could they be so closed-minded? Racism had all but disappeared since the Break, with humans of every shape and color working together freely because there was literally no one else to work with. Kira remembered one holdout in an outer fishing village, a man she'd met on a salvage run who'd called her a towelhead for her obvious Indian ancestry, but he was such a bitter, solitary man, and she had lived so long without any kind of ethnic hate, that the insult rolled off her almost humorously. It was joke, a thing to laugh about with her friends: *Was this guy for real?* On Long Island, everyone worked together, everyone got along, and no matter what you looked like, you were still human.

. . . unless you were a Partial.

She paused, a discarded power cable in her hand, suddenly seeing the situation from the other side. Just as Samm and Heron saw themselves as innately superior, the humans saw all Partials as innately evil—so different, and so lesser, that they didn't even qualify as people. Up until a few months ago she'd thought the same thing, but it had all changed when she met Samm.

Samm.

He was the one who'd convinced her, through his words and actions, that Partials were just as intelligent, just as empathic, just as angry and fractured, just as . . . human, really. They had different biology, but their thoughts and feelings were almost identical. She herself was the greatest proof of that: She had felt human for years—she still felt human. What the hell was she? In a sudden rush she felt the full weight of every mile she'd crossed from East Meadow to here, every river that separated her from her friends, every mountain that rose up to keep them apart. She felt tears flood her eyes, wondering what she was doing, why she was here, what she was trying to change. Her friends, her sisters, Marcus, all together, it had all been so happy and simple. Their lives weren't perfect, but they were lives. They were happy. She sat on the floor, sobbing and alone.

The generator stopped humming, and the room went suddenly dark.

She heard boots pounding on the floor, and Afa's sudden cry of alarm: "I lost it!" She looked up, saw the soft glow from his screen peeking through the gaps between the computer towers, and opened her mouth to ask what had happened.

But before she could, a burst of gunfire tore through the air, putting out the light with a tinkling shatter of glass. Kira dropped to the ground, crouching behind a computer tower.

The computer rooms in the data center were sealed from all outside interference; there were no windows, which meant that without the lights it had become nearly pitch-black. Random snippets of link data assaulted Kira, always easier to detect in a high-stress situation: the sudden shock of being ambushed, the confusion of not knowing where the attack was coming from, the alarm of a wounded comrade. Kira tried to piece it together: They'd been attacked somehow, by someone incredibly capable, but who? They hadn't seen any sign that Chicago was occupied. Was there some group hiding in there? Or had they been followed? By humans or Partials?

She was still frightfully amateur when it came to processing link data, but she tried to think hard about what it felt like when Samm and Heron had entered Afa's compound, trying to truly read the emotion behind it. All of it seemed to be coming from Samm and Heron, not the attackers. That meant the ambushers were either human or Partials wearing gas masks—a common tactic when Partials fought one another. Kira stayed still, listening, trying to figure out where each person was. The generator had been turned off, or outright destroyed, which meant that one of the attackers was there; Afa's screen had shattered, too, which meant one of the attackers had been somewhere with a clean shot at it. That would likely be two rows to her right, though whether they were in front of her or behind her, she didn't know.

Had Afa been shot as well? She felt something in the link about a wounded comrade, but she didn't know who or where.

Someone moved to her left: friend or foe? She couldn't tell; she listened to the footsteps, trying to tell which direction they were moving, and heard the unmistakable squelch of water. A wet boot, but whose? Unless they'd come in from the roof, the invaders would have shoes just as wet as Samm's and Heron's. Possibly wetter, since they'd been in the water more recently. That could be a clue in and of itself, but without more information, Kira had no way of knowing. She reached for her own boots, slowly easing them off, never making a sound. Her wet socks followed, leaving her barefoot. She'd be the only one in the room who didn't squeak and squelch as she walked.

Another flash of link data cascaded through her mind— THEY'VE FOUND ME—followed seconds later by another burst of gunfire. There was another sound behind it, like a gunshot but different. Kira couldn't tell what it was, but the gunfire stopped and a body fell heavily to the ground; Kira estimated it was about ten yards away, behind and to her left. She felt the sudden, confusing sensation of being sleepy and not sleepy at the same time, and interpreted it as another message from the link: One of her companions had been drugged or sedated. The not-quite-gunshot she'd heard had been a tranquilizer dart.

That means they're not trying to kill us, thought Kira. *Who wants to capture us? Dr. Morgan? But how does she know where we are?*

Kira rose to her feet, her back pressed tightly against the computer tower. She glanced up and down the row she was in, seeing nothing, and slipped forward to the next one as lightly as she could. Her bare feet made no sound on the concrete floor, but she felt cold drips on her legs and looked down in frustration; her boots had been left behind, but her pants were still soaked from the flood below, and she was leaving a dim trail of water showing exactly where she was. She heard another squelch, behind and to her right. Someone was getting closer. She slid to the floor and wrung her pants dry, twisting the legs as tightly as she could to get rid of the excess water. It was nearly impossible with her legs still in them. The squelch came closer—she guessed he was three rows away. She gritted her teeth, wringing out her second pant leg, trying to make them as dry as possible. Another squelch. She rose again, her pants cold against her legs but not dripping, and slipped lightly to the next row down. She left no trail this time. She moved another row, then another, slipping to the side, trying to put as much distance between her and the attacker as she could, in the direction he least expected.

The room erupted in noise again, shouts and automatic weapons and the harsh metallic rips of bullets tearing through computer towers. Two bodies slumped this time, and Kira felt again the faint of whiff of prescience from the link: sleep, pain, and victory. Her final companion was down but had taken at least one of the attackers down in the process. Kira was alone, and she had no idea how many enemies were left.

She heard a footfall, but she couldn't tell where it had come from. A voice, too soft to understand. A sudden sense of determined pragmatism: to find the last target and complete the mission. Had that come from her, or from the enemy? Kira was frustrated that she still wasn't adept enough to tell. She took a deep breath, crouching low in the darkness, sorting through her limited information: If that last impression was link data, then the enemy were definitely Partials, and at least one had removed his gas mask. The Partials worked in two-man hunting teams—she'd heard them constantly on the radio in the raid of Long Island—but they used larger teams as well, depending on the job. She might be facing a single combatant or a dozen. The reigning silence in the data center suggested that only a very small team had infiltrated; if there were more, they were waiting outside.

She thought further, looking for anything she could use to her advantage. Her rifle was on the far side of the room, but she still had her sidearm. Would it be of any use at all? Partial soldiers had vision enhancements, and better night vision in particular; it also stood to reason, given that they'd started the attack by cutting the lights, that they had some additional way to see in the dark, perhaps light amplification goggles. That would put Kira at a distinct disadvantage, but if she could turn it around, blinding them with the beam of her flashlight, she might be able to get off a shot before the target recovered. She drew her pistol in her right hand and her flashlight with her left, holding it across her body, aimed straight ahead with her finger on the switch.

A boot crunched down on something, echoing through the silence. One of the attackers had stepped on something, probably the shattered glass from Afa's screen. Was Afa okay? She shook her head. *Focus, Kira.* If someone had stepped on Afa's glass, then she knew where he was, and she could find him. She slipped from one tower to the next, crouching below the sight line as she moved from cover to cover. A moment later she felt a delayed link response: OVER THERE. This was definitely a Partial, and probably two, using the link to coordinate silently. Two against one, and both of them Partials. They would surround her and trap her, fill her with tranquilizer, and carry her back to Dr. Morgan.

Unless . . .

Kira remembered what Samm and Heron had said after their raid on Afa's building: She could feel them on the link, but they couldn't feel her. She was only beginning to learn how to use her link, but it was possible that she only had receptors for link data, didn't transmit any herself. This weakness was now her greatest advantage. She could link everything, and they couldn't link her at all.

Except for movement, Kira thought, cursing her lack of stealth training. *Heron couldn't link with me, but she could hear my movements.* She decided the best course of action was to move as little as possible. Instead, she reached for a spare ammo clip attached to her belt and slowly, carefully, making as little noise as possible, pulled a bullet from it. The bullets beneath were spring-loaded, designed to snap up and into place each time a bullet was fired, so she kept her finger in the way, letting the spring ease up instead of clicking. She dropped the bullet in her pocket and did it again, slowly, listening for any sign of the intruders. A third bullet. A fourth. She kept each one in a different pocket so they wouldn't clink against each other. Slowly she raised the first one in her hand, cocking it back, and threw it, arcing it high over the computer towers and into the far wall. It clattered against the plaster, bouncing back and into a computer tower before rolling to a stop on the floor. Through the link she felt her attackers snap to attention, alerted by the sound, followed a split second later by a tactical warning: IT'S A TRICK. Kira shook her head, angry at herself for thinking it would work, but an idea struck her. She pulled the second bullet from a pocket and threw it lightly at the tower nearest her, listening to it smack into the side and bounce across the concrete floor. The link lit up again, sending the same coordinating message: I HEARD A SOUND. IT'S A TRICK.

The next footstep she heard was moving away from her. Her double fake-out had worked.

She twisted to the side, peeking past the tower she was using for cover. One of the towers, maybe ten rows down, was mis-shapen in the darkness, lumpy and round. One of the attackers, she guessed, his knee or elbow disrupting the silhouette. She hugged the floor, readying her flashlight again, watching the malformed tower. It moved, expanded, separated into a vaguely human shape as the Partial stepped out from behind it. He was moving away from her, a thin pistol raised in front of him—the tranq gun. Kira rose to her feet and slipped after him, stepping slowly to keep her bare feet as silent as she could. He moved two rows and she moved two; if she could keep this up, she'd be in effective range to shoot him. There was still one other, though, and she didn't know where he was. Every time she crossed an open aisle, she ran the risk of exposing herself.

On her next step her foot came down on something and she froze, not wanting to put her weight on it. She looked down and saw faint lines in the dark, curves and twists like tiny snakes, and she cursed silently. *This is one of the rows we unplugged,* she thought. *The floor's covered with cords.* She moved her foot to the side, finding a safe place to put it down. The floor was a maze of looping cables, and she placed each foot strategically to avoid them: here, twisted this way, oriented just so. Each step seemed to take an hour.

The Partial she was following was getting farther away. Kira pulled out her third bullet and hurled it at the wall ahead of the Partial. He froze, and she crept forward while their link conversation cascaded through her mind: I HEARD A SOUND. IT'S A TRICK. IS IT A TRICK? He figured it out a second too late, turning to shoot her just as she stepped up behind him, shoved her semiautomatic pistol into the gap between his helmet and his chest armor, and fired. He fell to the floor, firing his dart gun harmlessly into the ceiling, and instantly she felt the pounding link message—DEATH!—and heard the sound of footsteps running toward her. She dove to the side, dropping her flashlight and ripping the ammo clip from her belt, popping the bullets into her hands as fast as she could, not caring about the noise. She hurled the entire handful into the air, her back pressed up against a computer tower, and then ran as fast as she could when the bullets clattered down, masking her movements in a raining metal cacophony. She felt frustrated snippets of the link from her last pursuer: SOLDIER DOWN. TARGET LOST. ANGER.

Kira realized she'd lost her flashlight, and with no more bullets to throw, she was out of tricks. She checked her pockets for something she could use, for anything—

FOUND HER. DEATH.

Kira gnashed her teeth—how could he have found her? She wasn't on the link; the first one had been three feet away from her and hadn't felt a thing!

DEATH.

She felt it again, the overwhelming feeling of death, and

cursed silently. *It's me,* she thought. *The link data is all phero-mones—tiny particles—and I was standing right next to him when he released a cloud of them. The death particles are on me, trailing behind me like a path, and he can follow them right to me.* She looked at her pistol, too small to make a stand against an alert Partial in a direct assault. She had nothing else. *If only I had my flashlight.*

The Partial's boot clicked against the floor, closer than before. He was almost on her. *I have one chance.* She closed her eyes, remembering the layout of the room, hoping she hadn't gotten turned around. She opened her eyes and ran.

She heard a soft whoosh of air, and something darted past her in the air, missing her by inches. She dodged to the side, running in a different row, then dodged back again. Another whoosh, and another tranq dart slammed into a computer tower right as she passed it, close enough that she flinched involuntarily. She leapt over a body, sensing rather than seeing that it was Samm. There were footsteps behind her, pounding heavily on the floor, charging toward her at top speed. *Almost there.* The Partial knew he had her, that she had nowhere to go. A great round shape loomed up in the darkness and she slid against it, searching fran-tically in the dark for the thick lever handle on the generator. She found it, slammed it down, and stepped back into the aisle.

The lights came on and the Partial stumbled just two yards away, blinded by the sudden burst of light overloading his night-vision faceplate. Kira raised her pistol and shot him three times in the helmet: crack, split, and through into his head. He dropped like a bag of sand.

DEATH.

CHAPTER TWENTY-FOUR

Afa had been shot through the thigh by a bullet from one of the invaders' guns—the only shot that had been an actual bullet. The rest of the shots turned out to be tranq darts, presumably intended to incapacitate their victims. The same bullet had also shattered Afa's screen, and Kira wondered which had been the true target: the man, or the data? Had the Partials followed them here to capture them, or to stop them from learning what was on the computer? Had it been both?

Kira couldn't help but wonder if it had been neither. She glanced at Heron, slowly regaining consciousness on the floor. Had she shot Afa? Had Samm? What motive could either of them possibly have for doing so, and why now? If they were colluding with the attackers, why go through the ruse of pretending to get tranqed? That would only make sense if they knew they were going to lose, and if they knew they were going to lose, why bother with the attack at all? It didn't make any sense, and Kira knew it; the most likely explanation was that the Partial attackers had come to kill Afa and capture the others. Even so, Kira couldn't shake the lingering doubts. How could the Partials have even found them, unless someone had provided them with a location? She cursed herself for not keeping one alive to interrogate, though she had to admit that she'd barely made it out alive as it was.

Kira finished binding Afa's wound while he was still unconscious, and checked each attacker in turn, pulling out their weapons to count the bullets. One of them, in fact, had a sidearm that was short one bullet. Kira couldn't tell how long ago the weapon had been fired, but it didn't seem likely that a trained soldier would enter combat with anything less than a full clip, and so this was likely the one who'd shot Afa. But "likely," she knew, wasn't the same as "true."

"Scavenging ammo?" asked Heron. Kira turned to find the Partial spy standing behind her, looking disheveled but alert. Kira slapped the clip back into the gun and dropped it on the fallen Partial's chest.

"This one shot Afa," she said, and rose to her feet. She tried to keep her voice casually curious. "Why do you think they shot him and tried to tranq the rest of us?"

"They were probably shooting the screen to kill the light," said Heron. "They were prepared for the dark and we weren't— standard ambush procedure. Those tranq darts don't have the penetrating power to shatter a piece of glass like that."

"That makes sense," Kira admitted, and it did. Maybe. She shook her head. "Shooting the screen almost guaranteed hitting Afa in the process. If they were trying to take us alive, why risk hitting him somewhere lethal?"

Heron smirked, and pulled the Partial girl's helmet off. Her face was Chinese, like Heron's, and strikingly gorgeous. "She's espionage. There was no risk."

"How many?" asked Samm. He came around the corner of a computer tower, still shaking off the effects of the drug; he was groggy, and his speech was slurred. Kira added "recovering from sedatives" to her long list of things Heron seemed to be better at than the other Partials. *She wasn't kidding when she said she was designed to be superior.*

"Three," said Kira, looking down at the girl's body. "One spy and two soldiers, I guess, though I'm obviously not as familiar with the model types as . . . whoa." She knelt down, seeing something strange under the folds of the Partial's hair. She brushed it back, revealing three rows of frilled slits on the girl's neck. "Heron, do you have gills?"

Heron crouched down, pulling the girl's head to the side to inspect her neck. "These are Morgan's," she said. "Special operatives, complete with Morgan's recent 'adaptations.' Check the others." They pulled the helmets off the two males, finding the same gills. Heron whistled. "Not exactly soldiers at all, then." She looked up at Kira. "And you killed two of them?"

"Skin of my teeth," said Kira. "These look like wet suits under their armor. Do you suppose they swam here? We're right on the shore of Lake Michigan, and unless there are any talking freshwater sharks you haven't told me about, traveling by water would be a lot safer than traveling by land."

"Part of the way, maybe," said Samm. "They'd still need to cross Michigan on foot, it's too wide to go around it."

"They seem perfectly capable of breathing on land," said

Kira. "They could have done both."

"It doesn't check out," said Heron. "If they'd followed us from Manhattan, they wouldn't have bothered sending gilled agents, because they wouldn't have known where we were going—for all they know we were headed to the plains, or west into the toxic wasteland. If Morgan had agents stationed here already, though, some kind of outpost in Chicago, what better agents to guard a flooded city than ones with gills?"

Kira nodded. "That's true. Or—" She stopped herself, not wanting to propose the other explanation so brazenly: *Or one of you is a spy, and used our radio to tell them exactly where we were and where we were going.*

"Or what?" asked Heron.

"Nothing," said Kira. She looked at the gills again, avoiding Heron's eyes, though the faint touch of the link hinted at her feelings: LACK OF TRUST. BE ON GUARD.

CONFUSION. Kira was pretty sure that was from Samm, and felt a wave of relief. If he was confused, then he wasn't in on it. She'd have to find a way to talk to him in private before Heron did.

"Take their gear," said Samm. "I'll dump the bodies in a closet upstairs." He and Heron began cleaning up the mess of the battle, but Kira went back to Afa. He was breathing better now, thanks to the painkillers she'd given him, but he was still unconscious. The shards of his screen lay around him in pieces, the gray side handle still attached to the server with a cable. The screen was like a smaller version of the glass desk upstairs; the glass was just the monitor, and all the processing and memory were housed in the frame; in this case, in the handle on the side.

The server itself seemed undamaged, and for all she knew the data transfer was still going, dumping all of ParaGen's secrets into the handle. Without a screen, though, they wouldn't be able to read it.

This is a data center, she thought. *It's filled with business computers, and since everyone who worked here was probably a tech nut like Afa, it will have other devices as well. There's bound to be another screen somewhere.* She checked Afa again, making sure he was okay, and swept the shards of glass away from him as much as possible before heading back upstairs to the offices. She started in the corner offices, hoping that their extra prestige might mean an extra computer or two, but found nothing: several docks, but none of the screens to dock in them. *They're designed to be portable,* Kira thought. *Anyone who had one probably took them home.* She kept looking, checking each office one by one before starting in on some of the cubicles. It reminded her of the offices she'd searched in Manhattan, and the memory gave her an idea. On a hunch, she left the cubicles and searched the back halls and rooms for anything marked with the initials Afa had had on his door: IT. Information technology. She finally found the IT office on the first floor, knee-deep in water. The IT director was still there, dead at his desk, his upper body covered with slime and his lower body stripped clean of everything but bone. She held her breath, sorting through his shelves, and found a screen slightly smaller than Afa's in the desk drawer. She fled back outside, gagging and closing the door behind her, and made sure to rinse herself off in the cleaner water outside before heading back upstairs, where she found Afa had woken.

"My screen got shot," he said. His voice was soft and vapid—he had again regressed to the "confused child." Kira sighed, knowing that an attack like this had made it inevitable, and sat down beside him to comfort him. He looked at her with worried eyes. "Where's my backpack?"

"It's right over there," she said, checking his pulse. Elevated but normal. "How do you feel?"

"My screen got shot," he said, trying to stand. He screamed in pain the instant he put weight on his leg, and collapsed back to the floor.

"Forget the screen," said Kira. "I've got a new one, but you've been shot, too. You need to take it easy."

"I need my backpack."

"You've been shot, Afa, right here in your leg—"

"I need my backpack!" His eyes quivered, on the verge of tears, and Kira stood up to bring him his backpack, wondering if maybe he had another screen in there and she hadn't had to actually spend all that time with the dead IT director. She dragged the pack over to him and he clutched it to his chest, rocking back and forth. "I can't ever leave my backpack," he said. "I'm the last human being on the planet."

"He looks bad," said Samm. Kira nodded, too exhausted to care about whatever Samm still thought about Afa; besides which, he was right.

"He's retreated inside his own head," she said. "It will be a while before we get him out again."

Samm jutted his head toward the server, and the screen handle still connected to it. "Did we get everything?"

Kira held up the handle. A small green light still shone at the tip of it. "I don't know. I don't dare disconnect it in case it's still transferring data."

"How long will it take?"

Kira shrugged, gesturing at Afa. "The only one who knows is currently singing a lullaby to his backpack. And he's losing blood, and I don't have the antibiotics I need to help him, and I have dead guy soaking into my pants, and I'm really starting to wish that a whole lot of things had gone differently." She took a deep breath, surprised at her own outburst.

"You're under a lot of stress," said Samm.

Kira felt tears coming close to the surface, and wiped one from the corner of her eye. "Yeah, what else is new?"

Samm stayed silent for a moment, and picked up the screen she'd brought up from downstairs. "You think we can plug this into the other one?"

"It only has one port," said Kira, wiping her eyes again and sitting up straighter. "We can't connect the new screen until we disconnect the server, and I don't want to mess with it if it's still downloading."

"Then we'll set up a perimeter and stay here for the night," said Samm. He glanced around the room, computer towers obstructing visibility in every direction. "We can't stay here, though—there's no good way to guard it, plus the generator was damaged in the battle. And the exhaust pipe. It's pumping the whole place full of burning paint thinner."

"Great," said Kira. "Life wasn't crappy enough yet."

Samm rose to his feet and held out his hand for Kira. She took it, standing to face him. They didn't turn away. She looked in his eyes and felt . . . *something*. The link was still hard to interpret sometimes.

Samm looked away first. "I'll grab his arms," he said, stepping behind Afa. "Let's get him somewhere safe."

▼ ▼ ▼

Kira jolted awake at two a.m., certain that something was wrong. She looked around wildly, grasping for her gun. "Who's there? Are we under attack?"

"Calm down," said Heron. "The generator just shut off. The change in background noise probably woke you."

"I'll go check it out."

"It's probably just out of gas, and we're not getting it restarted anytime soon."

"Then I'll get the screen handle," said Kira. "If we've gotten all we're going to get, I'd rather have it in here with us than down there by itself."

"Take your gun," said Heron. Her expression was unreadable in the dark, and the link, from what Kira could tell, was silent. "There might be more fish monsters."

"Thanks," said Kira. She checked Afa's pulse and breathing, almost by reflex at this point, and went downstairs. The poison gas, they'd discovered, was heavier than air, so the top floor was the safest place to be. Kira turned on the flashlight on the edge of her gun, comforted to have the rifle leading the way in case anybody was actually down there. The halls were dark, the stairs empty, the building silent except for the soft sound of drips and the lapping of water. Computer towers loomed around her in the data center, casting long shadows as the beam of her flashlight danced over them. The smears of blood from the earlier battle turned the scene from eerie to menacing, and Kira walked softly, holding her breath as she passed between the monoliths. Exhaust swirled around her shins and ankles, and the air tasted bitter. She found the handle, unplugged it from the server, and retreated upstairs as fast as she dared. When she got back to their camp she sat down on her bedroll, grabbed the second screen, and plugged in the cable.

"You're going to read it now?" asked Heron.

"What are we waiting for?"

"Good point," said Heron, and sat down behind her, peering over her shoulder.

Kira blinked as the screen flared to life, and dialed down the brightness to a tolerable level. A small icon in the center of the screen told her it was still trying to connect to the other handle, and she held her breath as the little hexagon spun around and around and around. It paused, then spun again. "Oh, come on," she whispered. A minute later it stopped. CONNECTION COMPLETE. She opened the download folder and scrolled through the massive list, eventually giving up and just opening the search tab. "What do I look for?"

"The Trust?" offered Heron. "RM? Expiration? Your own name?"

Kira typed in K-I-R-A and hit search. The little hexagon spun around but returned nothing. "What?"

"Maybe you're in there under a different name."

"I'll try my father." She typed his surname: D-H-U-R-V-A-S-U-L-A. The hexagon spun again, the machine thinking quickly, and soon it was spitting out results, file after file sliding by so fast she couldn't even read the titles. She stopped it at 3,748 results and cleared the search. "We'll have to narrow that down, I guess. How about . . ." She thought, chewing on her lip, then typed a new word:

F-A-I-L-S-A-F-E.

The hexagon spun. Twelve results. She opened the first file in the list and found it to be an email to her father from Bethany Michaels, chief financial officer of ParaGen. Kira read it out loud.

"'The joint chiefs have one final request for the BioSynth army; a sort of Failsafe. I know you insist on the unimpeachable loyalty of the BioSynths—I know that it's hard-wired into their brains and so on—but I think this is a very reasonable request, given the BioSynths' capabilities, and not one we could choose to ignore in any case.

"'In conjunction with the engineered army, we need an engineered virus. If the army malfunctions, or rebels, or in any way gets out of hand, we need to be able to push a button and, essentially, turn them off. We need a virus that will destroy the BioSynths without harming anyone or anything else. I trust your team will have no problem with the design or implementation.'"

Kira stared at the screen.

"The Failsafe is RM," said Heron. "Your own government ordered it."

Kira's voice was a whisper. "And then it killed the wrong people."

CHAPTER TWENTY-FIVE

Getting caught by the Partials had been easy. Marcus and Ariel packed their gear, started walking along the widest highway they could find, and got picked up by a patrol within the first two hours. The two-man team searched them, confiscated their weapons, and marched them toward East Meadow; a few miles later they met a truck, already half-full of human prisoners, which drove them the rest of the way in. The humans sat quietly in the back, their faces numb with terror, and Marcus didn't have to fake his own fear at the prospect of Partial occupation. They had gotten themselves caught on purpose, but they didn't have any idea what the Partials were planning to do with them. When they reached East Meadow they were dropped off, searched again, and interrogated. They didn't seem to recognize Marcus, or if they did, they didn't care. Near midnight they were released into the city with nothing but the clothes on their backs. They found an empty house and hid until morning.

They didn't risk going to Nandita's house until the following night, wary of being followed; when they arrived, they found that the Partials had already torn through it with a vengeance, searching every nook and cranny in meticulous detail. "If there's anything left, I'll be amazed," said Marcus, but they dove into it anyway, hoping to find a sign of Nandita's plans that the Partials had missed, if they even knew what they were looking for. They spent their days in the empty house, tearing it apart as carefully and as quietly as they could, and their nights hiding in nearby houses, a different one every night, doing their best to remain invisible.

The people who attracted too much attention always ended up dead in the evening execution.

They started by searching Nandita's room: all her drawers and closets, in the boxes under her bed, in the spaces behind the dresser and the large vanity mirror, even between her mattresses and hidden in the pockets of her clothes. They searched the hothouse as well, though in the months of Nandita's absence Xochi had already taken over much of it, and there were very few spaces not already filled by Xochi's ever-growing collection of herbs and sprouts. When they failed to find anything, they began searching the rest of the house, first looking in all the drawers and cupboards and eventually prying up floorboards, cutting open upholstery, and even digging holes in the garden. They found nothing.

"I think we have to face it," said Marcus days later, leaning tiredly on the kitchen counter. "These experiment logs either don't exist, or they're gone."

"They exist," said Ariel. "I saw them."

"She may have taken them with her," said Marcus. He stared

at the gaping hole they'd just punched in the kitchen wall; Nandita had repaired a section of Sheetrock there about a year before, something the Partials apparently didn't know, but when they broke it open they found nothing but a few dropped nails. "That might be why she left, to continue her studies or analyze the results or something."

"Or to hide them," said Ariel. "Or maybe just destroy them outright. Though I don't know what would have prompted her to do it."

Marcus shook his head. "You're assuming she left willingly. What if she was taken? Her and her records? That seems . . ." Marcus slowed, and laughed dryly. "I was going to say that seems needlessly paranoid, but under the circumstances it might actually be right. I don't think anything would surprise me at this point."

Ariel shook her head. "If they took her, they wouldn't be back here looking for her, right?"

"There are a lot of Partial factions," said Marcus. "It might have been one of Morgan's enemies."

"Nandita and Dr. Morgan were both performing experiments on Kira," said Ariel, nodding. "For all we know, they were working together."

"I certainly got the impression she was working for Morgan when Heron confronted me," said Marcus, "but I suppose Heron's not exactly the most trustworthy source. Consider this, though: As far as we know, Morgan's recent experiments on Kira were purely coincidental. She just wanted a human girl, she never went out of her way to get a specific one."

"As far as you know," said Ariel.

"As far as we know," Marcus agreed, "but I was there. I watched Kira go through this, making all her decisions in very Kira-like ways. If Morgan wanted a specific girl, all she had to do was raid the island like she's doing now, not set up some ridiculously elaborate con game to trick her into visiting the mainland of her own free will."

"But what about that photo you told me about?" asked Ariel. "You saw Kira and Nandita together before the Break, which is weird enough already, but then to see them at the ParaGen building? That's not like a huge red flag for you that something weird is going on here? There's got to be more to that relationship."

"Like what?" Marcus asked. "Of course it's a red flag, but for what? I've been trying to figure it out for weeks now, that's why we've torn your whole house apart, but what does it mean? Does seeing them at a ParaGen facility mean that Kira's different somehow? Most of us have some kind of gene mods from when we were kids—does Kira have a special one? Is she important in some way? I'm with you on this, Ariel, but I honestly don't know what any of it means." They heard a rumble, and immediately recognized the sound as an engine, probably a pretty big one. The Partials had brought motor vehicles back to East Meadow, thanks to their wealth of resources and energy, and the humans had learned to listen for the sound of approaching Partial "police." They dropped to the ground, trying to look as not-home as possible. It worked.

"That was the closest one yet," said Ariel. "I think they know we're here—that we use this house, I mean."

"The papers you saw in Nandita's hothouse," said Marcus.

"What else can you remember about them?"

"I told you," said Ariel. "It said 'Madison: Control.' It had a lot of physical information, height and weight and blood pressure and all that, not just single readings but changes over time. Madison and I would have been ten, maybe getting on to eleven, just starting to go through puberty, so there were a lot of changes to track. At least half of it, though, probably more than half of it, was chemicals—herbs, I guess, but she'd scrawled in some notes about different properties of each herb, and different mixtures in her droppers from one time to the next. She was trying to find the right combination for . . . something. I don't know. 'Control,' whatever that is."

"Oh damn," said Marcus, staring at the floor. He closed his eyes, slowly shaking his head as the realization washed over him. "Double dog damn it and around again for another damn."

Ariel smiled. "You watch your filthy mouth, Mr. Valencio."

"It's not about control," said Marcus, looking up at Ariel. "How much do you know about the scientific method?"

"I saw what I saw," she insisted.

"Of course you did," said Marcus, "but you were ten years old and you didn't know how to interpret it. When a scientist does an experiment, they always have at least two subjects: the experiment, which they screw around with, and the control, which they don't. It's a baseline, unmodified test subject intended only for observation, so that whatever happens to the experimental subject has something you can compare it to. Nandita could have been using Madison as a control subject to help her understand her observations of Kira."

"She'd never raised children before," said Ariel, seeing where he was going with the line of thought. "When Kira did something weird, Nandita had no way of knowing if it was weird because all kids are weird, or weird because of . . . whatever stupid thing we still don't know about Kira.

"So we were all control subjects," said Ariel, slowly understanding. "Three controls against one experiment." She frowned. "It makes sense, I suppose, but it doesn't answer anything. We don't know what she was testing for, or why, or what any of it has to do with ParaGen."

Marcus shrugged. "There are only three people who do know," he said. "Kira, Nandita, and Dr. Morgan. I'd bet you anything Morgan knows at least some of it, or she wouldn't be tearing this island apart trying to find the other two."

"Well I'm not going to go up and ask her," said Ariel.

"And Kira won't tell me anything," said Marcus. "I hear from her about once a week now, and never more than a few seconds. Wherever she is, the signal's incredibly weak."

Ariel looked around at the ransacked house, now more of a junkyard than a home. "If there was ever any sign of Nandita, the Partials got it before we did. Even if we find a hint of where she might be, we're weeks behind them, and we're hopelessly outnumbered. There's no way we're going to find Nandita before they do."

"Don't give up yet," said Marcus, and waggled his radio. "Most of the reports I get on here are Partial battles—one of the other factions is still attacking the ones who have occupied the island."

"So we get crushed between two Partial armies?" asked Ariel. "I thought you were trying to cheer me up."

"What I mean is that they're distracted," said Marcus. "They can't focus all their energy on finding her, because they spend half their time fighting off other Partials."

"And we spend almost all our time hiding from Partials," said Ariel. "They still come out ahead."

Marcus blew out a puff of air, deflating as he sank back and stared at the floor. "I was just trying to find a bright side, but I guess we don't have any of those left." He played with the broken Sheetrock, shifting the pieces with his foot. A thought began to dawn on him. "Maybe we do."

"We have a bright side?"

"We have a second Partial army."

Ariel raised her eyebrow. "That's the worst bright side I've ever heard of."

"No," said Marcus, growing more excited. "Think about it: Dr. Morgan has raised a massive army of Partials, with the express purpose of raiding our island and holding us hostage, and another army of Partials is attacking her for it. Partials don't just attack things for no reason—they're soldiers, not . . . barbarians. The only reason to cross the sound and attack Morgan's forces is because you're trying to stop her, and the only reason to try to stop this invasion is because you disagree with it."

Ariel frowned, obviously skeptical. "So the second group of Partials is on our side?"

"If A hates B and C hates B then A and C are allies," said Marcus. "That's the . . . transitive property of battlefield ethics, which I just made up. But it's true."

"The enemy of my enemy is my friend," said Ariel.

"I knew there was a phrase like that somewhere."

"So how does that help us?" asked Ariel. "I'm pretty sure one of us could get out of East Meadow, slip through the Partial patrols, if the other makes a big enough distraction, but what then? Head north through the most occupied territory on the island, into the middle of an inter-Partial battle zone, and hope you can tell which group is which? You'll end up back here in less than twenty-four hours, assuming you live through it at all."

"We go off the island," said Marcus, shaking his head. "We let the soldiers do the fighting, and we go around them to talk to the leaders in the back."

"You want to just march into the mainland, all alone, and find a group of Partials."

Marcus laughed. "Who am I—Kira? I'm not doing this alone, I'm going straight to the Senate."

"The Senate fled East Meadow in the invasion," said Ariel. "What makes you think you can even find them?"

"Because Senator Tovar used to run the Voice," said Marcus, "and I know where some of the old Voice hideouts are. You just help me escape, I need to get to the JFK airport."

CHAPTER TWENTY-SIX

Kira looked at her three companions, nodding as if to convince herself that her words were true. "The Failsafe was RM. It was created by ParaGen, under the direction of the government, as a way to control the Partial army."

Samm's face was solemn. "It was designed to kill Partials?"

"It was a kill switch," said Heron. "If the Partials ever got out of hand, boom: Activate the Failsafe, problem solved."

"That's a really good idea," said Afa, heavily doped on painkillers but still relatively lucid. His thoughts all seemed clear, but his voice was slurred and his inhibitions, if he had any, were missing altogether. "Aside from the genocide, of course. No offense."

"You're a sweetheart," said Heron, though her face told a different story.

"So the Failsafe was built into us," said Samm. "It was a biological self-destruct button."

"Which killed the wrong people," said Afa.

"I don't think so," said Kira. She held up the screen and

flipped through the file tree, looking for a specific one; when she found it, she held it up for all to see. "Here's a cached email from the earliest days of the RM epidemic, attached to an article about a mystery disease that seemed to appear out of nowhere; the records don't say exactly when the Failsafe was activated, or who did it, but my guess is that it happened about three days earlier. This particular email is from Nandita to my father." She turned the screen back toward herself and read out loud, "'New Super-Disease Claims Seven Human Lives in San Diego. Dozens of other cases may be related.'" She looked up. "The body of the email just says, 'Quicker than we thought.' Not 'Oh no, it's targeting the wrong people,' just 'Quicker than we thought.'"

"So they may have targeted humans on purpose," said Samm. "Which . . . doesn't make any sense at all."

"No, it doesn't," said Kira, "which is why I'm not sold on the idea yet, I'm just pointing out that it's a possibility."

"Are you going to speculate wildly on the rest of the information?" asked Heron. "Or just this part? I want to know when I should start paying attention again."

Kira mentally rolled her eyes, but stopped herself from doing it for real. "That's the thing," she said. "Most of the rest of the information is pretty clear. We don't get any sort of viral formula or anything, but there are records in here that detail almost everything else. We know how they did it: They designed the pheromone glands that run the link so that they could start pumping out viral spores when triggered by a specific chemical. We know why they did it: because they were worried the Partial army could rebel, or worse, and they wanted an easy way to shut it down; not the most ethical decision they'd ever made, but there you go." She put her hand on the glowing screen. "There are records in here where they debate it, there are records where they plan it, there are records where they talk about the specific details of contagion, trying to predict how quickly it would spread. But all those discussions were about Partials, and then the virus attacked humans, and there are literally no emails in the entire batch that talk about how weird that is. Nothing from the Trust, anyway. There is one email from Noah Freeman, the ParaGen CEO, to the board of directors, that seems to support this theory." She called up the email on her screen and read from it. "'We cannot confirm that the Partial team is working to undermine the Failsafe project, but just in case we've hired new engineers to imbed the Failsafe in the new models. If the team betrays us, the Failsafe will still deploy.'"

"That seems to confirm what you were just saying," said Samm.

"Right," she said. "We know the Trust built RM into the Partial genome, and this email tells us the board knew that part of it. But we also know the Trust built the cure into them as well, but they did it secretly. It never gets mentioned in any of the email discussions between the Trust and their bosses, and this email from the CEO implies that they knew the Trust was trying to undermine the Failsafe, but didn't know how. That 'undermining' must be the cure. It only gets mentioned between Trust members a couple of times, and only under powerful encryption. Without Afa to break it for us, we would never have been able to read them."

Afa perked up. "They used a Paolo-Scalini level six crawler with Dynamic—"

"We don't actually care," said Heron. "The point is that it's secret, which is weird. They didn't want their bosses to know they were building a Failsafe to the big scary Failsafe they wanted."

"Which seems like proof that the first Failsafe was designed to attack humans on purpose," said Samm. "If it was a mutation, the preconstructed cure wouldn't be able to stop it."

"Absolutely," said Kira, nodding in agreement. "The pieces all fit together a little too well to be an accident."

"What about expiration?" asked Heron. "That's ostensibly the other reason we're out here, right? Does it say how to stop it?"

"That's another thing that seems to have been a secret," said Kira. "Encrypted emails and everything. Some of the Trust knew about it; others, such as Morgan, apparently didn't. Without reading weeks of emailed conversations between the members of the Trust, I can't say why."

"Probably because some of them objected," said Samm. "You said there were arguments about the Failsafe, right? So I assume there were people who opposed it?"

Kira nodded. "There were. My father, for example, thought it was unconscionable to create new life forms with kill switches." She couldn't help but smile at this bit of goodness from her father, knowing that he opposed something she hated so strongly. Even knowing that she had no biological connection to him, or perhaps because she knew it, these other connections carried so much more weight.

Afa nodded, almost compulsively, drawing pictures on the floor with his finger as he talked. "So the Trust had a plan they didn't tell ParaGen, but between them they still disagreed, or they each had their own plan and they didn't tell each other.

Maybe both, or maybe somewhere in the middle."

"Right," said Kira. "There was a plan—at least one."

"But what about the expiration date?" asked Heron again. "You said there was something there—what was it?"

"Just theories and projections," said Kira. She held out the screen. "You can read them for yourself if you want: long talks about the need for a Partial expiration date, and how long the shelf life should be, and how it should work, and who was going to build. On and on and on. But no formulas, no genetic codes, no medical details of any kind."

"Just like the virus," said Samm. "I thought this data center had all of ParaGen's files?"

Afa kept doodling with his finger. "So did I."

"Then where's the rest of it?" asked Kira. "Another tower? I don't know if we're going to get that generator running again."

"I looked through their entire directory," said Afa. "Everything from ParaGen was on that tower."

"But it's obviously not," said Heron, "so where's the rest?"

"I don't know," said Afa.

"Maybe we need to check the directory again," said Samm, but Kira shook her head.

"It's clear they didn't want the most important pieces of their plan in the cloud, as Afa calls it. The rest of the files are exactly where we thought they were." She sucked in a breath, dreading the next part: "And we're going there."

Heron shook her head. "You don't mean Denver."

"Of course I mean Denver."

"We're not going to Denver," said Heron. "We gave this a shot and it didn't pan out, now it's time to be reasonable and go back home."

"There's nothing for us back home," said Kira.

"There's life!" said Heron. "There's salvation, there's rational thought. We talked about this before—"

"And we decided to go to Denver," said Kira. "That was our plan from the beginning. We thought we could get what we needed out of this place, but we couldn't—we tried and we couldn't. Now we have to keep going."

"My leg is broken," said Afa.

"I know."

"The bullet hit the shinbone—"

"I know," said Kira. "I know, and I'm sorry. What else can we do? Just turn around and give up because the long shot didn't pan out?"

"Denver was the long shot," said Heron. "Chicago was the only sensible part of the plan."

"We came out here to find the Trust," said Kira. "To find ParaGen, to find their plans, to find their formulas, all so we could cure these diseases—"

"We can cure them by going back," said Heron.

"No, we can't," said Kira. "We can delay them, we can work around them; maybe if Dr. Morgan gets really lucky studying me, there'll be something she can do about the expiration date. But RM will still be there, and babies will still die, and there is still nothing we can do about it."

Heron's voice was as cold as ice. "So if you can't save both, you're going to let both die."

"I can save both," said Kira. "We can save both, together, by going to Denver and finding their files."

Heron shook her head. "And if they're not there?"

"They're there."

"Where next?" asked Heron. "All the way to the coast? Across the ocean?"

"They're there," Kira said again.

"But what if they're not?"

"Then we keep going!" Kira shouted. "Because they're out there somewhere, I know it."

"You don't know anything! It's just what your desperate, messed-up psyche wants to believe."

"It's the only explanation that connects everything we've found so far. I'm not giving up and I'm not turning back."

The room was silent. Kira and Heron stared at each other, fierce as lions.

"I don't want to go to hell," said Afa.

"You're going to get us killed," said Heron.

"You don't have to come."

"Then you'll still get yourself killed," said Heron, "and if you're the key to correcting the expiration date, that amounts to the same thing."

"Then come with us," said Kira. "We can do this, Heron, I swear to you. Everything the Trust did, every formula they used, every genome they ever created, is all there just waiting for us to find it. We will find it, and we'll take it back, and we'll save everyone. Both sides."

"'Both,'" said Heron. She took a deep breath. "Us or the humans. You'd better do your damnedest, then, because if it comes down to one or the other, I assure you: It will be us." She turned and stalked out of the room. "If we're going, let's go, every minute we waste is another death back home."

Kira took a breath of her own, adrenaline still coursing

through her. Afa watched Heron leave and then spoke too loudly. "I don't like her very much."

"That's the least of her problems," said Kira. She looked at Samm. "You were awfully quiet that whole time."

"You know where I stand," said Samm. "I trust you."

Kira felt a rush of tears and wiped her eyes with her sleeve. "Why?" She sniffed. "I'm wrong a lot."

"But if there's any earthly way for you to succeed, you'll move mountains to make it happen."

"You make it sound so simple."

Samm held her gaze. "Simple isn't easy."

"We should call home first," said Afa. "That guy you keep talking to—we need to let him know we're gonna be late."

"No," said Samm, standing up. "We just got attacked—I don't know if they were a guard post or if they followed us, but either way, we're in more danger than we realized. We can't let anyone even know we're alive, let alone where we're going."

"We don't have to say where," said Afa, "we could use a code name. Like Mortorq—that's a screwdriver."

"No," said Kira. "Anything we say is too much of a clue. We go, and we go in secret." She looked at the screen in her hand, then shoved it in her backpack. "And we go now."

CHAPTER TWENTY-SEVEN

The ruins of the JFK airport were surrounded by a wide ring of flat, featureless runway, forcing any attackers to approach through the open. A dedicated assault with armored vehicles could take it easily, but there were few of those left in the world, and Dr. Morgan's guerrilla army had none of them. The Voice had held it against the Grid with just a handful of spotters and snipers, and now the outlaws and the Grid together were prepared to hold it against the Partials. Marcus crossed the open runways uneasily, praying that the defenders recognized him as a human. And that they bothered trying to recognize him at all.

The JFK expressway leading into the airport had been bombed out, along with most of Terminal 8, to give an advancing force less cover to hide behind. Marcus headed instead to Terminal 7, and as he drew close he saw snipers in the shadows, tracking him slowly with their rifles. "Stop there," a voice called out. Marcus stopped. "Drop your weapons."

"I don't have any."

"Then drop everything else."

Marcus wasn't carrying much, just a backpack full of rock-hard candy and a couple of liters of water. He set it down on the ground and stepped away, stretching out his arms to show that there was nothing in them.

"Turn around," said the voice, and Marcus did as he was told.

"Just a skinny little Mexican kid," said Marcus. "Oh wait! I forgot." He reached into the pocket of his jeans and pulled out a folded paper and stubby pencil. He held them up for inspection, then set them carefully on the ground.

"Are you making fun of us?" asked the voice.

"Yes."

There was a long silence, until at last he saw a man in a doorway wave him in. He jogged to the open door to find Grid soldiers waiting with machine guns. He looked at them nervously. "You guys are human, right?"

"Every Partial-killing cell of me," said the soldier. "You one of Delarosa's?"

"What?"

"Senator Delarosa," said the soldier. "Are you working for her? Do you have a message?"

Marcus frowned. "Wait, is she still . . ." He remembered meeting Delarosa in the forest, when he and Haru were retreating from the first Partial attack. She'd been hiding in the woods and attacking patrols. "Is she still fighting Partials?"

"With the full support of the Grid," said the soldier. "She's damn good at it, too."

Marcus pondered this, remembering her more as a terrorist than a freedom fighter. *I guess you hit a point where they all blend together,* he thought. *When things get desperate enough, anything goes—*

No, it doesn't, he thought firmly. *At the end of the war, we have to be as good as we were when we started it.*

"I'm just a guy," said Marcus. "No message or special delivery or anything."

"Refugee area is downstairs," said the first soldier. "Try not to eat much; we don't have a lot left."

"Don't worry," said Marcus, "I won't be staying long. I don't suppose I could talk to Senator Tovar?"

The soldiers looked at one another, then the first looked back at Marcus. "Mr. Mkele likes to debrief anyone new anyway. You can talk to him first." They led Marcus down through the airport, leaving the surface almost immediately in favor of the vast subterranean tunnels crisscrossing the entire complex. Marcus was surprised to find an entire refugee camp in the basements; he was apparently not the first person to think of retreating here.

"Do the Partials not know you're here?" asked Marcus. "They'd kill to get their hands on this place."

"They've sent a couple of patrols," said the soldier. "So far we've been able to make ourselves more trouble than we're worth."

"That's not going to last long," said Marcus.

"They're getting attacked on the flanks by Delarosa," he said, "and by another Partial faction. That's keeping their main force too busy to bother with us."

Marcus nodded. "That's exactly why I'm here."

The soldier led him to a small office and knocked on the door. Marcus recognized Mkele's voice when he told them to come in. The soldier pushed the door open. "New refugee. He says he wants to talk to the Senate."

Mkele looked up, and Marcus felt a twang of mischievous pride at the surprise in the security expert's eyes. "Marcus Valencio?" Surprising a man who prided himself on knowing things was an impressive feat indeed.

The pride was followed almost instantly by a wave of despair. Seeing Mkele not in control was somehow the most disturbing sign of just how much things had fallen apart.

"Hi," said Marcus, stepping in. "I've got a . . . request. A proposal, I suppose."

Mkele glanced at the soldier, his eyes uncertain, then looked back at Marcus and gestured to a chair. "Have a seat." The soldier left, closing the door, and Marcus took a deep breath to calm his nerves.

"We need to go to the mainland," said Marcus.

Mkele's eyes widened, and Marcus had the same feeling of uncomfortable triumph knowing that he'd surprised the man again. After a quick moment Mkele nodded, as if he understood. "You want to look for Kira Walker."

"I wouldn't mind finding her," said Marcus, "but she's not the goal. We need to send a group north to a city called White Plains, to talk to the Partials who are attacking Dr. Morgan."

Mkele didn't respond.

"I don't know for sure which faction is there," said Marcus, "but I know that they oppose Dr. Morgan's. A group of them raided the hospital Kira was trapped in a few months back, which is how we were able to get her out while they killed each other. Now they're attacking Morgan's forces again—they followed them all the way across the sound, which is a good indication they're trying to stop this invasion."

"And you think that will make them our friends."

"A equals B equals . . . look, Ariel had a much better idiom for it, I don't remember. But yes, we have a common enemy, so we might be able to get some help."

Mkele watched him a moment longer, then spoke slowly. "I admit that we have had similar thoughts, but we didn't know how or where to contact them. Are you sure about White Plains?"

"Very sure," said Marcus. "Samm told us all about it—they have a nuclear reactor that powers the whole region, so they stay there to maintain it. If we can make it up there, which is an admittedly difficult proposition, they might be willing to work with us to end the occupation and perhaps find some of the answers we're looking for before it's too late. It's worth a shot."

"Shots are exactly what you'll end up with," said Mkele. "This is a blind mission into hostile territory with no guarantee of safety. If you go, you'll be killed."

"That's why I'm coming to you," said Marcus. "I'm not Kira—I'm not ready to lead something like this, I just came up with the idea."

"So that when someone inevitably dies, it will be me instead of you," said Mkele.

"Ideally no one will die at all," said Marcus, "but you can plan your missions how you like. I recommend you live at least long enough to succeed."

Mkele tapped his fingers on the desk, a surprisingly mundane gesture that seemed to humanize the severe man in Marcus's eyes. "A year ago I would have chastised you for recklessness," said Mkele. "Today, as it happens, we're willing to try almost anything. I had a unit of soldiers already preparing for a mission on the mainland, and now that you've given us a clear goal, we can pull the trigger. It also happens that we have need of a medic, and of someone with experience behind Partial lines."

"And I suppose you're looking for a man to volunteer."

"This is the Defense Grid," said Mkele. "We don't wait for volunteers. You leave in the morning."

CHAPTER TWENTY-EIGHT

Kira and her companions were on their way to Denver.

They'd left the data center at first light, wrapping Afa's injured leg as tightly as they could before helping him to slog through two miles of filthy floodwater. The rowboat was right where they'd left it, and they paddled back to their horses in silence, Samm rowing with long, powerful strokes while Heron and Kira watched the overhanging trees for signs of attack. A lone dog stood on a bridge to watch them float by, but it didn't talk or even bark, and Kira couldn't tell if it was a Watchdog or simply a feral animal.

The horses were unhurt but terrified, and it took Samm and Heron several minutes to calm them down enough to be saddled. Kira rewrapped Afa's wound with dry bandages, and together they boosted him up onto Oddjob's back, where he swayed and grimaced in pain at the change of pressure on his shredded thigh muscle. Kira bit her lip, angry that they had to take Afa even farther from home—not angry at him, or at anyone really, just angry. *Angry that life is hard,* she thought. *Nandita raised me better than this. "If you have the strength to whine, you have the strength to do something about it."*

They were almost halfway from Long Island to Denver already, and it would be two full months out of their way to take Afa back home; two months they didn't have. They couldn't leave him, obviously, so they had to take him, hard journey or not. *Besides,* Kira thought, *if there's another computer system at the lab site in Denver, we'll need Afa to access it. He's the only one who can.*

We just have to make sure he survives.

When they were all mounted and ready, Kira led them not to the freeway but to a large hospital on the other side. "St. Bernard's," she said, reading the weathered sign at the mouth of the parking lot.

"Should we look for antibiotics in the pharmacy?" asked Heron. "Or in barrels hanging from the collars of giant shaggy dogs?"

"As long as the dogs don't talk," said Kira, "I don't much care." The talking dogs still freaked her out, and she'd dreamed about them again last night—of herself living with them, wild and feral, unaccepted in both human and Partial society. She knew it was unfair of her to hate them. They couldn't help being what they were any more than she could. She pushed the thought aside and entered the hospital, showing Samm how to sort the meds they needed while Heron watched Afa and the horses. They filled an entire satchel with antibiotics and painkillers, and mounted up to ride west.

Into the toxic wasteland.

The fastest way out of town was a railroad track, which cut across the river highway in a straight line south-southwest, high on an elevated beam that kept them well above the worst of the flooding. They followed it for miles, past rail yards and school-yards and old, sagging houses, past flooded churches and fallen buildings and across an overflowing river. The train tracks were straight and the way was mostly dry, but it was rocky and slow going for the horses, and they hadn't even made it to the freeway when it grew too dark to travel. They took shelter in a crumbling public library, letting the horses graze on the tall, marshy grasses outside before leading them carefully up the access ramp to the dry floor inside. Kira checked Afa's bandages, shot him full of painkillers, and cleaned his wound while he slept. Heron caught frogs and lizards in the bog outside and roasted them on a fire made of old chairs and magazines. The books in the library were old, rotted, and there was no one left in the world to read them, but Kira made sure that none of them went into the fire. It seemed wrong.

In the morning they found that they were just a short walk to Interstate 80, the same massive road they'd been following since Manhattan, but nearly a hundred miles farther west than where they'd left it at the eastern edge of Chicago. They got back on it, finding it higher and dryer than the railroad and much easier for the horses to walk on. The followed it all day, the city sprawling out endlessly on every side: building after building, street after street, ruin after ruin. Subcities came and went—Mokena, New Lenox, Joliet, Rockdale—their meaningless borders blurred together into a single, unbroken metropolis. When night fell again they reached the edge of Minooka, and the road curved south around it, and Kira looked out for the first time on open grassland stretching far into the west. The horizon was flat and formless, an ocean of dirt and grass and marshland. They slept in a giant warehouse, in what Kira assumed was an old break room for cross-country truckers, and listened as a rainstorm drummed furiously on the broad metal roof. Afa's wound was no better than the previous night, but at least it was no worse. Kira curled up on her bedroll and read by the light of the moon, a thriller novel she'd picked up in the library. *Sure this guy's being chased by demons,* she thought, *but at least he has a warm shower in the morning.*

She fell asleep with her nose in the book, and woke up wrapped snugly in a blanket. Samm was staring out the window as the sun rose over the cityscape, and glanced at her a moment before turning back to watch the sky grow light.

Kira sat up, stretching her back and shoulders and popping a stiff joint in her neck. "Good morning," she said. "Thanks for the blanket."

"Good morning," said Samm. His eyes were locked on the window. "You're welcome."

Kira stood, pausing to hang her blanket on a row of nearby chairs before squatting down to open her pack. Heron and Afa were asleep, so she kept her voice down. "What sounds good for breakfast this morning? I have beef jerky, an indistinguishably different flavor of beef jerky, and . . . peanuts. All pre-Break, picked up at that place we stopped in Pennsylvania." She looked again in her bag. "We're running low on food."

"We should forage through the city before setting out," said Samm. "We're not far from the toxic waste, and I don't know if we can trust anything we find there."

"We passed a grocery store last night," said Kira, grabbing all three of her food selections and placing them on the table next to Samm. She sat on the far side and opened the peanuts. "We can head back there before we move on, but for now, dig in."

Samm looked down at the food, selected a bag of jerky at random, and tore it open. He sniffed it carefully before pulling out a piece of black, twisted meat as solid as rawhide. "What do you have to do to meat to make it stay good for twelve years?"

"Define 'good,'" said Kira. "You'll be sucking on that thing all day before it's soft enough to eat."

He tore off a strip, long and whip-thin and almost hilariously fibrous. "We'll have to boil it," he said, dropping the strips back into the bag. "Still, though—edible food that's almost as old as we are. That cow might actually have been as old as we are, and he died before that tree was even born." He pointed at a twenty-foot poplar sprouting up through the cracks in the buckled asphalt parking lot. "And yet we can eat it. We don't have anything in the world today that can preserve food like that. We might never have it again."

"I don't know if we want to," said Kira. "Give me some fresh Riverhead jerky any day."

"It's just . . ." Samm paused. "One thing after another. Cars that won't run. Planes that will never fly again. Computer systems we can barely use, let alone re-create. It's like . . . time is flowing backward. We're caveman archeologists in the ruins of the future."

Kira said nothing, chewing on the soft peanuts as the sun peeked over the mountainous city beyond. She swallowed and spoke. "I'm sorry, Samm."

"It's not your fault."

"Not the caveman thing," she said, "or the jerky or . . . I'm sorry for getting mad at you. I'm sorry for saying things that made you mad at me."

He watched the sun, saying nothing, and Kira tried and failed to read him on the link. "I'm sorry too," he said. "I don't know how to fix it."

"We're in a war," said Kira. "We're not even in a war we can win—humans and Partials are killing each other, and themselves, and everything they can get their sights on, because it's the only way they know to solve problems. 'If we don't fight, we'll die.' What we need to face is that we'll still die even if we do fight, and we don't want to face that because it's too frightening. It's easier to fall back into the same old patterns of hate and retribution, because at least then we're doing something."

"I don't hate you," said Samm, "but I used to. When you first captured me, when I first woke up and saw you and realized that everyone in my unit was dead. You were there, so I hated you more than I even knew I could. I'm sorry for that, too."

"It's okay," said Kira. "I'm not exactly innocent either." She smiled. "All we need to do now is send each human and each Partial on a deadly cross-country trip together, so they can learn to trust and understand each other."

"I'm glad there's such a simple solution," said Samm. He didn't smile, but Kira thought she felt a whiff of one on the link. She ate another handful of peanuts.

"That's what you really want, isn't it?" Samm asked.

Kira looked at him, curious.

"A united world," he said, still looking out the window. "A world where Partials and humans live together in peace." He glanced at her from the side of his eye.

Kira nodded, chewing her peanuts thoughtfully before swallowing. It was exactly what she wanted—what she'd wanted ever since . . . Ever since she'd learned what she truly was. A Partial raised as a human, connected to both groups without really being a part of either one. "Sometimes I think—" and then stopped. *Sometimes I think it's the only way I'll ever be accepted. I don't belong to either group, not anymore, but if both groups joined, I wouldn't be the weirdo anymore. I'd just be one of the crowd.* She sighed, too self-conscious to say it out loud. "Sometimes I think it's the only way to save everyone," she said softly. "To bring them all together."

"That's going to be a lot harder than just curing our diseases," said Samm.

"I know," she said. "We'll find the ParaGen labs, we'll find their plans and formulas, we'll cure RM and the expiration date and everything else, and then it still won't matter because our people are never going to trust each other."

"Someday they'll have to," said Samm. "When it comes down to trust or extinction, to trust or oblivion, they'll see that they'll have to and they'll do it."

"That's one of the things I like about you, Samm," said Kira. "You're a hopeless optimist."

For the first few days the road was straight and flat, almost disturbingly so. Farms crept by on either side, reclaimed by grassland and herds of wild horses and cattle, but each new sight seemed the same as the last, a single farm repeated ad infinitum, until Kira began to feel that they were making no progress at all. Occasionally the Illinois River on the south swerved close enough to be seen from the road, and Kira began to track their progress this way. They traveled slowly, keeping the horses fed and watered and Afa well supplied with medicines. His wound was healing poorly, and Kira did what she could to keep his spirits up.

Three days outside of Chicago they came to an island city at the conflux of two rivers; they crossed the Rock River into a town called Moline, finding it swampy but navigable, but the river on the other side stopped her cold. It was the Mississippi, and the bridges were gone.

"Not good," said Kira, surveying the wide river. She'd heard of the Mississippi, more than a mile wide in parts. Here it was narrower, though its widest gaps looked to be at least half a mile if not more. Much too far for the horses to swim, especially with Afa. "You think this was the war, or just wear and tear since then?"

"Hard to say," said Samm.

Heron snorted. "Does it matter?"

Kira watched the water roll by and sighed. "I suppose not. What do we do?"

"We're not getting Afa across without a bridge," said Samm, "plus we'd soak the radio, and I don't trust its claim of 'water resistance.' I say we follow the riverbank until we find a bridge intact."

"North or south?" asked Heron. "This time the question actually does matter."

"According to our map we're still slightly north of Denver," said Kira. "We'll go south." They turned their horses around,

Kira whispering encouragements to Bobo and patting him softly on the neck. The riverbank itself was impassable, not just along the shoreline but several yards back from it, nearly a full quarter mile in some places. The ground was either too steep or too swampy or too dense with trees, and more often than not all three. They followed a narrow highway as far as they could, though more than once they found that it had wandered too close to the river and sloughed off, washing away into the relentless flood of water. When that road turned away they moved to a different one, though the story was similar there and occasionally worse. The first bridge they found looked across to the biggest city since Chicago, but this bridge was destroyed, just like the last one. The second day they found themselves trapped where the road had been completely washed away, surrounded on one side by the river and the other by a lake, and were forced to backtrack several miles. Here the wetlands stretched well over a mile from bank to bank, probably more than two, though Kira couldn't help but wonder how much of her estimate was accurate and how much was helpless frustration. It was beautiful, alive with birds and flowers and fireflies turning lazy circles over the marsh, but it was also insurmountable. They found a new road, prayed that it would take them to a bridge, and followed it south.

After two days of searching they came to the village of Gulfport, more under the water than over it. Heavy stone pylons marked where a bridge had once stretched across to the much larger city on the far side, but except for some girders peeking forlornly from the surging river currents, nothing but the pylons remained. Kira swore, and Afa slumped painfully in his saddle.

Even Oddjob, usually eager to wander during their pauses in search of green shoots to munch on, seemed too depressed to move.

"It's got to be the river that took out the bridge," said Samm. "These cities were too small to be a factor in the war, and none of them are military targets. I think the river's just too . . . big for its own good."

"Two big for our own good, too," said Heron.

"Somebody had to cross it first, right?" asked Kira. She nudged Bobo's flanks and walked him farther toward the water's edge, peering around the bend in the trees as far south as she could see. "I mean, somebody had to build the bridges, and somebody had to cross before that."

"Not with Afa they didn't," said Heron. Her tone of voice seemed to imply that they should leave him behind for the sake of the mission, but Kira didn't even bother to glare at her. She did shoot a glance at Afa, though, mostly asleep tied into his saddle, head bobbing in and out of consciousness as the painkillers warred with uncomfortable sitting position.

"We could build a raft," Kira said. "There are plenty of trees, and if we want to brave that sunken city, we could find planks and boards all over the place. If we build a raft big enough, we could ferry the horses across, and Afa with them."

"The current's a lot stronger than it looks," said Samm, but Kira cut him off.

"I know," she snapped, more harshly than she intended. "That's why we haven't tried crossing it before now, but what are our options? We're on a tight schedule as it is, even before we took a two-day detour in the wrong direction. We need to go west, so let's . . . go west. It's that or head south for another couple of weeks."

"You're right," said Samm, "but we don't build our own raft unless we have to, and if we get to the point where we have to, we'll know we're essentially doomed. Look at that town over there—these were all shipping towns, using the river to haul freight back and forth in the old world. All we have to do is find a boat that still floats and use that."

"So far all the big towns have been on the far side," said Heron. "Unless you want to head back north two days to Moline. I don't remember any convenient barges lying around up there."

"Then we keep going south," said Samm, and angled Buddy farther down the road. "We've come this far, we may as well keep going."

"Is that a good reason to keep going?" asked Heron. "'We're getting really good at failure, we may as well stick with it?'"

"You know I'm not very good at sarcasm," said Samm.

Heron snarled. "Then I'll put it more plainly: This is stupid. Kira has her own reasons for coming out here, but I'm here because of you. I trusted you, and I'm trying as hard as I can to keep that trust alive, but look at us. We're in a swamp, lost in a dead country, just waiting for the next attack, or the next injury, or the next little stretch of muddy road to just fall off into the river and drown us."

"You're the best one of us," said Samm. "You can survive anything."

"I survive because I'm smart," said Heron. "Because I don't get myself into the kinds of situations that could kill me, and frankly, that's the only situation we've even been in for weeks."

"We can do this," said Kira. "We just need to calm down a little."

"I know we can do it," said Heron. "As much as I complain, I'm not an idiot—I know we can cross the damn river. I just want you to assure me that we should."

Kira started to speak, but Heron cut her off. "Not you. Samm. And please tell me it's not because of this"—she waved her hand angrily at Kira—"whatever-the-hell-she-is."

Samm looked at Heron, then out across the river. "It's not enough, is it? Just to follow; just to have faith in someone bigger and smarter and better informed. That's how we're built, that's how every Partial is wired—to follow orders and trust in our leaders—but it's not enough. It never has been." He looked back at Heron. "We've followed our leaders, and sometimes they win and sometimes they lose; we do what they say and we play our part. But this is our decision. Our mission. And when we're done, it will be our victory, or our defeat. I don't want to fail, but if I do, I want to be able to look back and say, 'I did that. I failed. That was all me.'"

Kira listened in silence, marveling at the strength of his words and the force of his conviction. It was the first time he'd really explained himself—beyond the simple "I trust Kira" statements—and the sentiment was the opposite of "I trust anyone." He was here because he wanted to make his own decision. Was that really so important to him? Was that really so rare? And how could it possibly sway Heron, who was already so fiercely independent? She might have been a Partial, like them, but Samm was appealing to something in his and Heron's collective experience that Kira was realizing she didn't understand. Samm and Heron stared at each other, and she could only guess at the link data flowing between them.

"Okay," said Heron, and turned her horse to follow him. They started south, and Oddjob followed, and Kira brought up the end of the line, lost in thought.

The Mississippi led them to more flooded towns, most even smaller than Gulfport: Dallas City, Pontoosuc, Niota. Niota held another former bridge, reaching across to the first major hills they'd seen in weeks, a promontory bluff and a town called Fort Madison. Niota was in better condition than the last three villages had been, and they waded in as far as they dared, searching for anything they could use to float across. Samm found one end of a barge tipping up from the river at an angle, but nothing still holding to the surface. The current was, indeed, stronger than Kira had expected, and she waded back out of the eerie, underwater town as soon she as she could.

"Well," said Heron, flopping down beside her on the grass. "We're still stuck, but we're soaking wet. Remind me again how that's an improvement."

"Don't worry," said Kira. "As hot and muggy as it is here, you'll have something new to complain about any minute now."

"Let's get back to Afa and the horses," said Samm. "We can make it another ten miles today if we keep moving."

"Wait," said Kira, staring at the sunken city. Something had moved. She scanned it carefully, shielding her eyes from the bright glares and flashes reflecting up from the surface of the water. A wave surged, and it moved again, big and black against the glimmering water beyond. "The barge is moving."

Samm and Heron looked out, and Kira whispered to wait, wait, wait . . . and then another wave sloshed against it and it moved, almost lightly. "It's still buoyant," said Samm. "I thought it was sunken."

"It's moving too freely to be pinned," said Heron. "Maybe tied down?"

"And if we untie it," said Kira, "maybe we can use it."

They shucked their guns and heavy gear and waded back into the city, this time kicking off and swimming when the river grew too deep to stand in. The river was strong, but they kept to the lee side of the buildings, moving hand over hand along the roofs as they picked their way toward the barge. It flapped faintly against the current, nearly the farthest object from the shore. They hoisted themselves onto the last building out, watching the trapped barge from the roof.

"It's definitely moving," said Kira. "As soon as we cut it loose, it's going to pop right up and float away."

"We'll have to tie it to something else on a longer line," said Samm. "We'll want a safety line on whoever goes out there anyway."

"One-two-three not it," said Heron. "But I will get you a rope. The last building we passed was a hardware store." She slipped back into the water and Kira followed, not wanting to let anyone—even someone she vaguely mistrusted—enter a ruined, flooded building alone. They touched off from the wall and felt the current catch them, carrying them south between the buildings even as they tried to swim east to catch the next one. Heron caught hold of the rusted rain pipe with one hand and reached for Kira with the other, grabbing her as she rushed by. Kira felt something solid beneath her feet, probably a car or the cab of a truck, and pushed off from it as Heron pulled her toward the hardware store. Kira caught the windowsill, grateful there were no shards of glass poking out from it, and ducked her head below the surface to swim inside.

There was a foot or so of air in the building, trapped between the ceiling and the top of the river, though a faint breeze and a shaft of light showed that the air was kept fresh by at least one hole in the roof above. The damp atmosphere had covered the ceiling and the visible portion of the walls with moss, and Kira brushed some from her hair as Heron surfaced beside her. "Looks pretty well scoured out by the river," Kira told her, for most of the Sheetrock on the walls, and anything once attached to it, had long ago been washed away.

"There's bound to be something lower," said Heron, and they maneuvered to the widest stretch of southern wall—it was less likely here that the objects they needed, and indeed the swimmers themselves, would be swept out to the river beyond. Heron dove first, staying down long enough that Kira began to get seriously worried, before popping to the surface and brushing her coal-black hair from her face. "No rope," she said, "but I think I found some chain."

"Let me look," said Kira, and tucked herself into a duck dive down against the wall. She tried to open her eyes and found the water too dark and muddy to see in. She felt something heavy and coiled, slicker than rope but smoother than chain, and tried to lift it. It budged slightly, but was too heavy to move. She jumped up, breaking the surface and grabbing the wall for support. "I think I found a hose."

"Is that strong enough?"

"It should be, if it's long enough."

Heron pulled her knife from its sheath, popped it open, and bit it in her teeth before diving down. Almost a minute later she bobbed up with the knife in one hand and an end of the hose in the other.

"How long can you hold your breath?" Kira asked.

"Biologically superior," said Heron. "I keep telling you. Take this, the other end is still stuck to the shelf with a zip tie."

"Probably why it's still in here," said Kira, but Heron was already gone. She surfaced a while later and nodded: success. Kira began coiling the hose as well as she could, and stopped after the first twenty coils. "This has got to be at least a hundred feet."

"Then let's do it," said Heron, and gripped a portion of the hose as Kira ducked back out of the open window. Kira bobbed up farther south than she'd intended, looking up to see Samm watching from his roof. Was he smiling to see her? Of course he'd been worried with them gone so long, but Kira found herself hoping that he was worried about her, specifically, rather than just the success or failure of the search for rope.

She pushed the thought away and held up one end of the hose. "Hose," she said simply, short of breath as she struggled against the current. She worked her way back to Samm's roof, and he pulled her up. Heron clambered up behind her, not looking nearly as exhausted as Kira felt. Samm pulled up the looping lengths of hose and coiled them on the mossy shingles. He pointed back through the sunken city to the shore, where Heron's horse Dug was watching them solemnly.

"I think that's the best place to try to land it," he said. "We've got a pretty clear shot, depending on how deep it rides, but it looks like a pretty shallow barge. If we head back that way and tie off one end of this to . . ." He paused, studying the bits of architecture that poked up above the water. "That light pole. I can swim out from here, tie this off, cut whatever's holding it, and then we can tow it in to shore."

"Just that easy, huh?" asked Kira.

"Unless the barge is tied down with metal chains," said Samm, "yes. The hard part's going to be getting it back out again laden with horses without foundering against those buildings."

"I'm assuming we're the first people to try to dock a boat at that end of Main Street," said Heron. "I don't think they designed the city with 'barge maneuverability' in mind."

"We'll just use poles to push ourselves away," said Kira. "Against the pounding, bridge-destroying current of the mighty Mississippi River."

"Just that easy?" asked Samm. Kira looked up and saw that he was smiling—a tentative smile, as if he was trying it out. She smiled back.

"Yeah," she said. "Just that easy."

It wasn't. Samm could barely reach the barge with the hose tied off on the light post, and even after they moved it, he found the current almost too strong to work with as he dove for the docking ropes—not one, as they'd hoped, but five. He tied off the hose and spent nearly half an hour under the water, hacking on the series of ropes and coming up only briefly for air. Kira couldn't see him well, but he had lost most of his color and was shivering against the cold. Each time he dove back down she found herself holding her breath in sympathy, seeing how long she could last, and each time he seemed to stay down longer, dragging the time out impossibly, until at last she was certain he had drowned. With a sudden lurch the barge shifted, the cut ties making it less stable, and still Samm didn't come up. Kira counted to ten. Nothing. She waded in, counting to ten again, to twenty, and soon Heron was swimming with her, using the taut garden hose for balance as it stretched toward the breaking point. The barge moved again, spinning and slamming into the buildings downstream, and Samm erupted from the river, gasping desperately for breath. Kira caught him, holding his head above water as gulped down air.

"Got it," he said, his teeth clacking together. "Let's pull it in."

"We need to warm you up first," said Kira, "You could get hypothermia."

"This hose is going to snap if we wait any longer," said Heron.

"He could die," insisted Kira.

"I'll be fine," Samm said, shivering. "I'm a Partial."

"Back to the shallows," said Heron, "or it's all for nothing."

They worked their back along the hose, Kira watching Samm and praying he didn't shiver himself into a seizure. When they reached land shallow enough to stand on, she rubbed his back and chest, a quick furious burst of movement that probably soothed her conscience more than it did his condition. She felt a small thrill to be touching him—to feel the firm contours of his muscled chest—which seemed so enormously out of place she dropped her hands almost instantly, recoiling at the incongruity. She was a medic, not a schoolgirl; she could touch a man's chest without going all gooey. He was still shaking, his teeth chattering with the cold, and she rubbed him again, working her hands up and down his pecs and sternum to force some warmth back into his body. A moment later the three of them seized the rope and started dragging the barge up the flooded street. Afa watched listlessly from the shore, almost too doped on painkillers to stand. The barge drifted toward them slowly, and when they gained about twenty feet of slack, Kira untied the hose and waded back to the next secure point, tying it off and then starting over. The barge scraped along the houses, catching on one of them so firmly Heron had to swim out and dislodge it with a plank of driftwood. After more than two hours they'd moved the barge close enough to shore for the horses to board it. It was barely three hundred feet.

They tied it off again, snapping the hose and almost losing it; Samm wrapped the trailing end around his arm and grabbed a brick wall with his other, straining red-faced at the pain as Kira and Heron scrambled to secure the barge more firmly. A heavy wooden door ripped from a nearby frame served as a steep boarding plank, and they walked the horses up one by one, Kira leading them with soft words while Samm and Heron guided them from the sides to keep them in line. Samm was still shivering, and his horse Buddy seemed more spooked in response, shuffling and backtracking so nervously that the door cracked. They coaxed him onto the barge before it broke completely, and then had to find a new one to get Oddjob on board at the end. Afa came last, his face slack, his massive arms wrapped around his backpack like an overstuffed life preserver.

"I can't leave my backpack," he said. "I can't leave my backpack."

"We won't," said Kira. "Just sit here, and don't move, and you'll be safe."

Heron cut the lines and hurried to her place on the leading edge of the boat, reaching it just in time to pick up a board and push off against the row of buildings the current tried to carry them into. Samm was on the same side, his hands and arms still pale from the cold. Kira stood in the center, trying to soothe the horses; they whinnied in agitation at the instability of the barge, dipping and shifting exactly the way ground shouldn't, and became even more spooked as the barge slammed into the small hardware store.

"Watch the buildings!" cried Kira, trying to keep Bobo from rearing up and breaking away from her.

"Go to hell!" Heron shot back, her teeth tightly clenched as she tried to keep the unwieldy barge, now firmly caught in the river's sweeping current, from slamming into the building again. The river pulled them both into the buildings and out into the center, not quickly but powerfully; it was not a white-water river, but Kira was realizing that even a lazy river, when it got this big, had an immense amount of strength. Samm joined Heron at the back, and together they managed to keep the trailing edge of the barge from clipping the last building in the line, and suddenly they were out: free of the sunken city, free of the debris that cluttered the shores, free of the limited stability the buildings had granted. The barge spun slowly in the water, and the horses chomped and snapped in fear. Samm ran to help Kira control them, but Heron walked the edge, trying to keep herself at whatever part of the barge was the front.

"Sandbar," she called out, kneeling to grip the side for balance, and the barge shook with sudden impact, sending Kira reeling for balance. Afa fell on his side, closing his eyes and clutching his backpack tightly. Samm and Kira separated, each taking two horses by the reins and leading them a few steps away from each other. The sandbar spun them in the opposite direction as they bounced away from it, and for a moment they straightened out. Kira found solid footing, readjusting her grip on the horses, and Heron called out again, more urgently this time: "Fallen bridge!"

"What?" shouted Kira.

"Just hold on to something," said Heron, and suddenly the barge slammed into an outcropping of twisted steel supports, just barely visible above the water but solid and deadly below the surface. The horses screamed, and the barge screamed with them, metal scraping against metal. The barge tipped dangerously, then rocked back the other way as it rolled around the fallen bridge. Kira fought to keep control of her horses.

"We need to steer," she called.

"Yes, we do," said Samm, "but I don't think that's an option at this point."

"Here's another one," called Heron, and Kira held on tight as the boat rocked and splashed and shook. They were in the middle of the river now, the current faster and deeper, and Kira saw with dismay that it seemed to be carrying them straight through the path of debris from the bridge. They bobbed like a cork on the surface, thrown back and forth from stone to stone, steel to steel. A particularly bad hit brought a loud crack, and Kira looked around wildly to see if anything had broken. Heron scrambled across the floor and looked up angrily. "We're taking on water."

"That's awesome," said Kira. "Throw it back out!"

Heron glared at her, but found a discarded board and tried to stop up the hole—a crack in the side wall, thankfully, not the floor, or Kira thought they might have gone down almost immediately. The board didn't seem to help, and Heron gave up, trying to use it instead as a rudder. The barge ignored her and went where the river wanted it. They shook with another impact, then another, and Kira cried out as the floor rippled beneath her feet. *Floors aren't supposed to do that.*

"The floor rippled," she said.

Samm held his two horses tightly, though they looked ready to tear him in half. "Rippled or buckled?"

"I think it was just—" Kira cried out as the barge hit another obstacle, and the metal floor groaned in protest at some unexpected movement.

"Buckled," said Heron, bracing her board against the floor for stability. "This is not going to end well."

"How poorly are we talking," asked Kira, "assuming it at least ends with us on that side of the river?"

"Poorly," said Heron. "We lose some gear, maybe most of it. A horse if we're unlucky, Afa if we are."

"We won't lose Afa," said Samm. "I'll pull him to shore myself if I have to."

"You'll have to," said Heron. "This rust bucket is falling apart around us, and the river is doing everything it can to speed that along."

"Try to steer us closer to the side," said Kira.

Heron looked at her with wide, incredulous eyes.

"What in the hell do you think I've been trying for the last five minutes?"

"You're not trying it now," Kira snarled.

"You'd better hope you can swim," said Heron, shooting her an icy glare as she leapt back to the edge, "because Samm's saving Afa and I'm not saving you." She stuck the board back into the water, correcting the spin but failing to guide the boat in any particular direction. They almost hit a promontory on the far side, but the same current that had pulled them away from the east shore was now working to keep them from the west one, and even when they finally cleared the debris field, their barge was creaking and sinking and caught in a powerful current. The river turned south with water already lapping around Kira's feet, and she looked down the river to see that it was rounding a wide U-shaped bend before turning back east again.

"Keep steady on that rudder," she called to Heron. "The river's turning hard enough that we might get thrown onto the bank up there."

"That's not a bank, it's a dock," said Samm. "Getting thrown onto it will hurt."

"Just . . . save Afa," said Kira, keeping her eyes on the shore. The river moved surprisingly slowly for something so powerful, and it seemed to take them forever to round the bend. She worried they wouldn't build up enough momentum to get across at all, but slowly the west shore grew closer, their leaking barge turning just slightly wider than the river was. *We're going to make ground,* she thought. *Right in the middle of that city.* She could see it now, buildings and docks rising out of the overgrown riverbank, masked with trees and tall marsh reeds. The placement of the city seemed almost perfectly designed to catch things as the river carried them around the bend, and Kira briefly wondered if it had been built there for that exact purpose. Her thoughts turned more urgent as the shore drew closer, and the hope of landing became a certainty of crashing into the riverside wharf looming up to meet them. It was flooded, like most of the riverside cities, and Kira guessed their trajectory would carry them straight into a tangle of boats, logs, and other debris caught in a cluster of old stores and buildings. "Can we take another impact?" she asked.

"No, we can't," said Heron, standing up and throwing her rudder over the side. "Save what you can." She grabbed Dug's reins from Kira's hand and seemed to be readying the horse to jump over the side. Samm looked at the impending crash, then dropped both sets of reins and ran to Afa. The horses pranced back skittishly, and the sudden shift in weight caused the damaged barge to warp, knocking Kira off her feet and sending Oddjob completely over the side. Kira clung to Bobo's reins, trying to stand, when the barge slammed into the mass of debris and crumpled like a foil model. Kira went down, and the river swallowed her.

CHAPTER TWENTY-NINE

Water lapped against the sides of their boat as the soldiers pushed away from the dock. Marcus clung to the railing of what used to be a luxury yacht, retrofitted by the Grid soldiers and filled with a tank of the cleanest gas they could make. There were ten of them, including Marcus and Senator Woolf—though all the men here called him Commander Woolf, and Marcus could tell he was much more in his element here as a soldier than he was as a politician. They were setting out from the extreme southwest corner of Long Island, from an industrial wharf ominously labeled Gravesend Bay. Marcus tried not to think about the implication.

Their plan was simple. There were potentially some unfriendly Partials in Manhattan, but everything they'd learned from Samm suggested that Manhattan was about as far south as they ever ventured, being too busy securing their fragmented outposts in New York and Connecticut. Commander Woolf had charted a course across the Lower New York Bay, miles away from any watchmen on Manhattan, skirting the southern shores of Staten Island to the mouth of the Arthur Kill canal. From there they would travel north through the ruins of New Jersey, ideally staying well out of view to anyone watching Manhattan, all the way to the Tappan Zee Bridge and across into White Plains. If Morgan's Partials saw them, they were dead; if the other faction of Partials saw them at a bad time, or in the wrong light, or they were just in a killing mood, they were dead. The Grid soldiers were armed to the teeth, but Marcus knew that wouldn't matter if they met a platoon of Partials who didn't fancy a chat. Which was precisely why they were going so far out of their way not to encounter any.

The Lower Bay was a treacherous maze of sunken masts and scaffolds and radar antennas, jutting up from the water like a barnacled metal forest. Their pilot was the best they could find on the island, and he navigated through it with white-knuckled intensity. Their yacht was not the most maneuverable thing, and the controls were old and stiff. Marcus crossed the narrow boat—a braver act than he liked to admit—and gripped the far railing next to Woolf, who was looking at the ruins of the wrecked ships as they glided by.

"Please tell me these aren't what's left of your previous missions," said Marcus.

"In a manner of speaking," said Woolf, "but these missions failed twelve years ago. This is the last great NADI fleet, sailing north to attack the Partial stronghold in New York—quite possibly the one we're headed to now in White Plains. It was sunk by Partial aircraft before it could enter the narrows."

"And they're still here?" asked Marcus, looking around at the wreckage. "Some of these ships are sticking so far out of the water I don't know if we can count them as sunk, just grounded."

"The bay through here was only about forty feet deep," said Woolf, "more in the center where they dredged it as a shipping lane, probably much less now that it's collected more than a decade's worth of silt. The bigger ships are out there," he said, pointing to the southeast, "on an ocean shelf just south of Long Island. All the bigger ships that couldn't make it in this far."

"Why were any of the ships trying to get in this far?" asked Marcus. "Even if they weren't attacking a narrow river, a fleet this size would be overkill."

"I imagine overkill was exactly what they were going for," said Woolf, watching as another metal monstrosity floated gently past. They twisted up from the ocean floor like giant metal tentacles, the last, frozen remnants of a rusted kraken. "I know my unit was."

They left the worst of it when they passed south of Staten Island, crossing from the Lower Bay to the Raritan Bay, but even here there were shipwrecks and hazards. Their pilot watched the northern shore with a practiced eye, taking them into a small inlet that narrowed quickly to a kind of swampy marsh.

"Why are we stopping?" asked Woolf.

"This is it," said the pilot. "This is the Arthur Kill."

"This is the canal?" It looked more like a creek through a winding park than the deep shipping lane they'd seen on the map. "Are you sure?"

"Trust me," said the pilot, "I used to live around here. That thing west of us is the Raritan River—this is the Arthur Kill. It's man-made, and back before the Break they had to dredge it every year to keep it open. Now that it's not being dredged, I guess it just filled up with silt."

"Enough to grow reeds on the sides," said Woolf. "Can we still make it?"

"I can give it a shot," said the pilot, and cranked the engine into low gear. They putted almost lazily up the narrow passage, marsh birds screeching and singing and hooting back and forth around them, and Marcus felt like he was on a safari through a giant metal canyon. The buildings on both sides were oppressively industrial, not the once-shiny buildings of Manhattan but the weather-beaten processing plants of the Chemical Coast. The water everywhere around here had an oily sheen to it, and Marcus wondered how the birds could survive on it. A giant fish jumped in front of them, snapping at something near the surface, and Marcus couldn't help but imagine the reeds full of hungry, mutant crocodiles.

The driver took them as far as the Rahway River before making a detour; the Rahway was pumping enough water into the channel to keep the river south of it clear, but the tributaries farther north presumably had better outlets for their water than this artificial ditch, and the span between here and Newark Bay appeared to be sealed tight with sediment and reeds. They turned west up the Rahway, surrounded now on both sides by tall chemical silos, and wound through it until a series of massive bridges passed over them: a railroad and a multilane highway so broad it took four bridges to contain it. "That's the Jersey Turnpike," said the pilot, and brought them into shore near the base of the railroad. "I lived off exit 17E."

Woolf had the pilot steer them toward the coast, and the

Gridsmen gathered their equipment and starting wading to shore; Marcus eyed the reeds on the riverbank warily, still half expecting a crocodile, before jumping in after them.

The New Jersey Turnpike plowed straight through the city on the shore, a giant metropolis separated from Manhattan by yet another giant metropolis between them. "Either they're not watching us this far west," said Woolf, "or they see us no matter what we do. I say we screw stealth and make the best time we can."

CHAPTER THIRTY

"Just a few more minutes," said Haru. "They'll be here."

"And the Partials with them," said Private Kabza.

"We'll be fine," said Haru. "How many of these drops have we made, and how many times have you been murdered by Partials?"

"That's not an entirely fair way to frame it," said Kabza, but Haru cut him off.

"I said we'll be fine," Haru insisted. "Check with the rear guard again."

Kabza got on the radio and sent their rear guard a brief, coded message, whispering into the mic and then listening carefully as the man on the other end whispered back. He signed off and turned back to Haru. "Our exit route's still clear. I say we dump this stuff and run; the Voice can find it themselves without us here to hand it to them. It's not like they're paying us."

"Did you say 'the Voice'?" asked Haru.

"Of course I did," said Kabza. "What do you call them?"

"Delarosa hated the Voice," said Haru. "She'd never take on their name."

The radio blinked, and Kabza held it to his ear. After a moment he breathed a quick "Confirmed, over" and looked at Haru. "Point guard's spotted them. They should be here in a few minutes."

"Are they being chased by Partials?"

"He didn't say," said Kabza dryly. "I think he might have led with that if it was an issue, but I can call back to see if maybe it just slipped his mind."

"Just relax," said Haru, "this is what I've been telling you. We'll be fine."

"Fantastic," said Kabza. "I'm glad you have such unerring trust in this woman." He paused, watching the forest, then spoke again. "Speaking of which, why do you have such unerring trust in this woman? I thought you hated her."

"Delarosa and I . . . disagree on some things," said Haru. "When she first escaped, she was using innocent civilians as bait—including me, which I think made me a little justifiably upset. But her core principles I agree with completely: that our shores need to be protected, that the Partials need to be destroyed, and that desperate times call for desperate measures. Delarosa is willing to do what it takes, and she knows that as long as she doesn't put innocent humans at unnecessary risk, I'll support her."

"Define 'unnecessary risk,'" said Kabza. "I've spent the last three days in hostile territory, picking my nose and hoping nobody decides to shoot me while I hand Delarosa something we could easily have just left at a dead drop. Is that unnecessary?"

"She asked for something . . . unusual this time," said Haru, peering into the trees. "I want to know what she's planning on doing with it."

A moment later their perimeter guard flashed a silent hand signal, and Haru and Kabza watched as three cloaked figures stepped out of the trees. Delarosa pulled off her hood and stood silently, waiting. Haru stood up from cover and walked to her. "You're late."

Delarosa's face was stony. "You're impatient. Do you have my gear?"

Haru waved, and Kabza and another soldier brought out two heavy crates full of scuba equipment: masks, fins, wet suits, and four tanks of compressed air, recently filled. "The tanks are almost mint," said Haru. "Best condition you'll find on Long Island, and removed at great personal risk from the ruins of the Defense Grid armory." Delarosa motioned her followers forward, but Haru stepped in front to block them. "Before you take them anywhere, I want to know what you're going to use them for."

"For breathing underwater," said Delarosa. Haru didn't respond, and Delarosa cocked her head to the side. "You've never asked about my plans before."

"Because everything you've asked for has had an obvious purpose," said Haru. "Bullets, explosives, solar panels, radio equipment—that's all standard stuff for a band of guerrillas. But you know my rules, and the conditions on which I'll bring you these gear drops, so I want your assurance: No civilians will be harmed by whatever you're doing."

"Civilians are being harmed by every second we delay here," said Delarosa.

Haru kept his gaze steady. "What is the scuba gear for?"

"Scavenging," said Delarosa simply. "In twelve years we've picked a lot of this island clean, but there's still plenty to be found offshore. By giving me this, you're assuring that I won't have to ask you for nearly as many favors in the future."

"What's been underwater for twelve years that could possibly be so useful?" asked Haru. "Seems like any supplies or weaponry submerged for that long would be pretty corroded by now."

"I guess we'll see."

Haru stared at her, trying to decide what he thought. Finally he turned and walked away. "Don't make me sorry I helped you." He walked back to the rest of his men and signaled that it was time to leave. Private Kabza fell into step beside him.

"That's a relief," said Kabza. "The more they scavenge for themselves, the less we have to put ourselves at risk like this."

"Maybe," said Haru, still thinking about what Delarosa had said, and how she'd said it.

"What are you going to do?"

Haru furrowed his brow, plans already forming in his head. "We're going to follow them."

PART 3

CHAPTER THIRTY-ONE

Kira and her companions lost most of their gear in the river: Samm's rifle, Afa's radio, and almost all their food. Afa held on to his backpack, but the documents inside were soaked and useless, the paper disintegrating and the ink running hopelessly. His screen, thankfully, survived the trip, but the Tokamin to power it had washed away. Kira knew that this was potentially the most devastating loss, but it wasn't the one that made her saddest. That was Heron's horse, Dug, who'd broken both front legs in the crash. He'd survived, but all he could do was scream in pain and fear, his breath frantic and his mouth flecked in foam. Samm had ended his misery with a bullet.

They kept moving as soon as they recovered enough to do so, Samm and Heron and Kira taking turns on Buddy and Bobo while Afa, still wounded and nearly delirious, had to be tied into Oddjob's saddle to keep from falling off. Kira was convinced that his leg was infected, and they raided every pharmacy they passed, trying to replace their lost meds. As they traveled Kira was surprised at her ability to keep up with the others, matching not only the horses' pace, but their stamina as well. She had always known she was strong, and chalked it up to a lifetime of bitter survival—she had to work for everything she got, and that had made her physically fit—but she realized now that it was more than that. She could match the Partials stride for stride, mile for mile. It was a boon, but it disturbed her to learn it. Another piece of evidence that deep down inside, she was profoundly inhuman.

Their path took them north a few miles, back up past the river to Highway 34, and on this they struck out west. The land there was more of what they'd passed on the east side of the river, flat prairies as far as the eye could see, dotted here and there by stands of trees or dark lines of scrub and underbrush, marking a gully or a ditch or an old homestead. Kira thought it was pretty, especially when the sun began to set and the entire scene, both earth and sky, lit up in fierce reds and yellows and oranges. She looked at Samm, the beauty of the scene too much not to share with somebody, but his eyes were dark, and his face morose. She angled toward him and caught his attention with a nod.

"What's wrong?"

"What? Nothing."

"Samm."

He looked at her, then out at the glowing sunset. "It's just . . . this."

Kira followed his gaze. "It's gorgeous."

"It is," said Samm. "But it's also . . . I was stationed here, or I guess I just traveled through here, during the revolution. It was . . ." He stopped again, as if the memory was painful.

"You know how back home, in the east, everything's so broken, and run-down, and the buildings are all in ruins and overgrown with kudzu and weeds and everything looks . . . old? We're surrounded, every minute of our lives, by the evidence of what we've done, what we've destroyed. But out here . . ." He paused again. "Look around. There's not a house for miles, just a flat road that's still in pretty good condition. It's as if the war never happened."

"So you miss the reminders of destruction?" asked Kira.

"It's not that," said Samm, "it's just . . . I used to think the world was worse for what we've done, both our species, but out here I don't think the world even cares who we are. Or were. We came and went, and life goes on, and the land that was always here before us will still be here after we're dead and gone. Birds will still fly. Rain will still fall. The world didn't end, it just . . . reset."

Kira fell silent, thinking about his words. They seemed so pure, in a way, so unexpected from the Samm she thought she knew. He was a soldier, a fighter, a stoic wall, and yet here was a softer side, an almost poetic side, that she'd never known was there. She cast a long look at him as they rode: He looked eighteen, as all Partial infantry did, but he'd been alive for nineteen years. He'd been eighteen years old for nineteen years. But he'd started life as an eighteen-year-old, so did that make him . . . thirty-seven? The thought twisted her brain into knots, trying to figure out how old he really was inside. How he thought of himself, and how he thought of her.

There was that thought again, and she growled, shaking her head as if she could flick the thought away like water flying from her hair. *What does Samm think of me? What do I think of Samm?* She told herself it didn't matter, that they had more important things to worry about, but her heart didn't seem to care. She told herself there was no point trying to decipher their relationship, because she didn't even know what she wanted the relationship to be and therefore had no frame of reference. Her heart ignored all her reasoning. Her mind worked furiously on its own, thinking about who Samm was, about what he was, about where he came from and what he wanted and how Kira, the girl who kept risking his life, might fit into it. He talked about the world renewing itself, and all she could think about was being in that world together. It was the same talk she'd had with Marcus a hundred times, and she'd always yearned for something more. With Samm, though . . .

No. That's not why I'm here. That's not what I'm doing. Thinking about a future with Samm is a meaningless exercise when he's just going to die in a year because of the Partial expiration date. Find the answers. Solve the problem. You don't get a life until you make one worth living.

She rode on and watched the sun sink, watched the red sky turn pink, and then blue, and then the richest dark purple she'd ever seen. She watched the stars come out and shine until they seemed to light up the entire prairie. They camped in an open field, roasting rabbits Heron caught with a snare, and Kira closed her eyes and pretended that the world had never ended at all, that it was just beginning, that when she woke up in the morning the entire world would be like this spot: healed and whole, unscarred by human interference or Partial rebellion or any sign of civilization. She fell asleep and dreamed of darkness.

✌ ✌ ✌

The next day they saw their first poisoned tree.

The wind was changing, the strong easterly winds off the Great Lakes slowly replaced, more and more each mile they traveled, by southern winds up from the Gulf of Mexico. It hadn't gotten bad yet, but this twisted, stunted, stark-white tree was the first sign that the easy days were behind them. They were heading into the toxic wasteland.

The second day she smelled it—just a whiff, as a short tendril of wind brought it past her nose—the sour, almost metallic smell of the poisoned air, like a mix of sulfur and smoke and ozone. Just a hint and it was gone. The day after that she woke up to the smell, and it lasted most of the day, and here and there more bleached-white trees stood like haunting skeletons in the scattered groves by the side of the road. The grass that clung to the lees of the fence posts was paler now, more scraggly and desperate, and each day it grew worse. The next city they reached was a lonely place called Ottumwa, and in it they found the streets and walls and roofs all streaked with chemical residue, as if the runoff from the rain itself was stringent and deadly. A river cut through the center of town, not nearly as big as the Mississippi, but by extension, not blessed with impressive bridges. They had all fallen, whether to ancient sabotage or relentless weather Kira couldn't say. The water, at least, looked fresh, running down from the north where the land was cleaner. They stopped there for a few hours, scouring the ramshackle stores and restaurants for any meds they could find, and any cans of food that looked like they might still be good. Heron was a capable hunter, but now that they'd entered the wasteland it would likely no longer be safe to eat anything she caught. Kira checked Afa's wound again, no worse yet no better than it had been since the shipwreck, and murmured soothing reassurances in his ear.

"We're going to cross the river now," she said softly, dribbling some of the last of their fresh water over the bullet hole in his leg. "We're going to swim, but it's nothing like the last one. It will be easy."

"We'll ruin the radio," said Afa, his eyes half-focused through the blend of pain and painkillers. "We can't get it wet or we'll ruin it."

"We've already lost the radio," she said. "Don't worry about it."

"We can find a new one."

"We will," she said calmly, slathering the wound in Neosporin. "After we cross the river."

"I don't want to cross the river, we'll crash our boat again." And so they went, round in circles while Kira wrapped his wound in tight bandages and then covered it with plastic bags and duct tape, doing everything she could to keep it waterproof. She finished and walked to Samm.

"He's not even aware of where we are," she said. "We have no business taking him any farther—we have no right to do it."

"We can't just leave him—"

"I know we can't just leave him," she snapped, then softened her voice and looked away. "I know we're doing everything we can for him, I just don't like it. When 'everything we can do to help him' involves 'dragging him through a poisoned wasteland,' there's something intensely wrong with the decisions that got us here."

"What would you have done differently?"

Kira shot him a quick glare, annoyed by his relentless practicality, but she shook her head and conceded defeat. "Nothing, I guess, except maybe not getting attacked in the data center. And it's not like we had any control over that. I don't like having to put him through this now any more than I liked having to bring him in the first place, but we can't do this without him, and he can't survive without us. I just . . ." She looked at Samm, searching his face for some kind of sympathy. "I just feel bad for him. Do you?"

"I do," he said, nodding. "I can't help it."

Kira smirked and looked across the river. "You'd think they would have built their super-soldiers without any feelings at all, to make them better at . . . killing, I guess. War."

"They actually did the exact opposite," said Samm. Kira looked at him quizzically. "You didn't know?" he asked. "It was one of the earliest design laws that led ParaGen to create military-grade BioSynths. Afa has a copy of the UN resolution in his backpack, though I doubt you can read it at this point. They'd had some problems with automated drone soldiers and vehicles making decisions of . . . questionable morality in the field, and the only companies from there that could get contracts for autonomous military units were biotechnology firms that could create weapons with a human emotional response."

Kira nodded. "I guess that makes sense. I mean, I've always felt completely human, emotionally, so . . ." She shrugged, not knowing how to finish her thought. She paused, then frowned and looked back at him. "If you—we—were designed to know right from wrong and whatever, it seems like that would make us less likely to cross the line in battle."

"They taught us right from wrong, and then put us into an incredibly wrong situation," said Samm. "The rebellion was the most human of all our actions, I think. You have to understand—think about your own life, as the best example. You're completely driven, at every moment, to do what's right—you see people in trouble and you have to help them. You had to help me, even though everyone, including you, thought I was the irredeemable enemy. We weren't just designed with a conscience, Kira, we were designed with an overactive one, a heightened sense of empathy that would kick in to save lives and right wrongs and help the downtrodden. And then we became the downtrodden, and how else were we supposed to react?"

Kira nodded again, but as the implications dawned on her, she turned to stare at him in shock. "They gave you an acute empathy response, and then they sent you into war?"

Samm looked away, staring across the river. "Not really any different from having humans fight. Which was, I suppose, the point."

Heron walked up and dropped a pack of supplies on the ground between them. "This is the last of it—canned chicken and tuna, freeze-dried vegetables, and a new water purifier. It was still sealed, and the filter looks pristine."

"Perfect," said Samm. "Time to go."

They shoved their packs into plastic garbage bags from the grocery store, double and triple thick for maximum protection, and used more duct tape to seal it all as tightly as they could. They lifted Afa back into Oddjob's saddle, tied him down, and loaded their gear onto Buddy and Bobo's backs. The water was cold, but relatively slow, and the crossing was blessedly uneventful. The grass on the far shore was green and healthy, nourished by the clean river, but barely twenty feet up the bank they found more yellow, sickly weeds. The buildings on this side were as scoured by the chemicals as the buildings behind them. Kira checked Afa's waterproofed wrapping, determined that it was still sealed, and decided to leave it for now.

The clouds were gathering, and Kira worried about rain. They made it a couple of hours out of town, still on Highway 34, when the first drop fell.

It hissed against the pavement.

It was Kira's turn to walk, and she bent down to feel the heat coming off the asphalt. There was none. It was getting toward evening, and the overcast day had kept the ground relatively cool. Another drop fell and hissed, as if burning at the contact. "It's not hot," she said, straightening up. "The hiss isn't from steam."

Another drop fell, then another.

"It's not steam," said Heron, "it's acid."

A raindrop landed on Oddjob, and she whinnied in pain. More drops were falling now, and Kira felt a sharp burn on her arm. The drop of rain had left a small red mark, and the pain only increased as she looked at it. She shook her head and looked at the sky. "Those clouds came from the south, didn't they?"

"Run!" shouted Samm, and grabbed Oddjob's reins. Afa was screaming in pain and terror and clutching his sodden backpack. Kira looked around for her jacket, but she had taken it off to cross the river—it, along with everything they owned, was still sealed in the plastics bags and loaded on the horses. She grabbed Bobo and raced after Samm, pulling the horse behind her and trying to maintain control of him as the acid rained down and scaled his head and flanks. Heron ran past with Buddy in tow, and Kira followed as quickly as she could. The rain was heavier now, and Kira felt the acid on her arms and face, itchy and raw after only seconds. She reached back with her free hand and pulled loose her ponytail, shaking her long hair free until it formed a kind of hood protecting her ears and shoulders. She pulled some in front of her face, as well, terrified that she would get some of the scalding rain in her eyes, and fumbled forward through the limited visibility.

Samm had seen a farmhouse a ways off the road, and he was trying to force his way past the barbed-wire fence on the edge of the field while Oddjob tugged madly on the reins, screaming to escape the painful downpour. Heron reached them and pushed him aside, handing him the reins of her own horse; Kira saw that she'd done the same with her hair as Kira had, but Samm had no such luxury, and his face was streaked with long red welts. His eyes were bloodshot and puffy. Heron pulled out a knife in each hand and cut the wires in a vicious flurry, snapping all four and opening a hole in the fence. Kira rushed through the opening with Bobo, grabbing Buddy's reins as she passed. Heron followed with Oddjob and Afa, and Samm caught up with Kira and tried to grab Buddy's reins.

"Let me help!" he shouted. "You can't control them both!"

The horses were bucking madly, but Kira kept an iron grip on the reins and pushed Samm away with her foot. "Get yourself out of the rain! You'll go blind!"

"I'm not leaving you out here!"

"Get that house open so we can get inside!" she shouted, pushing him again, and after a moment he turned and sprinted toward the building, stumbling in the fallow field. Kira gritted her teeth, wondering how he could even see, and pulled the horses as hard as she could, using the leverage of one to keep the other in line, and hoping her shoulders would survive the strain. After a short struggle they seemed to realize that she was urging them to run, and in the open field they let loose, tucking their heads and galloping at top speed for the farmhouse, jerking Kira off her feet and dragging her forward. The slack in the reins pulled her toward Buddy's pounding hooves, and she let go and tumbled to a stop in the churning poison mud. The horses raced toward the house, neck and neck, and Kira surged to her feet and followed, realizing as she ran that she was yelling, half pain and half war cry.

Kira reached the house just as Samm and Heron were catching the horses, and she stumbled through the door in agony. The front room held a couch and an easy chair, each with a skeleton still staring at an old TV on the wall. Every inch of Kira's body seemed scalded by the acid, and she looked down to see that it had already eaten a hole in her shirt. She pulled the shirt off in a flurry, seeing half a dozen more holes in the back, and threw it across the room; Samm and Heron were inside now as well, slamming the door behind them to keep the horses from escaping back into the rain. The horses were terrified, still bucking and squealing and destroying everything in the room—the TV, the furniture, even the skeletons were trampled madly underfoot. Kira tried to reach Afa, still tied to Oddjob's saddle, but she couldn't get close. Heron crept around the perimeter of the room with Samm in tow, his face red and his eyes squeezed shut, dashing forward when the horses left an opening, and rearing back when they came too close. When she reached Kira, Kira too grabbed Samm and pulled him through the back door into the kitchen, away from the flying hooves. Kira could hear the sizzle of acid on their clothes and ripped Samm's shirt away from his chest; it parted like wet paper, already half consumed by the acid, and she threw it aside. Heron was stripping as well, and the pile of clothes smoked in the corner as the acid consumed them. Their skin was mottled with throbbing red sores. Samm's eyes were still shut tight, and he fumbled helplessly with his belt; Kira helped undo them, then pulled off her own. Soon all three of them stood in their underwear, gasping for breath, trying to think what to do next as the horses railed madly in the living room.

Afa was still screaming, sobbing hysterically, but at least he was still alive. She cast her eyes around the kitchen, searching for anything she could use—towels to wipe them dry or food to calm them down—and saw that the sink had two faucets, a normal one and a strange, industrial hand pump. She stared at it, caught by the incongruity, and then it dawned on her.

"This is a farmhouse!" she shouted, rushing toward the cupboards. "They have a well!"

"What?" asked Heron.

"They're too far out of town for the normal water system, so they have well water—their own aquifer deep underground, and their own pump to work it." She clattered in the cupboards, finding the biggest bucket she could and rushing it to the sink.

"There are a couple of these on farms back home, and they're the only running water on the island. These pumps are completely self-contained, so they should still work." She worked the handle, but it was stiff and dry; she threw open the refrigerator, found a jar of rancid pickles, and poured the pungent juice down the pump to prime it. She worked it again, up and down, up and down; Heron joined her, and suddenly the water came gushing out into the pot. Kira filled it while Heron grabbed another, and when it was filled they picked it up together and threw the water at the horses, washing some of the acid away. They pumped again, repeating the process, throwing bucket after bucket at the horses until Kira was sure the well would run dry. Little by little the horses calmed, the acid washed off their backs, and the two girls ran in to cut Afa loose and drag him, still sobbing, to the kitchen. His clothes, still on him, were nearly eaten away, and his back was a mass of welts and burns and blisters. Heron pumped another bucket of water, and Kira went back to the horses to unbuckle the saddles and bags and pull out the medicine. Afa was too hoarse now to scream, and only rocked back and forth on the floor; Samm looked unconscious, or deep in meditation to control the pain, and Kira wondered how damaged his eyes really were. She paused, exhausted, and looked at Heron.

Heron looked back, just as drained, and shook her head. "You still think we made the right decision, Kira?"

No, thought Kira, but she forced herself to say "Yes."

"You'd better hope so," said Heron. "We're only about twenty miles into this toxic wasteland. We've got another seven hundred to go."

CHAPTER THIRTY-TWO

Marcus and the soldiers traveled north, through the ruins of Jersey City and Hoboken and the vast metropolitan cityscape west of the Hudson River. Their plan was to swing wide around any hostile Partial lookouts hiding in Manhattan or the Bronx, and this required them to go much farther north than they strictly needed to, just to find a way back across the Hudson River. North of Manhattan it widened significantly, becoming more of a bay than a river, and the bridge they finally found crossed it at nearly its longest point: a white needle through the sky called the Tappan Zee Bridge. It was newer than any bridge Marcus had seen before, and he guessed it had been recently rebuilt sometime just before the Break. It was miles long, and took nearly a full day's march to cross. That it had survived at all was amazing; that it had survived in nearly perfect condition was a testament to the glories of the old world. It made him wonder if future generations, assuming they ever had any, would look at this impossible architectural feat with the same awe and reverence as the pyramids, or the Great Wall of China. A pathway through the sky. *They'll probably come up with some ridiculous religious explanation for it,* he thought, *like we built it as a road to get to heaven, and each pillar represents some aspect of our belief, and the length of the bridge times the height is the sign of the vernal equinox.* The bridge was covered with cars, many of them crashed or sideways or strewn together into arcane patterns, and they had to move slowly through the mess, stopping and starting and climbing over the hot metal relics as they baked in the sun.

The city on the far side of the river was called Tarrytown, and as they followed the bridge down toward the surface streets a loud voice rang out through the ruins.

"Stop!"

The soldiers raised their rifles, but Commander Woolf gestured for them to put them back down. "We mean no harm!" he said loudly, answering back. "We're here to talk!"

"You're humans," said the voice, and Woolf nodded, gripping his rifle by the barrel and holding it up in the air, demonstrating as clearly as possible that he was not holding it near the trigger.

"Our guns are for defense only," he said. "We're not looking for a fight. We want to talk to whoever's in charge."

There was a long silence, and when the voice shouted back, Marcus thought it sounded . . . hesitant.

"State your purpose."

"A Partial by the name of Morgan has attacked our settlement and taken our people hostage, and we know she's your enemy as much as she is ours. We have an old human saying: 'The enemy of my enemy is my friend.' We're kind of hoping that makes us friendly enough to talk for a minute."

There was another long pause, and then the voice said, "Put your weapons on the ground and step away from them."

"Do as he says," said Woolf, bending down to place his rifle on the ground. Marcus did the same, and all around him the other soldiers followed suit, some more reluctantly than others. There were ten of them, plus Woolf and Marcus, but the three Partials who emerged and walked up the bridge to meet them seemed confident that they were more than a match for twelve humans. Marcus agreed with them. The lead Partial was a young man, Samm's age, though Marcus realized that this was only natural: The Partial infantry were all the same age, frozen at eighteen years old. *I guess we'll meet the generals once we get into White Plains.*

"My name is Vinci," said the Partial, and Marcus recognized the voice as the man who'd been shouting to them a few minutes ago.

"We want to talk about a treaty," said Woolf. "An alliance between our people and yours."

If Vinci was surprised he didn't show it, though Marcus had always found the Partials hard to read. The man glanced over their group, then looked back at Woolf. "I'm afraid we can't help you."

Marcus started in surprise.

"Just like that?" asked Woolf. "You'll hear us, but you won't even think about what we say?"

"It's not my place to think about it," said Vinci. "I'm a rear-guard watchman, not a general or a diplomat."

"Then take us to the generals and diplomats," said Woolf.

"Take us to someone who can hear us out."

"I'm afraid I can't do that either," said Vinci.

"Are you not allowed to let us into your territory?" asked Woolf. "Then send a messenger—we'll camp here, we'll camp on the bridge if that's better for you—but tell someone in charge that we're here, and what we're offering. At least do that much."

Vinci paused again, thinking, though Marcus couldn't tell if he was thinking about agreeing or just trying to come up with another way of saying no.

"I'm sorry," he said at last, "it's simply too dangerous right now. The war with Morgan's forces is . . ." He paused, as if looking for the right words. "Spiraling out of control."

"We're willing to risk it," said Marcus.

"We're not," said Vinci.

"Why won't you at least hear us out?" cried Woolf, stepping forward, and suddenly the Partials swung their weapons up. Woolf was practically seething, and Marcus could tell that he was on the verge of starting a fight and hoping he had enough guys left to look for someone more helpful. Marcus racked his brain for something he could do to defuse the situation; he thought about Samm, and the way he had talked, and the things that did and didn't work with him. He had been unerringly pragmatic, and almost helplessly loyal to his leaders, even when he disagreed with them. Marcus thought back over everything, and leapt in front of Woolf right as the old man seemed to be about to make a move.

"Wait," said Marcus nervously, half expecting to get punched—from in front or from behind. "My name's Marcus Valencio," he said. "I'm kind of the designated 'Partials relations consultant' around here." He said it as much for Woolf's benefit as for the Partials, hoping it would slow them down and give him a chance to talk. "If you'll permit me to ask a politically sensitive question, what do you mean when you say you can't help us?"

"He means he *won't* help us," said Woolf.

Vinci didn't answer, but after a moment he nodded.

"See, I don't think that's actually the problem," said Marcus. Vinci was already looking at him, but now he focused in on Marcus with his full, laserlike attention, and Marcus was all too aware of the difference in intensity. He smiled nervously, assuring himself that this predatory look on the man's face was a sign that Marcus was right: There was indeed a secret here, and Vinci was too loyal to ever admit it.

"You're dying," said Marcus. "Not you personally, at least not yet, but your people. Your leaders. Every Partial has a twenty-year expiration date, and you didn't learn this until the first ones died, and by now you've lost a second or third or maybe even a fourth generation of Partials, and if I'm guessing correctly, that includes almost all your generals. Everyone in charge."

Vinci didn't agree, but he didn't deny it. Marcus watched his face for any change of emotion or expression, but they had such emotionless faces he couldn't tell what the man was thinking. He kept talking.

"I think what you're saying," Marcus finished, "is that we can't broker an alliance because there's nobody left in their nation with enough authority to broker one."

The group was silent. Marcus kept his eyes on Vinci's face, not daring to look behind himself for Woolf's reaction. The old man let out a breath and spoke softly. "Good heavens, son, if that's your problem, let us help—"

"We don't need your help," said Vinci.

"You're a nation without a leader," said Woolf, "a nation of young men—"

"Young men who defeated you," said Vinci hotly, "and who will do it again if you give us any reason to."

"This is not what I was trying to do," said Marcus, stepping back in between them. He knew he was cringing, preemptively flinching from an attack he was certain would come from one side or the other, but he stood there anyway, grimacing and hoping they'd stay calm. "Vinci, my commanding officer here did not mean to imply that you were incapable of making your own decisions, and that you need an old human dude to step in and run things for you." He looked pointedly at Woolf. "He knows exactly how offensive that would be, and he would never say it or imply it. Right?"

Woolf nodded, somewhat sheepishly, but Marcus could hear his teeth grinding as he spoke. "Absolutely. I did not mean to offend you."

"Sweet," said Marcus, and glanced at Vinci before looking back at Woolf. "Next, and furthermore: Commander Woolf, Vinci here did not mean to imply that help was out of the question entirely, or that he would sooner start another genocidal war than form an alliance with you."

"You don't speak for him," said Woolf.

Marcus turned to Vinci. "Am I wrong? You didn't actually mean to imply anything even remotely like that, did you? I mean, you know how similarly offensive that would be, right?"

Vinci took a deep breath, the first social clue Marcus had seen from him yet, and shook his head. "We don't want another war with the humans."

"Sweet baby James," said Marcus. "Now do you think you two can carry on a civil conversation, or do I have to mediate the entire thing? Because I'm seriously on the verge of peeing myself here."

Vinci looked at Woolf. "This is your Partials relations consultant?"

"He's unorthodox but effective," said Woolf. He rubbed his chin. "Is what he said right, though? That your commanding officers are all dead?"

"Not all," said Vinci, and Marcus could tell from his pause that he didn't want to say the next part: "But most of them, yes. We have one left. As you likely gleaned from our operations on Long Island, we're locked in a small-scale war with Morgan's faction; we're trying to cure this expiration date, as you call it, just like she is. But her methods have become too extreme."

"But time is running out," said Marcus. "We think that we can help you—we have some of the best medical minds on Earth, literally, slaving over the cure to our own extinction-level disease. With your help we can solve the RM problem in a matter of weeks, or at least we think we can, and then all that medical mind power can point straight at your expiration date. We can save each other."

"But we need to talk to this leader you spoke about," said Woolf. "Can you take us to him or her?"

"I can take you to her," said Vinci, "but I can't guarantee it will do any good."

Woolf frowned. "Is she dying, too? Is it"—he struggled for words—"her time?"

"She's a member of the Trust," said Vinci. "They're our leaders, and as far as we can tell, they don't expire. But General Trimble is . . . well, you'll see. Follow me, but leave your weapons. And it's dangerous, like I said: No offense, but a group of humans are nothing but dead weight on a Partial battlefield. If you see or hear anything remotely like gunfire, hide."

Woolf frowned. "Just hide? That's it?"

Vinci shrugged. "Well, hide and pray."

White Plains was like nothing Marcus had ever seen before, though the ride in should have prepared him: They didn't hike in or ride on a wagon, they rode in the back of a truck. A real truck, with an engine. The driver was a Partial named Mandy, presumably one of the pilots Samm had told them about, and she eyed them suspiciously all the way into town, despite the fact that they'd been disarmed and searched and even stripped of most of their gear. Marcus had seen self-propelled vehicles in action before, of course, but to see them used so casually was astonishing. In East Meadow they used them for emergencies only, when speed was paramount. Here they just drove around like it was nothing.

Then they passed another truck on a crossroad, and then another.

Then they got to the city itself.

Marcus had spent so much time in the ruins of a city that seeing one in prime condition was shocking, and somehow disturbing. Instead of pedestrians the streets were full of cars;

instead of lamps and candles the homes were lit with electrical light—porch lights, streetlights, ceiling lights, even light-up signs on the buildings. The entire city seemed to glow with them. More subtly, but more confounding once he noticed it, the buildings all had windows. Windows had been one of the first things to go after the Break, with freeze-thaw cycles shifting the frames of unheated buildings, and flocks of birds and other animals finishing off the rest. In East Meadow only the populated homes had windows, and the bottom few floors of the hospital where they worked to maintain them, but everywhere else they were broken. Nearly every window they'd passed in Brooklyn, Manhattan, and New Jersey had been broken. But not here. It was like a city from before the Break, pulled forward in time, untouched by the apocalypse that had destroyed the rest of the world.

But even that, Marcus told himself, wasn't quite true. The Partials were an army, and this was a city at war, without a civilian in sight. *Except me,* he thought. *I'm the first noncombatant this city's seen in twelve years.*

I hope I can stay a noncombatant long enough to finish this job and get out of here.

Mandy drove them to a large building in the center of town, ringed with sandbag barricades and topped with searchlights and snipers. The mood was dark, and every Partial soldier seemed to be watching for something—an attack, most likely, though Marcus couldn't help but worry about what could make even the Partials look so nervous. Vinci led them in, explaining to each new layer of security—and there were several—that he was bringing an envoy from the humans to talk with General

Trimble, and that he had already confiscated their weapons. Marcus felt, inversely, less safe with each new level of guards and protocols, as if they were walking into a prison instead of a government building. Running lights glowed softly in the walls and ceiling, giving the place an unearthly feel that only heightened his anxiety. Vinci brought them to a large room on the top floor, a kind of plaza with benches and low tables, ringed with apartments and topped by a wide, latticed skylight. A guard behind them locked the door to the outer hall.

"This is where you'll stay," said Vinci. "It's not the best accommodations, but on reflection, probably better than what you're used to."

"No question about that," said Marcus. "Where's the chocolate fountain? I'm honestly going to be a little disappointed if it's not strapped to the back of an enchanted polar bear."

"We're not here to stay," said Woolf. "We're here to meet with Trimble. Is she here?"

Vinci shook his head. "She's busy," said Vinci. "Just wait here."

"Wait how long?" asked Marcus. "An hour? Two hours?"

One of the outer doors opened, revealing a small but tidy apartment beyond, and a woman stepped out eagerly. Her face fell when she saw them. "You're not Trimble's men?"

"You're not Trimble?" Woolf asked her. He looked at Vinci. "What's going on here?"

"I've been waiting since yesterday," said the woman. She walked toward them, and Marcus guessed that she was somewhere in her late fifties—still fit and attractive, as all Partials apparently were, but not one of the young-looking pilots like

Mandy, or the supermodel serial killers or whatever Heron was. That meant, as far as Marcus knew, that this woman was a doctor, and he stuck out his hand to shake.

"Hello, Doctor."

She didn't take his hand, only looked at them sternly. "You're humans."

"You've been waiting since yesterday?" asked Woolf. He turned on Vinci. "Morgan is killing our people—we are dying, in war and in hospitals, every day. Every hour. You have to get us in sooner."

"But not before me," said the Partial doctor. "We all have business that can't be delayed." She looked at Vinci. "Are you her assistant? Can you get her a message?"

"I'm just a soldier, ma'am."

"Is she not here?" asked Marcus. "I mean, is she out on the front lines or something? Is she in a different city? We can go to her if that's easier."

"She's here," said the doctor, pointing at a set of wide double doors on the northern wall. "She just . . . isn't available."

"What is she doing that she can't even see us?" asked Woolf. "Is she busy? Who is she talking to if she isn't talking to any of the people who need her?"

"We're in the middle of a war," said Vinci. "She's leading that war from a central hub; she can't just leave it for everyone who comes to visit."

One of the human soldiers sneered, a huge man rippling with muscles. "We could force our way in."

"That's not the best tactic when we're trying to be diplomatic," said Woolf.

"Is there anything you can do to hurry it up?" asked Marcus. He gestured to the doctor. "I mean, I know you've probably thought of everything already, but . . . I don't know, can we send her a message? Can we tell her why we're here? We're the first humans in the city in twelve years, proposing a peace treaty and a medical alliance, that's got to pull some weight."

"I know it's important," said Vinci. "That's why I brought you here. But I warned you it would be hard, and you're going to have to be patient."

"That's entirely reasonable," said Marcus. "We'll wait."

"Except it's the same story they told me yesterday," said the doctor, raising her eyebrow. "My report is just as vital, almost certainly more so, but Trimble sees people on her own schedule, when she wants to, and not before."

"Then we'll wait," said Woolf. "As long as it takes."

Marcus wondered how many people would die, both here and at home, while they waited.

CHAPTER THIRTY-THREE

The doctor introduced herself as Diadem, but said no more than that. Her hostility toward Marcus and the rest of the humans was palpable, and not, it seemed, simply because they took her place in line to see Trimble. Add in the constant watch of the armed Partial guards, and the mounting threat of the imminent Partial war, and the room was starting to feel more and more like a pressure cooker. Marcus worried that if they didn't get in to talk to Trimble soon, the soldiers were going to explode.

Minutes turned into hours. Every time the clocked chimed they would roll their eyes or sigh as the time slowly trickled away; every time a door opened every head jerked up to see if it was finally their turn to see Trimble. The sun tracked a slow arc across the wide skylight overhead, and Partial soldiers would bustle in and out of the room, whispering anxious conversations that Marcus could only guess at. None of his guesses were happy. Commander Woolf was going stir-crazy, pacing up and down and trying, unsuccessfully, to ask their Partial guards what was going on. They wouldn't even let him get close, waving him off first with their hands and, when he pressed the issue, with their rifles. The background activity increased, and Marcus felt the tension in the room like an angry spirit, hot and ranting. He decided to try talking to Diadem again, asking her what was going on, but all she did was stare at the soldiers in what Marcus was beginning to realize was a Partial scowl.

"They're preparing for battle," she said at last. "The war is coming to White Plains."

"But Morgan's forces are all on Long Island," said Marcus. "Who are they fighting?"

Diadem refused to answer.

When night began to fall, Marcus despaired of ever seeing Trimble at all, and swore not to fall asleep and risk losing his chance in the middle of the night. He kept himself occupied by examining the various bits of technology scattered through-out the room—objects so arcane he could only barely recognize them, but that the Partials apparently used every day. On an end table he found a small plastic stick and picked it up, certain that he knew what it was but completely unable to remember—something out of his childhood, he knew, but what? It was covered with buttons, and he pressed a couple of them to see what happened, but nothing did. Diadem watched him with the calculating eyes of a hungry insect.

"Do you want to watch something?" she finally asked.

"No thanks," he said. "I'm trying to figure out what this thing is."

"That's what I meant," she said. "It's a remote—it runs the holovid."

"I knew I'd seen one before," said Marcus. "Most of the

houses in East Meadow had the wall units, all speech- and motion-activated; I haven't seen a hand remote like this since I was a kid."

"I have a wall mount at home," said Diadem, and it seemed she might be willing to make a little conversation. Marcus gave her his full attention. "But the waiting room is so big, and with so many people, the sensors would get confused with only voice or motion controls. It's kind of funny using these old primitive things, but whatever works, I guess."

"What you call primitive I call futuristic," said Marcus, still staring at the remote. "You have a nuclear power plant that gives you more energy that you know what to do with. We have a handful of solar panels that barely keep our hospital running. My friend has a music player, but I haven't seen a working holovid in twelve years." He stood up, searching the room for a projector. "Where is it?"

"You're standing in it." Diadem stood up and took the remote from him, pointing it at the skylight; one click dimmed the glass, keeping out the glare, and another click lit up a bright holographic mist in the center of the couches, projected down from hundreds of tiny lights in the skylight's latticed framework. Marcus and Diadem were standing in the middle of the gently shifting photonic mist, different vid icons moving lazily back and forth like sediment in a pool. Marcus stepped out to get a better view, grinning like a little boy as he recognized first one title, then another. He realized with amusement that all the titles he knew were the kid shows—*Windwhisper the Dragon*, *Nightmare School*, *Steambots*—the stuff he barely remembered from just before the Break. Most of the titles were "grown-up movies," the cop dramas and medical romances and alien invasion gore-fests his parents had never let him watch. As he looked through the menu, the other humans were clustering around it as well, as fascinated as he was. Marcus realized that they must have looked ridiculous, a bunch of slack-jawed yokels awestruck by a piece of commonplace technology, and wondered if Diadem had turned on the holovid just to be amused by their reactions to it. Just as quickly he realized that he didn't care. This was a part of his life that he'd lost, and seeing it again was almost heartbreaking.

"What do you want to watch?" asked Diadem.

Marcus's first impulse was *Windwhisper*, his favorite cartoon as a child, but the soldiers were all standing right there, and he felt a little foolish. He searched the shifting mist for an action movie, but before he could find one that looked good, the soldier beside him, the same giant bull from before, smiled broadly and said, "*Windwhisper*! Loved that show."

He's a soldier now, thought Marcus, *but he was only seven or eight when the world ended.*

Diadem swung the remote, scattering the holographic mist and grabbing the *Windwhisper* icon, and suddenly there it was, a giant hologram filling the center of the room as the cute purple dragon soared across the opening credits. "Windwhisper!" came the theme song, and Marcus and the soldiers sang the next line in unison with it: "Spread your wings and fly!" They watched the entire episode, laughing and cheering, reliving for half an hour the childhood they'd lost, but minute by minute the magic seemed to seep away. The colors were too bright, the music too loud, the emotions too broad, and the decisions too obvious. It was hollow and sickly, like eating too much sugar, and all

Marcus could think about was: *Is this really what I missed? Is this really all the old world was?* Life since the Break was hard, and the problems they had were painful, but at least they were real. When he was a kid, he'd spent hours in front of the holovid, watching show after show, effect after effect, platitude after platitude. The episode ended, and when Diadem looked at him with the remote poised for another, he shook his head.

She turned it off. "You look awfully sad for someone who just watched a friendly purple dragon knock a wizard into a lake made of marshmallow cream."

"Yeah, I guess," said Marcus. "Sorry."

She put the remote away. "You seemed to enjoy the beginning, but not the end."

Marcus grimaced, flopping onto the couch. "Not really. It's just that it's . . ." He didn't know how to phrase it. "It's not real."

"Of course it's not real, it's a cartoon." Diadem sat beside him. "A 3-D cartoon with photo-realistic backgrounds, but still—just a story."

"I know," said Marcus, closing his eyes, "that's not the right word, but it's . . . I used to love watching the Evil Wizard get it," he said. "Every week he'd have another scheme, and every week Windwhisper would stop him: one up, one down. Problem surfaced and solved in twenty-two minutes. I used to think that was awesome, but . . . it isn't real. The good guy's always good, and the Evil Wizard is always, well, evil. It's in his name."

"There were not a lot of children's shows about ambiguity and unsolvable moral quandaries," said Diadem. "I don't think most five-year-olds were ready for that."

Marcus sighed. "I don't think any of us were."

Vinci came and talked with them after dark, apologizing again that they weren't able to see Trimble yet, and bringing stories of the world outside: The war was going poorly, raging closer and closer to the city.

"But who's fighting?" asked Woolf. "All of Morgan's forces are on Long Island."

"There are other . . . issues," said Vinci.

"Issues?" asked Marcus. "I thought you were going to say 'other factions.' What does 'other issues' mean?"

Vinci said nothing, and Marcus couldn't tell whether he was thinking of a response or just refusing to answer. They waited, trying to decipher his actions, when a voice called out from the far side of the room.

"Trimble's ready for you."

They all looked up, surging to their feet. Diadem practically ran to the guard at the big double doors, but he stopped her with a look and, presumably, a burst of link data. "Not you, the humans."

"I've been here longer."

"Trimble wants to see them," said the guard. He looked at Vinci. "Bring their commander and their 'Partials relations consultant' and follow me."

The hallway beyond the double doors was wide and clean, nearly empty because of what Marcus was starting to recognize as the Partials' typically pragmatic style—they didn't *need* any plants or pictures or cute little tables in this hallway, so they didn't have any. At the end of the hall was another cluster of doors, one of which was surprisingly loud; Marcus could hear shouted arguments and . . . *yes, and gunfire. Why is there gunfire?*

The guard opened this door and a wave of cacophony rolled out to envelop them, shouts and cries and whispers and battle, and Marcus recognized it as the chaotic blend of multiple radios all blaring at once. The room itself, as they entered it, was lined with wall screens and portable screens and speakers of every shape and size and even, in one corner, another holovid depicting a giant glowing map of New York, including Long Island, as well as parts of New Jersey, Connecticut, Rhode Island, and even further north. It wasn't a multitude of radios, but of video feeds. Red dots blinked on the map, faces and bodies ran back and forth on the screens, Jeeps and trucks and even tanks rumbled through televised walls and cities and forests. In the center of it all, bathed in the light and sound of a hundred different screens, was a single woman sitting at a circular desk.

"That's her," said the guard, standing to the side and closing the door behind them. "Wait for her to talk to you."

Woolf and Vinci stepped forward; Marcus, more self-conscious, hung back by the door guard. The woman was facing away, so Woolf cleared his throat loudly to get her attention. She either didn't hear him, or ignored him outright.

Marcus looked at the screens lining the walls. Many of them showed the same scene, often from the same perspective, though he guessed that of the hundred or so screens there were still several dozen separate feeds. Most showed battle scenes, and he assumed that they were live; Trimble was watching the war unfold from a central location, the way Kira had done with her radios. He wondered again where Kira had gone, and if he would ever see her again. Most of East Meadow had given her up for dead, no one having come forward to end D Company's murderous occupation, but he still held hope—probably vain hope, he knew—that she would survive.

One of the largest screens was repeating a single scene: a running soldier, an explosion of mud and grass, and then it would all rewind in rapid motion. The flailing man would fly forward, land lightly on the ground, and run backward while the earth knit itself together again, and then suddenly the feed would reverse once more and the man would run forward and the ground beneath him would explode. After the fourth such cycle, Marcus realized that the speed and the stopping points were slightly different each time—it wasn't on a loop, someone was manipulating it, back and forth, searching for . . . something. He stepped forward, circling slightly to the side, and saw that Trimble was sitting at a faintly glowing desk-screen, her fingers sliding back and forth across a series of digital dials and sliders. She zoomed in and out, she wound the video backward and forward, and all the time the young man died in the explosion, over and over and over again.

"Excuse me," said Woolf.

"Wait for her to talk to you," said the guard.

"I've been waiting all week," said Woolf, and strode forward. The guard stepped up to follow him, but Vinci waved him off. "General Trimble," said Woolf, "my name is Asher Woolf, I'm a commander with the Long Island Defense Grid and a senator in the Long Island government. I've come to you as a duly appointed representative of the last remaining human population on Earth, to broker a treaty of peace and a sharing of resources." Trimble didn't respond, or even acknowledge him. He stepped forward again. "Your people are dying," he said, gesturing at the death and destruction that plastered the walls. "My people are dying, too, and we both know it's not just from fighting. We're sterile and diseased, both of us. In a few more years we will all be dead no matter what we do—no matter how many wars we win or lose, no matter how many times we shoot or shoot back or lay down our arms. Your people have two years left, I understand; mine will live longer but still be just as dead in the end. We have to work together to change this." He stepped forward again. "Do you hear me?"

The guard moved in as Woolf's voice rose, but Vinci ran forward to Woolf's side. "Thank you very much for seeing us, General," said Vinci. "We realize that you're very busy, coordinating so many different wars at once—"

"She's not coordinating anything," said Woolf quickly, gesturing at the screens dismissively. "She's just watching."

"Please check your tone or I will ask you to leave," said the guard.

"You want me to wait quietly?" asked Woolf. "I can wait quietly. I've been waiting for a day and a night out there, but we don't have time—"

"Be quiet," said Trimble softly, and Marcus stepped back in surprise as Vinci and the guard both staggered under the weight of her will. The guard regained his footing and stared silently at Woolf; Vinci opened his mouth, his face turning red with the effort, but he couldn't speak. Marcus had seen the same thing when Dr. Morgan had ordered Samm to obey her—the leader commanded, and thanks to the link the Partials had no choice but to obey.

"We're not Partials," said Woolf. "You can't just force our minds with your 'link.'"

"I'm not a Partial either," said Trimble.

This stopped Woolf in his tracks, confused. Marcus saw him struggling for a response and stepped forward with the first thing he could think of—anything to keep her talking.

"You're human?" he asked.

"I used to be."

"What are you now?"

"Guilty," said Trimble.

Now it was Marcus's turn to be shocked into silence. He cast about for something to say, and finding nothing, he simply walked forward, putting himself between Trimble and the view screen. Forcing her to look at him. She was an older woman, late sixties, maybe, the same age as Nandita and with similar coloring. *Nandita is the other reason we're here*, he thought. *We need to find her, too, just like Kira.* He seized on this thought, and when her eyes finally met his, he spoke softly.

"I'm looking for a friend of mine," he said. "Another human. A woman named Nandita Merchant. Do you know her?"

A spark of recognition lit up in Trimble's eye, and Marcus considered again her statement that she had once been human; no Partial he'd met was that visually expressive. Her hands came up to her face, half covering her mouth, her eyes going wide. "Is Nandita alive?"

"I don't know," said Marcus softly, still surprised that the woman seemed to know who Nandita was. "We haven't seen her in months. Do you know . . . anything about her? Maybe you've seen something on your screens to help us find her?" He paused, watching her face, watching her eyes grow moist with tears. He decided to push his luck just one step further. "We haven't seen Kira Walker, either."

An odd look passed over her face, like she was peering into a long-forgotten memory. "Nandita didn't have anything to do with Kira," she said, cocking her head to the side. "Hers was called . . . Aura, I think. Aria. No, Ariel; it was Ariel."

Marcus's eyes went wide, a thousand questions crowding his mind so abruptly that none of them managed to come out. Ariel? Trimble knew about Nandita and Ariel? That could only mean that Nandita had communicated with her at some point; maybe she'd even come here. And yet Trimble had asked if Nandita was alive, implying that even if she'd come here before, she was gone now. As he searched for words an alarm sounded, and Trimble swung her chair to the side, tapping a button on her console that sent a rippling cascade across the wall of screens, calling up a score of new videos and images: roaring artillery, crumbling buildings, long lists of names and numbers scrolling by so fast Marcus couldn't hope to read them.

"A new assault," said the guard, apparently recovered from his forced silence. He stepped forward to tap a small console of his own, glancing at the holovid map. "Inside the city this time."

"An assault here?" asked Woolf. He reached for his waist, grasping at something that wasn't there, and Marcus found himself doing the same—reflexively reaching for a weapon. If an army of Partials attacked, their band of humans was trapped in the middle without so much as a pointy stick.

And they still haven't told us who is attacking, thought Marcus. Knowing that they were covering something up scared him more than anything else.

"This isn't supposed to happen," said Trimble, her eyes only half-focused on the charts and videos that filled the wall before her. "None of this is supposed to happen."

"You have to help us!" said Woolf. "We have to help each other!"

"Leave me," said Trimble, and suddenly the Partials were walking for the door, grabbing Woolf and Marcus as they went. Their grips were like iron, and they pulled the humans outside as if they were children; Woolf and Marcus fought back, shouting all the way, but it was useless. The guard closed the door solidly behind them, and Marcus saw now that Vinci was panting for breath, flexing his empty hands and staring at the floor; Marcus couldn't tell if it was anger, exertion, or something else. Hatred? Shame?

"I'm sorry," said Vinci. "I'd hoped . . . I'm sorry. I warned you, but still. I'd hoped for something more."

CHAPTER THIRTY-FOUR

"Let us back in!" Woolf snarled.

"We're in the middle of a war," said Vinci. "There's fighting in the city—if things go poorly, there'll be fighting here, in this building. She doesn't have time to talk to you."

"But she's not doing anything," said Marcus. He looked around at the others, and the Partials didn't meet his eyes. "We all saw her, it was textbook traumatic stress. She's unfocused, she's acting by rote, half the time she didn't even seem aware of her surroundings. That can't be who you have leading your armies."

The Partials were silent.

"She said she was human," said Woolf. "Worse than that, she said she used to be human. What does that mean? I thought she was a Partial general."

"Except all the Partial generals are men," said Marcus, remembering Samm's explanation of the caste system. "Each model was grown for its ideal job. The older Partial women were all doctors."

"This was not a Partial woman," said Woolf. "She was human, or . . . she used to be." He had fire in his eyes. "Tell us what's going on."

"I'm sorry we pulled you out," said Vinci. "There was nothing we could do."

"You could disobey," said Woolf.

"No, they couldn't," said Marcus, realization dawning. "She used the link. She told them to leave and they were compelled to do it, whether they wanted to or not."

Woolf frowned. "What kind of human woman becomes a Partial general and has access to the pheromonal link?" He looked at the two Partials. "What is going on?"

When Vinci answered, the other soldier put a hand on his arm to stop him; Vinci ignored him and spoke anyway. "She's been like this for a while now. We've been fighting Morgan for years, mostly just little skirmishes, all stemming from one fundamental disagreement: what to do with you humans on Long Island. Whether or not your existence is a threat, or a necessity. Whether we had the right to exterminate your race, or leave you alone and let you live or die as best you could, or whether it would be in our best interest to keep a population alive . . . But when the expiration date kicked in and people started dying, it got worse. Morgan wanted to start using the humans as test subjects, experimenting on them, and Trimble didn't think it was right. Or, at least, didn't think it was the right time. But while Morgan's been getting stronger, rallying more Partials to her cause and becoming more violent in her methods, Trimble has been refusing to act. When she says anything, she says she doesn't want to condone a course of action that could lead to the eradication of the human species. But she is offering no alternative, no course of action whatsoever, and with more Partials expiring every day, Trimble's caution has begun to look more like fear and indecision. We've been losing soldiers to Morgan's faction in a massive flood, and still she does nothing to stem it." He looked at Marcus. "We want to help you—we've sent as many teams as we can to harry Morgan's rear flank, to disrupt her and avoid the elimination of the last of the human population, but without any real leadership from Trimble . . ." His voice trailed off, and Marcus heard an explosion in the distance.

"Who are you fighting here, though?" asked Marcus. "It can't be Morgan's company, and you've already confirmed as much."

"They're fighting themselves," said Woolf softly. Marcus looked at him, surprised, then looked at Vinci and the other soldier. They didn't answer, only looked at the floor.

"Your faction is fighting itself?" asked Marcus. The implications frightened him—he remembered the riots in East Meadow when the fight between the Senate and the Voice finally came to a head. He remembered how vicious it became when friends suddenly turned on one another, incensed by ideological differences. "The battlefront that's coming," he said, "that's a revolution? Soldiers from your company who now support Morgan? This city's going to tear itself apart."

"We should be safe in here," said Vinci, then hesitated. "We might be safe in here. Everyone in this building is a loyal to General Trimble."

Woolf frowned. "Why? Even if you disagree with Morgan . . . Trimble's useless."

"We're loyal because that's how they made us," said Vinci. "Because it's who we are."

The building rumbled from another explosion, and Vinci and the guard both fell into a ready posture Marcus had come to recognize as communication: They were scanning the link for news of what had happened. Marcus heard distant pops of gunfire.

"The fighting's getting close," said Vinci. "Get back to your men, I need to talk to the building's defensive force."

They hurried back down the spartan hall. "We can help," said Woolf. "I have ten trained soldiers in there—"

"Please," said Vinci, "this is a Partial battle. You'd only get in the way."

He led them back through the double doors to the waiting area and left them there, racing deeper into the complex. Trimble's guard closed the doors behind them, locking the doors tightly. Only one of Woolf's soldiers was in the waiting area, standing by the door of their sleeping quarters; when he saw them he waved them over, shouting urgently. "Hurry, Commander, you've got to see this." Woolf and Marcus ran toward him and he led them inside; the other soldiers were clustered around the outer window like children, watching the city in awed silence.

"Get away from there," said Woolf, "there's a battle going on. . . ." His voice drifted off as the soldiers cleared a spot for him, and he saw what they'd been watching. Thousands of Partials, seemingly with no battle line, running and shooting and killing one another in the city below—in the streets, on the rooftops. Their window was fifteen stories up, well above the majority of the fighting, which gave them a terrifying sense of the scale of the battle: Literally as far as they could discern through the city, battle was raging.

More frightening than the size of the battle, though, was the nature of it. Even the smallest, wounded, most ill-equipped Partial soldier was performing feats that would make any human the unquestioned hero of the Grid. Marcus watched in shock as an infantryman ran lightly along the roof of the building beyond, firing his rifle one-handed as he did and picking off snipers on the next roof over. When he reached the edge he leapt to another building, clearing the thirty-foot gap and landing in a machine-gun nest that was firing in another direction. More impressive still were the people he was shooting at, who despite his unerring accuracy were able to step to the side with inhuman speed, dodging the bullets by millimeters and returning fire almost casually. The machine-gun nest where the runner had landed became a swirling cauldron of knives and bayonets, each wielded with a controlled fury that made Marcus pale at the sight of it, and each blow turned aside with almost contemptuous ease. It was a war of supermen, every one of them too accurate to miss, and too fast to be hit.

Marcus pointed at the fliers that hovered and darted through the city, single-pilot fighters and five-man gunships, swarming like angry bees. "They have Rotors?" He hadn't seen a flying vehicle since before the Break.

"This city is just one horrible revelation after another," said Woolf. As if to prove his point, another Rotor hovered into view around a tall building, much bigger than the others. "That one's a transport," he said, backing away from the window. "It's coming this way—they must be coming for General Trimble." The soldiers dropped out of the window's field of view and backed away. A stray bullet cracked a hole in the window and shattered the wall above Marcus's head, and he threw himself prone on the floor. "Up and out," said Woolf. "We've got to get to the center of the building—into the waiting room." The soldiers ran through the door in practiced formation, staying low and finding cover with a trained fluidity that used to make Marcus feel safe, but now only seemed like a pale imitation of the Partials' superior precision. He followed them through, staying close to Woolf, wishing he had a gun and knowing it wouldn't do him any good.

A small Rotor darted over the skylight, machine guns firing, and Marcus heard an explosion as either it or its target went down. He had no idea which, or even which team was which. The coloring on the vehicles all seemed the same to him. He heard another explosion, from a different part of the city, and the sounds of gun and artillery fire ebbed and flowed in the background. It made Marcus feel blind and helpless, crouching behind a low bench, knowing that something was happening, without knowing who was shooting at what, or why, or where any of them were.

Another light Rotor flew past the skylight. A gunship followed moments later, in a perpendicular path. A dark shadow fell over the waiting room, and a deep thrum above them vibrated powerfully through the building.

"We don't want to be here," said Woolf.

The big transport Rotor hovered into view, filling the skylight, and too late Marcus realized that it was coming down, hard and fast through the center of it. The metal hull shattered the skylight in the same instant that the far doors flew open and the building's defenders flooded in. A turret gun on the transport unleashed a hail of fire on the defenders, but they had already moved to the side half a second earlier. Gull ports in the sides of the transport swung open before the hull even touched the floor, and armored Partials leapt out, guns blazing.

"Get down!" Woolf shouted, and the soldiers dove to the floor behind couches and tables, trying to make it back to the room they'd just exited. Marcus saw a moment of confusion in the attackers, a brief pause as they took stock of the new situation, and somehow, for some reason, they seemed to identify the fleeing humans as threats. A half second later they turned on the humans, gunning them down with cold ferocity. The humans shook and screamed as the attack ripped through their ranks, and Marcus closed his eyes as his companions' bodies fell to the ground around him.

More reinforcements arrived from deeper in the building, and Partials poured out of the transport in a seemingly endless wave. Marcus peeked up at the raging battle, quailed at the sight of it, and hid his head again, hoping he could just lie still and play dead until the fighting was over. The noise in the room was deafening, dozens of automatic weapons all firing at once, and he worried that he might lose his hearing permanently. A hand grabbed his leg, and he couldn't help the scream of terror that leapt from his lips. He rolled over in a flurry to see who it was, and recognized Commander Woolf. The man was talking, but Marcus couldn't hear it. Behind him were two more human soldiers, all crouched low behind the dubious cover of a waiting room couch. Woolf said something else, then gestured for Marcus to follow him and started crawling for the nearest door. The soldiers went after him, and Marcus started to follow. A bullet struck the soldier in front of him, dropping the soldier like a bag of meat, and Marcus scrambled forward in reckless fear, desperate to reach the open door. He felt a sharp sting in his arm, and then he was through, gasping and panting as Woolf and the last soldier threw the door shut behind them.

Woolf said something else, inaudible through the ringing in Marcus's ears. They kept low to the ground and crouched against a wall, hoping to put as many barriers between them and the gunfight as possible. Marcus couldn't use his right arm, and when he examined it he found a long groove in the meat of his triceps—a gunshot wound that had scraped the surface, shredding the muscle but too shallow to damage the bone. He stood up in a daze, headed to look for a first aid kit, but Woolf pulled him back down, yelling something Marcus could almost hear. Marcus shook his head, pointing at his ears to let Woolf know he couldn't hear anything; the commander frowned, puzzled, then shouted something obviously angry and dug in his breast pocket, pulling out a pair of orange foam earplugs and pressing them into Marcus's hand. Woolf and the last remaining soldier, a man named Galen, conferred with each other over something, and Marcus pushed the plugs into his ears.

We're going to die, he thought. *There's no way out of here—it doesn't matter who wins the fight in the waiting room, the entire city is a war zone.* Marcus considered again what they were up against: an army of the perfect soldiers. Humans are less agile, they have slower reaction times, they're less coordinated, they're not on the link—

"We're not on the link!" Marcus shouted, grabbing Woolf's arm. Woolf looked at him, confused, and Marcus explained his realization; his own voice sounded distant and muted through his ringing ears. "The link—the pheromonal system they use to communicate—they're all reading each other's minds. One guy picks up his gun to shoot, and on a battlefield he just shoots and the other guy dies, but in these tight quarters, the other guy's close enough to pick up the first guy's link data, so he knows he's going to shoot, and he gets out of the way. That's why none of them can hit each other."

Woolf said something in response, but Marcus still couldn't hear it. He pushed on anyway. "The Partials use the link to track each other, so when they want to hide, they wear gas masks. If you can't link with them, you can't defend against them. In the land of the Partials, we're like . . . stealth fighters."

Realization dawned in Woolf's eyes, and he turned back to Galen, speaking rapidly. Marcus couldn't hear him, but he could tell that at least some of his hearing was returning; the dull roar that had previously sounded like white noise had resolved into a chorus of gunfire, echoes from the battle in the other room. He hunkered down, trying to think of some way to use the lack of link to their advantage and escape. Samm had said that the link was so ingrained in the Partials that they'd forgotten, after twelve years, how to fight an enemy that didn't have it. *There has to be a way. . . .*

Woolf grabbed Marcus by his undamaged arm and gestured toward the equipment on the other side of the room. Marcus leaned toward, offering his ear, and Woolf shouted in it. "We have some shovels in our survival gear—we're going to try to hack through the side wall."

"What's on the other side?" asked Marcus.

Woolf sketched on the carpet with his finger, making an impression that looked vaguely like the waiting room and the surrounding doors. "If I've calculated it right, we're only two rooms away from Trimble's hallway. Cutting through is the quickest way out of the building."

Marcus nodded. "What if the walls are reinforced?"

"Then we think of something else."

The three men ran in a low crouch to their gear. The small survival shovels were some of the only gear they'd been allowed to keep; they couldn't hurt Partials with them, but they could certainly do some damage to the walls. The battle continued to rage in the room beyond, and Woolf used its cacophony to hide his assault on the wall.

"Here goes nothing." He slammed the shovel into the wall . . .

. . . and it cleaved through easily.

"It's just Sheetrock," said Woolf. He pulled his shovel back out, aimed another strike, and hacked out a chunk of the wall. Inside was a layer of pink insulation, and beyond that another Sheetrock wall. Woolf said something Marcus couldn't hear, presumably triumphant and vulgar, and handed spare shovels to Galen and Marcus. No one was coming through the door to stop them; the Partials were too preoccupied to follow them, and without the link to give them away, they could work with impunity. Marcus got to work on the wall, and soon the three men had opened a man-size hole they could squirm through into the next room.

The new room was empty, untouched except for a chaotic series of bullet holes in the wall where the Partials' battle had punched through. They ran to the far side and went to work on that wall, opening a ragged gap that Woolf peered through. He grinned. "It's the hallway, and it's empty. Move!" They tore into the wall with everything they had, Marcus hacking awkwardly with his left hand, his right still hanging uselessly—and painfully—at his side. He wanted to stop and patch it up, to at least give himself a shot of painkillers, but there was no time. He chopped at the wall as if he were escaping from hell itself, with all the devils behind him.

They crawled into the hallway and ran toward Trimble's room, gripping their shovels like axes. The noise of the battle was loud behind them. Vinci stood at the end of the hall, tucked behind an armored corner, and called out as they approached.

"Where are you headed?"

"Somebody landed a transport in the waiting—"

"I know," said Vinci. The double doors into the battle hall burst open and Vinci motioned them forward, dropping his questions and handing them some spare handguns. "There's no time!" he shouted. "Fall back into Trimble's room and lock the door!"

Woolf grabbed Marcus by his wounded arm. The pain was excruciating, and he couldn't stop the commander from dragging him through into Trimble's room. Woolf turned back to close the door, and Vinci slipped through, slinging his gun over his shoulder. They slammed the door shut and locked it tightly. They heard pounding on the other side almost immediately. "These doors will hold for a few minutes, but we need another way out."

"Is there another way out of this room?" asked Woolf.

"Let's hope so," said Vinci.

"Great," said Marcus. "The only guy we find to help us has the same 'hope for a miracle plan that we do."

"General Trimble!" shouted Vinci, jogging to the center of the room. The old woman sat in the same position as before, watching the citywide revolution play out on hundreds of screens, from dozens of different angles and viewpoints. "We have to get you out of here!"

"You must have a way out," said Woolf, close behind him. Marcus hurried after them, trying to stay close enough to hear.

"There's a Rotor in the room above us," said Trimble. Her voice was soft, and Marcus almost didn't catch it. She sounded even more disconnected than earlier, speaking through a haze of confusion.

"You have to stop this," said Marcus, pushing forward. He fumbled with a bandage from the medkit as he walked, trying to wrap his arm wound and stanch the bleeding. "Don't run away, just do something. Send out orders, coordinate the war, do . . . something!" He stopped in front of her, and her eyes half focused on his. She seemed dazed, or maybe half-asleep. "These people have stuck with you for years, waiting for you to lead them. That's a kind of dedication I've never even imagined—if they were humans, they'd have thrown you out on your ear years ago, but they're Partials, and Partials are loyal to the chain of command. To, apparently, stupidly ridiculous extremes, which is where we are now. They will follow you anywhere, but only if you lead them."

Her head shifted slightly, and Marcus realized he now had her full attention, intense and vague at once.

"I've destroyed the world once already," she said. "I won't

condone a course of action that will destroy it again."

"Failing to act is no less a crime than acting incorrectly," said Woolf, but the second half of his sentence was lost in a sudden boom as the locked door behind them exploded. Partials poured through the opening, taking positions with trained precision. Vinci raised his rifle to fire, and a dozen rifles zeroed in to fire back. Marcus dropped to the ground, his entire life literally flashing before his eyes: his job at the hospital. Kira. The school. The Break. His parents, more clear in his mind now than in all the years before.

"I'm sorry, Mom," he said. "I guess I'm going to see you soon."

The rebel Partials screamed a death sentence on Trimble. Vinci moved to block her with his body. Woolf and Galen raised their handguns.

Trimble rose to her feet, turned to the Partial invaders, and spoke a single word:

"Stop."

It looked to Marcus as if an invisible wave had struck them, rippling across the crowd and freezing them in their tracks. Where before they'd been still, now they were rigid, so motionless they looked like statues. Even Vinci was rooted to his spot, as if her word had turned him to stone.

The link, thought Marcus. *I've never seen it this powerful.*

"I have a Rotor in the room upstairs," said Trimble, turning to Marcus. "Can you fly it?"

"I can," said Woolf.

"Then go," said Trimble. "It's short range, but it should get you to Manhattan at least." She tapped a code onto the glowing screen closest to her hand. "No one will follow you."

"What will happen to you?" asked Marcus.

Trimble nodded to the frozen Partials. "They will kill me."

"They can't even move."

"I had hoped to guide them," said Trimble, "but all I've done is hold them back. Now holding them back is all I can do. Go now."

"And Vinci?" asked Marcus. "Are they going to kill him, too?"

"I won't be able to stop them."

Marcus looked at Woolf, who nodded and spoke. "We'll take him with us."

"Hurry," said Trimble.

Marcus grabbed his medkit and headed for the stairs at the side of the room. Woolf and Galen lifted Vinci—his body was stiff as a board—and carried him up after. Marcus stopped at the top of the stairs. "Thank you."

"If you find Nandita," said Trimble softly, "tell her . . . that I tried."

"I will." He slipped through the door into a small hangar beyond, and when Woolf and Galen passed through with Vinci, he sealed the door behind them. The Rotor was small, but looked like it would hold four people if they squeezed in tightly. As they maneuvered Vinci into position, he went abruptly limp, gasping for air and croaking out a plea.

"We have to go back." A chorus of voices rose up behind them, a sign that the other Partials were also free. "We have to help her, they're going to—" Gunshots echoed up from beyond the door, and Vinci hung his head. "Never mind," he murmured. "Open the windows and spread the data. Let everyone know that a general has fallen."

CHAPTER THIRTY-FIVE

Kira kept one eye on the sky as they traveled, watching for rain, and one eye on the fields around them. They could never afford to be far from shelter in the toxic wasteland, but in the great plains of the Midwest, they were often far from everything.

They lost another horse in the first acid rainstorm—*But no, Kira reminded herself, we didn't lose Buddy in the rainstorm, we lost him in the house—the house that I brought him into.* The mad kicking of the horses, thrashing wildly with their hooves as the acid burned their flesh, had destroyed the room and everything in it, and by the time they'd washed them clean and calmed them down, Buddy had been kicked too hard, and in too many places; he had a broken foreleg, two broken ribs, and a shattered jaw. Kira herself put him out of his misery. *There was nothing else I could have done,* she told herself, probably for the hundredth time. *It was either bring him inside or let him die in the acid, and I couldn't do that to him.* It didn't soothe her conscience, but she pushed it aside anyway. The worst part of all was that it wasn't even the biggest problem on her mind.

Kira and Heron were both burned by the acid, though the blisters had healed into angry welts after a few days. Samm was much worse off, and spent three days near blind before his Partial accelerated regeneration was able to fight off the poisons and rebuild the damage to his corneas. Afa, the only human in the group, had it worst of all: He'd survived the harrowing fifteen minutes tied to the back of the kicking, thrashing horses, but in the process his back and arms and legs had been horribly burned by the acid, and his eyes, burned even worse than Samm's, showed no sign of having healed. Kira stopped in every city they passed to scrounge for ointments and painkillers, but most of the time they kept him doped and tied to the back of Oddjob, trying to make the travel as easy as possible for all of them. They didn't know what they'd find at the ParaGen complex in Denver, but Kira hoped it would have, at the very least, adequate shelter and a clinic they could scavenge for supplies. Afa deserved better than they could give him on the move.

Highway 34 took them through the state of Iowa, a vast, flat checkerboard of farmland that was now marked only by bleached-white fences and sickly yellow trees. The poison wind blew steadily from the south, broken by the occasional acid rainstorm or, even more terrifying, vast black dust storms that swept across the land like swarms of locusts, blotting out the sun and scouring the last desperate leaves from those few bushes strong enough to draw strength from the toxic earth. Kira had tried at first to use their water purifier on the oily yellow streams that flowed here and there across the land, but they gave up when the purifier itself started to break down under the caustic onslaught. Instead they searched every grocery store and shopping center they passed for bottled water, loading as much as they could on their own backs and using Bobo, the last remaining horse aside from Oddjob, as a pack animal to carry their few remaining supplies. Clean feed for the horses was even harder to come by, and as the journey wore on Kira was forced to spend more and more of their rest stops swatting their mouths away from the poisoned grasses sticking up through the dust. Their good traveling clothes were left in a smoking heap on that first farmhouse's floor, and they were dressed now in the farmers' family's clothes. They were too big, but Kira joked that at least now they were properly dressed for the Midwest country they traveled through. It was the kind of joke she thought Marcus would have made.

When the Missouri River appeared before them, cutting a deep, treacherous border between Iowa and Nebraska, Heron growled, "If I never see another river again, it will be too soon."

"That doesn't make linguistic sense," Samm started, but Kira cut him off.

"It's an expression," she said, staring at the river. She sighed. "And one I agree with in this case." The Missouri was thick and putrid, a gray-green river laced with streaks of yellow and pink. It smelled like burned detergent, and the air around it tasted strangely metallic. Kira shook her head. "It's not as big as the last one, but it's not one I exactly want to take any chances with, either. Where's the nearest bridge?"

"I'm looking," said Samm. He had found a new map in a bookstore, replacing the one they'd lost in the Mississippi crossing, and he stood now carefully unfolding it. Kira patted Bobo on the neck, soothing him gently, then moved to Oddjob and Afa. The big man was asleep, lolling precariously in the harness they'd rigged to keep him strapped to the saddle. He hadn't fallen yet, but Kira checked the straps anyway, talking softly to Afa as she did. "You want to go north or south?" asked Samm, peering at the road map. "There's a crossing north in Omaha and another south in Nebraska City, and we're about halfway between them both."

"Omaha will be bigger," said Heron. "Better chance the bridges are still up."

"It's also out of our way," said Kira, checking the bandage on Afa's still-broken leg. "We need to get off the plains soon or Afa is going to die. We're going to eventually have to turn south anyway, so I say we do it now."

"If we don't have time for a detour," said Heron, "we don't have time to head back north again when the bridge in Nebraska City turns out to be at the bottom of the river. We should go for the sure thing."

"Heading north takes us across a second river," said Samm, still looking at the map. "The Platte merges with the Missouri just a few miles north of here, and if we go to Omaha, we'll have to cross them both."

"All right, then we go south," said Heron. "The second river can bite me."

"I agree," said Samm, refolding the map and looking up. "Nebraska City still looks pretty big, and if the bridges are gone, we can just head farther south to Kansas City. The bridges there were huge—they're bound to be up."

"Unless someone destroyed them in the Partial War," said

Kira. She ran her hands through her hair—far too greasy, after weeks of travel with no clean water to wash it in. She shrugged, too exhausted to think. "I just hope this wasteland doesn't get any worse the farther south we go."

The bridge to Nebraska City was indeed still standing, and Kira made a silent prayer of thanks as they trudged toward it. A sort of levee to the south had become clogged with debris, and the river below the bridge had swelled to create a small lake, stinking of chemicals and topped with a layer of stagnant foam, like an ice cream float. It hurt just to breathe the air above it, and Kira tied a spare shirt across her mouth—and another across Afa's—to try to filter the worst of it. Halfway across they found themselves trapped by a cluster of cars, crashed into a snarl that completely blocked the road. Kira and Samm strained to shift them out of the way while Heron scouted ahead, and by the time they cleared a hole wide enough for the horses to pass through, Heron was back, reporting that portions of the bridge were unstable, corroded by the river or the rain until pieces had started to slough off. They proceeded carefully, controlling their breathing; at one point Kira could look down through the cracks by her feet and see the multicolored water drifting lazily below them, iridescent in the pale sunlight. She kept a firm hand on Oddjob's reins, hoping no more cracks appeared until they were safely across. They reached the far side after nearly half an hour, and if the ground hadn't been poisonous, Kira would have kissed it.

The land west of the river was, if possible, even more featureless than the land east of it. They followed the map to rejoin

I-80 in a town called Lincoln, and made good time on a stretch of highway so remarkably straight it didn't deviate more than an inch for days. They hit the Platte, but they didn't have to cross it, and when the road curved north to follow the river, they plunged south instead, eventually rejoining Highway 34 on the banks of the Republican. They kept between these two rivers, traveling in a wide corridor through bleached fields and corroded cities. During the day the sun baked the toxic chemicals on the ground, and acrid smoke and steam rose up in wisps like ghosts in the fields. At night the land was eerily silent, stripped of crickets and birds and howling wolves until nothing remained but the wind, rippling through the pallid grasses and sighing through the shattered windows of the houses they camped in. Kira kept her eye on the rain, thinking of Buddy and Afa's blistered face.

Afa was asleep most of the day now, with or without the sedatives they gave him, and Kira grew more worried than ever. His broken leg was refusing to heal, as if all his body's strength was routed to some other purpose. In a town called Benkelman she used most of their water to wash him, head to toe, cleaning his hair and his leg wound and the sores from the acid and shooting him full of antibiotics; she didn't know if it would do any good, for the surface wounds, at least, seemed uninfected, but she didn't know what else to do. In the East Meadow hospital she would have had more options, but in a crumbling farmhouse in the middle of nowhere, there was nothing to do but hope. She wrapped him tightly and covered him with blankets, and the next day they tied him back in his saddle and headed west again, leaving the road—it tried to cross the river, but the bridge was gone—and striking out across the fields themselves. They passed a town called Parks, and a bigger town called Wray, and soon the river petered out to nothing and the fields stretched out to nothing on every side, as if the world had run out of terrain altogether and there was nothing left but land and sky, a lost limbo of never-changing nothing.

Afa died days later, the travelers still lost in the pale yellow wasteland.

They buried him in dirt that smelled like broken batteries, and crouched in a fiberglass shed while the acid rain poured down to dissolve his flesh and bleach his bones.

"What the hell are we doing?" asked Heron. Samm looked up at her; Kira, too tired to move, lay in the corner with her eyes closed.

"We're saving people," said Samm.

"Who are we saving?" asked Heron. Kira looked up, her head loose on her neck, her movements shaky and uncoordinated from weeks of malnutrition, exhaustion, and fear. "Have we saved anybody? We've killed somebody. We killed two horses. Afa lived for twelve years on his own, completely alone, in the one of the most dangerous parts of the world, and now he's dead." She spit onto the ground and wiped her mouth on her sleeve. "Let's face it: we've failed."

Samm peered in the dark at his careworn map, nearly falling apart at the creases. Poison rain drummed down on the fiberglass over their heads. "We're in Colorado now," he said. "We have been for a few days. I'm not a hundred percent certain of where in Colorado, but based on how fast we were traveling before, I'm pretty sure we're . . . here." He pointed at a spot on the map, far from any roads or cities.

"Yay," said Heron, not even looking. "I've always wanted to be here."

"Heron's tired," said Kira. She was herself on the verge of tears, practically broken by Afa's death. But she couldn't quit now. She sat up to take the map from Samm and her own hand shook with the effort. "We're all tired. We're genetically perfect super-soldiers, designed to keep going under the harshest conditions, and we can barely move. We need to conserve our strength if we're going to get to Denver."

"Are you kidding?" said Heron. "You aren't still planning on completing this idiotic mission, are you?" She turned to Samm, incredulous. "Samm, you know it's time to do what we should have done weeks ago. Turn around."

"If I'm right," said Samm, "we're barely a day's journey to Denver. We could get there tomorrow."

"And do what?" Heron demanded. "Find another ruined building? Risk our lives to get its generator running? Beat our heads against the computer because everything we want to look at is trapped behind firewalls and encryptions and passwords and who knows what other kinds of security? Afa was the only one who knew how to get past that; without him we don't even know how to navigate the filing system."

"We're too close to give up," said Samm.

"We're not close to anything," said Heron. "We're going to go, and we're going to find nothing, and this entire trip has been a waste of everyone's time. We're not going to cure RM, we're not going to solve the expiration date, we're not going to do anything but die in a wasteland."

She lurched to her feet. "I'm not even going to say it."

"Say what?" Kira demanded. "'I told you so'? 'We should have turned around after Chicago'? 'We should never have left New York in the first place'?"

"Take your pick."

Kira struggled to her feet, panting with the exertion. "You're wrong. We came here with a job to do. If we don't do it, Afa will have died for nothing. All of us will have. And we'll take the whole planet with us."

"Come on," said Samm, but the girls ignored him. Heron reached Kira's side before Kira even realized she was moving, and her fist slammed into Kira's chin like a sledgehammer. Kira staggered back, already bracing herself to pounce back and attack before her mind had fully processed the punch, but before they could go any further Samm shoved himself between them. "Stop it."

"She's out of her mind," said Heron. "We had a chance if we'd gone back east after Chicago—we could have gone to Dr. Morgan, we could have even gone to Trimble. Anything would have given us a better chance than this. What're you looking for, Kira?" she asked, looking at Kira over Samm's shoulder. "What is this about? Is this even about saving our race? Or the humans? Or is this whole insane expedition all just so you can figure out what the hell you are? You selfish little bitch."

Kira was speechless. She wanted nothing more than to bash Heron's head against the ground, but Samm kept himself solidly between them. He faced Heron solemnly, keeping Kira back with his arm.

"Why'd you come with us?" asked Samm.

"You said you trusted her!" Heron snarled. "You told me to come, so I came."

"You haven't done what you're told since the day I met you," said Samm. "You do what you want, when you want, and if anyone gets in the way, you take them out. You could have stopped us at any time. You could have incapacitated me and kidnapped Kira and brought her to Morgan and done everything exactly the way you wanted, but you didn't. Tell me why."

Heron looked at him fiercely, then scowled at Kira. "Because I actually believed her. She talked about researching everything ParaGen had done to find some sort of cure, and for some stupid reason I thought she meant it."

"I did," said Kira, thought the fight had gone out of her voice. She felt drained and empty, as hollow as the fiberglass shed they were hiding in.

"And you," Heron spat, looking at Samm. "I can't believe you're still siding with her. I thought you were smarter than this—I thought I could trust you. That's what I get for believing in something, I guess."

Heron's words were clearly meant to cut Samm deeply, and it broke Kira's heart to hear them, knowing how they must make him feel. But if they did affect him, he didn't show it. Instead, he held up a hand to silence Heron and turned to Kira, his eyes dark with fatigue. "You say you *did* mean it. Do you still?"

Kira was reeling from Heron's accusations, and felt even more empty as she searched for an answer. Was she really doing this—putting them through all this hell, starving her friends and torturing the horses and killing Afa—just for her own selfish reasons? She didn't know what to say, and they stood in tense silence for what felt like an eternity.

"Intentions are all I have left," she said at last. "We're going to go there, and whatever we find, it'll be more than we have now.

At least there's a chance. At least . . ." She trailed off. She had run out of words.

"You're out of your mind," Heron said again, but stopped when Kira turned away and sat, collapsing in a heap as her legs buckled. She lay down on the floor of the shed and wished she could cry.

CHAPTER THIRTY-SIX

Haru Sato slunk through the warren of tunnels under JFK, keeping far from the other soldiers when he could, and nodding to them passively when the tight hallways made it impossible to keep his distance. He kept his weather-beaten hat pulled low over his face, avoiding eye contact, hoping no one would talk to him or ask where he was going. If they found out he'd fled his unit, he'd be arrested—or worse. It was not a good time to be a traitor.

Mr. Mkele's office was in the middle of a long hall, what looked like it used to be a shipping office, now converted to the last, dying nerve center of human civilization. Morgan's forces had taken East Meadow, had rounded up every other human they could find on the island; in a matter of days, they would come for this hideout and the human world would end. Their time as the dominant species was over. And what pitiful resistance they could mount was managed out of this failing office.

Well, thought Haru, *this office and Delarosa's roving base camp. And Delarosa's more dangerous than we ever knew.*

A single soldier stood guard in front of the closed office door, his uniform wrinkled and dirty. There was no time for pleasantries anymore. Haru glanced up and down the hall, seeing it relatively empty; most of the remaining Grid soldiers were upstairs on defense, or out in the wilderness attacking Morgan's flanks. For the moment, Haru and the guard were alone. Haru glanced around again, set his resolve, and walked toward him.

"Mr. Mkele is busy at the moment," said the guard.

"Let me ask you a question," said Haru, stepping in close. At the last minute he turned to the right and lifted his arm, like he was pointing at something, and as the guard turned his head to follow, Haru slammed his knee into the man's gut, bringing his left arm behind to catch the rifle slung over the man's shoulder. The guard reached for it, still doubled over and too shocked to breath, but Haru maneuvered him swiftly into place for another knee, in the face this time, and the man collapsed. Haru opened the door, shoved the unconscious man through it, and stepped in after him. Mkele leapt to his feet, but Haru had already locked the door tightly.

"Don't call out," he said. "I'm not here to hurt you."

"Just my guards."

"I went AWOL last night," said Haru. "I couldn't risk him raising an alarm." He laid the man gently in the corner. "Just give me five minutes."

Mkele's office was full of papers—not cluttered, as if he simply failed to throw anything away, but full, and from the looks of it very efficiently organized. This was a man who used his office not for show or for storage, but for long hours of work and study.

Mkele was sitting behind his desk with a map of Long Island spread out before him, marked here and there with the sites of Partial attacks, Grid counterattacks, and—Haru couldn't help but notice—some of Haru's own allegedly secret activities with Delarosa and her warriors. *I guess I'm not as good at keeping secrets as I thought. Maybe he already knows.*

No, thought Haru. *If he knew what Delarosa was planning, he wouldn't be nearly this calm.*

"You're turning yourself in," said Mkele.

"If you want to look at it that way," said Haru. "I'm delivering intel, and if some of that intel reflects poorly on me, I'm prepared to face the consequences."

"It must be very important intel."

"What did you do before?" Haru asked. "Before the Break?"

Mkele stared at him a moment, as if deciding how to answer, then gestured at the map before him. "This."

"Intelligence?"

"Mapmaking," said Mkele. He smiled faintly. "In the wake of apocalypse, we must find new areas of endeavor."

Haru nodded. "Were you familiar with the Last Fleet? I don't know its real name, I was seven when it happened. The fleet that sailed into New York Harbor and got bombed to hell and back by the Partial air force. They call it the Last Fleet because it was our last chance to defend ourselves against the Partials, and when it was gone, the war was over."

"I know it," said Mkele. His face was calm—intent without appearing nervous. Haru pressed forward.

"Do you know why the Partials destroyed it?"

"We were at war."

"That's why they attacked it," said Haru. "Do you know why they attacked it with such overwhelming force that they sank every ship in the fleet and killed every sailor onboard? They'd never done that with any other attack or counterattack in the war. I've heard the stories a thousand times from the older guys in the Defense Grid—how the Partials who had typically been much more interested in pacification and occupation, suddenly decided to obliterate an entire fleet. They say it was a message, the Partials' way of saying, 'Stop fighting now or we'll make you regret it.' That always seemed pretty reasonable to me, so I didn't question it. Yesterday I learned the truth."

"From who?"

"From Marisol Delarosa," said Haru. "She'd started requesting strange equipment, stuff that didn't fit any of her known methods, so I followed her."

"What kind of equipment?"

"Scuba gear," said Haru. "Acetylene torches. Stuff that didn't make sense from one drop to the next, but they all started adding up to the same thing."

"Underwater salvage," said Mkele, nodding. "I assume this means she's been exploring the Last Fleet?"

"The Last Fleet wasn't destroyed as a message," said Haru. "It was carrying a nuclear missile."

Mkele's face tensed immediately, and Haru continued. "It was the US government's 'final solution,' to land a nuke on the Partial headquarters in White Plains and knock out the majority of their military operation in one move, even at the expense of one of the most densely populated areas in the entire country. They needed to sail in close to bypass the Partials' missile defense systems; it was a suicide mission even before the Partials figured out what they were doing. Some old man in Delarosa's team was a navy chaplain before the Break, and he started talking about the same final solution. That's what gave her the idea. He knew all kinds of things once she started asking the right questions. The missile was on an Arleigh Burke–class destroyer called *The Sullivan*." He leaned forward. "I tried to warn you by radio, but my unit sided with her. I can't stop her alone, so I came as fast as I could. If nothing goes wrong with their operation, they'll have the warhead in hand by tonight."

Mkele whispered, "God have mercy."

CHAPTER THIRTY-SEVEN

They saw the mountains first—massive peaks that rose up from the plains of the Midwest like the wall at the edge of the world. The tops were white with snow, even in the summer. They reached the outskirts of the city soon after, a suburb called Bennett, washed pale by the acidic rainfall, the streets stained a sulfurous yellow and the brown plants dry and brittle. The dead plains lapped at the edge of the city like an ocean of poison grass, and no birds perched on the eaves or the power lines. The cities Kira had grown up with, even the massive ones like Chicago and New York, had stood like monuments in an overgrown cemetery, marking the site of death but covered with vines and moss and the signs of new life. Denver, in contrast, was a mausoleum, lifeless and bare.

The travelers had distributed their gear between the horses, Kira leading Bobo while Samm led Oddjob; the mare seemed morose without Afa strapped onto her back, and Kira wondered if even the animals' diet of canned vegetables and instant oatmeal—the only clean food they could find in the toxic waste-land—was starting to take its toll. If they'd lost Afa back in Chicago, or sent him back on his own, they could have loosed the horses and spared them the horrors of the journey completely, but to loose them in the middle of the poison plains would have been the height of cruelty, and Kira wouldn't hear of it. They had lost Afa, but she would save his horse if it meant her own life.

Except I know that isn't true, she thought. *If it really comes down to it, I'll save myself.* It made her feel guilty and nauseous to think of it, and she did her best to think of something else.

The city they passed through was, if anything, bigger than Chicago. The suburb of Bennett stretched west into the suburb of Nieveen, then Lawrence, then Watkins and Watkins Farm, and on and on in an endless sea of housing developments and shopping malls and parking lots. Lonely wind rustled through the piles of brittle leaves and broken glass that clustered in the gutters and collected against the walls of crumbling buildings. Heron ranged far ahead, scouting their path more out of habit than necessity, doubling back at regular intervals to report that they were coming up on first one airport, then another, then a golf course. There was nothing meaningful to report; nothing to see but the bleached bones and rusted metal frames of the millions of people and buildings destroyed in the Break. Samm found another road map in a broken-down gas station, folding it out on the hood of an empty car. The roads coiled together on the page like a cluster of nerves.

"According to Afa's records," said Kira, "the ParaGen complex was here, tucked up against the mountains." She pointed to the western edge of the city, in an area called Arvada. She read the name off the map. "Rocky Flats Memorial Preserve. Why would they build an industrial facility on a preserve?"

Samm pinpointed their current location and measured out the distance. "That's forty miles away. How big is this city?"

"Forty miles across," said Heron. "We're walking from one end to the other. It's at least twice that north to south, so be grateful we came the way we did."

Kira looked at the sky, estimating the position of the sun. "It's already . . . three in the afternoon? Three thirty? We're not making it forty miles by nightfall."

"Not even tomorrow by nightfall if the horses don't perk up," said Heron. "I tell you, we need to just leave them and move on."

"We're not leaving them," said Kira.

"Guilt won't bring Afa back," said Heron.

"And callousness won't make the distance any shorter," said Samm, folding the map. "Let's keep walking."

Kira had held a vain hope that the toxic wasteland would be better here, shielded in some way by the mountains or the skyscrapers or some foible in the weather patterns, but the city proved to be somehow more dangerous than the land they had already crossed. Acid runoff collected in potholes and dips in the road, forming caustic lakes where drainage grates were too clogged with garbage to let the slurry escape. Truck beds open to the weather had formed miniature salt pans, evaporating the poison particles out of the rainfall in an ongoing cycle until they were filled with crystalline masses that kicked up in the wind and burned the travelers' eyes and throats; they wrapped their faces with spare clothing and peered cautiously through their eye slits, always on the watch for danger. Some of the chemicals that saturated the city were flammable, and fires smoldered here and there as they passed, sometimes reigniting in the heat, all the time feeding the poisons in the air with a never-ending stream of smoke and ash.

They stopped for the night in what looked like it used to be a luxury hotel; the rich green carpet in the lobby was bleached at the edges and covered with windblown dust. They led the horses through a wide double door and made camp in a former five-star restaurant, sealing the way behind them to keep out as much of the toxic wind as possible. Samm built the horses a corral from old hardwood tables, and they fed them from a massive store of canned apple pie filling they found in the kitchen. Kira ate canned tuna mixed with canned beef bouillon to hide the flavor; if she never saw another can of tuna again in her life, she'd count herself lucky. They didn't bother setting watch, collapsing on the deep pile carpet without even untying their bedrolls.

Kira rose the next morning to find Heron already gone, presumably scouting ahead, if she hadn't already abandoned them completely. They hadn't talked much after the fight, and while Heron seemed resigned to go with them to Denver in the end, she had not been her usual self since.

Samm was searching boxes stacked along the wall next to the kitchen for anything they could take with them. "Most of the cans have gone bad," he said, tossing Kira a bloated metal can of tomato paste. "Hotels are always crappy anyway—they use too much fresh food, and most of the canned stuff is bulk."

Kira nodded to the five-gallon can of tomato sauce on the table beside him. "You don't want to haul that thirty miles today?"

"Believe it or not," he said. He paused in his work, turning to face her. "I'm sorry about Afa."

"So am I."

"What I mean to say," said Samm, "is that I'm sorry I was so . . . pretentious. In the beginning."

"You were never pretentious."

"Arrogant, then," said Samm. "Partial society is so regimented, we always know who we report to and who reports to us—who we're above and who we're below. I didn't treat him like an equal because . . . I guess I'm just not accustomed to the concept."

Kira laughed hollowly, collapsing in a nearby chair. "Okay, that actually does sound kind of pretentious."

"You're making it very hard for me to apologize."

"I know," said Kira, looking down at the floor. "I know, and I'm sorry, and I didn't mean to. You've been more than helpful, and Afa wasn't exactly the easiest person to take seriously."

"What's done is done," said Samm, and continued to work on the food supplies. Kira watched him, not because it was interesting but because it cost too much effort to look away.

"You think we'll find what we're looking for?" she asked.

Samm continued to search for usable cans of food. "Don't tell me you're starting to pay attention to Heron."

"I used to think there must have been a plan," said Kira. "That even though I didn't know how RM and expiration and whatever I am all fit together, they still did, somehow. But if there was any plan, I can't help but think it went wrong a long time before now.."

"Don't say that," said Samm, setting down the cans and

walking over to where she was still sitting. "We won't know until we get to ParaGen. No point in doubting yourself now. For the record, I never have."

Kira smiled, in spite of everything. She had begun to wonder if Heron was right, if this was more about her own frustration about her entire existence being an accident or an evil plot or an outright lie than it was about saving the races. And yet, Samm didn't. She found herself again at a loss for words. He reached a hand toward her cheek.

They heard noise in the lobby, and Samm had his gun in his hand before Kira even realized he'd brought it over with him. He lowered it quickly, though, when Heron appeared. She paused for a moment in the doorway as she saw them together, but only for a moment.

"Pack up," she said. "We move out now."

Samm looked at her, silent, then quickly rose to finish packing the food. Kira followed Heron from the kitchen to the main room of the restaurant, where she began saddling Oddjob. "You saw something?" asked Kira.

Heron pulled the buckles tight on Oddjob's saddle and moved on to Bobo. "Green."

"What do you mean 'green'?"

"The color," said Heron. "I assume you're familiar with it?"

"You saw the color green?" asked Kira. "You mean, like, grass?" Heron nodded, and Kira's jaw fell open. "How far did you go?"

"Twenty stories," said Heron, finishing with Bobo's saddle. "You gonna help?"

"Sure," said Kira, jogging to her bedroll and packing her

sparse gear as quickly as she could. "Just keep explaining things so I don't have to stop every five seconds to ask another question."

"This is one of the tallest buildings in the area," said Heron, "so instead of scouting out into the city I climbed to the top to see what I could see. And I saw green—grass, trees, everything—in the direction of Rocky Flats. A little patch of it pressed up into the foothills of the mountains."

"Right where the ParaGen building is supposed to be?" asked Samm.

"I couldn't tell," said Heron, throwing her gear onto her back. "But I'm pretty sure I saw smoke over there as well."

"There's smoke everywhere," said Kira. "Half this city's on fire."

"Those are chemical fires," said Heron. "This one looked suspiciously like a cooking fire. That's why I want to make sure I get there before dark—if there's someone there, they might find us before we find them, and that could be a problem. You can try to catch up, but I'm not waiting for you." She slipped out the door, rifle in hand, and ran through the lobby to the city beyond.

Kira looked at Samm. "People?"

"I don't know."

"Then let's go find out."

They finished packing in a frenzy, wincing with stiff, ragged muscles as they secured their final pieces on the horses' backs and raced out into the city. It had rained in the night, and the city was even more treacherous because of it: Showers of acid dripped off the roofs, and twisted, alien plants had bloomed like tumors from the cracks in the street, soaking in the poison like sponges and streaking it in painful burns against the legs of anyone who stepped too close.

They followed the best landmark they could find—a tall, dark building that seemed to rise up more or less in the right direction. As the day wore on, they began to suspect that the black skyscraper might actually be the ParaGen building—nestled at the base of the mountains, a lonely spire beckoning them onward. Samm and Kira made the best time they could, pushing the horses beyond their limit, but when night fell again, they had only reached the outskirts of Arvada. The city here was as acid-washed and desolate as the rest.

"We can't just stop," said Kira. "It's, like, right there." She pointed at the black spire and the mountains beyond, now so close that they towered over them. "I can't just camp down for the night if the thing we've been looking for is right there, just . . . We have to keep going."

"We can barely see," said Samm, glancing at the myriad streetlights, useless in a world without electricity. "It's dark, the horses are beat, and that much cloud cover means rain."

Kira growled in frustration, clenching her hands into fists as she turned, casting around for anything she could find that might solve her problem. She spied a grocery store and pulled Bobo toward it. "There. We'll leave the horses and go on foot." They unsaddled the horses in a break room in the back of the store, filling a plastic tub with as much bottled water as they could scrounge, and closed the door to keep them from wandering away. Kira emptied most of her pack as well, bringing only the essentials: water, a heavy tarp for protection, and the depowered computer screen with all the information they'd downloaded at the Chicago data center; she didn't want to go anywhere without it. Samm brought his rifle and several clips of ammunition, and Kira realized she should do the same. Prepped and ready, they stole out into the night. The sky was clearing, and the starlight made the city look blank and colorless.

Arvada was less industrial than much of the city they'd walked through, though this only made it more depressing in the toxic fallout—instead of bleached buildings, they walked through dry, dusty parks and residential streets full of drooping houses and stunted, misshapen trees. Samm seemed more nervous than eager, but his mood turned when they came upon a wide lake of fresh water—not just saltless but literally fresh, completely clean of the poisons and chemicals that had plagued all water they'd passed in a month. A breeze blew gently from the mountains, and Kira smelled clean air for the first time in weeks: green leaves, fresh fruit, and . . . *Yes,* she thought, *just a hint of baked bread.*

What's going on here?

The land beyond the lake was green—they couldn't see it, but they could smell it in the air, and feel it in the soft give of the healthy grass beneath their feet. Somehow, against all logic, there was a patch of healthy grass at the base of the mountain, stretching out from the fence that marked the borders of the Rocky Flats Preserve. Kira frowned and approached the fence carefully. It was old and rusty, but the land beyond it was rich and verdant, even in the darkness. An oasis of life, thriving in the midst of desolation. The black spire rose up like a gash in the sky. Lights flickered through the trees, and Kira raised her gun protectively.

Samm nodded to the right, and they followed the fence as quietly as they could, slipping through the healthy grass and bushes that surrounded the mysterious complex. Soon they came upon a wide gate, open and empty, and they watched it from the shadows for nearly ten minutes before determining that it was, indeed, unguarded. Thick undergrowth around the base of the gate made Kira suspect it hadn't been closed in years.

"Does somebody live here?" Kira whispered.

"I . . ." Samm seemed lost for words. "I have no idea."

"Is there an outpost here?" she asked. "Some kind of . . . Partial base or . . ."

"I would have said something if I'd known."

"Well, who else could it be?"

They stared at the open gate, trying to work up the nerve to enter.

"We still haven't found Heron," said Samm. "She could be in there, or she could be hiding and waiting for us."

"Only one way to find out." Kira crept forward, gun ready. She wasn't about to stall, not when they were so close, not if there was a Partial settlement here. After a moment, Samm seemed to agree and follow her.

They walked past the fence into the bizarre paradise beyond. Kira marveled, awestruck by the vibrant plant life that surrounded them, and again they saw the lights—fires, Kira was certain, but unlike the smoldering disasters in the city, these seemed small and controlled, just as Heron had said. Campfires, or bonfires. They crept through the darkness, and soon they heard them.

Voices. Happy voices, laughing and singing, with another

sound in the midst of it, something Kira had thought she'd never hear again. She broke into a run, all caution forgotten, and when she saw them she dropped to her knees, too overcome with emotion to run or speak or even think.

Children.

The bonfire leapt and crackled in the middle of a clearing, surrounded by low buildings and a crowd of dancing people, and dancing through the midst of them were children—infants and preteens, ten-year-olds and toddlers. Dozens of children of every age and size, laughing and whooping and clapping their hands, singing as a small band played pipes and fiddles in the firelight. Kira sank into the grass and cried, weeping and sobbing and trying to talk, but there were no words. Samm knelt beside her and she clung to him, holding him, pointing to the children, and Samm was trying to pull her away but all she wanted to do was get closer, to see them for herself, to touch them and hold them. They had seen her now, the children and the adults and everyone; the music had stopped, and the singing, and they were rising to their feet in shock and surprise. Samm tried again to pull Kira to her feet, and she finally managed to speak to the crowd of strangers inching toward them.

"You have children."

A semicircle of strangers spread loosely in front of them, and Kira noticed now that they were holding spears and bows and here and there a gun. A young woman about Kira's age stepped forward with a hunting rifle, aiming it with practiced expertise at Kira's chest.

"Drop your weapons."

PART 4

CHAPTER THIRTY-EIGHT

"**W**ho are you?" asked Samm.

The girl with the rifle kept a perfect bead on Kira's chest. "I said drop your weapons."

Samm dumped his rifle on the ground. Kira was too shocked to move, still staring at the children, and Samm pulled her rifle from her shoulder and threw it down in the grass. "We're not here to hurt you," he said. "We just want to know who you are."

The girl lowered the hunting rifle slightly, no longer sighting down the barrel but keeping it pointed in their general direction. She had long blond hair pulled back in a ponytail, and her leather vest seemed rough and homemade. "You first," she said. "Where'd you come from? No one's crossed the mountains in twelve years."

Kira shook her head, finally finding her voice. "Not the mountains, the wasteland. We're from New York."

The blond girl raised her eyebrow, and the crowd of people around her murmured in disbelief. An older woman stepped forward, holding a small child in her arms, and Kira stared at the little boy like he was a miracle in human form: three years old, plump and rosy-cheeked, his face streaked with dirt and whatever sticky food he'd had for dinner. He stared back at Kira in perfect innocence, studying her as if she were the most normal thing in the world, and then smiling as he caught her eye. Kira couldn't help but smile back.

"Well?" the woman demanded. "Are you going to answer?"

"What?" asked Kira.

"I said that you couldn't have come from the Badlands," said the woman, "because the wasteland is all that's left."

Samm put a hand on Kira's shoulder. "I think you tuned out, staring at the child."

"I'm sorry," said Kira, and rose to her feet. The crowd stepped back, but kept their weapons ready. Samm stood beside her, and she gripped his hand for support. "It's just that . . . it looks like we have a lot of explaining to do. On both sides. Let's start over." She looked at the blond girl. "Start with the basics—are you humans or Partials?"

The older woman narrowed her eyes, and there was no mistaking the anger in them. Kira knew at once that this woman was human. *Best to pretend we are, too*, thought Kira.

"My name is Kira Walker, and this is Samm. I'm a medic from the human settlement on Long Island, on the East Coast—up until five minutes ago we thought it was the last human settlement in the world, and from the way you're talking, I bet you used to think more or less the same thing about this place. We had no way of knowing there were survivors out here, but . . . here you are. And here we are." She held her hand out, ready to shake. "Greetings from—" She stopped herself right before saying *another human being*, and felt a sudden pang of loss deep in her gut. She couldn't say that anymore. She swallowed and mumbled out an alternate end to the sentence. "—another human community."

Kira kept her hand out, wiping her eyes with her other hand. The armed settlers stared at her in silence. After a moment the blond girl jerked her head toward the east. "You crossed the Badlands?"

Kira nodded. "Yeah."

"You must be starving." She lowered the rifle completely and took Kira's hand; it was just as rough and calloused as her own. "My name's Calix. Come over to the fire and have some food."

Samm collected their rifles, and he and Kira followed Calix back toward the bonfire; some of the locals were still watching them warily, but they seemed more curious than scared. Kira couldn't help but reach for the nearest child, a girl of about nine, but pulled her hand back before touching her curly black hair. The girl saw her, smiled, and grabbed Kira's hand.

"My name's Bayley," said the girl.

Kira laughed, too overcome with joy to know how to respond. "It's very nice to meet you, Bayley. You remind me of my sister. Her name is Ariel."

"That's a pretty name," said Bayley. "I don't have a sister, just brothers."

Everything about this place seemed magical—that Kira was talking to a child, and that the child had brothers. "How many?" asked Kira, barely able to contain her excitement.

"Three," said Bayley. "Roland's the oldest, but Mama says I'm more responsible."

"I don't doubt that for a minute," said Kira, and sat down on a low bench by the bonfire. A handful of children ran up to gawk at the newcomers, then scampered off, too full of energy to stop for more than a second. A portly man in a greasy apron handed her a plate of mashed potatoes liberally whipped together with garlic and chives and covered with a gob of smoky white cheese, and before she could thank him, he ladled on a pile of rich, meaty chili. The smell of hot peppers tickled her nose, and her mouth watered, but she was too overwhelmed to eat a single bite. Another little girl poured her a glass of cool water, and Kira guzzled it gratefully. Samm thanked everyone softly, nibbling politely on the food, but kept his focus on the people and the area around them, ever wary.

Calix and the older woman who'd spoken before pulled up a bench and sat in front of them. The three-year-old boy in her arms wriggled to the ground and ran off to play. "Eat," said the woman, "but talk between bites. Your arrival is . . . well, like you said. We didn't think there were any other humans left. And giving you dinner doesn't mean we trust you. At least, not yet." She gave a tight smile. "My name's Laura; I'm kind of the mayor around here."

Kira set down her food. "I'm so sorry about before, Laura—I didn't mean to ignore you, it's just that—how do you have children?"

Laura laughed. "Same way everybody does."

"But that's the thing," said Kira, "none of us can." She had a sudden thought and leapt to her feet in terror, afraid of what she

434

might have brought into the settlement with her. "Do you not have RM?"

"Of course we have RM," said Calix. "Everybody does." She paused, frowning at Kira. "Are you saying you don't have the cure?"

"You have a cure?"

Calix seemed just as surprised as Kira. "How can you survive without the cure?"

"How did you do it?" asked Kira. "Is it the pheromone—have you been able to synthesize it?"

"What pheromone?"

"The Partial pheromone," said Kira, "that was our best lead. Is that not how you do it? Please, you have to tell me—we have to get this back to East Meadow—"

"Of course it's not a Partial pheromone," said Laura. "The Partials are all dead, too." She paused, glancing back and forth nervously from Samm to Kira. "Unless you've got some bad news to go with the good stuff."

"I wouldn't necessary call it 'bad,'" said Samm, but Kira cut him off before he could say any more; the people here were suspicious enough already, there was no point in telling them their newcomers were Partials until they'd built up a little more trust.

"The Partials are still alive," said Kira. "Not all of them, maybe half a million, give or take. Some are . . . nicer than others."

"Half a million," said Calix, obviously shocked by the sheer size of the number. "That's . . ." She sat back as if she didn't know what to say.

"How many humans?" asked Laura.

"I used to know exactly," said Kira, "but these days I'd guess about thirty-five thousand."

"Thank God," said Laura, and Kira saw tears streaming down the woman's face. Even Calix seemed pleased, as if the second number was a match for the first. Kira grew suspicious—it was almost as if the girl didn't really understand the size of either number.

Kira leaned forward. "How many of you are here?"

"Almost two thousand," said Laura, and smiled with bittersweet pride. "We expect to pass it in the next few months, but . . . thirty-five thousand. I've never dreamed there would be so many."

"What's it like?" asked Calix. She addressed the question to Kira, but kept stealing glances at Samm. "The world outside the Preserve? We've explored some of the mountains, and we've tried to explore the Badlands, but it's too big. We thought it covered the whole world."

"Just the Midwest," said Samm, "and not even all of it. From here to the Mississippi River, more or less."

"Tell me about the cure," said Kira, trying to steer the conversation back to this most important element. "If you didn't get it from Partials, what is it? How do you make it? How did any of you survive the Break in the first place?"

"That's Dr. Vale's work," said Laura. "Calix, run and see if he's still up, he'll want to meet our visitors." Calix stood, taking a last look at Samm, and ran into the darkness. Laura turned back to Kira. "He's the one who saved us when RM first hit—well, not right away. It was a few weeks later, about the time everyone started to realize that this was really the end. He grabbed as many of us as he could, friends of friends and whoever we could find that was still alive. And he gave us the cure, which I guess he must have synthesized himself, somehow. Then we holed up here in the Preserve."

"You've had the cure that long?" asked Kira. She stammered for a minute, uncertain how to ask the next question politely, then gave up and asked directly. "Why didn't you tell anyone? Why didn't you save as many people as you could?"

"We did," said Laura. "I told you, we found every single person we could find, young and old, everyone who wasn't already dead from the war or the virus. We scoured the city for weeks, and we sent drivers out in every direction. We brought back everyone we found, but there weren't many left alive at that point. I wasn't lying to you, Kira, we honestly thought we were the only humans left in the world."

"We all went east," said Kira. "The last bits of the army gathered us all in one place."

Laura shook her head. "Apparently they missed a few."

"And what made you think all the Partials were dead?" asked Samm. His voice was typically emotionless, but Kira could tell something was bothering him, and had been since they'd arrived in the Preserve. She strained to pick up his feelings on the link, but without the heightened awareness of combat, her senses were too weak.

"Why wouldn't they be dead?" asked Laura. "RM killed them the same as us."

"Wait, what?" asked Kira. This was news—not just news but an outright shock. "RM doesn't affect Partials," said Kira. "They're immune to it. That's . . . that's the whole point of it." She felt a moment of panic—if this part of the world had a mutant, Partial-killing strain of RM, they were in terrible danger.

But if that was so, then they were already exposed. Better to stay calm and learn what they could.

"That's all true," said Laura, "but then the virus mutated. It happened here, in Denver—a new strain that appeared out of nowhere and burned through the Partial army like wildfire."

Kira couldn't help but glance at Samm, looking for a sign of recognition on his face, but he was as impassive as ever. He was listening so intently that Kira thought this must be the first time he'd ever heard the story, but she couldn't be sure, and she couldn't just ask him here in front of everybody. She filed it away to bring up later.

Kira turned back to Laura. "If a new strain hit in Denver, they must have quarantined those forces and kept it from spreading. Back east, no one's even heard of an RM strain that targets Partials."

Calix ran into the firelight, breathless and pointing back deeper into the Preserve. "Dr. Vale's awake," she said between breaths. "He wants to see you."

Kira leapt to her feet. If this Dr. Vale had cured RM, maybe he knew more about Partial and human physiology than she did; maybe he'd already found the records they were looking for, and he could tell them more about the Trust, and the expiration date, and maybe even about who and what Kira was. She practically ran ahead of Calix as the girl led them through the village—a sprawling campus of office buildings that had long ago been converted to apartments. There were people here who hadn't been at the bonfire, but apparently word had spread, and

Kira found herself watched by hundreds of curious eyes, standing in doorways and leaning out of windows and clustering at the street corners. They stared at Kira and Samm with the same wonder Kira had felt on first seeing them, and she couldn't help but wave as she passed. There were more people, and they had a cure, and they lived in a paradise. It was the single brightest hope she'd felt in possibly her entire life.

In the distance, behind the office building village, a massive tower rose up, as high as anything Kira had seen in Manhattan. It was pitch-black, like a hole in the night sky, and she could see it only as a patch of darkness moving against the snow-covered mountains behind. She thought Calix was leading them there, but she stopped them instead at a low building that looked like it had once been a warehouse, and had since been converted to a hospital.

"He's in here," said Calix, opening the door. Kira saw that it was glass, and realized with a start that almost all the windows in the Preserve still had glass in them—a classic sign of human habitation, and a phenomenon that Kira had only ever seen in East Meadow. It made her feel even more at home, and the fact that she was going into a hospital only reinforced the feeling. Samm, however, hung back, and after an awkward moment Kira walked back to drag him.

"Come on," she said, "this is it. This is what we've been looking for."

"We left the horses," said Samm, his voice barely above a whisper. "We shouldn't leave them overnight—let's go get them and meet this guy tomorrow."

"Is that what's been bothering you?" asked Kira. She tugged

on his arm. "Come on, the horses will be fine, we can get them in the morning."

"They let us keep our guns," Samm whispered, jostling them for emphasis. "I know that makes it seem like they trust us, but it's creepy as hell—they have no way of knowing if anything we say is true, and that means that behind all their smiles and accommodations there's some higher level of security we can't see, and I don't like it at all. Let's come back in the morning."

Kira paused, studying his face. She thought she could feel his worry through the link, and if she could feel it, it must be powerful. "You're really nervous, aren't you?"

"You're not?"

Kira glanced around; they were still being watched, and Calix was still waiting impatiently by the door. No one was close enough to hear them—at least not with human senses. She leaned in closer and whispered. "This is a group of people who are alive, who have found a cure, and they're living around the building that holds the secrets to RM, expiration, and whatever the hell I am, Samm—this is what we've been looking for."

"Something's not right here."

"No one has threatened us—"

"And where's Heron?" he asked. "Heron went ahead of us, to investigate this exact place, and yet she's not here—that means she either saw something she didn't like, and she's holding back, or they saw her first and took her down. That is, they couldn't have done anything good with her if they're pretending to us that they've not seen her. And I do not want to meet the enemy that can see Heron first and take her down."

He's right, thought Kira. *This is suspicious, and dangerous, and too good to be true, and yet* . . . "They have the cure," said Kira. "Whatever they're lying about, they're not lying about that—there are children everywhere. And if they have that, they might have more. I have to go into that building, Samm, I *have* to. If you want to wait outside, that's fine."

"I'm not leaving you alone," he said, and looked at the glowing hospital before them. "I guess we're going in, then."

CHAPTER THIRTY-NINE

Calix led them through the halls, and Kira discovered that the hospital was not a converted warehouse but a converted laboratory, full of state-of-the-art equipment—this must have been part of the old ParaGen facility as well. The halls were relatively empty, but Kira's heart leapt into her throat at the sound of crying babies—not sick, screaming infants like she'd always known in East Meadow, but healthy babies and happy, cooing mothers. She wanted to run and see them but blinked back her tears and followed Calix. She needed the cure first; then she could get some answers.

Samm stiffened suddenly, his head jerking around to look for something, and Kira instinctively dropped into a combat stance, ready for attack. Samm breathed deeply, scanning the hall, and finally caught Kira's eye. She started to speak, but he shook his head and nodded toward Calix. The blond girl had stopped by an office door and was looking back at them oddly.

"Is everything okay?" Kira couldn't help but notice that she was asking Samm. He started to answer, but Kira cut him off.

"Is that his office?"

"Yeah," said Calix, and knocked on the door. A gruff voice on the other side shouted for them to come in, and they followed Calix through. Dr. Vale was short and average-looking, old but healthy; Kira couldn't actually tell if he was older than Dr. Skousen or not, and wondered if he'd had any of the longevity gene mods that some of the older, richer people had gotten before the Break. If he had, there'd be no real way to guess his age—he could be anywhere from sixty to a hundred and twenty. Samm stared at him a moment, and Kira couldn't help but feel a faint wave of suspicion wash through her. Samm didn't like the doctor, she didn't even need the link to tell her that. Kira cleared her mind and prepared herself for the conversation, ready for whatever happened.

"Please sit down," said Dr. Vale, gesturing at the chairs in front of his desk. Calix began to sit with them, but Vale stopped her with a kind smile and a gesture toward the door. "Would you be so kind as to wait outside, dear? Our guests are going to have a lot of questions, and I want to make sure we're not disturbed."

Calix seemed none too pleased about this, but sighed and left the room—making sure to flash Samm a quick smile on her way out. Samm didn't even seem to notice, focusing all his attention on Vale, and Kira felt a glow of inexplicable satisfaction.

Calix closed the door behind her, and Vale looked at Samm and Kira. "So," he said. "You're the two wanderers from across the Badlands."

"Yes, sir," said Kira. "We came here looking for . . . answers.

And we need to find a cure for RM, and we understand you've synthesized one."

"That I have," said the doctor, "that I have. Tell me, how many of you did you say there are?"

"Humans or Partials?" asked Kira.

Vale smiled. "Both."

"Thirty-five thousand humans," said Kira. "Roughly. And about half a million Partials."

Vale practically beamed. "Then this is a bittersweet meeting, isn't it? To learn in one short second that one's entire picture of the world is obsolete. I admit I'm not prepared for this revelation, and I pride myself in being prepared for everything."

"Please, sir," said Kira. "Tell me about the cure."

"It works," said Vale, raising his hands in a contented shrug. "What else is there to say? We inoculate each child as he or she is born, and RM can never harm them again. Not the best long-term solution, I'll grant you—I'd hate to think that a hundred years from now we're still giving shots to every human child ever born—but then that's what we did before the Break as well, isn't it? Vaccinations and antibiotics and a whole chemical stew. Even before RM, the world had become far more hostile to our species than we like to admit."

There was something odd about him that Kira couldn't quite put her finger on. She'd grown up as a medical intern, spending her entire life around doctors, and this Dr. Vale was . . . different. He didn't talk like a doctor.

"What we need," he continued, gesturing toward the darkened window behind him, "is a cure that works like our Preserve."

"What do you mean?" asked Kira.

Vale smiled again. "The paradise we live in was once so deadly it was restricted territory, devoid not only of humans but of plants and animals as well. A barren wasteland, much like the one you crossed, but now the tables are turned, aren't they? What nuclear technology destroyed, biotechnology resurrected."

Kira frowned. "This place was nuked?"

"No, no, no," said Vale, "or at least not in the way you're thinking. The Rocky Flats Plant was a nuclear weapons facility for World War II, the first site chosen for the production of hydrogen bombs. More radioactive material passed through here than through the entire city of Hiroshima, but technology, as we have seen, has a way of getting out of hand. The facility became such a health hazard it was completely dismantled, and after decades of cleanup efforts it was finally deemed safe for habitation—not by humans, of course, it wasn't that safe, but who likes deer anyway? Let them have cancer, we don't insure them. Thus was born, in the year 2000, the Rocky Flats Wildlife Preserve, and thus it stayed for more decades, clean enough to mollify our consciences without actually being clean. Such is the human capacity for altruism."

"You mentioned biotech," said Kira. She wasn't sure where he was going with any of this, but at least he was talking. Kira pushed him along, trying to learn more. "I'm guessing that's when ParaGen showed up."

"You guess correctly," said Vale. "ParaGen, the front-runner in a burgeoning new industry. We weren't always here—we started on the south side, in Parker—but our first foray into the realm of biotechnology was a series of hungry microbes designed to eat things that no one else wanted—"

"You worked for ParaGen?" Kira blurted out.

"Naturally," said Vale. He glanced at Samm, still stiff in his chair, then looked back at Kira. "It was my background in biotechnology that made the cure possible."

Kira had to force herself not to leap up out of her chair—a biotechnologist from ParaGen? Was he part of the Trust? She was bursting with questions, but wasn't sure yet how to approach him: If she just came out and asked about the Partials or the expiration date or the Failsafe or anything else, would he answer her? Would he clam up? Would he fly into a rage? She decided to keep him talking, to get a read on his personality. "You built microbes?"

"Microbes that ate waste products," he said, practically giddy to be discussing the topic. "Radiation. Heavy metals. Poisonous chemicals. All very different things, but all, in their own way, a perfect energy source for an organism designed to use it. A couple of government contracts, a few years for the microbes to work their magic, and all of a sudden the poor, bedraggled Rocky Flats was a Garden of Eden. A success like that leads to more contracts, bigger projects, bigger checks; a few more successes and you can start writing your own checks, and one of them turned out to be Rocky Flats itself, a vast tract of perfect real estate that nobody else would ever want. Our karmic reward for saving it, and still the microbes churn away in the soil, holding back the toxic wasteland and maintaining our little corner of paradise."

He loves to talk about this stuff, thought Kira. *Should I push him a little further?* She cleared her throat. "So you were part of the research team that created new organisms."

"That I am," said Vale. He glanced at Samm again, still as cold and silent as a statue. Kira wondered what was wrong, but Vale looked back at her with a kind smile. "I'm a geneticist, to the extent that any genetics work is even possible these days. The cure I have is workable, for now, but I need something that works like those microbes—something that lives under the surface and spreads itself out and protects us without any guidance or intervention. Something that passes from mother to child."

"But what you have now is still a cure," said Kira. "It still works. Where we come from in New York, we haven't had an infant live past three days since the Break. We found a way to cure one child a few months ago, but that's it. We have one miracle child, but you have hundreds. We've been trying to reproduce our cure and we can't do it, but you could give us a future. Please—I'm a medic, I've trained for this exact moment my entire life. Take me to your lab, show me how you do it, and we could save tens of thousands of children. An entire generation." Kira felt herself crying. "We could have a future again."

"The cure isn't portable," said Vale.

"What?" She furrowed her brow in confusion. "How could it not be portable?"

"You'll see," said Vale.

Kira stood up. "Right now."

"Be patient," he said, waving her back to her chair. She didn't sit down. "I want to help, but we have to be careful.."

"What is there to be careful about?"

"We have a delicate balance here in the Preserve," he said. "I'll help you, but I need to do it without upsetting that balance."

"Then let us help you," said Kira eagerly. "I've studied RM, we've crossed the wasteland, we know the terrain and the politics and everything else. What do you need to know?"

"Nothing tonight," said Vale. "I'll talk to you tomorrow."

Kira clenched her fists in frustration. "What about the expiration date?" she asked. He looked up, eyes wide and curious, as if he didn't understand. "The Partial expiration date," she said again, "the mechanism in their genome that kills them after twenty years. Do you know anything about it? Have you figured out how it works?"

"The others will find you a place to stay," said Vale, rising from his chair and walking to the door. His voice was less certain now, his joy at discussing the microbes replaced with a mumbling uncertainty. "It's going to rain tonight, and microbes or not, you don't want to be caught outside."

"Why won't you answer me?" Kira demanded.

"I'll answer you tomorrow," he said. "Follow Calix, and I'll send for you in the morning." He opened the door and gestured toward the hallway.

"First thing in the morning," said Kira. "Promise us." Samm stood to follow her.

"Of course," said Vale. "First thing."

Calix had been sitting on the floor in the hallway, and rose quickly to her feet. "We need to hurry," she said. "The acid rains are coming soon; everyone else will be inside." She looked at Samm. "You can stay at my place—both of you—but we'll have to hurry."

Kira looked back at Vale, his maddening smile still pasted to his face. "First thing," she said, and turned to follow Calix as she ran down the hall.

They reached the front door and Calix looked out carefully, peering up at the thick black storm clouds that filled the sky. "No rain yet. Come on." She ran out, and Kira moved to follow her, but Samm caught Kira's arm.

"Wait," he said, and leaned in to whisper in Kira's ear. His voice was so soft she could barely hear it. "Did you feel it?"

"Feel what?"

"Dr. Vale," said Samm. "I felt him on the link. He's a Partial."

CHAPTER FORTY

Calix lived a few buildings away, and they made it just as the first acid drops fell and splatted on the ground. "The stuff ParaGen put in the dirt helps keep the plants safe," said Calix, "but you don't want the acid on you." A large man stood in the doorway, holding it open for them to race inside, and chided them for cutting it so close.

"Are you trying to get yourself killed, Callie?"

"Never been hit yet," said Calix, slapping him affectionately on the arm as she walked past. "Thanks for getting the door."

"Anytime. These the travelers?"

Samm surveyed the lobby of the building, packed with eager onlookers. He looked back at the big man and nodded. "We are. We need a room for the night, if you have one."

"He means 'please,'" said Kira. "And thank you very much for your hospitality."

"I have plenty of space," said Calix, and pushed the button for the elevator.

Kira walked past her, looking for the stairs, and jumped slightly when the elevator doors slid open. "Holy crap."

Calix raised her eyebrow. "You okay?"

"Where I come from I just . . ." Kira shook herself slightly and followed her gingerly into the elevator. "We don't have enough juice to run elevators back home. I've never actually been inside one."

"Neither have I," said Samm, though Kira knew it was a lie. He was probably trying to avoid the inevitable question of why their past experiences had been so different. Calix pushed a button on the inside wall of the elevator—the highest floor—and the doors slid closed.

"This whole complex is powered," said Kira. "Not just the hospital but everything. Where do you get the juice?"

"ParaGen had gone fully self-sustaining a few years before the Break," said Calix. "We have power, running water, and of course the Preserve itself to protect us from the wasteland. There's even enough land to ranch cattle, if we could find any live ones."

"The chili at dinner had beef in it," said Kira.

"Actually venison," said Calix, and looked at Samm proudly. "I tracked the deer myself. I've been a full-fledged hunter for two years now."

Samm nodded, which was a huge display of emotion for him. "Very impressive."

Kira tried not to scowl. It wasn't like Calix had hunted some monster, like that thing that had chased Kira back in New York.

The elevator let them off on the top floor, which Kira immediately recognized as an office block, though most of the cubicles had been cleared away. The remaining desks were set up along the walls, stacked with potted plants and piles of books and board games. A number of rubber balls sat idly in the corner. "This is our courtyard," said Calix. "My place is back here: Conference Room Two." Each office and conference room they passed had been remade as a small apartment, many of them occupied, and Calix waved familiarly at her neighbors as she passed each one. The neighbors gawked at the newcomers but didn't approach them. Conference Room 2 was more sparsely decorated than most of the others, and Kira wondered if Calix was simply less of a decorator than the others, or less experienced, or if somehow she was poorer. Their society didn't seem to use money, but she was beginning to realize that almost nothing here was what she expected it to be.

Like the fact that their doctor was a Partial.

There was a single bed, which Calix graciously offered to Kira, but Kira insisted on sleeping on the floor—on the other side of the room, where she and Samm could talk in private once their host finally fell asleep. After the first hour of excited questions about the world outside the Preserve, though, Kira realized that Calix was far more likely to outlast them than the other way around. After the second hour Kira was too sleepy to care, and felt her eyes closing as Samm continued to answer question after question.

She slowly drifted off to sleep in her tangle of blankets on the floor, only inches from where Samm sat. A few moments passed, her breathing becoming deep and even, and she felt something touch the back of her hand.

He'd placed his hand on top of hers.

She woke in the morning with a start, sitting up straight and reaching for something, though she couldn't remember what it was. Sunlight peeked through the curtains in the window, and Calix's bed was empty. Samm lay asleep, as straight as a corpse, on the floor next to Kira. Kira rolled to her feet, checked the hallway, then closed the door firmly and shook Samm awake.

"Samm!"

He woke up like a predator, whirling into a combat stance so swiftly Kira had to duck to avoid getting hit. He paused, scanning the room, then looked at Kira. "I'm sorry," he said. "This place has me on edge."

"Same here," she said. "We need to figure out what's going on; we're alone for now, but I don't know how long until Calix gets back."

"The doctor's not a Partial," said Samm.

"You said he was."

"He doesn't match any Partial model I've ever seen," said Samm. "I've been thinking about it all night—he's not a general or a doctor or anything else, which means there are two possibilities. One, he's a model like you, one we haven't seen yet and wasn't mass-produced. I think this is unlikely, most obviously because you don't emit link data, and he does, and you age, and he clearly couldn't be as old as he is if he started as a child seventeen years ago. The second, more likely scenario is that he's like Morgan, a human with gene mods to use the link. Which leads to one pretty obvious conclusion."

"He's also a member of the Trust," said Kira. "Given everything he said about his history with ParaGen, that makes a lot of sense; he'd worked for them since the beginning. He was probably one of their senior scientists."

"It also means he can incapacitate me if he chooses," said Samm. His voice was calm and matter-of-fact, despite the seriousness of his words. "He didn't give me any orders last night, but if he ever does, I don't know if I'll be able to disobey him."

"You disobeyed Morgan."

"And it took me a few minutes to do it, and with extreme concentration," said Samm. "Their control is almost impossible to break, the Trust even more so than the regular officers. If he really exerts himself, at close range, I don't know that I'll be able to do anything about it. Even in the best-case scenario, he can incapacitate me long enough to come after you."

"And in the worst-case scenario," said Kira, "he can control me, too. Assuming he even knows what I am."

"Morgan didn't," said Samm. "But that doesn't mean anything—obviously your father and Nandita knew that you were a Partial, but Morgan didn't. We don't know what Vale does or doesn't know."

"I'm beginning to realize the Trust couldn't have been very . . . trusting," said Kira. "It's as if there were at least two different groups, with two different agendas."

Samm nodded. "That explains some the existence of some contradictory evidence, but it doesn't exactly explain what any of that evidence means. We need more information."

"Which is probably in that center spire," said Kira. "The building we were in yesterday seemed like it was exclusively medical. If Vale gives us the runaround again, that spire is our next priority."

Samm nodded in agreement, then paused for a moment.

"Did Nandita ever control you?"

"You mean with the link?"

"Yes," said Samm. "Did you ever get the impression that you were being forced?"

"Not that I remember," said Kira. She looked at him, feeling a pang of sadness for some of the things he'd been through. "What does it feel like?"

Samm let out a breath. "It can be hard to recognize," he admitted. He paused, and the barest hint of a smile crept over his face. "Of course, for someone as pathologically independent as you, it might stand out a little more."

Kira slapped him lightly on the arm. "I didn't know Partials could tease."

"I'm a good learner."

"Either way," said Kira. "I don't think Nandita ever controlled me with the link, and I don't know if Vale will even try." She paused for a moment, suddenly concerned. "Whether or not he knows about me, though, he has to know you're a Partial, right?"

"I can't imagine he wouldn't," said Samm, "but then I can't imagine why he wouldn't say anything about it, either. What does he have to gain by keeping it secret? Unless . . . maybe he knows we're both Partials, but doesn't know if we know he knows?"

Kira glanced at the door again, still closed. "It's very possible. I think we need to operate as if he's hiding something. Even if it's just in his own self-interest. He couldn't expose you as a Partial without exposing himself as one of the scientists who created us. These people aren't as militant as we are in East Meadow, but they still don't seem to like Partials, either. If they found out their doctor helped build the rebel army, they might not take it very well."

"That's the best guess I've come up with, too," said Samm. "Either way, it's bad news for us. He has a good thing going here, with a perfect little society, and our arrival—our very existence—threatens all of it. If the Partials follow us here, he's done. If the humans follow us here, he's done. If the truth about you or me or him ever gets out, all the secrecy falls apart and he's done. His best possible courses of action would be to kill us or to keep us here indefinitely. Which is perhaps why he didn't offer to help us understand the cure for RM yesterday."

Kira frowned, troubled by the apparent inconsistency. "Unless he was being truthful earlier," said Kira. "He said it wasn't 'portable.' That might mean it needs to be refrigerated. Obviously we can't haul something like that back across the whole continent. That said, at the very least he could give us the formula, or teach me the process. But he refused. Whatever's going on, you're right about the danger."

"And we still don't know where Heron is," said Samm.

"Right." Kira drummed her fingers on the floor, trying to sort through the mess of possibilities. "If she got too close, he'd detect her. He might have used the link to capture her."

"Heron is much higher on the link hierarchy than most of us," said Samm. "It's part of the independence built into the espionage models." He paused, thinking silently, then sighed—a distinctly human action that he must have picked up from so much time spent with Kira. She found it fascinating. "Still," he continued, "she was subordinate to Morgan, and I imagine Vale is similar in his command of the link. He could have her imprisoned somewhere."

"It's also possible that she detected him first," said Kira, "and stayed back. Knowing Heron, that seems more likely to me. For all we know, she might be trying to find the answers we've been looking for in another part of the compound."

"The central spire," Samm said again. "Since all the buildings here are apparently powered, she'd be able to access the computers pretty easily. That doesn't mean she can access the information, though. Without Afa to hack through the security, I don't know how any of us are going to do that."

"Then she'd start with physical records," said Kira. "Assuming Dr. Vale hasn't just destroyed them all—if he's trying to hide his identity, he might have destroyed a lot of old data."

"Assuming he's even trying to hide," said Samm. "There's always the chance that we've just completely misinterpreted everything about this place—maybe everybody knows who he is. We could learn a lot more if we had somebody here we could trust for straight answers."

"I don't trust Calix," said Kira quickly, cutting him off before he could suggest it. "She's clearly loyal to Vale."

"He's their leader," said Samm. "Why wouldn't she be loyal him?"

"That's my point," said Kira. "I'm not saying she's a spy or anything, just . . . if we ask a lot of questions, it'll get back to him."

"And now you're assuming there's a conspiracy," said Samm. "Just because Vale is shifty doesn't make everyone here an enemy. The most likely scenario is that everyone here is just happy and oblivious."

Kira shook her head. "Likely but not guaranteed. I don't want to trust anyone until I know more of what's going on."

"That's the one thing this society isn't ready for," said Samm. Kira looked up, and Samm smiled, just slightly, in the corner of his mouth. "You're a rebel, Kira Walker. Even when there's nothing to rebel against."

Kira smiled back. "Maybe I was made this way. Are there any rebel-model Partials?"

"We started the Partial War," he said simply. "Rebellion is the most human thing about us."

The latch on the door clicked open, and Kira looked up in a rush, momentarily terrified about being caught before realizing that nothing they were doing was outwardly suspicious. Why wouldn't the two newcomers be talking to each other? She only hoped no one had heard what they were saying.

Calix pushed the door open with her hip, carrying a pair of plates piled high with eggs and hash browns; both were liberally laced with red and green chili peppers, and after the chili last night, Kira got the distinct impression that whoever made the food around here liked it spicy. "You're awake," said Calix, setting the plates on a table by the wall—an oddly shaped remnant of the much larger conference table that once filled the room. She pulled forks from her pocket and gestured to the meal grandly. "Breakfast is served. And I invited a friend, if you don't mind; I couldn't carry everything by myself anyway."

As if on cue there was a soft knock on the door, and Calix opened it to reveal a short young man with a broad face and a wicked grin. His arms were full of thick plastic cups and a hefty jug of water. "Thanks, Cal. Hey, guys, I'm Phan."

"Hey," said Kira. Her stomach growled audibly, and she grimaced in embarrassment. "Sorry. We haven't had real food in months—this looks delicious."

Phan laughed. "No problem, dig in." He unscrewed the jug and started pouring cups of water. Kira realized that despite his height he was about her same age. "Sorry to barge in on your breakfast, but you're kind of the most amazingly interesting thing that's ever happened here in the history of ever."

Kira chuckled. "I could say the same about you. We've always hoped there were more survivors, but we'd never been able to contact any."

"Sit down and eat," said Calix, guiding Samm to the table with a light touch on his arm. "Don't worry about us, we already ate."

"Take turns eating so one of you can talk," said Phan, passing out the water. "Start with how on earth you were able to cross the wasteland—none of us has even made it as far as Kansas. We figured if we ever found a settlement it would be west, across the mountains."

Kira swallowed her bite of potatoes—incredibly spicy, but nothing Nandita's cooking hadn't prepared her for—and asked a question of her own. "Has anyone crossed them?"

"They've never come back if they have," said Calix. "We've gone far enough to know that the toxic wastes don't go very far west. The mountains stop the wind, keeping most of the bad stuff out here on the plains, but even without the acid storms, the mountains are pretty dangerous. You've got to cross some pretty high passes to get over them, and a lot of the roads have washed away."

"The best bet would be an excursion up north," said Phan, "through Wyoming and around the tip of the range, but Vale won't approve it. It's as empty up there, and there's no good place to hide from the storms. He has to make rules like this, since people like Calix are dumb enough to try it."

"Shut up," said Calix, throwing a wadded sock in Phan's face.

"Do you always have to do what Vale says?" asked Kira. "I thought Laura was the mayor."

"I didn't become a hunter by ignoring good advice," said Phan. "Vale, Laura, the other adults, they're all just trying to keep us alive."

Samm popped a thick slice of pepper in his mouth, apparently unfazed by the heat. "You're a hunter, too?"

"I taught him everything he knows," said Calix.

"And then I improved on it," said Phan with a grin. He nodded toward Samm. "How about you?"

"We don't really have hunters," said Samm, "at least not as a caste. I'm a soldier."

Calix frowned. "Is it really that bad? With the Partials, I mean—do they attack you so often you need full-time soldiers?"

"We have to maintain some sort of defensive force," said Kira, jumping in, "but most of us are other things—farmers and medics and stuff like that. We don't have the cure, like you do, so a pretty big chunk of everything we do is dedicated to finding one."

"How are you alive if you don't have the cure?" asked Phan.

"Same as you," said Kira, "we're just immune. It's the newborns who need the cure."

"You're just automatically immune?" asked Calix. "Just like that?"

Kira frowned. "You're not?"

"Everyone in the Preserve was inoculated twelve years ago," said Calix, "right after the Break. We've never heard of a . . . natural immunity. I though RM just killed everybody."

It still boggled Kira's mind that the people here had had a cure for so long—not that there'd been any way to get it from them, but just knowing that it was out there, that all the infants she'd watched die could have been saved, nearly broke her heart all over again.

"If people are naturally immune, there could be survivors everywhere," said Phan. "We could bring people in from all over the continent—all over the world."

Kira stole a glance at Samm, then looked back. "Would you let new people in? If we could bring people here?"

"Are you kidding?" asked Phan. "That's like a dream come true. We'd probably make a red carpet just so we could roll it out for you."

"They never let us explore too far, though," said Calix. Her face and voice were more somber, suddenly, and she looked at Kira as she spoke—the first time she'd addressed her instead of Samm practically since they'd arrived. "We keep pushing for more expeditions into the Badlands, the younger generation especially, but the leaders don't like it—they want us to stay close, where it's safe. They say the Preserve has everything, but . . ." She gestured at Samm and Kira. "You're the proof that it doesn't. That's why you need to tell us what's out there, and who's out there, so we can convince them to let us explore. Paradise or not, we can't stay here forever."

"That sounds like someone else I know," said Samm, though Kira didn't respond. It would take more than a mistrust of authority for Calix to earn her trust.

"Tell us about the Partials," said Phan. "We were told stories about them when we were kids, hiding here after the Break. Can a Partial really throw a car?"

CHAPTER FORTY-ONE

Marcus and the soldiers flew as far as they could in the stolen Rotor, but the rioting Partial army was hot on their trail. A lucky shot clipped their left wing somewhere over New Rochelle, and Woolf managed to coax another few miles out of the flier before an antiaircraft emplacement on the coast forced them into an emergency landing in Pelham Bay. Vinci wanted to head southwest, crossing the Throgs Neck Bridge to Long Island, but Woolf said it was too dangerous—the bridges were covered with traps and explosives, and there was no way they could cross them safely. Instead they found a motorboat on City Island, filled it with as much good gas as they could find, and made the crossing that way; Partial pursuers fired at them from shore as they raced across the water, but nothing hit. They landed in Queens near the ruins of the Defense Grid base.

It was a blackened husk, bombed to oblivion and burned to the ground.

"Welcome to the last human refuge," said Woolf. "As you can

see, we're not really equipped for visitors."

"Great," said Galen. "We got away from one Partial army just to end up behind the lines of another."

"But at least we got away," said Marcus. "What's the next move?"

"It seems like a fair guess to say that the pro-Morgan faction won the civil war back there," said Vinci. "With Trimble gone, Morgan's cemented herself as the single greatest power in the region, but there are other factions, and they might be sympathetic—even if they didn't take a side before, Morgan's actions may have tipped them in our favor."

"Enough to mount a resistance?" asked Woolf.

"Maybe, maybe not," said Vinci. "It depends on how quickly we could unite all the remaining factions—and if any of them have already joined Morgan outright. I'm afraid I don't have any reliable intelligence on that."

"Then we need to get back there," said Marcus. "We need to find them all, and we need to recruit them."

"If they still oppose Morgan," said Woolf. He looked Vinci. "Twelve years ago your people nearly exterminated our race in a rebellion. Do you really think they'd ally with humans now? Against their own people?"

Vinci paused a moment before speaking. "I have recently learned to make my allies along ideological, rather than racial lines. That was a lesson you taught me. I do not agree with Dr. Morgan, and I don't know if I'll agree with whoever wins the civil war in White Plains, but I agree with you. You said you wanted to work together and cure us—our expiration date and your disease. Is that still correct?"

Woolf didn't answer, but Marcus nodded firmly. "Absolutely. We'll do everything we can."

"Then I'm with you for now," said Vinci. He looked at Woolf. "We started a war but never intended to end the world—the virus did not come from us. We've been struggling with the guilt of what happened for twelve years. There are many Partials left who might just be looking for a reason to trust humans again, or at least a reason to live in peace. The hell we just escaped from should be proof enough of that." He held out his hand. "I can't speak for every Partial, but if you're ready to trust me, I'm ready to trust you."

Woolf hesitated, staring at the Partial's hand. Marcus watched the old soldier's eyes, guessing at the battle of memories and hatreds and hopes that must be going on behind them. Finally Woolf reached out and grasped Vinci's hand. "I never thought I'd see the day." He looked in the Partial's eyes. "As commander of the Defense Grid and a senator of the last human nation, consider this an official treaty."

"You have my support," said Vinci, "and the support of any other Partials we can recruit."

"I want to kiss you both," said Marcus, "but this touching moment doesn't mean anything until we get some more people behind it. Where to next?"

Woolf looked around at the devastated ruin. "Before we try to raise a Partial army, we should at least check in with the human forces—we've been gone long enough we don't even know what's going on here. Even if we could find a radio, though, I don't know how much we can share. Morgan's forces are monitoring all frequencies, and the last thing we want is to let Dr. Morgan know we're raising a combined army of Partials and humans."

"Where to, then?" asked Vinci. "Do you still have a base of operations Morgan hasn't conquered?"

"I honestly don't know," said Woolf. "The Senate fled to an old outlaw hideout, but if I had to guess, I'd say Morgan's already taken it. Our best bet is a guerrilla named Delarosa."

"You're sure about that?" asked Marcus. "She might not take kindly to a Partial in the ranks."

Vinci looked at Woolf. "You want to ally with a racist?"

"More of an extremist," said Woolf. "After the invasion, her extreme methods made her one of our most effective forces in the field. She knows the island better than the invaders do, and if anyone's managed to stay free, it's her."

"And you're sure you can trust her? That she won't just shoot me on sight?"

"She's a pragmatist," said Woolf. "She'll use the weapons she has, and she'll use them as effectively as possible." He slapped Vinci on the back. "What better weapon could she want than a Partial?"

CHAPTER FORTY-TWO

Calix spread her arms wide, gesturing toward the entirety of the Preserve. "What do you want to see first?"

"Dr. Vale," said Kira.

"Not till this afternoon," said Calix. "I checked with the hospital, and he's got a birth this morning."

Kira's heart soared at the thought of a birth, and she longed to see the cure administered firsthand, but she forced herself to stay focused. They had a lot of other things to investigate. "That big black spire in the middle," she said.

"Too dangerous," said Phan. "That was ParaGen's main building, and the Partials blasted the shiz out of it during the rebellion. I'm amazed it's still standing."

It was worth a shot, thought Kira. *But if Heron hasn't been captured, that's got to be where she is.*

Samm bent down to examine the grass, probing it gingerly with one finger before pressing his whole hand down to touch it. "How does this survive the rain?"

"Engineered microbes in the soil," said Calix. "It absorbs the poison too fast for it to do any real damage to the plants."

Kira knelt down as well, running her fingers through the soft, lush grass. "They're not even discolored. The microbes must come right up into the leaves."

"Maybe," said Calix. "I'm not a scientist, I wouldn't know."

"But they do teach you science," said Kira, standing up. "I mean, they have a school here, right?"

"Sure," said Calix. "You want to see it?"

Kira shot another glance at the central spire, towering over the Preserve like a blackened tombstone. That was where she wanted to go, but they'd have to wait until the time was right. She felt ready to explode with frustration, but took a deep breath and hoped Calix and Phan couldn't see how stressed she was. *The time will come,* she told herself. *We need to earn their trust first.* "Sure, let's see the school."

"The school's great," said Phan, falling into step beside Kira as they walked. He had more energy than anyone Kira had ever met, ranging back and forth as they walked, smiling and waving at everyone while inspecting each tree and wall they passed, all while carrying on a conversation. "You learn all the basics first, like reading and writing and math and all that. Vale saved a bunch of schoolteachers, so they know what they're doing. I was actually with the teachers during the Break. I was in kindergarten, and we were all hiding in a bomb shelter after a Partial attack during the first wave of the war. They hit so fast they didn't even have a chance to cancel school, so I don't know what happened to my family, but I guess that's the only reason I'm still alive. Sucks to be my parents, obviously, since they weren't at school and we could never find them afterward, but you say some people are just naturally immune, so for all I know, they're still alive. That's awesome; that's like the best news ever."

Kira couldn't help but smile, struggling to keep up with the dizzying pace of his conversation. "I'm sorry you lost your parents."

Phan looked at her quizzically. "You still have your parents?"

Kira shook her head. "Good point—I guess none of us have our parents anymore."

"Some do," said Phan with a shrug. "Families Vale was able to find and inoculate all in one bunch. Doesn't bother me, though—I never would have made it twelve years if I'd spent all my time missing dead people. You gotta move on."

Kira glanced at Samm and Calix, deep in a similar conversation. She hoped Samm could keep his head and not spill any secrets about who he was; Calix was certainly doing her best to distract him, smiling and laughing and touching him now and then on the arm or shoulder, just lightly. Kira felt a sudden surge of paranoia, convinced that Calix was trying to seduce Samm and learn the truth, but even as she thought it, she realized it was stupid. Calix was probably just giddy at the sudden introduction of a hot teenage guy into a very, very small dating pool.

Somehow, that thought only made Kira angrier.

"Being a hunter is not the most important job," said Phan, "but it's definitely one of them, because it's one of the only ways we get protein. Protein that's not eggs, I mean. There are deer in the Rockies, and elk and mountain goats, and this is the best place for them to find food, so we keep the gates open and tore a bunch of the fences down and welcome them in—which makes it sound easy, but sometimes they don't come in, and sometimes we get wolves coming after the chickens or the kids or whatever, so the hunters are the ones who set traps and follow tracks and keep the food chain moving in the right direction."

There was something incredibly cheery about the way he talked—his bragging didn't seem arrogant or pushy, he was just proud of what he did and genuinely happy to be doing it, and his excitement over each new topic of conversation seemed infectious rather than overbearing. Kira soon gave up trying to squeeze a word into the torrent of eager babbling, and listened as Phan talked about everything from wolf pelts to wasteland survival to the finer points of converting an office building to living space. They passed several more of the big buildings, and even a fountain in a grassy courtyard, and Kira marveled at the strange mix of affluence and survivalism that permeated their society—they had running water and electricity and showers and even a grounds crew, patiently mowing the grass and trimming the bushes, but on the other hand they had none of the salvage opportunities that Kira had grown up with. All the clothing stores within easy reach had been ravaged by acid storms or incinerated in chemical fires, so the people wore a mixture of frontier homespun, animal hides, and patchwork oddities hand-stitched from old curtains and sheets. Kira realized that they would probably find her own background equally bizarre, a parade of high-fashion divas using candles and wood-burning stoves in their giant, decaying mansions. Was there anywhere on Earth where life was normal? Did "normal" even mean anything anymore?

The school was in another office building, filling the two

lowest floors with hoots and hollers and the happy shrieks of children. Kira's heart beat faster as the sound grew louder, still shocked by the existence, let alone the sheer number, of children in the Preserve. *This is what I've been working for,* she thought. *This sound—this crazy, wonderful chaos. A new generation discovering the world and making it their own.* Tears filled her eyes, and she felt torn between the desire to stop and stand and soak it in, absorbing the happiness as slowly as she could to make it last that much longer, or simply to race forward and throw open the doors and drown herself in the joy of so many children. Her reverie was cut short when Samm spoke.

"You go in," he said. "I'm going to go get the horses."

Kira looked at him in surprise. "Alone? Let me go with you, it's too dangerous in the ruins for one person."

"It's okay," he said. "I can tell you want to see the children. Calix said she'll go with me—this close to the Preserve, she knows the ruins well."

Calix was smiling, and Kira was so shocked she couldn't read the expression on the other girl's face. Did she look pleased? Too pleased? Victorious? Kira stammered, trying to form a response: On the one hand, Calix almost certainly knew the territory better, and for that reason would be a better companion for the trip. On the other hand, a trip into the ruins for Kira and Samm would be another chance to speak in private, and to look for Heron—or for Heron to contact them. If she was trying to stay hidden, she wouldn't approach with Calix standing right there. And . . . Kira still didn't trust Calix, for reasons she couldn't quite put her finger on. Kira wasn't going to keep denying to herself that Calix's evident crush on Samm didn't rub her the wrong way. But it was more than that.

"We'll be fine," said Calix. "I've been through there dozens of times. I think I know exactly which store you left them in. And I haven't seen a horse since before the Break. I'm dying to meet them."

"Weather's clear," said Phan. "Go now and you'll be back in time for lunch—I bet those horses'll be excited to eat some real grass for a change after walking in the wasteland. How long were you out there anyway?"

"Um . . . three or four weeks," said Kira. She was still trying to form a plausible protest as Samm and Calix walked away.

"Come on inside," said Phan. "This is great. You're going to love it. They're doing a play today, all the third and fourth graders. Something about fairy tales or something; they do it every year." He pulled Kira into the school, and she followed blankly, watching Samm and Calix disappear around the corner.

The city of Arvada looked different in the daytime—it seemed more desolate, somehow, with the sun beating down from a cloudless sky. Samm took deep breaths, vigilant for any sign of Heron on the link, but all he smelled was dirt and sulfur and bleach. The toxic scent of the wasteland.

Calix steered him around a wide, hazy intersection, pointing to faint wisps of smoke with an expert eye. "Toxic fumes," she said. "The rain last night reacts with some of the dry chemicals that collect in the shallow pans like that, and it makes a poison gas. When the wind gets bad, it blows right into the Preserve, but on a still day like this you can just go around them." She led him onward, sometimes speaking softly about the city—its hazards and its opportunities—and sometimes just walking in silence. Her knowledge of the wasteland and how it worked was impressive, and Samm thought about how helpful she would have been on their journey out here. They would have traveled much more easily, and perhaps even managed to save Afa's life. *I wonder if she'd want to come back with us,* he thought. *She talked about trying to leave, and she'd be an asset on the road, knowing what she does about surviving in the wasteland. Of course, she might not want to come at all if she knows what's it like there, and it would be a change for her, going from the bliss of the Preserve to the horror of war back east. I'll ask Kira what she thinks before I suggest it.*

"That's it up there, right?" she asked, pointing down a wide, ramshackle street. Samm recognized the shopping center at the end of the road and nodded.

"That's right." They walked easily, without fear of enemies or predators because there were none anywhere in the area. *The same wasteland that imprisons them,* thought Samm, *also protects them from any other threats. It keeps them safe, and it keeps their lives easy, but if a real threat ever appears, they won't be ready for it.* He watched the way Calix walked, sure and confident but wary only of very specific dangers—she could spot the poison gas, for example, and yet walk right past a prime ambush point without even noticing. *They wouldn't last a day against a real enemy. They should pray that Dr. Morgan never finds them.*

The horses whickered hungrily when Samm approached; their food was gone, and their water was almost depleted. He spoke to them simply, trying to emulate Kira's soothing tone, but his words were still direct and matter-of-fact, like he was talking to another Partial soldier. "Sorry we were gone overnight," he said. "We found a group of people in the ParaGen complex. They have real grass and an apple orchard, and clean water to drink. We've come to take you back." He pointed at Calix. "This is Calix. She's a friend." The horses stared back with deep, dark eyes, stamping their feet impatiently.

"They're huge," said Calix. "Bigger than any elk I've ever seen."

"They're hungry," said Samm, "and they want to get outside. They don't like being stuck inside with their own droppings, this one especially." He patted Oddjob on the nose and brushed her back with his fingers to calm her. "This one's Oddjob, and that's Bobo. Kira named them." He showed her how to soothe them, and then how to load them up with the equipment—first a blanket, then the saddle, buckled tight enough to stay on without cinching too close and hurting them. They were skinnier now than when they'd started the journey in New York, and he hoped that a short stop in the Preserve could give them some strength back, and a bit more weight. They'd need it for the return journey.

Calix seemed to be thinking the same thing, for she asked him a question as she worked on Bobo's saddle. "How long are you staying?"

"I don't know," said Samm, though the question had been troubling him ever since they'd found the settlement. He had to be careful what he revealed to her. "We can't stay long—we came looking for ParaGen's headquarters in the hopes to find a cure for RM, and now that we've discovered one exists, we need to take it back as soon as we can. Our people are at war, and we need . . ." He paused, not sure how to say what he needed without giving too much away. "To be honest, we're looking for more than just the cure for RM," he said. "We need information on the Partials themselves. We're trying to . . ." How much should he say? How much was Calix prepared to hear? The people in the Preserve didn't seem to think much one way or the other about Partials, but they likely still blamed them for the Break. How would she react to the idea of peace between the species? She was staring at him, her eyes full of . . . trust? Friendship? He couldn't read human emotions, and wondered again how they ever managed to get along without the link. He'd seen the look on her face before, on Kira's face, but he wasn't sure what it meant.

He decided to be direct, at least in part. Maybe they could trust Calix more than Kira thought. "We're trying to help the Partials," he said. "They have a problem of their own, a sickness that's killing them, and if we can cure it, it might mean a chance at peace between our species. That's why we came to the Para-Gen complex, to see if we could find something to help us—and to help them."

"You'll have to talk to Dr. Vale," said Calix. "He knows all kinds of stuff about RM and disease. Maybe he knows something about what's happening to the Partials."

"We have very similar doctors at home," said Samm, thinking of Morgan. *Do Vale and Morgan know each other? Is Vale truly a part of the Trust?*

"But Dr. Vale cured RM," said Calix, "like, twelve years ago. Your doctors haven't been able to do that yet."

"Does that seem odd to you?" asked Samm. "He had a cure for RM almost as soon as it appeared? Within weeks?"

"I guess no one really asked," said Calix. "I'm not sure what you're suggesting . . . that he had sinister motives? How could saving people's lives be sinister?"

If he already had a cure prepared before the Break, Samm thought, *and kept it for himself and his "Preserve." But the rest of the Trust didn't have it, did they? Morgan or Nandita, or Trimble from B Company—where was their cure?* It didn't make sense, and Samm found the discrepancy intensely troubling. There was more going on here than he could grasp, and he didn't like it.

"I'm sorry you had to live so long without a cure," said Calix, leaving Bobo and stepping toward Samm. "Naturally immune or not, that must have been horrible, to watch everyone you know die, to watch all those babies, year after year. . . ."

"Yes, it must have been," said Samm, almost immediately realizing what he'd said—his phrasing made him sound like an outsider from the human society. But Calix didn't seem to notice; instead she took his hand in her own, rough and calloused but warm and gentle. He tried to smooth over the mistake with a firmer statement. "Every infant has died since the Break."

"You have no children at all?" There was a look of deep sadness in her eyes as she contemplated the life in East Meadow. "No wonder Kira seemed so overwhelmed." She paused a moment, looking at Samm's hand. "Are you . . . ? Are you and Kira . . . ?"

"Leaving?" asked Samm.

"Together?" asked Calix. "Are you . . . married? Dating?"

Samm shook his head. "No." But before he could say another word, Calix was kissing him, her lips pressed against his, soft and supple, her body warm against him and her arm wrapped behind his head, pulling them closer together. Samm froze in surprise, his brain melting under the sensation of her lips, but he regained control and gently pushed her away. "I'm sorry," he said. "I'm not very good at this."

"I could teach you."

"I mean, I'm not very good at communicating," said Samm. "I don't always understand . . . It's not important. What I mean to say is I'm sorry if I . . . led you to believe something I shouldn't have."

Calix's face was a mix of surprise and confusion. "I'm sorry," she said. "You seemed . . . interested."

"I'm sorry," he said again. "I think I'm in love. . . ." He paused. "I don't think she even knows."

Calix laughed, a hollow sound that seemed more sad than amused. She wiped a tear from her eye and laughed again. "Well. I look like a big stupid idiot now, don't I?"

"I'm the idiot," said Samm. "You didn't do anything wrong."

"That's very kind of you to say," said Calix. She took a deep breath and shook her head, wiping another tear. "If you could do me a favor and not tell anyone I, uh, threw myself at you like a moron, that would be very kind as well."

"Of course," said Samm. He felt suddenly embarrassed to be looking at her, and cast around for something else to occupy his eyes. He chose the floor, and stared at it awkwardly. "You're much more forward than she is."

"Apparently so," said Calix. Samm watched out of the corner of his eye as she walked back to the horses. "You crossed the entire continent together, and yet neither of you ever made a move?" She huffed another short, hollow laugh. "No wonder you don't have any children."

"That's not the reason," Samm began, but Calix cut him off

with another nervous laugh.

"I know, I know, it was just a stupid joke. I'm sorry, I'm really making an ass of myself today, aren't I? Good old Calix."

"You're very attractive," said Samm.

Calix groaned. "That's not what I want you to say right now."

Samm felt terrible, first because she felt terrible, and more so because he didn't know how to talk to her. *Damn link,* he thought. *I know how to talk to Partial girls, but humans are so . . .* He rolled his eyes. *They're like a whole different species.* He felt horrible for giving Calix signals he wasn't aware he was giving, and now he couldn't even console her.

"I wish I knew what to say," he said. "I'm really, like I said, a terrible communicator. I'm not good at talking—"

"It's okay," said Calix quickly.

"It's not okay," said Samm. "I'm sick of it. I want to be better at this, but I'm just not built for it. I didn't want to cross an entire continent with Kira without ever saying anything, but I did, because I don't know how to say it. There are a lot of things I'm stuck with, but . . . I'm just sorry. I am."

He looked up, and saw that Calix had stopped her work on the horses and was staring back at him. Her voice was soft. "What is it you want to say to Kira?"

Samm stood still, emoting a thousand different bits of data that Calix didn't even know were there. Right now wasn't the time to say things like this to Kira, they had more important things to do. And yet . . . *Kira thinks I'm a statue,* he thought. *An emotionless mannequin.* He deliberately imitated the signs of sadness and resignation he'd seen in other humans, drawing in a breath and letting it out slowly. A sigh. "I don't know what she wants," he said at last. "You made your intentions clear. Kira is a mystery to me."

"You don't know if she loves you back."

"We're too different," said Samm. It was hard to talk without saying too much. "I don't know if she wants . . . what I am."

"Sure," said Calix. "For all we know, she might really get turned off by handsome, competent, kindhearted guys."

"You're very kind," said Samm.

"Lot of good it's doing me," said Calix. She sighed as well, moving away from the horses and sitting cross-legged on an old, weathered table. "Look. You and Kira was not the relationship I'd hoped to be discussing today, but I've done this enough times with Phan that I'm pretty sure I've got some pointers you could use. First of all, everything you said about not knowing what she wants? She feels exactly the same way—I haven't talked to her or anything, but I guarantee it. Ironclad. I've been watching you ever since you came into town, and you never gave a single sign that you were interested in her. That's why I made a move. If I couldn't tell, neither can she."

"I'm very bad at commu—"

"I know," said Calix firmly. "I am very quickly becoming an expert in how bad a communicator you are. We've established that, and we're moving past it. Step two: You said you were grateful to me for being so up-front about my feelings, and frankly, I'm grateful to you for being up-front about yours. Once I forced it out of you. I'd rather know how you feel than hope and wonder and delude myself for weeks on end—which is exactly what she's been doing."

"You can't know that," said Samm.

"Of course I can," said Calix. "Not everyone's as bad at this as you are, Samm. Anyone with eyes to see can tell she's got a thing for you."

Samm stood stock-still, but any Partial linking with him would have been stopped short by the intensity of his emotions. He wondered if it was true—if Kira really had feelings for him, a Partial, one who'd attacked her people, betrayed her to a madwoman, and caused her more trouble than he cared to think about. A man with barely a year left to live before the Partial expiration date erased his life and his future in a single stroke. He didn't think it was possible.

"She has a boyfriend," said Samm. "Another medic, back in New York."

"New York's pretty far away."

"But we're going back."

"And if you get all the way back there without saying anything, you deserve to lose her," said Calix.

Samm couldn't help but agree with that. "Marcus makes her laugh," he said. "I can't do that."

"You could always try just lunging in for a kiss," said Calix with a wry smile. "Didn't work so hot for me, but you never know."

"I don't think that's my style."

"Your style is silent celibacy," said Calix, "and I can guarantee that won't work either. Just talk to her."

"I talk to her all the time."

"Then start saying the right things," said Calix.

CHAPTER FORTY-THREE

"Vale still won't see us," said Kira. They were sitting in a small park—a cluster of picnic tables in a small grove of trees in the Preserve. Samm and Calix had returned in time for lunch, and Calix had abandoned them almost immediately to play a game of football with a larger group of teens on the field nearby. Phan was playing with them as well, and paused every few plays to cajole Kira and Samm into joining them, but Kira had too much to discuss, and welcomed the relative privacy. Samm, for his part, seemed even more quiet than normal, but Kira took this as a renewed focus on the task at hand. He insisted that Calix wasn't hiding any secret motives, but said little else about their trip into the ruins.

"Vale is obviously hiding something," Kira continued, "and even if we sit around waiting for him to give us the meeting he promised, he'll probably just give us another runaround. He's hiding something, and I don't like it, and we still haven't heard anything from Heron, and I'm sick of it. It's time to go to the spire." She glanced at it, a tall black peak jutting up behind the other buildings. "Phan took me around earlier, just kind of showing me the complex, and some of the buildings get pretty close to it. We could get most of the way there without arousing any suspicion and then, I don't know, try to sneak in without anyone noticing. I honestly don't know if anyone would even care—Phan said it was structurally unsound after the Partial bombings, but they don't exactly seem nervous living next to it. They don't really seem to think of it at all."

"Is there a fence?" asked Samm.

"A low wall," said Kira, "mostly made of junk and old furniture. They're trying to keep the kids from wandering in by accident, but they don't seem to have any active security—that's pretty typical of this society as a whole. They don't expect anyone to attack, or rebel, or break the law at all, and as far as I can tell, no one ever does."

"And naturally this makes you suspicious," said Samm.

"That would make anyone suspicious," said Kira. "There is no perfect society—there's always going to be unrest, or criminals, or something sinister underneath, making it run. Maybe Vale is using some kind of mind control to keep everyone in line. Like the link, but for humans." Samm looked at her with a reasonable attempt at skepticism on his face. She smirked. "I don't know, but it's something."

There was a cry of triumph from the field, and Kira looked up to see half the football players jumping in excitement. A young man was lying on the ground, moaning softly, the ball lying next to him, and Calix was walking away from what appeared to be a brutal tackle, a small dribble of blood on her cheek. Kira's eyes widened in surprise. "Wow. I had no idea she was that intense."

"She's got some stuff to work through," said Samm. He narrowed his eyes as he peered at the field. "I hope she doesn't hurt anyone."

"Now's our chance," said Kira, putting a hand on his arm. "Wait till they set up for another run, and then follow me. If we go behind these trees and left to that building, we'll be out of sight before they even notice we're gone."

"And if somebody else sees us?"

"We've never been specifically forbidden," said Kira. "If somebody sees us, we play the 'new folks in town' card and thank them for keeping us out of a dangerous building, then we regroup and go back at night. But if there's even a chance we can get in now, I want to at least try."

"Okay," said Samm. "You armed?"

"Semiautomatic in the back of my waistband."

"Ankle holster," said Samm. "Here's hoping we won't need them." They sat in silence, watching the game; Phan got on the line of scrimmage, ready to run, not pausing as he had so often to call Kira and Samm into the game. The rest of the players lined up as well, the quarterback called hike, and Kira and Samm slipped away. They were around the corner before the play had even finished.

"This way," said Kira, and led Samm along the building toward the center of the complex. The spire reared up behind the building, so tall it was visible from almost anywhere in the Preserve. People said hello to them here and there, but nobody Kira recognized from her brief tour with Phan. She waved back, hoping no one would stop them for conversation, and no one did. Two buildings later they were at the edge of the large central clearing. Beyond them was the low wall, a mishmash of broken tables and filing cabinets and here and there a boulder or a fallen tree, and beyond that was the massive, blackened shape of the ParaGen spire. The outer wall was a lot like so many other skyscrapers Kira had seen—once covered with windows, now a checkerboard skeleton of shattered glass and dangling wreckage—but unlike those other buildings, this one had been directly attacked and then pounded with years of corrosive rain, and portions of it were blackened or twisted or pocked with grotesque holes. It was also shaped oddly, tapering into weird juts and angles that might once have looked modern and beautiful, but now only added to its strange, brooding menace. Kira could almost imagine she saw lights inside, and imagined for a fleeting moment that they were the ghosts of old office workers, still toiling endlessly in their forgotten tomb. She chided herself for being silly, and thought of more plausible explanations. Was the power that still ran the complex still running in the spire as well? What was left in there to be powered? The clearing looked blocked and overgrown, as if no one had entered the building in years.

"Heron was here," said Samm.

"Was or still is?"

"The data's too faint to tell," said Samm.

"Now we know Vale's hiding something," said Kira. She looked around. "If we can make it over the wall, we'll be completely hidden in the underbrush beyond," said Kira. "We can probably get in without being seen."

"It would be better to wait for night."

"And have Phan and Calix tied to our necks again?" asked

Kira. "This is the best chance we'll ever have." She looked around. "I don't see anyone else—they're all eating lunch, or playing football, or whatever these people do in this creepy place."

"It's called 'living normal lives.'"

"And it could all just be a show for our benefit," said Kira.

"Do you really think . . ." Samm shook his head. "Never mind. Let's go."

"I'm sorry about all this," said Kira softly, feeling the sudden weight of their never-ending quest crushing down on her shoulders. "I'm sorry I dragged you into it."

"You know I believe in this as much as you do," said Samm. "Other people's normal lives are what make our crazy ones worthwhile."

Kira felt a flush of emotion. "I promise you that as soon as we're done saving the world, we'll eat lunch and play football."

"Deal," said Samm.

Kira looked back at the spire. "Ready?"

"Try to keep up," said Samm. He looked around for observers, then looked back at the spire and narrowed his eyes. "Go."

They sprinted across the open clearing, dodging the stumps of fallen trees that dotted the lawn. Samm reached the wall first, vaulting over into the tall desert grass beyond; Kira followed, dropping to the ground in the tall brush. They held still, listening for cries of pursuit or alarm, but Kira heard nothing.

Samm was panting.

"Are you winded?" Kira whispered. "I didn't think you could even get winded."

"We're still weak from crossing the wasteland," said Samm.

"Our bodies aren't functioning at peak capacity."

"I'm fine," said Kira.

"So am I," said Samm. "Let's go."

They crawled on their bellies through the underbrush, staying out of sight below the tall grass. Samm seemed back to normal again, and Kira forged ahead, determined to reach the building as quickly as possible—hidden or not, they could still be discovered until they were inside and away from prying eyes. Soon she grew nervous, afraid that the slow pace of crawling was taking too long, and rose up to a crouch to take a peek above the grass. The Preserve complex seemed quiet and still. She dropped back to her hands and knees and scuttled forward more quickly, the building now nearly in reach. Samm followed, his face grim and determined. When they reached the building he was breathing oddly again, not panting but taking long, slow breaths.

"Are you okay?"

"I feel strange," he said. "Exhausted, like I haven't slept in days."

Kira couldn't help but feel a twinge of guilt. *I don't feel tired at all—was Samm really pushing himself this much harder than I was? Was I pulling so little of my own weight on this journey, and didn't even know it?* "Do you need to rest?"

"Not here," said Samm. "We need to get inside."

The tall brush extended nearly to the edge of the building, where they could enter through any number of floor-to-ceiling openings—giant windows destroyed in the Partial attack. Almost the entire ground floor was open around the perimeter, supported by a series of central pillars. There was nothing but reception desks and waiting areas; any records they could find would likely be in the offices above, and Kira spied a stairwell door standing partly open. She pointed it out to Samm, and he nodded, his chest rising and falling in slow, deliberate rhythm. She counted softly under her breath: "One, two, three," and then they leapt up and ran, bolting across the rubble-strewn floor to the door beyond. Kira reached it first, several steps ahead of Samm, and when he staggered through, she slammed it shut behind him. He leaned heavily against the wall, gasping for breath, his eyes closed.

"I don't think anyone saw us," she said. "We can rest here for a minute before moving up."

"If I rest, I'll fall asleep," said Samm. He struggled to open his eyes, but his lids seemed heavy and unresponsive. "Keep moving."

"Are you going to be okay?"

"We have to keep moving either way," said Samm, "so it doesn't matter."

Kira tried to protest, to tell him that they could come back later, but he wouldn't listen. "We won't get another chance at this. I can make it." He gripped the railings with his hands, one on either side, and raised a leg that looked as heavy as lead. Kira inserted herself under one of his arms, wrapping his hand around her shoulders, and put her own arm around his waist, helping him along. His breathing was deeper now, almost as if he were already asleep. His steps were arrhythmic, and sometimes it took him three or four tries to find the right height for a stair.

"You're doing fine," said Kira, though she knew something wasn't right. *What the hell is going on?* "Just a few more." She held him tightly, supporting almost his full weight as they climbed. "That's right, just a few more." At the top of the first flight of stairs she opened the door, and he collapsed through it onto the floor. The smell of earth and plants filled the air, and she saw footprints of cats and birds in the dust that covered the carpet. "Samm, are you okay?" It didn't look like anyone outside could see them in this spot; it was as good a hiding place as any. "Samm, talk to me."

"Not . . ." His voice was slow and weak, as if he had to force each word through a heavy screen, and they had no force left when they emerged. He rolled his head back and forth, opening his eyes as wide as he could, struggling to stay conscious. She waited for him to finish the sentence, but when he finally spoke again, it was something different. "Heron . . . here." Another pause. "Asleep." He turned his head toward her, but his eyes were dazed and unfocused. "Find . . . it."

"Find 'it'?" she asked. "Find what?" She shook him, whispering urgently in his ear, but nothing roused him. *He's asleep—he told me he was asleep. And apparently Heron's here somewhere.* Kira willed herself to use the link, to detect some sign of Heron's data anywhere in the air around her. She'd never been able to use it at will; only in combat could she actually rely on it, when her adrenaline seemed to amplify its effect. *But my adrenaline's high now,* she thought. *This thing with Samm has me scared to death, and I'm not detecting anything. Are the combat pheromones simply stronger—or am I just designed to detect the combat pheromones and nothing else?*

She checked Samm again, his pulse and his breathing. They were normal. Now that he'd stopped fighting and settled into sleep, his body functions seemed to have normalized. She stood up, trying to figure out what she should do next—should she stay until he woke? Should she leave him here and keep going? The latter seemed like the only viable option, but she didn't like it—what if something happened to him while she was gone? She dragged him over to the wall and propped him up on his side, his back to the wall and his front held up by a pair of desktop computer towers she pulled from nearby cubicles. He was sleeping so soundly she worried that if he threw up or drooled he'd be too inert to react, and would choke to death. This would at least keep him safe from that.

It's almost like he's been sedated, thought Kira. *But why would someone do that to him—and how could they have done it? Did Calix slip him a drug? Why drug him and leave?* She shook her head. *I can ask him more when he wakes up. Right now I'm here, at the end of our search, and I don't know how long we have before they come looking for us. And if we leave now, Samm is right, there's no guarantee we'll have another chance to find what we came for. I have to find the records.*

She silently apologized to him, and then rifled through the desks on the floor, searching for a directory or a map—some hint of where to start looking. Obviously the Trust wouldn't be mentioned by that name anywhere, at least she didn't think so, but she knew most of their names from the records they'd found in Chicago. She repeated them again in her mind: Graeme Chamberlain, Kioni Trimble, Jerry Ryssdal, McKenna Morgan, Nandita Merchant, and Armin Dhurvasula. My father. She found a small directory and scanned it for their names, but found nothing.

She decided to try another tack, approaching the problem from another angle: What clues had she already gathered, and what pieces did she already know? It took her a moment to align her thoughts; she had been so busy getting here the last few weeks and had thought of little aside from survival. She had to remind herself of the mysteries she was trying to solve. Dr. Morgan had been assigned to create the Partials' incredible physical attributes: their strength, their reflexes, their resistance to disease, and their incredible ability to heal. Jerry Ryssdal had worked on their senses. Kira's father had created the link, and the entire system of pheromonal communication. She still didn't know about Trimble. Last of all came Graeme Chamberlain and Nandita, who had been assigned to the Failsafe project. The world-ending plague they had come to know as RM. They'd learned in Chicago that the Failsafe was designed to kill the Partials if they ever got out of hand—it had been requested by the American government, and mandated by the ParaGen executives, and that mandate seemed to be the defining incident that sparked the lead scientists to form the Trust in the first place. And somehow, when the virus finally appeared, it killed humans instead. That couldn't possibly be what the Trust decided to do—she couldn't allow herself to think that anyone, let alone her father and the only mother figure she had ever known, would willingly, knowingly, unconscionably destroy so many people. And Graeme had killed himself, which didn't tell her anything but still left her deeply unsettled.

Still, she thought, *the Trust had been fractured, even as they tried to make their plans.* Dr. Morgan knew nothing about the expiration date, for example, but somebody must have programmed it into their DNA, someone with a plan. There were others, too, the names Morgan had screamed when she thought Kira was a spy: Cronus and Prometheus. *Were they code names for some of the people on this list? Or new people altogether?* And where did Dr. Vale fit into this?

Kira turned back to the directory, searching for anything that might relate to the Trust's plan: expiration. Failsafe. Virus, virology, pathology, epidemiology—she searched for every synonym she knew. She searched for "laboratory," for "research," for "genetics," she even searched for RM. . . . *Wait.* She stared at the directory. There was no RM, but there was an RD. *Is that a reference to the virus? Maybe an earlier version of it? But there is no way something so secret would be here on a directory so general it doesn't even have the lead scientists' names.* She remembered her confusion with the term IT, and how it had turned out to be an acronym: information technology. *RD must be the same thing, maybe . . . reference database? Research database?*

Research and development.

If the Trust were anywhere, they were there. But where is Floor C? The floors here are all numbered. She looked for a map, scrounging through every desk she could find, but on her third pass through the main hallway she stopped at the top of the stairs, staring not at them but at the doors beside them. Three sets of double doors, all in a row.

Elevators.

The Preserve had an ongoing, self-sustaining power grid. The elevators in the other buildings still worked. If they still worked here, finding Floor C would be as easy as looking at the buttons. Getting there would be as easy as pressing one. She stepped forward, her finger hovering over the call button. She pushed it.

Deep in the bowels of the building a motor hummed to life, and Kira felt the floor vibrate as the gears and pulleys turned. Clanks and groans echoed through the elevator shaft, and Kira stepped back as the door before her wrenched halfway open with a loud screech. The elevator beyond was only partly lined up with the door, leaving a wide gap at the bottom that plunged deep into darkness. *Having power to run them doesn't mean anyone's been maintaining them for the last twelve years,* Kira thought. It's amazing the elevators still work at all. The doors tried to close, but had damaged themselves so much in opening that they couldn't shut again. Kira hesitated in the doorway, trying to decide if she trusted the stability enough to climb in and look at the buttons. She peered into the pit below, seeing dark red lights at the bottom of a shaft that looked to go down at least seven stories. *That's five levels below ground,* she thought. *There must be one for maintenance, maybe two. And three full subterranean stories.*

A, B, and C.

She decided to avoid the elevator, and instead peeked into the shaft and around the corners, searching for a maintenance ladder. She found one she could reach relatively easily, but she still had a moment of terrifying vertigo as she stretched out over the deep black pit. With her hands firmly on the metal rungs, she swung the rest of her body out into space, found the ladder with her feet, and began climbing down. Each floor was marked, and she breathed a sigh of relief when she climbed down past 1 and found A waiting below it. She kept going, stopping on Floor C, and searched for an exit. Next to the ladder was a maintenance door; she twisted the handle, and it opened smoothly.

The hallway beyond was brightly lit. The air was fresh and well circulated. Far away, a faint echo in the emptiness, she heard footsteps.

Kira's heart caught in her throat, and she found herself suddenly paralyzed with fear. Was that Heron—was she already here? Or was it somebody else? Had they heard all the noise she'd made with the elevator? Was there one set of footsteps, or more? Were they coming or going? She didn't know, and not knowing made her too afraid to move. After a moment she paused, forcing herself to think. *No matter what it is, I should go through the door. I can't just leave, and this could be my only chance to find out what I am.* She hesitated, trying to psych herself up, wondering if there was a security system inside that would attack her. She hadn't set off any alarms by opening the door. She took a deep breath and drew her handgun from where she'd hidden it in the back of her pants. She stepped through.

The hallway was bright, not just because of the lights, but because the walls and floors and ceiling were white, like a hospital. She could feel the faint hum of something through the floor, like the motor of the elevators but constant, like a background buzz. *The power generator?* she thought. *Or an air circulator.* There was definitely a faint breeze, neither hot nor cold but simply air in motion. She heard another cluster of footsteps, so small she thought it had to be just one person. She strained at the link, trying to see if it was Heron, but felt nothing. Kira fumbled in her waistband for her handgun, pulling it out and checking the chamber and magazine, making sure it was loaded and ready to go. She held it before her carefully, walking softly on the balls of her feet. She could hear somebody walking, but she was determined they wouldn't hear her.

Floor C was a lab, far more intact than the upper stories. Whatever the Partials had done to this place, the destruction hadn't penetrated this deep. Kira walked past offices and conference rooms, past laboratories and showers, past clean white rooms full of equipment she didn't even recognize. Was this where Vale was making his cure? That would make sense; ParaGen would undoubtedly have the best genetic engineering equipment in the Preserve. Was this equipment the reason he said it wasn't "portable"? Maybe it was Vale she could hear down here. Kira quickened her pace.

She heard the footsteps again, and as she drew closer she heard a voice, murmuring and indistinct, someone talking softly. Kira walked as quietly as she could, still wary of who she might find, or what he or she might be doing. Would they attack an intruder? Would they take her presence as a threat? What equipment were they using, and how were they using it? Would they kill her to protect their secret?

It doesn't matter. I've come this far. I need to know.

She rounded the final corner, stepping into a vast room, and gasped. Before her in two long lines were ten metal tables, each bearing an emaciated, almost skeletal man. Snaking up from each was a cluster of tubes and cords and cables, some dripping nutrients into the bodies while others bore away what looked like waste or recirculated blood. Their faces were uncovered, but a small tube sprouted up from the neck of each figure, punching straight through the skin and curling up into the tangle of tubes that hung above them. In any other situation she would think they were dead, but she could see a frail rise and fall of their chests, see their hearts thumping slowly inside their fragile ribs. They were living corpses, unconscious and lost to the world. They looked like they'd been there for years.

"What's going on?" she whispered.

"They're Partials," said Dr. Vale. Kira looked up to see him on the far side of the room; her pistol rose up almost involuntarily to point at him, and he raised his hands. "You wanted to know how I synthesize the cure," said Vale. "I don't—I harvest it directly." He motioned toward the tables. "Behold: the cure for RM."

CHAPTER FORTY-FOUR

Kira stared in shock. "What is this?"

"This is salvation," said Vale. "Everyone you've met here, every child you've seen, what you've called a miracle . . . It's here because of these ten Partials."

"This is . . ." She stopped, stepped forward, and shook her head, still struggling to process what she was seeing. "Are they asleep?"

"Sedated," said Vale. "They can't hear or see you, though I suppose our voices might drift through the back of their dreams."

"They dream?"

"Perhaps," said Vale. "Their brain activity is not an important part of the process; I haven't paid any particular attention to it."

Kira stepped forward again. "They never wake up?"

"What would be the point?" asked Vale. "I can tend them more easily in their sleep—they're far less trouble this way."

"You don't 'tend' them," said Kira. "They're not plants."

"By strict biological definition, no, but the metaphor is apt."

Vale walked toward one, checking the tubes and wires that connected him to the apparatus in the ceiling. "They are not plants, but they are a garden, and I tend them carefully to harvest the crop that keeps the human race alive."

"The pheromone," said Kira.

"The technical name is Particle 223," said Vale, "though I've taken to calling it Ambrosia." He smiled. "The food of life."

"You can't do this," Kira found herself saying.

"Of course I can."

"Of course you can, but . . . we'd always known this was a possibility, but . . . it's not right."

"Tell that to the thousands of lives they've saved, and the hundreds more they'll save this year alone." Vale's smile faded, and his face grew solemn. "Ten for two thousand, that's two hundred lives each. We should all be so benevolent."

"But . . . they're slaves," said Kira. "They're worse than slaves, they're . . . your creepy human garden."

"Not human," said Vale firmly, "things. Living things, yes, but mankind has used living things as tools since his first sentient thought. A bush in the wild is simply a bush—under human care it becomes a hedge, a wall to keep us safe. Berries become inks and dyes, mushrooms become medicine. Cows give us milk and meat and leather, horses pull our plows and carriages. Even you used horses to cross the toxic wasteland, a job I'm sure they would never have chosen on their own."

"That's different," said Kira.

"Not different at all," said Vale. "A horse, at least, is a part of the world. They exist today because a million years of natural selection failed to kill them: They earned their right to live. The

Partials were grown in a lab, made by and for the aid of humanity. They're . . . seedless watermelons, or blight-resistant wheat. Don't let their human faces fool you."

"It's not just their faces," said Kira hotly, "it's their minds. You can't talk to one and tell me they're not real people."

"Even computers could talk, by the end," said Vale. "That didn't make them people either."

Kira shook her head, closing her eyes in anger and frustration. She was so repulsed by the revelation she could barely think. "You have to free them."

"And then what?" asked Vale. Kira looked up to see him gesturing broadly, encompassing not just the laboratory but the Preserve, perhaps the entire world. "Should we go back to the way your people live? Struggling in vain to cure a disease that can't be cured, watching thousands of your own children die so that ten men—ten enemies, who rebelled and murdered you— don't have to suffer?"

"It's more complicated than that," said Kira.

Vale nodded. "That's exactly what I'm saying. You say it's cruel to keep them like this, unconscious and emaciated; I say it would be crueler, and to more people, to let them go free. Do you know how I keep them sedated? Come over here." He walked to the end of the first row of tables, gesturing for Kira to follow. The Partial on the last table looked similar to the others, but his equipment was different. Instead of the tube poking out from below his jaw, his entire throat had been fitted with what looked like a respirator. Kira approached slowly, her gun forgotten in her hand, and saw that he had a small set of fans set into his neck.

"What is it?" she asked.

"It's a ventilation system," said Vale. "I call this one Williams, and he was my last creation before time and wear rendered our gene mod equipment unusable. Instead of producing Ambrosia, he produces another particle of my own design, an extremely powerful sedative that only affects Partials. The biomechanics behind that were monumental, I assure you."

Kira's voice caught, thinking of Samm, and Vale nodded as if he guessed exactly what she was thinking. "I assume your Partial friend is upstairs somewhere, sound asleep?" He gestured at the ceiling. "The ventilation system in the spire still functions admirably well, and pumps the Partial sedative throughout the building and out into the Preserve. I'd be interested to know how far he got before succumbing; Williams here may well become our primary defense if the other Partials you spoke of ever attack us."

Kira thought back: Samm hadn't felt the effects until they'd approached the central clearing—she'd guess fifty yards from the spire at most—but he'd been oddly lethargic all afternoon. Was that from the sedative, or something else?

And how far would she have to take him before the effects wore off?

She looked back at Vale. "You can't just do that."

"You keep saying that."

"You can't just turn a person into a weapon."

"Child," he said, "what do you think the Partials are?"

"Well . . . of course that's what they are," said Kira, "and look how that turned out. Didn't you learn anything from the end of the world?"

"I learned to protect human life at all costs," said Vale. "It's an edge we danced much too close to, trying to have it both ways."

"You're not doing this to protect humans," Kira snarled, stepping back and raising the pistol. "You're doing this for power. You control the cure, so you control everything, and everybody has to get in line."

Vale laughed out loud, so unexpected, and so genuinely amused, that Kira couldn't help but take another step back. *What am I missing?* she thought.

"What human oppression have you seen here?" he asked. "What iron boot am I wearing that no one else can see? Are the people of the Preserve unhappy?"

"That doesn't mean they're free," said Kira.

"Of course they're free," said Vale. "They can come and go as they please, we have no guards or police. We have no curfew but the inherent dangers of acidic storms; we have no walls but the deadly expanse of the Badlands. I don't demand tribute, I don't control the schools, I don't keep any secrets at all except this one." He gestured at the comatose Partials.

Kira bristled. "Phan and Calix said you won't let them leave."

"Of course I told them not to leave," said Vale. "It's dangerous out there. Phan and Calix and all the hunters are vital to our community. But they are still free to go anytime they choose. Just because they made the choice I recommended doesn't make me a tyrant." He pointed at Kira. "Even you've been free to leave, this entire time—the rabble-rousing newcomer and her dangerous pet Partial. No one's stopped you from leaving, no one's shadowed your movements. Tell me, Kira: What are you railing against?"

Kira shook her head, confused and defensive. "You're controlling these people."

"By a loose interpretation, I suppose," said Vale. "You come from a land where control, from what I gather, comes at the point of a gun—where the government buys your obedience through scarcity. Through what they hold back. I maintain order by giving people exactly what they want: a cure for RM, food and shelter, a community to be a part of. They accept my leadership because I lead them well and effectively. Not every authority figure is evil."

"That's very self-righteous talk from a man in a secret lab full of half-dead prisoners."

Vale sighed, staring at her for several moments. Finally he turned, walking to the side of the room, and drew a syringe of clear liquid from a tray. "Come with me, Kira, I want to show you something." He walked to a door in the far side of the room, and after some hesitation Kira followed. "This entire complex is connected by a series of underground tunnels," said Vale. "Let me remind you, before we rejoin the others, that they don't know about the Partials. I would appreciate your discretion in the matter."

"Because you're ashamed of it?"

"Because many of them would react like you have," he said, "and some would try to punish the Partials further."

"You don't know me very well, Doctor, but I'm not really the kind to stay quiet about things I don't like."

"But you are good at keeping secrets," he said.

Kira glanced at him sideways. "You're talking about Samm?"

"Do you have other secrets, too?"

Kira studied him a moment, trying to see if he knew, or even suspected, what she was. *Probably not,* she decided, *or he would have asked why I'm not affected by the Partial sedative. Unless he knows more about me than I do. . . .*

Of course he knows more, she thought, *he's part of the Trust. He knows everything we came here to learn. I can't stop what he's doing by myself, not now, but if I get the answers I need, I may not have to.* She pondered a moment longer before speaking.

"I'll keep your secret—for now—but you have to give something to me."

"The cure?" he asked. "As you can see, it's the same cure you've already discovered—and, as I told you before, it's not exactly portable."

"Not the cure," she said. "It's evil, and whatever you're about to show me won't change my mind about that."

"We'll see," said Vale.

Kira persisted. "What I want is information."

"What kind of information?"

"Everything," she said. "You helped build the Partials, which means you know about RM and expiration, the Failsafe. I want to know what your plans were, and how everything fits together."

"Whatever information I have is yours," he said. "In exchange, as you said, for secrecy."

"Agreed," said Kira.

"Good," said Vale, stopping beside a door in the hallway. "But first, we go up."

Kira read the label on the door. "'Building Six.' That's the one you converted to a hospital."

"It is."

"I've already seen the hospital."

Vale opened the door. "What you haven't seen is the baby born this afternoon. Follow me."

He climbed a set of stairs, and Kira followed, suddenly nervous. Of course there would be a new baby—why else would he go to the spire to retrieve a syringe of the cure? Her stomach tightened involuntarily; she had spent so much of her life in the East Meadow hospital, toiling in maternity while infants died and mothers wailed in despair, that she couldn't help but feel the same tension again. But it was different now—Vale had the cure. This child wouldn't have to die. Except she knew where the cure had come from. She closed her eyes and saw the Partials' gaunt, withered faces. Keeping them like that was wrong, no matter what Vale said to excuse it. *And yet . . .*

They came out into a hallway, locking the door carefully behind them. People bustled back and forth, and Kira was shocked to see that most of them were happy—they laughed and talked and smiled, cuddling tiny warm bundles to their chests. Mothers and fathers, brothers and sisters. Families, real, genetic families, like she'd never seen them before. The maternity ward she'd worked in was a place of death and grief, a place of exhausted struggle and a relentless, implacable foe. It was the only kind of maternity she'd ever known. Here, though, everything was different. The mothers who came to give birth knew that their children would live. This was a maternity ward full of hope and success. Kira had to stop for a moment, steadying herself against the wall. *This is everything I've ever wanted,* she thought. *This is what I want to create at home—this is what I want to bring them. Hope and success. Happiness.*

And yet . . .

Behind all the sounds of activity was one that Kira knew all too well—the wail of a dying child. She knew from intense personal experience exactly how the virus would progress; how it would attack the child from moment to moment. If the child had been born just a few hours ago, as Vale suggested, then RM was still developing in its bloodstream. The child would have a fever, but not yet a deadly one; the virus was slowly replicating itself, cell by cell, building more viral spores, eating the tiny body from the inside until finally—tomorrow, perhaps—the child would practically cook itself alive trying to keep up. This early in the process the pain could be assuaged, the fever controlled, but the process could not be stopped. Without the pheromonal cure, death was inevitable.

Vale walked through the hall toward the sound, nodding politely to the people he passed, and Kira followed numbly behind. Is this what he wanted her to see? The cure in action, saving an innocent life? She didn't know what he hoped to accomplish with that—she already knew the stakes, probably better than he did, thanks to living so long with no cure at all. It wouldn't sway her opinion on the captive Partials, and it wouldn't buy her silence or compliance. Dr. Vale pushed through the last door, entering the room, and Kira saw the mother practically collapse in joy at the sight of him. The father, equally grateful and nervous, shook Vale's hand enthusiastically. Vale reassured him with small talk and a smile, prepping the syringe, and all the while Kira stood against the wall, watching the baby squall and scream in the bassinet. The parents glanced her way but quickly dismissed her, their focus turning back to the child. Kira watched them as they held their child, looking for all the world like Madison and Haru. Like every set of parents she had ever seen.

It doesn't matter, she thought. *They can't justify what they're doing to those men in the basement. If these parents knew that living, breathing people were suffering like that, would they be so glad to see the cure? Would they even accept it?* She wanted to tell them, to tell them everything, but she felt frozen.

Vale finished prepping the shot and turned to the parents, shooing them from the room. "Please," he said softly, "we need a moment of privacy with your child."

The mother's eyes went wide in fear. "Will he be okay?"

"Don't worry," said Vale, "it will only be a moment." They were reluctant to leave, but they seemed to trust him, and with a bit more gentle urging and another quizzical glance at Kira, they left the room. Vale locked the door behind them and turned with the syringe—not toward the infant, but toward Kira, holding it out to her like a gift. "I told you that I lead these people by giving them what they want," he said. "Now I'm doing the same for you. Take it."

"I don't want your cure," said Kira.

"I'm not giving you the cure," said Vale. "I'm giving you the choice—life or death. That's what you wanted, right? To decide for everyone what is right and what is wrong. What is justifiable and what is irredeemable." He offered her the syringe again, walking toward her, holding it up like a grail. "Sometimes helping someone means hurting someone else—we never like it, but we have to do it because the alternative would be worse. I have destroyed ten lives to save two thousand: a better ratio, I think, than most nations could ever hope for. We have no crime, no poverty, no suffering but theirs. And mine," he said, "and now yours." He held out the syringe again. "If you think you know better than I do how to weigh one life against another, if you feel like you should decide who lives and who dies, then do it. Save this child or sentence it to death."

"This isn't fair."

"It isn't fair when I have to do it either," said Vale harshly. "It still has to be done."

Kira looked at the syringe, at the screaming baby, at the locked door with the parents on the other side. "They'll know," said Kira. "They'll know what I choose."

"Of course," said Vale. "Or are you suggesting that your choice will be different depending on who knows about it? That's not how morality works."

"That's not what I'm saying."

"Then make your choice."

Kira looked at the door again. "Why'd you send them out if they're just going to find out anyway?"

"So we could have this discussion without them screaming at you," said Vale. "Make your choice."

"It's not my place."

"That didn't bother you ten minutes ago when you told me what I had done was evil," said Vale. "You said that the Partials ought to be released. What's changed?"

"You know what's changed!" shouted Kira, pointing at the screaming baby.

"What's changed is that your high-minded morality is suddenly faced with consequences," said Vale. "Every choice has them. We're dealing with the very real threat of human extinction, and that makes the choices worse and the consequences horrible. And sometimes with the stakes this high a choice you would never make before, that you would never consider in any other circumstance, becomes the only moral option. The only action you can take and still live with yourself in the morning." He pressed the syringe into her hand. "You called me a tyrant. Now kill this child or become a tyrant yourself."

Kira looked at the syringe in her hand; the salvation of the human race. But only if she dared to use it. She'd killed Partials in battle—was this any different? Taking one life to save another. To save a thousand others, or maybe ten thousand by the time they were done. In some ways this was more merciful than death, for the Partials were simply sleeping—

But no, she told herself, *I can't excuse this. I can't justify it. If I give this child the cure, I will be supporting the torture and imprisonment of Partials—of people. Of* my *people. I can't pretend like that's okay. If I do this, I have to face it for what it is.*

Is this what is left, at the end of everything? A choice?

She held the baby's foot, pushed in the needle, and gave him the shot.

CHAPTER FORTY-FIVE

Ariel was surviving the Partial occupation the same way she survived everything: by being alone. The conquering army had scared many of East Meadow's residents into community shelters, clustering together for strength, and stockpiling their food and water in a single place. This had only made them easier to capture when the Partials started raiding the city, swooping in to snatch victims and then carrying them off for experiments or executions, it was impossible to tell which anymore. The groups' sheer size and noise made them easy to find and prey on, and really, no amount of untrained civilians could fend off a Partial attack. With Marcus gone, Ariel stayed on her own, moving from house to house, eating food left behind by others and always staying one step ahead of the raiders. It had kept her hidden, and it had kept her safe.

Until the Partials found her.

Ariel gasped for breath, struggling to keep going. She knew the city like the back of her hand, but the Partials were faster than she was, their senses keener. She could hear their feet pounding on the road behind her, heavy boots slamming down, one after another, a relentless rhythm getting closer and closer with each gasping breath. She dodged to the left through a gap in a fence, cutting right and then doubling back to the left again, around another wooden fence. Her feet were quieter than theirs, barely a whisper in the darkness, and she held her breath as she tiptoed through the grass, her eyes straining in the dim light for any twig or branch or bottle she might step on and give herself away. She heard one set of heavy footprints run past her, crashing through the hole in the fence and thrashing wildly through the yard beyond. The second pair followed, and she nodded. *Just one more. Just one more Partial fooled and I'm free.* She crept forward silently, almost to the end of the grass; there she would slip down a stairway to a basement safe house she'd used a time or two before, and hide there until the raiders gave up and left in search of easier prey. All she had to do was make it to the stairs—

The third set of Partial footsteps stopped, nearly even with her on the far side of the double fence. Ariel froze, not moving, not making a sound, not even breathing. The Partial took a step in one direction and stopped. Back in the other direction, and stopped. *What is he doing?* But even as she asked the question, she knew, somehow, what he was doing. He had stopped because he had spotted something. And he knew where she had gone.

She heard a deep chuckle. "Oh, you're good," the Partial laughed, and vaulted the fence directly toward her. Ariel cursed under her breath and sprinted again, all thoughts of stealth gone in a flat-out race for survival. The Partial vaulted the second fence and ran after her, just a few yards behind, almost close enough to stretch forward and grab her by the neck. Ariel ran as fast as she could, her mind trying desperately to figure out how he'd found her—she'd been quiet, she'd been hidden, she'd done everything she'd learned to do, and yet it was like he'd known she was there, almost like a sixth sense. Marcus had told her about their link, and the way it let them find one another, but everything he'd said told her that it wouldn't work on humans— that humans were a blind spot in a sensory system they relied on too much. She'd used that to her advantage before, and it had always worked. How had she given herself away?

The Partial was almost on her, his heavy breathing sounding so loud in her ears, she thought for sure he must be only inches behind her, toying with her. She could smell his sweat, and the sour stink of his breath in the air. *That's it,* she thought, *it's my scent. I've been running so hard, and hiding so long, I must stink. He didn't see me or hear me or feel me on the link, he smelled me, like a bloodhound.*

But I'm not giving up.

She lowered her head, pushing herself into the hardest sprint of her life, when suddenly her body went into a spasm and she sprawled forward on the ground, rolling end over end as her muscles failed her, and her inertia carried her in a tumbling crash. Her senses flickered and jumped; the world was upside down and backward. She struggled to right herself, but her entire body throbbed in pain. It was like she'd been hit full force with a baseball bat, but she couldn't tell from where. Slowly her eyes focused, and she saw the Partial standing over her with a shock stick; he clicked it a few times, letting bright blue light arc back and forth between the contacts.

"You're a fighter," he said, dropping the stick back into a ring on his belt. He knelt down and smiled, his teeth flashing white in the moonlight. "I might have to have a little fun before I turn you in to the boss." Ariel tried to move, but her limbs still wouldn't obey her. The Partial reached for her neck.

"Stop," said a voice, and the Partial froze. His hand hovered inches from Ariel's face, motionless. "Stand up," said the voice again, a woman's voice, but Ariel couldn't see the speaker. There was something familiar about it, but she couldn't place it. The Partial stood, staring blankly forward. "Pull out your weapon." The Partial obeyed. "Shock yourself." The Partial clicked the shock stick on, raising it toward his own chest, but stopped a few inches away. His eyes seemed harder now, as if he was struggling, and Ariel could see sweat pouring down his face. "Do it!" the voice commanded, and the Partial's defenses collapsed. He slammed the taser into his own chest, falling instantly to the ground, his limbs flailing as his nervous system short-circuited. Somehow his hand managed to keep the taser pressed to his chest, even as the rest of his body twitched and jumped, until finally he lost all control and slumped into unconsciousness. The taser fell inert to the ground.

It's Dr. Morgan, thought Ariel, still trying to move. She managed to get one arm under her, raising her head slightly off the ground, but her vision swam and she struggled to stay up. *When Morgan was controlling Samm, that same thing happened—that was exactly how Marcus and Xochi described it. Dr. Morgan's here. She has come for me herself, like a vampire in the night.* She got her other arm under her and lurched up, still woozy, her eyes wandering in and out of focus. She turned and saw a figure in the darkness behind her, but her leg throbbed and she couldn't run. "Dr. Morgan," she croaked, but her voice wouldn't obey, and the words were meaningless mush. The figured stepped into the moonlight.

It was an old woman, hunched and dark, not a vampire but a wild-haired witch.

"You," said Ariel.

"Hello, child," said Nandita. "Come, we must find your sisters. Our world is about to end again."

CHAPTER FORTY-SIX

Kira walked in silence through the dark subterranean hall, feeling the weight of the empty syringe in her hand. It seemed heavier now than it ever had when it was full.

"I don't know you how you do it," said Kira.

"That much was obvious," said Vale, "since you kept insisting that I couldn't do it at all. Now, I think, you have a glimpse of what it costs to be a leader."

"That wasn't right," said Kira. "It wasn't the right thing to do. But . . . it was the only thing I could do."

"Whatever helps you sleep tonight," said Vale. He sighed, and his voice became distant, pensive. "In twelve long years, every hour I haven't spent tending the Partials and harvesting the cure, I've spent trying to figure out how to do it without them. They won't last forever, but this colony needs to. These children will grow up and have children of their own, and what will save them then? I can stockpile enough Ambrosia for another generation, maybe two, but then what? Even a 'cured' human is still a carrier—RM will be with us forever."

"You have a year to figure it out," said Kira. "Eighteen months at the most, before every Partial dies and we lose them forever."

"The expiration date," said Vale, nodding. "It's as tragic as the Failsafe."

Only the Trust knows about the Failsafe. It's time to confront him. "You're one of them, aren't you?" asked Kira. "The scientists who made the Partials. The Trust."

Vale paused in midstep, casting her a glance. When he started walking again his voice was different, though Kira couldn't discern his mood—was he curious? Defensive? Had she made him angry?

"You know a great deal about what I thought was secret," said Vale.

"The Trust is why we're here," said Kira. "I . . ." She paused, not sure if she should reveal everything. She decided to play it safe and keep everything as vague as she could. "I knew a woman named Nandita Merchant. She told me to find the Trust, with the implication that they'd have the answers we need to save both species. She disappeared before I could ever ask her about it directly."

"Nandita Merchant," said Vale, and this time Kira had no problem reading his emotions—he was struck with a deep sadness. "I'm afraid she'll never be able to recover from what she did with the Failsafe. She is as guilty as the rest of us."

It was Kira's turn to stop in surprise. "Wait," she said. "The Trust did this? The Failsafe was a virus, we learned that in Chicago, but you're saying . . . you're saying that Nandita, that all of you, built it to target humans? On purpose?"

"I didn't build it at all," said Vale, still walking. "I built the Partial life cycle, their growth and development, the way they accelerate to an ideal age and stay forever—until, of course, they reach the expiration date. Sheer poetry, I assure you, one of the most sophisticated bits of biotech in the entire project."

Kira's mouth fell open. "You created the expiration date?"

"It was a kindness, I assure you," said Vale. "When the government requested a Failsafe, I posited the expiration date as a more humane alternative—"

"What's humane about killing them?"

"It's not humane, it's 'more humane.' Humans, of course, have an 'expiration date' as well, when we'll die of old age. It's the same principle. And expiration doesn't put any humans in danger, which a Failsafe might have—and eventually did. But my arguments about the Failsafe and the expiration date were all in the beginning, before we could see the entire picture. Graeme and Nandita, who were tasked with creating the Failsafe, saw it long before the rest of us did. They were the ones who built RM."

"I knew Nandita," said Kira. "I . . ." She hesitated again, but decided there was nothing wrong with a little more information. "I lived with her for years—she ran a kind of orphanage, and I was one of the kids she helped. She's not a mass murderer."

"No more than any other human in her position," said Vale, cryptically. "But by any measure imaginable, she, and the rest of us, are indeed mass murderers."

"But that doesn't hold together," said Kira adamantly. "If she wanted the human race dead, completely eradicated, she could have betrayed us to the Partials, or started spreading poison, or a million other things to kill us, but she didn't. It had to be her partner," said Kira, following him breathlessly as she sorted through the clues in her head. "Graeme Chamberlain, the one who killed himself. Could he have, I don't know, re-engineered the Failsafe behind everyone's back?"

"You're still not seeing the entire picture," said Vale, never looking at her as he walked briskly down the hall. There was something he was keeping from her, something he was reluctant to tell. Kira pressed on.

"But Chamberlain acting alone doesn't add up either," said Kira, slowing a bit as she thought deeper into the problem. She ran to catch up. "The cure was part of the Partials' design, embedded in their genetic makeup. Why would he make a virus obviously intended to kill every human on Earth, and then also build a cure perfectly designed to stop it? It doesn't make sense. But it does make sense if . . ." The answer was right there, on the tip of her brain, and she struggled to grab it—to force it to coalesce into a simple, understandable thought. *There were so many of them working,* she thought, *on so many different pieces. How do they fit together?*

Vale walked a few more steps, dragging slowly to a stop. He didn't turn around, and Kira had to strain to hear his voice. "I was against it in the beginning," he said.

"But it's true?" Kira approached him slowly. "You and the rest of the Trust—you did this on purpose? You altered the Partial Failsafe to kill humans instead, and you built them to carry the cure so that . . . Why?"

Vale turned to face her, his face once again tinged with deep anger. "Think about the Failsafe for a minute—about what it is, and what it represents. We were asked to create an entire species of sentient creatures: living, breathing individuals who could think and, thanks to the UN Resolution on Artificial Emotional Response, feel. Think about that—we were specifically instructed to make a being that could think, that could feel, that was self-aware, and then we were told to strap a bomb to its chest so they could kill it whenever they wanted. Ten minutes ago you wanted to free ten comatose Partials, and you couldn't stand to kill a single human child. Would you be able to condemn an entire race to death?"

Kira stammered under the sudden onslaught, searching for words, but he carried on without waiting for an answer. "Anyone who could create a million innocent lives and, in the same moment, request a means to kill all of them, without mercy, is not fit for the responsibility of those million lives. We realized what we were creating in the BioSynths—creatures every bit as human as ourselves. But the ParaGen board and the US government saw mere machines, a line of products. To destroy the lives of these 'Partials' would be an atrocity on par with every mass genocide we've seen in human history. And yet, we could tell, even before we released the first of them for combat testing, that they would never be regarded as anything other than weapons, to be cast aside once they were no longer useful."

Kira expected his face to grow harsher as he spoke, more furious at this remembered horror, but instead he became softer, weaker. Defeated. He was repeating an old argument, but with all the fervor drained out of it.

"At the most fundamental level," he said, "humanity would not learn to be 'humane,' for lack of a better term, unless their lives quite literally depended on it. So we created RM, and with it the cure, both embedded in the Partials. If the Failsafe was never activated—if humanity never got to the point where they felt the need to destroy the Partials in one moment—then no one would have been the wiser. But if humanity decided to push the button, well . . ." Vale breathed deeply. "The only way for humans to survive, then, would be to keep the Partials alive. Just as disenfranchising the Partials would cost humans their humanity, so destroying them like defective products would cost them their lives."

Kira could barely think. "You . . ." She searched in vain for the words to make sense of it all. "All of this was intentional."

"I begged them not to," said Vale. "It was a desperate plan, one of terrible consequence—even worse, in the end, than I'd prepared myself for. But you have to understand that we had no other choice."

"No other choice?" she asked. "If you objected so strongly, why not go to the executives, or to the government? Why not tell them it was evil, instead of going through with this horrible . . . punishment?"

"You think we didn't try?" asked Vale. "Of course we tried. We talked and persuaded and kicked and screamed. We tried to explain to the ParaGen board of directors what the Partials really were, what they represented—a new sentient life form introduced to the world without a thought for how they would live in it once the war was over. We tried to explain that the government had no plans for their assimilation, that there was no possible outcome but apartheid, violence, and revolution, that it would be better to shut down the entire program than to condemn humanity to what was going to happen. But the facts, as they saw them, were simple: number one, the army needed soldiers. We couldn't win the war without them, the government was going to get them from somewhere. Number two: ParaGen could build them those soldiers, could build them better than any other company in any other industry. We were miracle workers; we made giant trees with leaves like butterfly wings, delicate and perfect, and when the wind blew they fluttered like a cloud of rainbows, and when the sun set behind them, the world lit up with iridescent shade. We made a cure for malaria, a disease that killed a thousand children a day, and we erased it from the world. That's not just expertise, little girl, that's power, and with that kind of power comes greed. And that's fact number three, and the most damning fact of all. The CEO, the president, the board of directors . . . The government wanted an army, and ParaGen wanted to sell them one, and what good were the Trust's arguments in the face of five trillion dollars in revenue? If we didn't build their Partial army, they would have found someone else with more malleable morals to do it instead. You don't remember the old world, but money was everything. Money was all that mattered, and nothing we did would stop them from buying, or ParaGen from selling.

"We could read the writing on the wall. This army was going to be built, and there would be no plan to give these Partials rights equal to humans. There were only two outcomes: either the Partials would be killed with this Failsafe in a genocide on par with the Holocaust, or a violent revolution would break out, which the Partials, superior in every way, would win, destroying humanity as we knew it. Any way you sliced it, one species would be decimated, and the death of one would come at the expense of the soul of the other. All we had left was to try to, somehow, provide for a way in which both species could work together—that they had to work together just to survive. And so when Armin pitched us his plan we . . . well, we didn't like it, not at first and not ever. But we knew we had a responsibility to see it through. It was the only plan in which both species made it out alive."

Kira's breath caught in her throat. "Armin Dhurvasula."

"You know him, too?"

She quickly shook her head, hoping her face didn't give her away. "I've heard of him."

"A genius among geniuses," said Vale. "This entire thing was his plan—he devised the pheromone system, and designed the entire interaction of the Failsafe and the cure and everything else. It was a masterpiece of science. But despite his plan and our best efforts, the worst still came to pass. I promise you that we didn't mean for it to be this devastating; we don't even understand how RM turned out as ruthlessly efficient as it did. I suppose it's small consolation that, when it comes down to it, this was unavoidable. From the moment we created the Partials, from the moment we thought about creating them, there was no other possible outcome. Humanity will destroy itself, body and soul, before it will learn a simple lesson."

Kira was too stunned to speak. She had expected a plan, she had hoped and prayed that the Trust had a plan, but to learn that it was a plan of mutual annihilation—to force both species to work together or die apart—was too much. When she finally spoke her voice was small and scared, more childlike than she'd sounded in years, and the question she asked was not the one she thought she would. "Have you . . . seen him? Anywhere?" She swallowed, trying to look less nervous. "Do you know where Armin Dhurvasula is now?"

Vale shook his head. "I haven't seen him since the Break. He said he had to leave ParaGen, but I don't know where, or what he's doing. As far as I know, Jerry and I are the only ones left— and Nandita, now, I suppose."

Kira thought back on her list of the Trust. "Jerry Ryssdal," she said. "He was one of you, too. Where is he?"

"South," said Vale solemnly. "In the heart of the wasteland."

"How can he survive?"

"Gene mods," said Vale. "He came here once, in the night, and I barely recognized him—he's more . . . inhuman, now, than even the Partials are. He's trying to cure the Earth, so there's something left for the meek to inherit; I told him he'd do better helping me cure RM, but he was always single-minded."

"And there are two more back east," said Kira. "Two factions of Partials are led by members of the Trust: Kioni Trimble and McKenna Morgan."

"They're alive?" His eyes were wide, his jaw open. Kira couldn't tell if he was glad to hear it or not. "You say they're leading the Partials? That they've sided with them, against the humans?"

"I think so," said Kira. "They . . . I've never met Trimble, but Dr. Morgan's gone completely mad, kidnapping humans and trying to study them so she can cure the Partial expiration date. She didn't know about it until Partials started dying, apparently, but she's convinced she can solve it with human biology." *And with me,* she thought, but she didn't say it out loud. She still didn't know what she was, or what Vale would do when he found out. And she had to ask him. She felt torn between paranoia and desperation.

"Trimble knew about our plan," said Vale. "Morgan and Jerry didn't; they designed most of the Partials' biology, but we weren't sure we could trust them with the issue of the Failsafe, and since it didn't touch their work, we didn't need to."

"Who are the others?" asked Kira.

"What others?"

"I found all those names in my research," said Kira, "but I never found yours, and I've heard of two others that I still don't know anything about."

"My name is Cronus Vale," he said, and Kira nodded in recognition.

"Cronus I've heard," she said, and shot Vale a careful glance. "Dr. Morgan seems to think of you as a threat."

"Don't tell me you've met her."

"It was not the most pleasant experience of my life."

"She's petty and arrogant and heartless," said Vale. "By the end, she had all but given up on humanity as a species."

"That sounds like her."

"If she ever finds this place," said Vale, "we're all doomed. My philosophies are, as you've seen, somewhat opposed to hers."

"You're trying to protect humanity, even if it means the enslavement of the Partial race," said Kira, and the truth was beginning to dawn on her. "What happened to your ideals? What is your plan now? For the survival of both races?"

"After twelve years, I've finally come to understand

something," said Vale. "Extinction has a way of making you choose sides," said Vale. "I don't want to hurt anyone, but if I can only save one species, I've made my choice."

"It doesn't have to be one or the other," said Kira. "There's a way to save both."

"There was," said Vale. "But that dream died with the Break."

"You're wrong," said Kira, and she could feel tears welling up. "You, Armin, Nandita, and Graeme . . . all of your work was about this, about both races surviving. There must be something that I can do!"

"I promised you information," said Vale, "and I'm a man of my word. Tell me what you need to know, and I'll give you everything I can."

They climbed the stairs to the hidden lab in the spire, and Kira considered the question: She had so many; where should she start? She wanted to know how RM worked, and what exactly the relationship was between the virus and the cure. If the same being produced both, how did they interact? She also wanted to know about the expiration date: how it functioned, how they might be able to work around it. Vale had been working on RM for years without cracking it, but he seemed to have no interest in the expiration date; he might know something valuable that he hadn't followed up on yet. "Tell me about the expiration date," she said.

"It's really just a modification of my own work on the life cycle," he said. "I designed the Partials to accelerate to a certain age and then sit there, freezing the aging process by continually regenerating their DNA. At the twenty-year mark, that process reverses, and the DNA is actively degenerated. They're essentially aging a hundred years in a matter of days."

"Samm didn't say they age," said Kira, "they just . . . decay. Like they're rotting alive."

"The effect is the same at that speed," said Vale. "It's not the nicest way to die, but it was the most elegant, biologically speaking."

Kira furrowed her brow, still searching for the stray pieces to complete the puzzle. "How did you keep the expiration a secret from Morgan?"

"ParaGen was a maze of secrets," said Vale. "Nobody trusted anybody else, and the board of directors trusted our primary scientists even less. That's why we had to build two Failsafes."

Kira raised her eyebrow. "Two?"

"A Partial killer, like they wanted, and the human flu that Graeme and Nandita built as part of our plan. The Partial Failsafe was never put into production, of course, but I still created it, as a cover for the rest of our plan. The board could see the Partial Failsafe, could get progress reports and testing data, and content themselves that we were following orders; meanwhile, the other Failsafe is what we eventually incorporated into the mass-produced Partial models."

"Wait," said Kira. She opened her backpack and rooted around for the old computer handle from Afa's broken screen— the one with all the info they'd downloaded in Chicago. "Do you have a monitor I can plug this into?"

"Of course." He offered her a cable, and she powered up the handle.

"Before we came here," she said, "we pulled a bunch of records from a data center in Chicago. One of them was a memo from the ParaGen chief executive officer to the board of directors; we read it because it mentioned the Failsafe, but it didn't make sense at the time. In light of what you just said, though . . ." The list of files appeared on the screen, and Kira scrolled through it quickly, looking for the one sent by the CEO of ParaGen. "Here." She opened it and read the pertinent line: "'We cannot confirm that the Partial team is working to undermine the Failsafe project, but just in case, we've hired engineers to imbed the Failsafe in the new models. If the team betrays us, the Failsafe will still deploy.'"

Vale's jaw dropped. "They went behind our backs."

"That's all we thought when we read it," said Kira, "but after what you've told me, it's got to be more than that—if the board didn't know about the human Failsafe, then the only one they could add to the new models was your decoy. The one that kills Partials. That means it might still be out there, and if it kills the Partials, it will kill everyone, since that's our only source for the cure."

"True," said Vale. "But look at the time stamp: July 21, 2060. That was two full years after the final batch of military Partials was created. I can only imagine that this email referred to the line of Partials that was never put into mass production."

"New models . . . ," said Kira, trailing off. *It's me,* she thought. *That's what I am—a new Partial model. That's even the year I was born, five years before the Break. It's talking about me.*

I'm carrying the Partial Failsafe.

"You look terrified," said Vale.

Kira brushed her hair from her face, trying to control her breathing. "I'm fine."

"You don't look fine."

Kira looked at the ten Partial prisoners lying inert on their tables. *If something triggers me, I'll kill them. I'll kill Samm.* She tried to keep the quaver out of her voice. "What was the trigger?"

"For the Failsafe? It was triggered by a chemical, administered either through the air or by a direct injection. Only some of the Partials were carriers—viral factories, essentially, that could be turned on at a specific moment. We could turn on the cure the same way."

"Yes," said Kira, "but what is the trigger? Specifically? And would it be the same for the new models?"

"None of that matters," said Vale. "The president triggered the Failsafe to stop the Partial rebellion, and when I saw how vicious RM had become I triggered the cure. It's over and done. Those new models that were mentioned in the email were only prototypes, and as far as I know, none of them survived the Break. They were young children at the time."

"But what if they did survive?" asked Kira. *What if something triggers her accidentally, and she destroys every Partial left on the planet?*

Vale stared at her, his face confused and pensive. Slowly his expression changed, and Kira couldn't help but take a step backward.

Vale took a step back as well. "You said you lived with Nandita, right?" he asked. "An orphanage. How exactly did she find the girls she adopted?"

Kira watched his face warily, trying to guess if he'd guessed what she really was. He seemed suspicious, but how much did he know for sure? How much did he need to know before he acted—and what actions would he take? If he thought she was a threat, would he kill her right here?

She opened her mouth to speak, but couldn't think of anything that wouldn't give herself away. *I can't look like I know too much,* she thought, *but I can't look like I'm dodging the topic, either.* "She had four girls," she said. "She found us the same way as every other foster parent on the island. I think some of us were assigned by the Senate." She wasn't sure if it was true, but it sounded good without professing any specific knowledge. "Why do you ask?"

"Some were assigned," he said, "but not all?"

"Nandita raised us like any other kids," she said, but suddenly Marcus's questions about experiments flashed through her mind. *That's it, it's me,* she thought, *it makes too much sense.*

He watched her closely, taking another step back. Kira glanced over his shoulder—was he backing away from a threat, or slowly inching toward an alarm? *How much time do I have?* The tension in the room was thick enough to choke on, and she felt a thick bead of sweat run down the small of her back.

"Do you realize," he asked softly, "how much damage the Partial Failsafe could do in the open at this point? To the Preserve, to East Meadow, to the entire world?"

"Please," said Kira, "think about what you're doing—" But it was the wrong thing to say, and Kira knew the instant the words were out of her mouth that a plea was as good as a confession. Vale spun around, diving for the table behind him, and Kira didn't even wait to see what he was reaching for. She turned and ran, sprinting as fast as she could from the room. A gunshot rang out behind her, and sparks flew from the door frame just inches from her head. She ducked around the corner and hurtled toward the end of the hall.

There were more shots behind her, but she was faster than he was, and already too far away for his unpracticed aim. She stumbled around each corner, barely slowing to change direction, racing back to the elevator shaft she'd come down through. Only when she reached it did she realize she'd left her computer handle back in the lab, plugged into Vale's computer. "No time," she muttered, leaping onto the ladder and hauling herself up. "I'll come back for it later." She might be able to take Vale—she might, depending on his gene mods—but he could have sounded an alarm by now, and called for backup, and she couldn't face the entire Preserve. Her only hope was to get to Samm and carry him out, before anyone on the outside knew what was going on.

But how far would she have to take him before they escaped the sedative's influence? And how long before the dose in his system wore off?

She reached the second floor and clambered out through the elevator door, still wedged half-open. Samm lay nearby, right where she'd left him, and she pulled his backpack on over her own before heaving him to his feet. He hung limp and heavy from her arms, two hundred pounds of muscle turned to dead, useless weight. She threw his arm over her shoulders and lifted, grunting with the effort, listening all the time for noise of pursuit. There was nothing behind her, and she couldn't hear anything outside. She hobbled to the stairs, half carrying and half dragging Samm. She reached the ground floor and leaned against a wall to rest, looking out across the overgrown clearing that surrounded the spire. There were two people talking to the west, resting in the shade by one of the makeshift apartment buildings, but they didn't seem to be on alert. Kira readjusted her grip on Samm and hauled him through the lobby to the other side of the building, slipping out the eastern edge where no one was waiting. The ground was uneven, broken by roots and gopher holes, and she was forced to move slowly with Samm weighing her down.

If only I knew where the horses were, she thought, but there was no time to find them. If she carried the Partial Failsafe, then it could mean the death of Vale's Partials, the death of the Preserve, and the eventual death of all humans and Partials. Kira was a living bomb, and destroying her before she went off would supersede every other goal he had. He would sacrifice his secrecy, his authority, whatever it took to preserve the human race. She had to escape or die.

She reached the end of the clearing just as a man came around the corner of the nearest building. He stopped in surprise; she clenched her teeth, nearly borne down by Samm's weight, and forged past him. "Hello," he said. "Is he okay?"

"He fainted," said Kira. "He just needs some fresh air." *We just need to get to the gate,* she thought, *just reach the gate and we'll be fine.*

"You're the newcomers," he said, matching pace with her. "Were you in the spire?"

"We're just out walking," said Kira, looking ahead. Another clearing loomed before them, and another building, and beyond that the fence and the edge of the city. *If we can just get to the city, we can hide . . . but I need to get rid of this guy.* "Do you know Calix?" she asked.

"Of course."

"Find her," said Kira, "and tell her we left a valuable medicine in our bags in her room—a red bottle, wedge-shaped, with a green ring around the lid." It was an antibiotic, but this man didn't need to know that; she just needed to draw him away. The man nodded and ran off, and Kira struggled on. She reached the next building, and now there were more people around, adults and children. *Just a hundred feet,* she thought. *We're almost there.* A few of the people asked about Samm, their faces concerned, and Kira did her best to play it off without attracting more attention, but the crowd began to grow.

"What's wrong?"

"Where are you going?"

"What's happening?"

And then another voice, in the distance behind them. "Stop them!" The crowd looked up, confused. Kira pushed through them. "Stop them!" the voice cried again, and Kira recognized it as Vale. She kept walking, struggling to keep Samm from falling. A woman in the crowd grabbed her arm.

"Dr. Vale wants you to stop," she said.

Kira drew her gun, and the woman backed off quickly. "Dr. Vale wants to kill us. Just let us leave." *Only fifty feet.*

The woman retreated, hands up, and Kira crept forward, hunched far to the side to keep Samm's weight centered over her. She clung to him with one hand, dragging him forward and warding off the crowd with her gun. She stole a glance behind her and saw Vale approaching with a group of armed hunters.

Samm groaned, groggy but awake. "Where are we?"

"We're in bad trouble," said Kira. "Can you walk?"

"What's going on?"

"Just trust me. Wake up."

"Stop them!" shouted Vale again. "They're spies, come to destroy the Preserve."

"We're leaving," said Kira through clenched teeth, struggling step by step for the open gate. Samm was still leaning on her heavily, trying to walk but too unsteady to do it effectively. The townsfolk hadn't stepped in to stop her, still wondering what to do. "Just let us go."

"Let them go and they'll return with a thousand more like them," said Vale. "They're Partials."

Samm's speech was slurred. "So the recon trip didn't go as planned?"

"You're not helping," said Kira. "Can you walk yet?"

Samm tried to stand up, reeling slightly, and fell back onto Kira's shoulder. "Not well."

"Is it true?" asked a voice. Kira turned to see Phan, and the look of betrayal on his face struck Kira through the heart.

"I'm a person," she said. "The Partials—"

"The Partials destroyed the world," said Vale, catching up to them. "And now they're here, trying to finish the job."

"You're lying," Kira hissed. "You destroyed it, and now you're living in a fantasy, trying to pretend like the past never happened."

"Don't listen to their deceptions," said Vale.

The crowd moved in on them, the open path to the gate become smaller and smaller as the crowd closed in. Kira swung her gun around wildly, trying to balance Samm with her other arm. "Please, Samm, I need you to wake up."

"I'm awake," he said, the crowd now mere feet away from them. "I can walk."

Kira let go of him, and he stayed steady enough. "We have to—"

Vale fired.

CHAPTER FORTY-SEVEN

"I apologize for my absence," said Nandita. "I was trying to save the world." She stood in the living room of her old house—the one Ariel had run away from so many years ago, and swore she'd never come back to.

Ariel clenched her fists and snapped back. "You lied to us before," she said. "What makes you think we'll believe you now?"

"Because you're adults now," said Nandita, "or close enough. Children need to be protected from the truth, but teenage girls need to face it."

Five faces stared back at her, all the women in Ariel's life: her sisters Madison and Isolde, her friend Xochi Kessler, and Xochi's mother, the former senator Kessler. Even Arwen was here, the miracle baby. All trapped by the Partial army, brought back here to simmer and worry and die. They'd gathered in Nandita's house because it was the only home they had left. *If they knew how close we were to Kira,* Ariel thought, *we'd be in even more trouble than we are.*

"The Grid's been searching for you for a year," said Senator Kessler. "Where the hell have you been, and what are your ties to the Partial army?"

"I created them," said Nandita.

"What?" Kessler stammered, the first to manage a response. Ariel was too shocked to say anything. "You created the Partials?"

"I was on the team that built their genetic code," said Nandita, taking off her coat and shawl. Her hands were wrinkled, but missing the calluses Ariel had always seen on her. Wherever she'd been, she hadn't been working in a garden, or in any kind of manual labor.

Kessler seethed with anger. "You just admit it? Just like that? You created one of the greatest forces for evil this world has ever—"

"I created people," said Nandita, "like any other mother. And the Partials, like any other children, have the capacity for good or evil. I'm not the one who raised them, and I'm not the one who oppressed them so harshly they were forced to rebel."

"Forced?" demanded Kessler.

"You'd have done no less in their place," snapped Nandita. "You're more eager to fight what you don't agree with than anyone I know; anyone but Kira, perhaps."

"Just let her talk, Erin," said Xochi. Ariel had never heard the girl call her mother by anything but her first name.

"So you created the Partials," said Isolde. "That doesn't explain why you disappeared."

"When we created them, we built them to carry the plague," said Nandita. "Not exactly what came to be known as RM,

534

mind you: The plague that was released was more virulent than even we intended, and for reasons we don't fully understand. But we also made a cure, carried by all Partials, that could be activated by a second chemical trigger. And then, as you can see, everything went to hell."

"You're still not telling us where you've been," said Ariel, her arms folded tightly across her chest. She was so used to hating Nandita that this string of confessions was leaving her deeply confused: On the one hand, it gave her more reasons to hate the woman, and to justify all her suspicions and accusations. On the other hand, though, how could she trust anything Nandita said? Even when it was self-incriminating?

"Have patience," said Nandita. "I'm getting to that. You need the proper setup first."

"No, we don't," said Ariel. "We need answers."

"I taught you better manners than that."

"You taught me to distrust everything you say," said Ariel. "Stop trying to win us over and just answer our questions, or every woman in this room will gladly turn you over to the Partials."

Nandita stared at her, fire lighting up her ancient eyes. She looked at Ariel, then at Isolde, then back to Ariel again. "Fine," she said. "I was gone because I was trying to re-create the chemical trigger to release the cure."

Xochi frowned. "That actually seems pretty easy to understand."

"That's because I gave you the context for it," said Nandita. "I worked on it for eleven years, as best I could with the facilities I had, using herbs to distill the chemicals I needed. Last year while I was out searching for ingredients I found something I never imagined still existed—a laboratory with operable gene-mod equipment, and enough power to run it. I tried to get back here, to bring you to it and explain the entire thing and solve the problem once and for all, but a civil war and now a Partial invasion have made safe travel very difficult."

"But why us?" asked Ariel. "Why take us to the lab—why use us for your experiments?"

"That's the part you don't yet have the context for," said Nandita. "The chemical trigger was for you—the cure is in you. Kira, Ariel, and Isolde."

"What?" asked Madison.

Isolde stared in shock, covering her nine-month swollen belly with her hands as if to protect it from Nandita's words.

Ariel smiled thinly, her confusion and terror leavened by a victory so long in coming she couldn't help but revel in it. "So you were experimenting on us."

"I had to re-create the trigger from scratch," said Nandita, "which required a lot of trial and error."

"Back up," said Xochi. "You said the cure was built into the Partials—why were you trying to get it from these three?"

"You've answered your own question," said Nandita.

"We're Partials," said Ariel, keeping her eyes fixed on Nandita. "Your little Partial orphanage." Her mind reeled at the revelation, but her anger kept her focused—she'd hated Nandita for so long, concocted so many theories about her behavior, that this new shock was all too easy to believe. "How could you do this to us? We treated you like a mother!"

"I can't be a Partial," said Isolde, the hurt obvious in her voice. "I'm not, I'm . . . I'm pregnant. Partials are sterile." She was shaking and laughing and crying all at once. "I'm a human, like everybody else."

"I've watched them grow up," said Kessler. "Partials don't grow."

"These are new models," said Nandita. "The first generations were created for the war, but everyone knew the war couldn't last forever. ParaGen was a business, and Partials were a product, and the board of directors was always looking ahead to the next season's hot new thing. What do you do with BioSynth technology when you don't need any more soldiers?"

Ariel felt nauseated, feeling suddenly alien in her own skin. "We were children." She grimaced. "You were selling children?"

"We were creating Partials that people could love," said Nandita. "Strong, healthy children who could be adopted and raised just as human children—filling a market need, which is how we could convince our bosses to pay for it, while at the same time assimilating Partials, and the thought of Partials, into the ranks of humanity. The children we created were the missing link that would take Partials from an alien horror to a simple part of everyday life. They were as human as we could make them—they could learn and grow, they could age, they could even procreate." She gestured at Isolde. "On top of that, they had all the benefits of being a Partial: stronger bodies and bones, more efficient muscles and organs, better senses and sharper minds."

"And a death sentence after twenty years," said Xochi.

"No," said Nandita, "no expiration date. Everything about the new models was designed to match or improve on human life; there were no limitations, no hedging our bets with a Fail-safe."

"You weren't just building children," said Ariel, "you were rebuilding the human race."

Nandita said nothing.

"It's not true," said Isolde, her voice rising. "None of what you've said is true. You're a crazy old woman and you're a liar!"

Ariel looked at her adopted sister, her hatred for Nandita slowly giving way to the kind of horror that was destroying Isolde. If they were Partials, they were monsters. They'd destroyed the world—maybe not personally, but they were a part of it. Other people, everyone they'd grown up with, would think they were a part of it. Already Senator Kessler was inching forward, placing herself between Xochi and the Partial freaks that used to be her friends. What did she think they were going to do? Now that Ariel knew she was a Partial, was she suddenly going to start killing people? What would the rest of the island think of her: that she was a traitor? A sleeper agent? A fool or a monster? At least Ariel had no friends to betray, already isolated by years of living on the outside; Isolde had friends, family, a job—a job in the Senate, in the heart of human government. Would they think she was a spy? What would they do to a Partial spy, pregnant or not?

What would the Partials do if they found out? Did they already know? Could Ariel go to them for help, or to help end the occupation? Maybe if they heard it from one of their own . . .

One of their own. A Partial. Ariel's mind rebelled, and she felt herself get sick, running to the kitchen and vomiting in the sink. A Partial. Everything she'd ever thought about Nandita was true. It was even worse.

No one came to the kitchen to help her.

"What about Isolde's baby?" asked Xochi. Her voice was uncertain. "Is it a . . . which is it? Human or Partial?"

"I'm not a Partial!" Isolde screamed.

Ariel wiped her face and mouth, staring out the kitchen window into the darkness beyond.

"I assume it's both," said Nandita. "A human/Partial hybrid. We assumed this could happen, but . . . I'll need to do more studies to find out exactly what it means."

Ariel walked back into the room. She felt different. Apart. More so than she'd ever felt before.

"So you spent years trying to activate the cure," said Madison, "and then . . . what, you left to go activate it somewhere else? Without the girls?"

"I found a laboratory, like I said," said Nandita. "Powered and self-sustaining. I would have come back for the girls, but the political climate was not exactly friendly at the time."

Kessler growled. "We're not stupid—if you'd told us you were working on a cure—"

"You would have stonewalled me like you stonewalled Kira," said Nandita. "And if I'd ever told the story I told you just now, you'd have thrown me into prison or killed me outright."

"So stop talking and do it," said Isolde. "You're back because you have the cure, right? You can unlock it and we can save everyone." She touched her belly again, and Ariel felt a surge of hope, but Nandita shook her head.

"What?" asked Xochi. "You didn't find it?"

"Of course I found it," said Nandita. "I had eleven years of biological data on the girls, I worked on the original project, and I had an ideal laboratory. I knew there was a trigger, and I found the exact chemical blend to pull it." She brought out a small glass vial from a pouch around her neck and held it up; it glittered in the light. "But it's not the cure. Someone already triggered the cure, in every Partial who has it." She looked at Madison. "Kira discovered that while I was gone, that's how she saved your baby."

"So what did you find?" asked Isolde. "What does that vial unlock?"

"I have an inkling," said Nandita. "But it's not good."

CHAPTER FORTY-EIGHT

"**I** think we lost them," Kira whispered, panting with exertion. They'd been running through the ruins for nearly an hour, with what felt like the entire Preserve following closely behind them. She was so tired she could barely walk, and they'd taken refuge in an old bank. "I don't know if I can run another step. Now I know how you felt in the spire."

"How I still feel," said Samm. He collapsed against the wall and sank slowly to the floor, leaving a smear of blood from the wound in his arm. "Whatever sedative he used in there is an absolute killer. Patch me up."

Kira stayed by the window nearly a minute longer, watching the road for any sign of movement or pursuit. Still nervous, she retreated to Samm's wall and hauled out the remnants of her medkit—not a full kit, for that was back in Calix's room, but the essentials she'd kept in her backpack with the other things she didn't want to leave her sight: her gun, now out of ammo; a handful of water-stained documents from Afa's stash; the computer handle, though that was now lost in Vale's secret lab. She swabbed the gash in Samm's arm, a bloody groove where Vale's bullet had grazed his triceps, and gave him a handful of antibiotics to swallow.

"You're probably not going to need these," she said, "from what I've seen of your immune system, but take them anyway. It makes me feel better."

"This isn't your fault."

"He was aiming at me," said Kira. "I'm the one who pissed him off."

"And I got in the way on purpose," said Samm. "I told you, he's on the link—I knew who he was going to shoot before he did it."

"That doesn't make me feel any better," said Kira, searching her bag for bandages and finding that she didn't have any. "All back in the Preserve," she said. "Hang on, let me see what I can find." They were hiding in the bank's back offices, away from the street, and she stood up to search for some kind of cloth.

"Now that we have some time to breathe," said Samm, "you can tell me why he suddenly wants to kill us. I assume we got caught slinking around in the spire."

"I found his secret," said Kira, opening the drawers in an old wooden desk. *Plus, he found out mine,* she thought, but she didn't want to share that with Samm just yet. *What would he say if he knew I was carrying the disease that could kill every Partial in the world?* "He doesn't have a new cure. He's harvesting the phero-mone from a group of Partials locked up and sedated in the spire. One of them has been modified to produce a powerful Partial sedative, which is why you passed out as soon as you entered the building. It's how he keeps them incapacitated."

Samm was silent a moment before speaking. "That's horrible."

"I know."

"We have to stop him."

"I know," said Kira, "but we've got other things to think about first. Like you not dying of blood loss." She found a suit jacket in a small closet and pulled it out to examine it. On Long Island it would be half mildew after twelve years in the humidity, but here in the wastes of a desert city, it was fairly well preserved. She brought it back to Samm and sat on the floor with her knife, cutting it into wide strips. "I've always wanted to see you in a suit."

"We have to free them."

Kira stopped mid-cut. "It's not that simple."

"We can go back. At night. We need to figure out a way to rescue Heron anyway; she's been gone too long to not be in there somewhere. We can find her, and free the people that he's captured, and get everyone out of there."

"I know," said Kira, "but it's not that simple. The captured Partials are practically skeletons. I don't know if they could survive outside the lab, let alone a daring nighttime rescue attempt."

"Would you say the same thing if they were human prisoners?"

Kira felt like she'd been slapped. "I'm not saying you're not right, I'm just saying it's not that simple. Why are you so mad at me?"

"This is the same thing Dr. Morgan tried to do to you," he said. "To turn a living being into a petri dish for a science experiment. I risked my life and destroyed my friendships to free you."

"You helped capture me."

"And then I freed you," said Samm. "There's a very real possibility that whatever Morgan wanted to do to you would work—that she could learn something from your biology to help stop the expiration date—but I freed you. Tell me right now that the reason you won't go back there with me doesn't have anything to do with the fact that those Partials are being used to save human lives."

Kira opened her mouth to deny it, but she couldn't. She couldn't lie to Samm. "So you're saying we should just let all the human children here die." She didn't phrase it as a question.

"You don't know that's what would happen—"

"I know damn well that's exactly what would happen," she shot back, stopping him before he could even finish. "In East Meadow that's happened every day for twelve years, and for one of those years I was right in the maternity ward watching it. If we take those Partials out of that lab, the human children being born will die. I'm not going to let that happen."

"But you'll let those Partials be used like machines?" he said. She had never heard him this angry before. He sounded almost . . . human. "You're a Partial, Kira. It's about damn time you start to come to terms with that."

"That's not what this is about."

"The hell it isn't. What is it, shame? Are you ashamed of what you are? Of what I am? I thought you were in this to save both races, but when push came to shove you went right back to the humans. Heron has been explaining from the beginning how we might be able to save the Partials, but you wouldn't do it; you had to come out and here look for a way to save the humans first."

"It's not that simple!" Kira shouted. "Take away those Partials and these children will die. This community will disintegrate. I don't want this to be about numbers, but in this case it is: ten people for two thousand, for ten thousand or twenty thousand as the community grows. If they were humans in that lab who were keeping alive a hospital filled with Partial children, I'd be saying the same thing."

"Then why not treat them like humans?" Samm said. "For all you know, the Partials would stay willingly. Did he even ask them? Did he even explain the situation? We're not heartless monsters, Kira, and we don't deserve to be treated like it."

"Would you stay?" she asked, turning it back on him. "Give up everything you have, every hope and ambition, to become a . . . milk cow? You'd stay here and do nothing and let them harvest your pheromones? At least you'd have Calix to keep you company."

"Kira, you don't know what you're talking about."

"How about this?" she asked, too angry to stop the tirade. "The Partial who produces the sedative; his name is Williams. He's a living weapon who cannot, by definition, coexist with any other Partials. Vale altered his DNA, and he can't alter him back because the equipment broke. The only way to really free them is to—" She stopped suddenly, realizing that she wasn't just talking about Williams anymore. She was talking about herself. The living weapon that threatened every other Partial merely by existing. "The only way they can be free," she said softly, "is for him to die." Her voice choked up, and she forced herself to ask the final question. "What do you do with him?" *Please don't say you'd kill him,* she thought. *Please don't say you'd kill me.*

"I think . . ." He stopped, and Kira could tell he was thinking deeply. "I hadn't thought of that yet," he said. "It's not simple, but it's . . ."

Please let him say no, she thought.

"I guess that sometimes one person has to suffer so everyone else can be free," he said, and Kira's face went pale.

"So you would kill him?"

"I'm not happy about it," said Samm, "but what's the alternative? Sacrificing a whole community for one person? You have to do what's best for the group, or all you have are tyrants."

"So you'd sacrifice one guy for the other nine," said Kira, "but you won't sacrifice ten guys to save a few thousand. That's a weird inconsistency, don't you think? This town full of humans isn't one of those groups you have to do what's best for?"

"What I'm saying is that we can't use people," said Samm, "because people aren't things. Though I guess I shouldn't be surprised, since that's exactly the way we treated Afa."

"Excuse me?" asked Kira. "I'm the one who defended him— I'm the one who stood up for him the entire time, who did everything I could to keep him healthy, to be nice to him—"

"We dragged him into a situation he had no business in," said Samm, "because we needed him. We used him for our own ends, and I'm not saying you did it—we all did it, we all brought him along. But we were wrong to do it, and now he's dead, and we have to learn our lesson from that."

"And our lesson is to let more people die?" she asked. "I

know that Afa's death was our fault, and mine more than any-body's, and I don't want that on my conscience, but no matter how much I couldn't save him, I can save the next generation of human children. I'm not happy about it, and Vale's not happy about it, but these are impossible choices. Everything we pick is going to be horribly, tragically wrong for somebody, somewhere, but what's our alternative? Don't pick? Sit back and let everyone die? That's the worst choice of all."

Samm's voice was softer now, no longer aggressive but simple and sad. "I don't believe in impossible choices."

"Then what's the answer?"

"I don't know yet," he said, "but I know it's out there. And we have to find it."

Kira realized she was crying, and wiped the tears away with the back of her hand. She was still holding a ripped strip of the suit jacket, and waved it feebly. "Give me your arm," she said. "I still need to wrap it."

"Do it nice and slow," said Calix, and Kira and Samm jerked up, whirling around to find the blond girl standing behind them with a drawn pistol. Her rifle was slung over her back. "Thanks for having such a heated discussion," she said. "It made it much easier to find you."

"I'm out of bullets," said Kira, shooting a glance at her discarded gun and backpack on the far side of the office room.

"I have one," said Samm, "but I'm pretty sure she could shoot us both before I can get to it."

"That's the truest thing you've ever said," said Calix. "How about you pull that gun out nice and slow and kick it over to me." Samm grabbed his pistol with two loose fingers, nowhere near the trigger, and dropped it on the floor. "That's right," said Calix, "over to me." He kicked it, awkwardly from his slumped position, and she bent down to retrieve it, keeping her semiautomatic trained on them the entire time with her other hand. She made sure Samm's safety was on, and dropped the gun in a satchel by her waist. "Now, let's answer a few questions before I take you back to the Preserve. First"—and here her voice wavered slightly—"are you really Partials?"

"We are," said Kira, "but that doesn't make us enemies."

"Dr. Vale said you were trying to take away our RM cure."

"That's . . ." Kira looked at Samm, then back at Calix. "We don't want anyone to die."

"But you're talking about shutting down his lab."

"Do you know what the cure is?" asked Samm.

"It's an injection," said Calix.

"But do you know how he makes it?"

Calix's confusion faded, and her face grew grim and determined again. "Why does this matter?"

"The cure comes from Partials," said Kira. "He has ten of them in a basement lab, where they've been living in induced comas for twelve years."

"That's not true," said Calix.

"I've seen them," said Kira.

"You're lying."

"Dr. Vale created the Partials," said Samm. "There's a lot about him you don't know."

"Stand up," said Calix. "I'll take you back, and we'll talk to Dr. Vale, and he can show everyone exactly how wrong you are."

"That's going to be a lot more eye-opening than you think,"

said Kira, rising to her feet, when suddenly a gunshot blasted through the building and she dropped to the floor, covering her head. *Did she shoot me? Samm?* She heard another shot, and a cry of pain, and Calix slumped to the floor. Kira looked up in surprise, then glanced at Samm; he seemed just as confused as she did. Calix was rolling on the floor, clutching her chest in a growing pool of blood. Kira cried out and ran to her. "Calix!"

Calix groaned through clenched teeth, a snarl of pain and anger. "What did you do?"

"I didn't do anything. Who shot you?" She peeled the girl's hands away from her bloody chest, looking for a bullet hole, and found that the wound was in her hand itself. The excess blood came from a second hole in the girl's thigh. "You keep pressure on this," she said, folding the girl's hands back into her chest. "Samm, I need your help with this leg."

"Who shot her?" asked Samm, holding Calix's shoulders to keep her still.

"Who do you think?" asked Heron. Kira wheeled around to see her running in from the ruined street. "It was long range and this handgun isn't as accurate as it could be. Get out of the way so I can finish her off."

"We don't want you to finish her off," said Kira, throwing herself in front of Heron's gun. "Where have you been?"

"I've been doing my job," said Heron. "You've seen the spire?"

"Of course," said Kira, "and the lab in the basement."

"I couldn't get close enough," said Heron. "There's some sort of sedative that works on the link. But I've been tracking a man named Vale for the last two days, and I'm reasonably certain he's part of the Trust. There are also some Partials here, somewhere.

Is that building what I think it is?"

"Do you think it's a pheromone farm of ten brain-dead Partial coma patients?"

"Actually no," said Heron, looking surprised, "that's . . . I knew it was bad, but that's . . . surprisingly bad. Either way, I hate being right." She looked at Calix, still groaning in pain and thrashing on the floor. "Seriously, let me put her out of her misery."

"No more killing!" said Samm forcefully, and Kira and Heron both looked at him. He'd muscled past the pain from his wound and stood up. Kira nodded. "Absolutely, no more killing. Help me hold Calix down so I can look at that wound."

"Why do you want to save—this human?" asked Heron. She looked at Samm. "I suppose I don't even have to ask you anymore, though, do I?"

"She's a hunter," said Samm. "She's not an enemy combatant. They don't have soldiers—until we showed up, they didn't even know war still existed. And no one but their leader knew about the Partials in the basement; I won't punish Calix for something Vale did."

Kira felt a surge of emotion in her chest. "Exactly."

"Then we won't kill any of them," said Heron. "We can slip in at night, when their guard is down, and Samm and I will cover you while you get the prisoners. You're the only one of us that's immune to the sedative."

Samm spoke before Kira could. "We'll free them," he said firmly, "but we're not leaving—or at least I'm not."

"What?" asked Kira and Heron at the same time.

He looked at Kira. "That's the answer to the impossible

choice. I'm doing what you said: I'm staying with them."

"That's stupid," said Heron.

"I can't sacrifice anyone's life," said Samm, "anyone's freedom, if I'm not willing to sacrifice my own. We'll free the Partials who have been imprisoned, and the humans can get the pheromone from me."

"You . . ." Kira was stunned. She cast about for some way, any way, to argue with him. "You only have a year," she said. "You can only help them for a year before you expire."

"Then you have one year to solve it," said Samm. "Better get to work."

"This is all very heartwarming," said Heron, "but it's meaningless. You're not staying here, Samm."

Kira opened her mouth to argue, but stopped when she saw the look on Samm's face. He must have sensed something over the link. Heron wasn't disagreeing with him. She was stating a fact.

"Heron," Samm said slowly. "What did you do?"

"What I should have done a month ago," said Heron, her expression dark and penetrating. "I reported back in."

Utter silence fell over the room. Even Calix was quiet, gritting her teeth as she clutched her wounds.

Kira looked at Samm, but she already knew exactly what he was thinking. His confusion, heavily mixed with anger, burned so brightly on the link Kira could feel it clearly.

Calix hissed through her teeth, "What report is she talking about?"

"You called Morgan?" asked Kira. "You betrayed us?"

"If that's what you want to call it," said Heron. "I've put up with your emotional self-discovery long enough, and it's time to stop shut up and get things done. If Dr. Morgan can use your biology to solve expiration, then I'm giving it to her."

"When are you going to understand this?" asked Kira. "This is what Samm just said—we can't pick sides anymore!"

"And he was very impassioned," said Heron.

"What did you do?" Samm demanded. "Specifically."

"I located a working broadband radio and called back to D Company on the repeaters we had set up," said Heron. She looked at Kira. "I gave you your chance, and I did everything I could to help you, but the answers you're looking for aren't here. I'm done screwing around."

"This is a peaceful community," pleaded Calix. "If you bring a Partial army here, they'll destroy us."

"There it is," said Samm, looking up. Kira looked at the ceiling, saw nothing, and looked back at Samm to see him tilting his head. He wasn't looking, he was listening. She frowned and did the same, trying to hear what he'd heard.

"What is it?" asked Calix.

"I don't hear anything," said Kira, "just a—a droning sound, like a buzz. It's very faint."

"That used to be one of the most recognizable sounds on the planet," said Heron, "but you haven't heard one in almost twelve years."

"What is it?" Kira demanded.

"A turbine engine," said Heron. "On a cargo plane. Morgan's army is already here."

CHAPTER FORTY-NINE

Kira ran for the pile of strips she'd torn up for Samm's arm. "Sorry, Samm, you're going to have to wait a little longer for that bandage."

"The meds were enough," he said, through clenched teeth.

Kira dove back to Calix's side, pressing a wadded sleeve of the suit coat against her leg wound and wrapping it as quickly as she could with the makeshift bandages.

"Why bother?" asked Heron. "You don't even know—"

"Shut up," said Kira. She tied the strips firmly, putting as much pressure on the bleeding hole as she dared without turning the bandage into a tourniquet. "How does that feel?"

"Fine," said Calix. "How long before I can kick this Partial girl in the ass?"

Heron raised her eyebrow.

"Stay here," said Kira, wrapping another bandage around Calix's hand. "I have painkillers in my bag—don't take too many. Someone will be back to find you."

"Where are you going?" asked Calix.

"Out to meet them." Kira shook her head. "If no one comes, look for antibiotics, and get as strong as you can before trying to cross the wasteland. It isn't kind to people with leg wounds."

"Please," said Calix. "Please, don't let them hurt anyone."

Kira took the girl's rifle and ran for the street, Samm and Heron close behind.

"What are you expecting to accomplish?" asked Heron, catching up to her.

Kira scanned the sky for any sign of the plane.

"There," said Samm, pointing to the east. Kira followed the line of his finger and found it, a small black cross in the pale gray sky. "It looks far away, but it's moving fast."

"Then we run," said Kira. "Back to the Preserve. There's no telling what Morgan is going to do with the RM-resistant people she finds there. We need to get as many of them out of there as we can."

"Smart way to spend your last few minutes," said Heron.

"Who asked you?"

"I don't want them dead any more than you do," said Heron, "though admittedly I don't necessarily care if they live, either. As far as I know, all Morgan wants is you."

"You don't know what she's going to do to those people," said Kira.

"We should be running the other way," said Samm. "We can get lost in the ruins and save you, Kira."

"I'd like to see you try," said Heron.

"We're not running away," said Kira. "I ran away when Morgan invaded Long Island, and she started killing hostages to flush me out. I thought I made the right choice, but . . . I'm not letting her do it again."

"What are you saying?" Samm asked, but Kira pointed up at the giant plane looming low in the sky.

"We need to get to the Preserve, now!" She took off, racing through the now-familiar streets that led through the outskirts of the city to the edge of the Preserve, with Samm and Heron right behind her. Kira kept looking up, trying to judge the plane's speed and distance. *We're not going to make it in time*, she thought, *it's coming too fast.* She pushed herself, never daring to slow down or deviate from her path. The plane grew larger in the sky, lower to the ground, and soon she could hear it, a low drone that built to a deafening crescendo as Kira finally reached the Preserve. There were guards by the gates, a new posting to keep the intruders out, but they were too preoccupied with the giant airplane roaring toward them to notice Kira and the others. The plane had wide rotors in the wings for a vertical landing, and it swooped down across the fence at the same time Kira pelted through the gate.

She shouted to get the attention of the interior guards, though she could barely hear her own voice above the sound of the rotors. She grabbed the nearest guard and spun her around, shouting in her ear. "That's a Partial army—you need to get everybody out of the Preserve and into the ruins now."

"We're—" the guard stammered, looking from Kira to the plane and back again. "Supposed to—"

"You don't want to be here when they land," Kira shouted. "Get everyone you can and hide them in the city!" She let go of the woman's arm and ran deeper into the Preserve. In the corner of her eye she saw the guard regain her bearings and rush into the nearest building; soon a crowd of people spilled out, terrified children and parents with babes in arms, screaming in terror as they ran for the toxic ruins of Denver.

Kira and Samm ran toward the plane, shouting at everyone they passed to evacuate. Heron slowed behind them, blocking any retreat they might try to make. Partial soldiers were already piling out of the plane when it landed in the grass, securing a perimeter with ruthless efficiency and then expanding it from cover to cover, each team watching the next. They trained their rifles on Samm and Kira, but they didn't fire.

"They've linked me," said Samm. "They know it's us."

"Drop your weapons," said the soldier at the edge of the landing zone. Kira held her hunting rifle out to the side, not dropping it but showing that her hands weren't near the trigger.

"I surrender," she said. "I'll come willingly."

"Drop your weapons," the soldier repeated. Wind from the rotors whipped through the air, smothering their words and lashing Kira's face with dust and her own flailing hair. Kira grimaced in frustration, but dropped the rifle. Samm still wasn't armed.

"Don't hurt the civilians!" Kira shouted.

"Kira Walker," said a voice, and Kira looked up to see Dr. Morgan descending from the plane. Her lab coat was gone, replaced by a crisp black business suit. "Nice to see you again."

"Do not hurt them," said Kira. "These people are innocent."

"Samm," said Morgan, stopping in front of them. "It's not every day I get to meet a rebel soldier from my own command."

"You haven't responded to her," said Samm.

"And I don't intend to," said Morgan. "You're a traitor and she's an enemy combatant; hardly the kind of people to whom I feel beholden to listen."

"I don't want to fight you," said Kira.

Morgan smiled. "I wouldn't either. You took us by surprise last time, but now you have no rebel Partial army to flank us while your friends make a messy rescue attempt. I have all the power here, and I'll thank you to remember that."

"Not all," said Vale. He approached from the far side of the clearing, a cluster of Partials surrounding him in a way that looked more like an honor guard than a prisoner escort. "I have to say, your soldiers are very obedient."

Morgan frowned, and Vale gritted his teeth. Kira wasn't sure what was happening until she saw the soldiers fidgeting uncomfortably, torn in two directions by the competing authority of two members of the Trust. She looked at Samm and saw him swaying, a bead of sweat rolling slowly down his brow. She took his hand.

"You're stronger than they are," she whispered. "You don't have to obey either one of them." He gripped her fingers tightly, so tightly she felt they were ready to crush under the weight.

The contest of wills carried on, Vale and Morgan staring each other down, the soldiers wavering in the middle. Kira saw their knuckles turn white as they clutched their rifles desperately, and one reached up to grasp his forehead.

"Enough!" said Kira. "This isn't getting anyone anywhere. Dr. Morgan, what do you want?"

Morgan stared at Vale a moment longer, then looked away and released a shallow breath. Vale did the same, and the alignment of the soldiers didn't seem to have changed at all; they remained loyal to whoever they were standing closest to. Kira looked at Samm, but read nothing on his face. She felt her heart race, terrified that she'd lost him back to Morgan's control, but he squeezed her hand.

She realized, in that moment, that she'd never been more relieved in her life.

"I am here for my esteemed colleague," said Morgan. She looked at Vale and smiled. "I'm putting the band back together, Cronus. Enough is enough, it's time we reversed your expiration date once and for all."

"Are you trying to do it with gene mods?" he asked. "You saw what they did to Graeme; what they've done to Jerry." His put his hand on the shoulder of the Partial soldier in front of him. "Our minds can't take it, and neither can theirs."

"We can make them into anything we want," said Morgan. "We've done it before, and we can do it again. They're the future. Our children. Made in whatever image we'd like."

"Gene therapy is not the answer," said Vale.

"You would know," said Morgan. "But I don't have time to solve your genetic riddles on my own." She looked at Kira. "That's why I've come for you, and for her. The new model. The one without all those pesky genetic limitations."

"I won't let you take her," said Samm.

Morgan started to answer, but Kira cut her off. "I'll go," she said quickly.

Samm started to protest, and Morgan looked genuinely shocked, but Kira nodded, taking a deep breath. "Dr. Vale's knowledge, Doctor Morgan's research, my biology. Heron was

right. It's the only real chance we have of ever curing expiration."
She looked at Samm. "It's the same thing you said before—the
only moral choice is to sacrifice yourself. Somebody has to step
up." She had come to Denver looking for answers, a plan, any
sort of hope that she was part of something larger, something
that could save both humans and Partials. But that plan had
gone wrong long ago, and she was nothing. A failed experiment.
She'd dedicated her life to saving the world, but now she realized
that dedicating her life wasn't enough. She had to give it.

She looked back at Morgan. "I'm ready."

"I . . ." Morgan's voice trailed off, and she peered at Kira
closely. "That's not what I was expecting at all."

"Me neither," said Kira. She clenched her jaw, trying not to
cry. "Let's go," she said softly. "Now, before I lose my nerve."

"You don't want to do this, McKenna," said Vale. "Any experimentation on Kira could release the Failsafe."

Morgan looked at him quizzically. "Excuse me?"

"The Partial Failsafe," said Vale. "The decoy we built to fool
ParaGen, the one that kills Partials. The board embedded it into
a new line of Partial prototypes without our knowledge. If you
stumble onto the chemical trigger, you could release it."

"What are you playing at, Cronus?" asked Morgan, though
Kira could see a hint of doubt in her eyes. "I've seen her medical
scans—I've combed through every cell in her body for months
now. If there were another viral package, I would have seen it."

"You didn't know what you were looking for," said Vale.

Morgan stared at him, then shot a glance at Kira. "Is this
true?"

"I . . ." Kira kept her eyes locked on Morgan, too afraid to look at Samm. "I think he's right."

Morgan nodded vaguely, her eyes distant. "We'll have to be careful, then." She turned to the plane. "Take her. Let's get out of here."

"What are you going to do with the Preserve?" asked Vale. The soldiers around him, fully under the sway of his link, made it clear from their positioning that they were ready to fight if he gave the word. But they were surrounded, and Kira doubted his small group, no matter how loyal, could really stop Morgan from doing anything.

Morgan glanced around her, at the intact buildings and thriving grass and trees and the families surrounding the plane, as if noticing them for the first time. "Assuming you come with me, I don't see any reason why your little ant farm shouldn't be allowed to die in peace."

"Then I'll join you," said Vale.

"And I'm staying," said Samm.

Morgan rolled her eyes, clearly irritated. "What makes you think you can make requests?"

Samm stood firm, looking more fierce than Kira had ever seen him. "It's not a request."

Morgan thought for a moment before answering. "Fine," she said, dismissing him with a wave. "Exile here is worse than what I had planned for you anyway." She looked at Heron. "How about you? I'd say you've earned your way back into the inner circle, my dear."

"I'm staying, too," said Heron.

This surprised Morgan even more. "What about your expiration?"

"I'll be back east in time," said Heron, and glanced at Samm. Kira couldn't be sure, but it looks like they were sharing something over the link. She expected her to mention the Partials trapped in the spire, and thus was surprised at the vagueness her next words. "I have some loose ends to tie up first."

"Fine, then." Morgan turned back to the plane, signaling for the soldiers to bring Vale and Kira after her. Kira could see the humans of the Preserve cowering here and there in the background, watching in terror and fascination as this enemy from the sky from the sky took their leader and left them alone.

I have to go with them, she thought. *I have to take a step, and then another, and then up onto the plane and away to . . . to I don't even know. The end.* She shook her head. *I want to go, but . . . I don't want to leave.*

"Kira," said Samm, and she felt a tear in the corner of her eye.

"Samm," she said, "I . . . I'm sorry, I don't know . . ." She turned to face him, trying to find the right words to tell him what she felt, but she didn't even know it herself, and suddenly he was embracing her, holding her in his arms, kissing her more passionately she had ever been kissed before. She kissed him back, feeling their bodies melt into each other, lips and arms and chests and legs, a single person in a moment of perfect unity. She held him as long as she could, and when he pulled away to breathe, she pressed her face against his chest.

"I'm sorry for bringing us here, for everything I've done," she said. "I'm so sorry."

"I chose to follow you," he said, and his voice was deep and rich. "And I'll find you again."

They kissed one more time, and then the Partial soldiers were pulling her to the plane. She turned and looked at him from the steps, and he stared back, motionless.

And then the doors were closed and the giant rotors spun up with a hum she could feel in her bones.

CHAPTER FIFTY

Isolde's baby was born two days later, in her bedroom in Nandita's house. The Partial raiders had long ago pillaged the hospital for gear and meds, and so they had nothing to help her other than themselves. Madison held Isolde's hand, coaching and encouraging her; Senator Kessler caught the baby, and Nandita watched both mother and child for signs of trauma. It was a boy, and Isolde named him Mohammad Khan. Within hours he was sick. His skin broke out in a scaly rash, hardening in patches as tough as cowhide, and then swelling into blisters. Isolde watched in tears, cradling her baby with no hope of saving him.

But this was not RM.

Senator Kessler studied the blisters from behind a paper breath mask. "This has never happened before." She shook her head, trying to force away the fear. "Tens of thousands of RM cases, and nothing ever like this."

"The first human/Partial hybrid," said Nandita. "This is

the first Partial to ever contract RM. We don't know how it will affect him—or how he will affect it." Nandita stared at the squalling child, lost in thought. "'What rough beast, its hour come round at last . . .'" She turned and walked away.

Ariel watched the child, and trembled.

ACKNOWLEDGMENTS

I love writing these acknowledgments because I have so many people who help me, and they deserve all the credit I can give them. At the same time, I hate writing these because I'm terrified I'm going to leave somebody out. I'll keep it brief this time. Thank you to my editor, Jordan Brown, my agent, Sara Crowe, my publicist, Caroline Sun, and everyone else at HarperCollins and Balzer + Bray. You're amazing.

Thank you to all of the authors who let me join them for awesome book tours and events, and thank you to the many amazing booksellers who organize those events and have become, over time, good friends. Most of all, thank you to the readers who come to all of these events. You're what makes them great.

On a personal level, this book would not exist without my wife, Dawn, who is the most wonderful person I know. This book would exist, but would not be very good, without the input of my brother, Rob, and my friend Ben Olsen, who both contributed valuable bits of storytelling gold. I'd tell you which bits, but it's kind of a spoiler.

Last of all, I want to thank the human race for being stupid and painful and wonderful and inspiring. People are the most amazing things the universe has ever created. Embrace your complexity, stretch your creativity, and live up to your potential. You are what makes the world great.